SOMETHING IN THE WATER

SOMETHING
IN THE
WATER

Peter Scott

DOWN EAST BOOKS
CAMDEN / MAINE

FOR HOLLIS

Copyright © 2000 by Peter Francis Scott, Jr.
ISBN 0-89272-517-6
Printed at Versa Press, Inc.; East Peoria, Illinois

1   3   5   4   2

Down East Books
P.O. Box 679
Camden, ME 04843
BOOK ORDERS: 1-800-685-7962

Library of Congress Cataloging-in-Publication Data

Scott, Peter, 1945–
     Something in the water / by Peter Scott.
          p. cm.
     ISBN 0-89272-517-6
     1. World War, 1939–1945—Naval operations—Submarine—Fiction. 2. World War, 1939–1945—Naval operations, German—Fiction. 3. World War, 1939–1945—Maine—Fiction. 4. Submarines (Ships)—Fiction. 5. Submarine warfare—Fiction. 6. Fishing villages—Fiction. 7. Islands—Fiction. 8. Maine—Fiction. I. Title.
     PS3569.C675 S65 2000
     813'.54—dc21
                                        00-064509

IN MEMORIAM

CAPTAIN MAURICE E. BARTER

1914–2000

At least I know that many spirits live,
And circulate among us at odd times;
I don't know why they come; perhaps they are
The bashful ones who hate to leave the earth
Like folks we know that never leave the town
Where they were born—and I incline to that;
They tended children when we went away,
And now I think they're taking care of us.
                    —"Cyrus" Wilbert Snow

PART ONE

Drums Along the Rum Run

President Roosevelt: "Enemy ships could swoop in and shell New York; enemy planes could drop bombs on war plants in Detroit; enemy troops could attack Alaska."

Newsman: "Mister President! Aren't the navy and air force strong enough to deal with anything like that?"

President Roosevelt: "Certainly not."

White House news conference,
March 2, 1942

CHAPTER ONE

MISTER KEEN, TRACER OF LOST PERSONS WAS SCRATCHY, FAINT, and raspy—washing ashore, drawing back out. Amos knelt in front of the radio's walnut console and caressed the dial, listening closely, his head cocked like that of a wary bird. But all he could get was the Jell-O jingle receding into the distance behind a dying hiss of static.

"Open the window," Uncle Lew used to say, "so's the radio waves can get in."

"Waves, hell," muttered Amos. "It's the batteries."

He lit a lamp, unlatched the trapdoor, and let himself carefully down the steep cellar steps. In a house that old, everything was a size too small for a man built like him, especially stairs and ceilings. He stood on the dry plank that spanned the muddy cellar floor and stooped over to check the wires and the liquid levels in the big blue battery jars. While he topped them off, some twenty in number, his lamp heated a hole in the cobwebs above the shelf. That done, he headed back upstairs.

Amos did not care too much about hearing *The Tracer of Lost Persons*—they would repeat the episode on Thursday—but he did not want to miss the news and Walter Winchell. He planned his supper around Winchell's report to, "Mr. and Mrs. America, and all the ships at sea."

He lit two more lamps and carried them to the table by the radio for the brightest meal. What he wanted was a fresh codfish, soaked and baked in milk, and potatoes—white food. Instead, he made some biscuits, filling the house with their thick smell, fried some bacon and eggs, and sat down in the lamplight to listen.

Headline News was scratchy and weak, too, so that once in a while he had to stop chewing to hear. As on every night in the months since Pearl Harbor, there was one piece of bad news after another, with something hopeful saved for the end.

The destroyer *Kearney* had been torpedoed south of Iceland.

Walt Disney had announced the release of a movie about a baby elephant that flies with his ears to save his mother.

The island of Malta had been bombed again, for the five hundredth consecutive day.

But the RAF had dropped bombs that weighed two tons each on the German defense works in Essen, and . . .

The destroyer *Roper* had sunk a German U-boat in the Chesapeake Bay.

While a woman sang the Palmolive jingle, Amos mopped up the last of the yolk with a biscuit.

"How the hell can an island stand up to bombing like that, for more than a year, from the whole German Air Force?" He talked with his mouth full. "Could they even surrender? How? Wave bed sheets at the bombers? Christ."

He drained the full cup of cold tea in a gulp and stood up facing the radio, one huge pink speckled fist opening and closing on a shriveled lemon he had taken from his pocket without noticing.

"That's bad all right. Sure, go ahead and sing, soap woman. It's bad, but we haven't seen the worst yet. What about the merchant ships coming up the coast, the tankers on their way to Halifax? Unarmed and full of oil?"

Amos cleared the table, turned off the radio, then snuffed one lamp and turned the other down before setting it in the window. Pulling on his heavy wool coat, still damp in the shoulders, he stepped out onto the front stoop and sat down in the gray twilight with a toddy of sweetened water, lemon, and a generous three fingers of dark Demerara rum. A lone gull scaled over the bare oak, cried, then turned out toward the sea.

Amos's house was the smallest of the four in the cove, separated from the others by a high granite ledge and a thicket of spruce beneath which were laid to rest almost everyone who had lived in the island cove since great-great grandfather Stillman Coombs, a Cornish man, sailed in and planted himself in 1802 with an ox, a bride, and a fishing boat. Stillman's wife, Experience, would hold the long iron drilling pole while he struck it with the sledgehammer—one strike, one quarter turn of the drill in the granite, another strike—to cut blocks for the house and barn foundations. Experience gave Stillman four sons. Sammy, the eldest, built his own house, where Amos now lived, on a foundation as sound as Stillman's.

In the next two generations Stillman's offspring built two more houses in the cove, along with three wharves, several fish shacks, and a store. When Amos was growing up, the cove was a busy little village of Coombses—cousins and aunts and uncles everywhere, horses and oxen and Model T's, five fishing boats, and twice that many sailing peapods moored together. Grammy Helen had so many children that her husband slept on a cot in the store and called her the old lady who lived in a shoe. By 1920 most of the cousins had grown and moved off to the mainland, crowded out. Those who stayed, stayed forever. Experience Coombs's grave, marked by a tall, white marble obelisk, stood in the center of the cove cemetery; gathered around her lay her sons and their families, still within her reach.

Out in the cove, Amos's boat swung slowly on her mooring, disturbed by the coming tide. He could hear a flock of small birds over toward the meadow. It was either the goldfinches or the grosbeaks, the first ones to stop on the island for a rest on their way north. Aunt Ava used to say that if the grosbeaks returned first the lilacs would bloom late, and it would be a raw spring with no time for painting boats. Or was it the goldfinches that were bad luck, he wondered?

"Two goddamn tons," muttered Amos as he tucked the rum bottle under his arm. "A bomb big as a trawler."

Normally his legs and arches pained him some at this time of the day, but not this evening. Even though he had a slight hitch from a twist in his hip, he walked and stood straight for a man his age; he was careful to do so. He knew that once a man who works with his back and hands starts stooping, he never straightens up—not after age forty, which he had already passed. He hummed the Palmolive jingle as he started up the road—at first patches of it, softly; then more of it, louder. Amos was not musically inclined; his neighbors used to tease him about how bad his singing was, but now it did not matter because they were all gone: Lew and Walter to fish with, Aunt Ava to take care of their appearances and manage everything above the high-tide line. One by one he had lugged them from their houses to the graveyard, leaving him alone in the cove, alone on the east side of the easternmost island in Penobscot Bay, with the high spine of the mountain between him and the rest of America.

The moon would soon be over the horizon and then it would get clearer; the sea would darken to steel. Amos thought it should be a dry moon, but he could not remember. He went along the path, instead of the road, and as he neared the field below Ava's window, he instinctively tucked the bottle inside his shirt, where it rode warm and sloshing, half full. The goldfinches saw him first and rose from the trees on the edge of the field in long draping ribbons. In the last evening light they were not as bright as in years past, but still he marveled at the dull golden mass in the trees and watched them speed alone or in groups across the field, where they settled in the bony sumac for the superior view.

The path to the cabin on the cliff skirted Ava's dooryard and led past Uncle Lew's empty house. The blinds in the darkened windows were tattered now, so they looked like gray eyelashes on closed lids. No one had been inside Lew's house for years and years, not since they went through it to remove the furniture. No one would ever go inside again, Amos thought: Let it stay empty and sink under its own weight.

He kept up Aunt Ava's and Uncle Walter's house. He mowed the grass, pruned the fruit trees, patched the roof—even swept and dusted the inside in the spring. He had finished the preserves in the cellar long ago, but he still borrowed tools and kitchen utensils—borrowed and returned them.

As Amos crossed her yard, he saw Ava sitting in her wicker throne in the parlor window. The light that revealed her seemed to come from the parlor door, but the parlor window was dark. He stopped, scared stiff for a moment, as he always was when this happened. Tonight she sat still, looking out at him over the rims of her spectacles as she had in life whenever he disturbed her at her tatting. She wore her nightcap, and her white shawl over her shoulders against the chill.

For years she sat just like that at this time of day to watch for her brother Walter coming up the meadow path. If he approached the house like a man negotiating a heaving deck, she would berate him for drinking again and serve him a cold supper in silence. Finally Walter built the little cabin up on the cliff where he could go have another drink in peace or sleep off the ones he had already downed. Only a year after he built the cabin, Walter drowned outside the ledges below it. Amos was the one who found the boat going around in circles with Walter hanging on the washboard, stone dead and going black in the face. He had been a hefty, laughing man, Amos's favorite.

The bulkhead's double doors lay open beneath Ava's window, offering the dark, open maw of the cellar. Amos wondered if he had forgotten to close them.

You left them open the day before yesterday, said the

ghost. Her voice was low and strong; it seemed to issue from the cellar hole.

"I thought I closed them," Amos replied.

The birds fell quiet at the sound of his voice.

Maybe you're getting old, forgetting things, she said.

Was that twinkle from her eyes, he wondered, or the light where it touched her spectacles? It must be her spectacles, Amos decided; she's dead.

"Maybe I could blink and make you go away, or snap my fingers, like that." He showed her.

Maybe, but I doubt it. She smiled.

You wouldn't though. It was Walter's voice, though he was not to be seen. *You could always lie down and join us, as if you hadn't thought of that already,* he added.

You could break your neck wandering around those cliffs in the dark, Ava warned. *I notice you didn't even bring a lantern.*

"That wouldn't get rid of you, though," Amos said. "Then we'd all be—"

Certainly it would, she interrupted. *What is it that keeps us here but you?*

"At least you two stay in one place. Uncle Lew, he wanders around everywhere." Amos looked around in the increasing shadows. Was that something moving by the well?

Lew's lucky, came Walter's voice. *He always was.*

Ava glared into the dark parlor to shush Walter, but it did not work.

Where you going with that lemon? Walter wanted to know.

Amos opened his fist, surprised to find the half lemon still there.

You're going to have yourself a toddy up on the cabin porch. Walter's voice was wistful now.

"I might." Amos put the lemon in his coat pocket and turned to go.

What kind of a man talks to a radio? Ava resumed her tatting.

"The same kind of a man that talks to ghosts." He walked over and shut the bulkhead doors, as steady as a minister. The birds stirred in the trees on both sides of him and scooted over his head, lost souls flying across the darkness.

It's goldfinches that are good luck, and it's not for spring, but for winter, Ava said. *You got them mixed up because you forgot that it's the way goldfinches fly—falling, then flapping to rise up, then dropping and rising again— that predicts it won't stay cold long enough for the sea to freeze. How you could think it was grosbeaks, and the spring, I'll never know.*

Amos spat over his shoulder—she'd always hated that, and turned to leave.

Go ahead, Ava said. *Don't listen to me. But remember what happened last time you went up to the cabin to sit at night. You believed what you thought you saw from there.*

Then you went and told everybody about it, said Walter. *What the hell, Amos?*

"I only told Cecil, so he could report it to the mainland; he's the constable now, if you remember." Amos was sarcastic. He was surprised and hurt to hear Walter take her side.

So he could also report it to the whole island, which already thinks you're daft and laughs about how you live alone in a ghost town talking to shadows and guzzling rum. For pity's sake!

"So the hell what," said Amos. If Walter wouldn't stand up to her, he would. "Let them laugh. I saw an explosion. Like I said, it was like a kitchen match flaring up and then a smear of orange fire. Three points north of the lighthouse, maybe twenty miles beyond it."

Why didn't the lighthouse report it, then? Walter had asked this before.

"What makes you think they didn't? Maybe they didn't see it."

I hope you stay to home, Ava said, softer now.

I hope you didn't tell Cecil the whole of it, said Walter. About seeing the sailors in the water afloat and on fire. What was it you called them, bobbing torches? Seen them from more'n thirty miles away. After hearing that, who's going to believe anything you say?

Amos showed them his back and started home. He felt tired and resentful. They were the lucky ones. To them the cove was still alive with boats and people, the way it once was. Vergil was down on his wharf off-loading barrels of soused tripe and tubs of lard for the store. One of the children, his turn having come, was driving the oxen and cows in from the meadow. To them Japan was still a shiny black lacquer, and Hitler was a German version of Charlie Chaplin. No matter how hard Amos tried to explain what was going on in the present, they could not understand it. He was foolish to think that they could.

When he poured another toddy on his front stoop, the rum was warm from the trip inside his shirt. The evening star flickered in the east. With another run of good days, he would have his deck painted and loaded with lobster traps, then he and the boy could start setting them out.

Richard Snell gave the breakwater light a wide berth and steered into Rockland harbor. A big gillnetter, the *Holly B.*, passed him to port with a wave from her skipper, and Richard cut back his throttle to dance in her wake. He blinked and squinted through his window, then wiped it clear with his sleeve. It had been seven months since his last run to Rockland—five since Roosevelt had declared war—and Richard had heard that the Coast Guard station was gearing up. He had not, however, imagined so much traffic and noise and confusion. The fishing boats and moorings had been moved out to make room for a huge, rusted dredge that ground and squealed as it loaded a deep barge with bottom mud. A quarry crane and its swarthy crew from Stonington was setting granite blocks for a new pier. Two Coast Guard cutters were rafted up at the far end of the town wharf; a third, tied alongside, was getting her hull scraped and painted by men in dungarees. A pile driver groaned, hesitated, then struck with a thud that Richard could feel in his deck planks. Where all these people had come from, he could not imagine.

"Christ," he muttered.

He found Dennis Kehoe's *Kingfisher* moored north of the sardine factory and drifted in alongside her. Prentiss Phinney, his full gray beard stained brown around the mouth by tobacco and rum, threw Richard a line and watched while he tied it off.

"I almost didn't recognize the place," said Richard. "What a god-awful mess. You'd think—"

"You have lobsters?" Phinney spat and wiped his mouth with the back of his hand.

"Yes, but not many this early in the season. You got my rum? It's good to see you, Phinney; it's been a while."

"I guess it has. We saved out two cases for you. Come on aboard."

Phinney hauled up Richard's first lobster crate and helped him up after it. Dennis Kehoe stood in the door to the wheelhouse wiping his hands on a blue rag. The *Kingfisher* was a lobster smack out of Boston, one of the few still operating on the Maine coast in the spring of 1942. She bought lobsters from outlying fishermen and sold them in the city. Dennis also carried Demerara rum from the Barbados to sell to the lobstermen on his route. Demerara was the favorite among the older fishermen. They had inherited a taste for it from their grandfathers, who once bought it in small wooden barrels from schooner captains. Dennis did not go any farther east than Rockland until later in the summer, so Richard bought Demerara from him there to sell to the fishermen on the islands in Penobscot Bay. The younger fishermen were satisfied to drink blended whisky or thinner rum, but the old ones still insisted on Demerara: it lin-

gered sweetly on the tongue and spread through the whole body
to ease back pains and loosen cramped legs.

Dennis Kehoe had inherited the *Kingfisher* and its customers from his father, with Prentiss Phinney thrown in. Dennis
had inherited his father's looks too, but the blue eyes had lost
their kindness and the wide mouth its easy smile. He avoided
Richard's outstretched hand by holding up his own, still wrapped
in the oily rag.

"You just caught us," he said. "We was about to pull up
bumpers and head home. You got two cases of rum. We
thought we'd have to sell them in Boston."

You weren't going to wait for me the way your father would
have, Richard thought, or offer up a cup of rum to celebrate the
trade.

Phinney weighed one of Richard's lobster crates and poured
the skittering contents into the smack's watery hold.

"Save out a half dozen from that second crate, if you would
Mister Phinney," said Richard. "They're for my friends here at
the Coast Guard station."

Phinney grunted in reply and set about packing the empty
crates with rockweed and then rum, two bottles at a time.

"The bad news is that the rum's up 15 percent this time,"
said Dennis. "The good news is that lobsters are up 10 percent." The *Kingfisher*'s skipper seemed to be looking at something perched on Richard's shoulder as he talked. "Butter's up
more than 50 percent, if you can get it."

Richard lifted the flannel ear flaps of his hat and tied them
together on top while Dennis wrapped a rubber band around a
wad of bills and tucked it into the pocket of his overalls. "A lot
of people are using the war to get rich," Richard said.

"If you mean me, you're mistaken," said Dennis. "I've joined
the navy. Phinney here will be making the runs from now on."

"I didn't mean you. I'd join up too if I was your age. I guess
me and Phinney can keep this trade going until you get back—
us old fellows, eh, Phinney?"

"Step onto your deck, and I'll hand these crates down to you," Phinney said. "I'll be back the first Friday in June."

"Maybe next time you won't be in such a hurry, and we can have a drink or two the way we used to." Richard took the crate by its rope handle as it slid toward him over the boat's washboard.

"Perhaps we will," Phinney said.

Richard knelt on the seat of his skiff, facing the bow so he could see where he was going and rowed cautiously through the harbor's boat traffic to the public landing. His long johns and shirtsleeves were pushed up above his elbows, revealing the bulging forearms of a man who had hauled heavy traps hand over hand for twenty years. He pulled and sculled his way through a confusion of other skiffs and tied off. The sun had gone down behind the distant hills leaving the noisy harbor in shadow. But at what seemed the exact second that Richard set foot on the pier, the dredge's dozens of mounted floodlights were switched on as the vessel took its place for the night shift. Two Portuguese quarrymen were fixing dog-toes to a granite block, while a third—a darker, older man in a leather muffin hat—smoked and watched. Richard knew the crew was from the Crotch Island quarry at Stonington; he did not recognize any of them but thought they might know him, so he nodded in their direction as he swung the heavy gunnysack over his shoulder. Then he started for town, eager to get away from the howl of the dredge and the awful pounding that made him wince.

The bar at the Harbor Inn was just barely lit by imitation ships' lanterns with little bulbs inside them. The place was dark, and when the door swung shut behind him, it was quiet too. The only two customers, both young men with slicked-back hair and baggy trousers, were seated at the bar watching Reggie Lombard as he exchanged their empty beer bottles for full ones, and poured their shot glasses full. Richard set his gunnysack on the floor at the end of the bar and took the stool next to it. The drinker closer to him watched him, then looked over his shoulder at the sack on the floor.

Reggie said, "Look what the cat drug in," and brought Richard a cold draft.

"This is the only quiet place I've been all day," Richard told him.

"You wait," Reggie said. "In an hour, when the day shift's over, you won't be able to hear your own voice in here." He motioned to the empty tables with a folded newspaper. "Half of them will be your Portagee friends from Stonington. They make more money here than they do on Crotch Island, and they spend every penny of it, too."

"They're not my friends," said Richard, licking foam from his upper lip. "My friends are white."

"Portuguese are white," Reggie said. "They wouldn't be coming in here if they weren't."

"You'd call Mexicans white if you could sell them a drink."

"You haven't changed a damned bit." Reggie resumed his seat on the stool by the cash register and disappeared behind his newspaper. Someone had written "Loose Lips Sink Ships" in lipstick in the corner of the mirror behind the bar. Richard thought of the red lip prints on Iris Weed's coffee cup.

"Whatcha got in the bag there, cap'?" The nearest drinker had turned toward him; the other watched their reflections, only partly interested.

"Seaweed," Richard said.

"He looks like somebody that would be carrying around a bag of seaweed," the other man sneered. He let smoke drift out of his mouth and inhaled it through his nose.

Richard would have said something if he had not noticed the headlines on Reggie's newspaper. A destroyer had sunk a U-boat off the coast of North Carolina. No German survivors. The long-awaited dawn of Victory in American waters.

"You mean to tell me they finally sunk one of them submarines? How'd they do it?" Richard asked.

"You just found out? Where've you been? It's all anybody's talking about," said the nearest drinker.

"I've been lobstering is where I've been." Richard glanced over at the man then turned back to Reggie, whom he had been talking to. Reggie was looking at Richard over his newspaper.

"They say the ship was a destroyer that sank it with gunfire then finished it off with depth charges. Off of Cape Lookout. Most of the Germans had abandoned ship and was in the water, but the depth charges killed them. It's about time they got one. Now maybe—"

"What's that then, one submarine for how many merchant-men sunk in the last couple of months up and down the coast—several every day?" Richard slid his empty mug toward Reggie. "People stand on the pier at Atlantic City and watch them blow our ships to blazes; the lights of the amusement park give the U-boats a clear silhouette. It's disgusting. What do we have, one destroyer for every twenty U-boats? And them building more every day."

"And we are too." The near man had turned toward Richard. "That destroyer was the *Roper*, one of the new Wickes-class flush deckers, radar equipped. There's two more just like it coming off the ways at Bath right now."

"How do you know so much? You guys in the navy?"

"Coast Guard. This is Ed Murphy. I'm Dave. Dave Jones."

Murphy nodded at Richard's reflection.

"I'm Richard Snell." He and Jones reached across two stools to shake hands.

"Snell?" said Murphy. "That's a goddamned German name isn't it?

"It's an American name." Richard's voice went flat. "My people arrived in this country two hundred years ago. They were farming on land they bought from the Mohawks a hundred years before your people gave up digging potatoes and came over here, Mister Murphy. My grandfather moved back east, to Maine, and he fought in the Civil War with the Deer Isle regiment. Don't go calling me a German."

"Snell? That means slow, doesn't it?" asked Murphy.

"That's *schnell,* and it means fast, or quick, for your information."

"Snell rhymes with smell. Dick Smell." Murphy laughed.

"Goddamn you." Richard set his cap on the bar and stood up.

"Cut the shit, Murph," said Jones. He held up his hand to Richard. "Sit down, cap'. Don't pay any attention to him. He gets nasty when he drinks. Let me buy this next one, bartender; we'll drink to the crew of the *Roper.*"

One of the lobsters in the gunny sack flapped his tail in a last desperate attempt to escape. Richard stirred the sack with his foot to quiet the critter but only disturbed the others.

"Would those be lobsters in that bag, cap'? How many you got?" asked Murphy.

"They would be," said Richard. "There's six of them."

"Would they be for sale?"

"They might be."

"What else you got in there? I mean that sack looks pretty hefty for just six lobsters. I thought I heard something clink when you kicked it just now. If you're looking for customers, you found them."

"Not in here," said Reggie. "I don't want anything to do with this."

Richard lifted the gunnysack over his shoulder and led the way out the side door, thinking that the son of a bitch would pay in dollars for his smart-ass remarks. Behind an old flatbed truck that rested on cinder blocks, its tires gone, Richard set the sack down in the gravel and untied it. He drew out one bottle, pulled a strand of rockweed from its neck, and pointed to the label.

"This is Demerara, from Guyana. You won't find rum this good in any barroom. There's four bottles, at ten dollars each." He slipped the bottle back into the sack. "The lobsters are sixty cents."

"How big are they?" asked Murphy. "Show us one."

Richard fished around for a fair-sized lobster and held it in front of Murphy's face, so close the critter could smell his hair oil. The lobster waved its war claw and climbed in the air on its skinny legs.

"We don't have that kind of money," Jones said. He bent down and picked up the sack. "But since we're in the service, you can call it your contribution to the war effort. Here, just drop that one in with the others, Dick Smell."

Murphy was laughing when Richard drove the lobster—legs and claws first—into his face with all the force he could muster. The Coast Guardsman fell backward, his throaty cry muffled by crunching shell and squishing flesh. Richard drew back the lobster for a second blow again, but Jones caught him with a fist to the temple, and he collapsed to his knees. He saw Murphy on the gravel next to him, covering his own face with bloody hands. Richard felt another blow to the same side of his head, then another on his cheekbone, then nothing more.

Amos opened the fish shack door with his foot and turned the trap sideways to get it through. He had taken off his shirt and unbuttoned his long johns in the warm shack, but out on the wharf, where he added the trap to the top row, he shivered all over like a wet dog, rolled down his sleeves, and buttoned up his shirt. It was cold for mid-May and unusually clear. From the way his boat was riding on her mooring the wind appeared to be westerly, but Amos knew it was northwest by the cold forest smell of it; light northwesterly winds like this one often got baffled by the mountain and the high cliffs around the cove, coming across as westerly by the time they got to his mooring. Still, he thought, it was christly cold and bright, more like late October.

He counted thirty-nine traps in the tiered stack of those with their warps cut to fifteen fathoms. One more fifteen, he thought, then he could start on the tens for inshore fishing. Since the boy had started to go lobstering with him, he had taken better care of his gear. He tucked his hands into his armpits and allowed himself some satisfaction in the sight of the freshly painted buoys and their warps tarred and coiled inside each trap. The new oak laths and bows with which he had replaced the weaker ones gave the old, weathered traps a sturdier look. Amos decided that he'd build the last fifteen brand new, from the bottom up, and set it out first for good luck.

The two windows over the workbench in the fish shack looked out over the wharf and the cove, facing south to collect the light and warmth of the sun. Amos laid out pieces for a new trap frame on the bench. He lifted one of the heavy oak runners and sniffed it.

"This batch is pretty green," he said out loud.

Uncle Walter did not answer. He was standing at the bench, resting his bulk on a tilted stool. He did not like to sit because he overflowed the stool and his ass hurt him. The sunlight made his hair look extra red and his body look hazy. Walter's attention was fixed on something out the window.

A boat was approaching from the south; Amos had not heard it because it was downwind. It was Richard Snell in the *Lucille,* and he was cutting back the throttle as he came into the cove. He had not been out lobstering, and he had no business down in Head Harbor, so he must be coming from Rockland with the rum. Amos had expected him yesterday and had watched for him, but today he did not feel like talking to Richard, or rather listening to him talk about his new Chevrolet engine and his hotshot friends in Stonington.

Amos opened the damper on the stove so Richard would not see smoke and tie up to the wharf.

Christ, you'll roast us to death, Walter said.

Amos reached through Walter for his old spyglass and perched on the stool in the shadow under the drying buoys, where the *Lucille*'s skipper could not see him watching.

Richard tied up onto the far side of Amos's boat, which—on a whim—he had named the *Tuna*. He did not step out onto his deck and hail the cove or even look around as he usually did. At first Amos could only make out Richard's shape and his red flannel cap in the wheelhouse, but as he stepped over the washboard onto the *Tuna*, the breeze swung both boats toward shore and put Richard—full bodied and face first—into Amos's view. The lobsterman held four bottles of rum pressed against his chest and carried two by their necks in his free hand—only six quarts instead of the eight Amos had ordered. But it was Richard's face, not the number of bottles, that made Amos gasp. One whole side was swollen like a ripe pumpkin and was the pale purple color of a sheep's intestines. His right eye was lost in a little black hole, and his lower lip was puffed out like that of some Africans Amos had seen in *National Geographic*. There was a row of black stitching over his eyebrow, and another followed the border of his nose from bridge to nostril. Richard ducked quickly into the cabin of the *Tuna*.

He looks like a goddamned jack-o-lantern, said Walter.

"Jesus what do you suppose happened to him? He must have mixed it up with somebody and gotten the raw end of it. He's only wearing one mitten; I wonder what that's covering up," whispered Amos.

Richard came up out of the *Tuna*'s cabin and plucked the envelope from its clothespin on the bulkhead next to the wheel. He stuffed it into his jacket pocket with his left hand without bothering to open it and count the money. And, Amos soon saw, he did not leave any change, and he did not come back aboard with two more bottles. Richard took money for eight quarts but left six, and he roared off at full throttle, rocking the *Tuna* with his wake as if to remind Amos how tippy and unseaworthy his little boat was.

Amos lowered the spyglass.

"Now isn't that a goddamned Snell for you. Poachers and crooks, all of them. His uncle still has those two wrenches he borrowed, what, twelve years ago? Richard'll say that prices went up again, so six costs the same as eight. He'll say he gave me a deal. Tonight we'll drink a toast to the guy who fixed his face that way, by Jesus."

Richard ran a broomstick through the spokes of his wheel to keep it steady and unwrapped the linen bandage on his right hand. Of the dozens of cuts on his fingers and palm, only the one just below his thumb had been deep enough to take stitches. The swelling had gone down, but the hand still throbbed when he moved it, and the cuts from which he had picked pieces of broken shell still stung. He wished he had seen that Murphy's face before he had blacked out; he hoped it was mashed up like deviled ham. In fact, Richard hoped he had put at least one of his eyes out with a spiny leg. The son of a bitch wouldn't be eating lobster for a while, at least not one of those they stole. Richard smiled and winced when his face moved.

He bent over the washboard, scooped up a bucket of salt water, and stood soaking his hand, watching Barter Island recede over his stern. It had been six years since Richard and his mother moved off the island and bought a house in Stonington on Deer Isle. When the bridge over Eggemoggin Reach was built, connecting Deer Isle to the mainland, Lucille said she wanted to move up there, where she could get to a doctor when she needed one and to the hospital if she had another fall. He bought her a little house near her friend Claire, on Hill Street, and lived with her there—except during the lobstering season, when he stayed overnight often at their old house on Barter Island.

It was not until after they had settled in Stonington that he realized how isolated and backward life on Barter Island had been. No movies. No electricity except for a few who had generators. No running water. No telephones. In Stonington he could take Lucille for Sunday drives—to Bucksport or to Southwest Harbor to watch the sailboats. When he was not at home, she had a phone to call her sister or the doctor if anything went wrong or if she wanted to gossip with her friends. Tonight he would wait until it was dark so nobody would see his face when he went into Stonington Harbor; he would call her from the town landing and say he had engine work to do and would be late. Maybe by morning the swelling would be down, and it wouldn't scare her so much. He touched his fat lip with his pinky.

When Richard came around Merchant's Island and drew within sight of Stonington and the quarry, he saw Cecil Barter's store boat coming toward him and cursed his luck. Cecil was loaded with groceries from the mainland, and Richard had no doubt that he would want his rum.

"My God, Richard. What happened to you?" Cecil stood bug-eyed, holding onto the *Lucille*'s washboard with his gaff. Richard had never before seen Cecil surprised.

"I got robbed in Rockland. Robbed and beaten."

"How? By who? What did the police do? Who sewed you up?" Cecil was First Selectman on Barter Island, a deacon in the Congregational Church, and a glutton for news of improprieties.

"I got jumped in the alley behind the Harbor Inn, the bar. It was three guys, strangers; they followed me out. They took six bottles of Demerara and a dozen lobsters. Two of them grabbed me from behind, but I got a good lick in on one of them; I bashed his goddamned face in with a lobster." Richard held up his wounded hand.

"Mercy. And you didn't report it because of the rum. The wages of sin," intoned the deacon. He clucked his tongue and straightened his tie. It was just this posture of moral authority that Richard knew so well and had wanted to avoid this afternoon, of all times. He had suffered it at town meetings when he had lived on the island, then heard more just recently in America First committee meetings in Stonington. There Cecil had presided, preaching in high-toned indignation against American involvement in the European war, as if he was Lindbergh himself.

"I was unconscious," continued Richard. "Reggie Lombard, the bartender, he took me to the hospital. I don't know who it was that sewed me up. The ones that robbed me got away, the bastards."

"And people complain that we don't have barrooms in this county," said Cecil. What he did not say—and did not need to—was that one of those complainers was standing right in front of him with a face that looked like spoiled meat.

"We don't have barrooms in this county because the county is run by women," Richard grumbled.

"There aren't any women in the county government," said Cecil. "I know that for a fact."

"Then the men running it are taking orders from their wives like everybody else in this sorry state does," Richard said. "Do you want your rum? You didn't pull me over to pass the time of day. Ten quarts."

Cecil nodded and took the rum, two bottles at a time, stowing them under a box of canned peas. He did not drink it himself but kept a few bottles in the back room of the island store to sell to fishermen for a fair profit. He hated dealing with Richard Snell, hated himself when he was polite to the man, as he was now. He had heard that Snell had ties of some kind to the German-American Bund, a bunch of shady fellows in Deer Isle. Worse, Richard reminded him of his own father—an unwashed, ignorant, opinionated man.

"Did you make a delivery to Amos?" asked Cecil. "I haven't seen him in two weeks; I don't think anyone has."

"I delivered his rum, but I didn't see him. He was watching me though, I could feel it. He gets queerer and queerer. If he wasn't your father-in-law, I'd say he was daft, living in a ghost village all alone—miles from anybody—peering out of windows and talking to himself or maybe even to the dead."

"I don't have any cash on me," said Cecil. "I can give you a slip of credit for the store, or an IOU."

"I'll take the IOU." Richard knew the storekeeper had the cash; he just could not stand parting with it. To pay Cecil back for the wages-of-sin sermon, Richard wondered aloud about Amos as the two boats drifted apart.

"What's he got in that cove? Four or five houses, two wharves, and a coupla hundred acres of good land. He ought to sell it—all but his house—or pass it on to Leah and you to sell if you want; he doesn't need money. She shouldn't have to wait for her inheritance till he dies."

"You ought to put an ice pack on your face when you get to your mother's; that'll bring the swelling down," Cecil replied.

The storekeeper pushed the boats apart and opened his throttle. He was glad he had mentioned Amos, whose mere existence galled Richard so. But it made him cringe to think that Richard knew so much about Amos's affairs, that he was so interested. Like Cecil's own father, Richard Snell was the kind of man who discovered other people's weaknesses and filed them away for some future use, some profit, or some meanness.

CHAPTER TWO

WHEN AMOS CROSSED THE YORK LEDGES INTO OPEN WATER, HE swung the *Tuna*'s bow into the wind and cut her back to half throttle for a look around. The sun had risen a hand above the horizon and was still a hazy orange. The air was brisk but on so clear a day, when the breeze was light and coming off the mainland, it would soon be warm enough to shed his mittens. There was not another boat in sight, not a soul, just as he had hoped.

In a couple of weeks there would be plenty of lobstermen, a dozen or more, setting out traps in the waters off the east side of the Barter Island; there would be men from the west side, and more and more were coming each season from Stonington, as well. Years ago, when there had been five Coombs boats fishing in these waters, no one contested the family's ancestral claims to the best lobstering grounds: the deeper, sandy-bottomed area between the Black Horse and Fog Island early in the season, and more important, the rocky shore along the Battery and Boom Beach, and in the Turnip Yard later in the season, when the lobsters came in to shed. But this year, he had heard, the Stonington men were grumbling that he claimed more territory than he needed with just 250 traps. At the garage in town the boy had overheard Melvin Brill telling somebody he was going to move two strings of his traps into the Turnip Yard this year; to hell with Amos Coombs.

If he does, thought Amos, he'll get the same reception his father got twenty years ago when he tried it.

Amos had to stand on tiptoe to take the top trap down from the pyramid he had built on the stern. These traps had twenty-fathom buoy lines, and he would set the first string of ten in a line running north to south, where the bottom was sand and eel-grass. When the lobsters started to come crawling in toward shore, the oily herring bait would draw them into his traps, and when the Stonington men started to set out their gear east of the island, his buoys—red and yellow and freshly painted—would be there to mark his territory. The first trap that he set on the washboard was sturdy oak like the rest, and having dried out all winter long, it seemed as light as an empty well bucket. He placed two smooth ballast stones, each the size of a splayed hand, in the bottom of the trap; hefted it; added another stone; then baited it, tied it shut, and spat on it for good luck. In moves made so many times they had become instinctive, he pushed the throttle forward, nudged the trap overboard, and watched the coiled line at his feet as it ran out. The trap floated for a minute, tilting slightly, then slowly began to sink. Being so dry and light, it would travel some in the current before it settled on the bottom, but Amos had allowed for that. In two weeks the trap would be waterlogged; then he could remove the ballast stones, and it would sink straight down on its own.

When he had finished setting the second string, he cut her back to an idle, brought his stool up from below, and poured himself a little drink. From his dinner pail he plucked a bright blue hard-boiled egg that he held up between thumb and fore-finger to examine before he cracked it, peeled it, dunked it over-board for the salt, and chewed it appreciatively.

He hadn't heard them until they banged on his front door, he remembered. He never did. He had fallen asleep with a Sears catalog open in his lap, so he had not noticed Leah's Chevy turning around up on the road or heard her when she and Gus tiptoed across the gravelly dooryard. When the banging snapped him out of sleep, he knew immediately what it was; he opened the door, took the May basket from the knob, and shouted into the darkness: "Leah! Gus! I know it's you! Come back here. I caught you this time."

He heard them giggling in the spruce by the creek bridge. He smiled to imagine his girl Leah—more than thirty years old, with a husky teenage son—scampering around in the dark like a kid. While he looked through the contents of the little woven basket—two blue eggs in a sphagnum nest, a bouquet of swamp buttercups and forget-me-nots tied with a red ribbon, a block of fudge in waxed paper—he wondered once again if she knew that it had been a May basket that had led to her being born and had led to a decade of misery for him. But she didn't know, he thought, and she never would. Perhaps if her mother had lived longer, she would have told Leah, but he thought not. Why would she mention it to her daughter when she never said a thing about it to him, the boy who chased her into the Turner graveyard after leaving a basket on her doorknob. What would she say? That two weeks after her sixteenth birthday she and Amos lost their virginity in a cemetery? That their first coupling was clumsy, fully clothed, messy, and over before they knew it had begun? That she, Leah, was born of such an unpleasant ex-perience? That she was named Leah because Leah was the weak-eyed, unwanted daughter?

Amos shook his head and unwrapped the fudge. He did not like the way his engine was idling, with little in-sucks as if it was catching its breath; he resolved to adjust the butterfly choke when he went in to pick up another load of traps. Riding the coming tide and helped along by a light southerly breeze, he had drifted within sight of the cove. He shook the teabags out of his thermos and—still sitting on the stool for the sake of his legs—turned toward his wharf.

• • •

He pushed the last trap of his second load overboard in mid-afternoon. He had thought that he might finish this early, so he had brought along the box of seed packets and three bottles of rum that he had promised Jake Gardiner, the keeper at Mount Desert Rock light, eighteen miles out. He had only known Jake for about ten years, since he took the keeper's job, and he rarely saw him. But as Maggie said, Amos had an "affinity" for Jake, which, she explained, meant that Amos enjoyed his company. It was true. When the lighthouse tender from Bar Harbor made its spring delivery, it carried a load of topsoil with which Jake and his crew filled the crevices in the rock around the keeper's house, shallow troughs that had been washed clean by winter storms. They planted a vegetable garden by the house and put in flower gardens all around the lighthouse; the flowers, which were Jake's great pleasure, took the hard edge off the bare little rock in the summer. The rum, Amos thought, would do much the same for Jake.

If he ran the *Tuna* at three quarters throttle, he could be out to the light and back by dark, or close to it. The weather was calm and clear, there were no signs of the wind backing to change that, and the moon would be nearly full.

Three years before, when the Coast Guard had taken over the Lighthouse Service, Jake had been offered a commission as Chief Petty Officer and had accepted it. His assistant keeper, Gooden, a Gloucester man with a mouth like a shit house, had not been invited to join the Coast Guard but had stayed on the lonely rock anyway. How Jake, a man who kept himself and his lighthouse buffed and polished and in Bristol fashion, could stand the nasty Gooden, Amos did not know. But with the handing over of the station to the Coast Guard came a 600-meter band radio and Seaman First Class Ernest Morales from Boston to operate it. A handsome, laughing young man with perfect white teeth and an irreverent, big-city manner, Morales was a hero to the boy, who would be sore that he had not been with Amos for this visit. Jake had once told Amos and the boy that Morales was hornier than a three-peckered billy goat, adding that the Coast Guard had sent him out to Mount Desert Rock as a courtesy to the police departments in the major cities of the East Coast and as a way to protect the female population of the entire region. This claim made Morales shine and made the boy gaze at him in admiration.

Out past Amos's fishing grounds, eight miles from the lighthouse, the sea gave over to low rolling swells. He passed over Grumpy Ledge and knew the bottom was dropping off to three hundred feet. The sea beneath him was black and dark as night; without the shore to give him some perspective, his boat seemed tiny on the water's huge, blank surface.

When he was young, Amos asked Walter why some people kept their houses so hot in the winter: the older the person, the hotter the parlor. Those rooms were stifling. Walter said that such people had had the chill. Once the cold gets into you, he explained, once it seeps into your bones, the chill is always there, and you cannot get warm enough ever again. Walter told his nephew that he, too, would have it one day and understand. Since then, Amos had had the chill, of course—more than once—and his uncle was right: once it set in, it was with you for life. What he did not know at the time, but had learned later, is that the fear of the water works the same way. Once you have had the feeling of complete helplessness, the awareness that only thin planks stand between your feet and the horrible deep darkness beneath, once you had that, it never went away. The older Amos got, the worse it grew, especially in deep water or threatening weather. He could make excuses, but he could not get rid of the fear; he just had to live with it, like the aching arches and the deepening cold in his bones. When the boy was with him, he could hide it pretty well; when he was alone, it was the only thing out there with him, and it was damn poor company. There was no point in complaining about the fear to the ones already gone; cold and dark and death didn't mean a thing to them.

Amos held onto the *Tuna* with both hands. The boat was round-hulled and quite tippy; she was fine for inshore waters, but out at sea she was awfully hard to handle. She bobbed around like a cork, and if Amos did not run along a trough the right way, she would not steer at all.

He heard a low groaning noise—or felt it in the planking under his feet. Amos thought there was something wrong with his engine and stuck his head in the cabin door to listen. But the sound, or the feeling of sound, was all around. He came up and looked out again to see a shiny black pipe rising straight up out of the water, making its own little wake, not more than a hundred yards to starboard. The sea moaned and lifted beneath him, raising his little boat on a slow, sinuous swell. Then the rest of the giant machine broke the surface in a splash and heave of water. First he saw the conning tower of the submarine, then the deck and glistening black hull, as it surfaced and steamed south by east away from him, as indifferent as a passing humpback.

Amos ducked beneath the gunwale and on his knees watched her sail away. The sub was a German, he knew, and it was huge. After the vessel had been up on the surface for a few seconds, it let out a great gushing blowing noise, like a sleek, black iron whale. Amos shivered in terror and stared, his mouth wide open, his bowels loosening dangerously. Pushing the *Tuna* up to full speed and making for the lighthouse, he never took his eyes off the sub as it shrank out of sight on its way offshore.

Harvey Gooden was on the upper gallery of the light, polishing the glass, when he saw the *Tuna* pull into the slip and tie off on the launch. He watched her skipper scamper up onto the rock, headed for the house; from fifty feet up Amos looked like a little toy soldier wound up too tight and let loose. Harvey cupped his hands over his mossy teeth and hollered:

"What's the hurry, Cappy? I never seen you move so fast!"

Amos stopped at the foot of the lighthouse and leaned back. "You see anything to the south? You got binoculars up there?"

"Sure I do," said Harvey. "Just you wait. What am I looking for?"

Amos did not wait. He found Morales in the radio room, giving the hourly weather report. Amos shook his shoulder. Morales turned around grinning, still talking into the headset, "wind southwest, five to ten knots; waves two feet," and shooed him away.

Amos hurried through the kitchen, where supper was cooking, and ran headlong into Jake, coming out of the pantry with an armload of tin cans and a pie. Thrown off balance, the lighthouse keeper lost control of the cans but managed to save the pie. He flattened his hand against Amos's chest to steady him and stop him from doing more damage, feeling his friend's heart sputtering like an old one-cylinder engine. Jake had just bathed and had combed his hair with Wildroot Cream Oil.

"Jesus, Amos, you stink of bait."

"I just got nearly run over by a goddamn German submarine. Right out there." Amos pointed out the kitchen window.

Jake set the pie on the shelf and collected the cans. He held out one with a dented rim. "This one's going to be a bitch to open."

"You didn't hear what I said."

"Yes I did. I'm no psychiatrist, but I can tell by the look on your face that you've sure as hell seen *something*. What you need to do right now is settle down. Let's go to the radio room. I thought you'd be delivering rum; we looked for you yesterday."

"I am delivering your rum—and your seeds too, for that matter; it's a piece of luck that they're not blown to bits and me and my boat with them."

Harvey followed them into the radio room. "I didn't see nuthin. What was it I was looking for anyway?"

"Let's find out," said Jake. "Those binoculars are supposed to stay up in the light; you know that."

Jake sat Amos down in Morales's chair, cleared a space on the table, laid a large black book before him, and opened it to "German Ships: Submarine." Harvey and Morales exchanged a look and closed in to look over Amos's shoulder.

On the second page, the lobsterman put his finger on a silhouette labeled *Standard Atlantic Boat, Type VII.* "Sure," he said, and sat back. There it was. Right there. It eased him somewhat to see his apparition in a Coast Guard book. Now he knew he had seen it.

"That's the bridge I saw, with a gun inside the railing aft of it, and that bigger one on the deck forward. Two hundred twenty feet long? I tell you it looked every bit of it. He can travel at seventeen knots? He was going maybe six or seven. I'll tell you the reason I thought it was a whale—it blew like a whale. *Pfooo!* And instead of smelling like metal or fuel oil, it stank of living things. No not living . . . dead things, things rotten, stale food, meat that's gone by. . . ."

This made Morales mutter solemnly in Spanish and Jake rub his hands together as if he were drying them.

"Jesus, how can you be so calm. You might have got your ass killed," said Harvey.

"I'm not calm, you goddamn fool. I nearly shat myself out there."

Harvey's face sank in disgust. "I'm taking these binoculars back," he said.

"He's been lying on the bottom all day in the sand out of the current, using his electric motors and breathing the same air since dawn," said Morales. "Now he's come up to go hunting out in the sea lanes, so he's back on his diesels and blowing off stale air. That was German shit you smelled—and cabbage, I bet. Sauerkraut. He's on his way out to sink a merchantman going from Boston to Halifax."

"Like a compost heap when you stir it up; like . . ."

Jake led Amos across the room so he could show them the sub's position on the chart.

"Here. Right there," he pointed. "He was heading south."

"Right out to the Halifax run, just as Morales said, and nobody can do a damn thing about it." Jake smoothed his mustaches.

"What do you mean?" asked Amos. "Why can't you get Pancho here to get on that radio and call an airplane to come bomb him? He's on the surface out there right now. Just bomb him."

"Fuck you, carrot top; don't call me Pancho."

"Relax, Morales," said Jake. "Get on that set. There just might be an aircraft patrolling in the area, though probably not one that could do anything. It's worth a try, but I doubt they could send a plane out here if you saw Hitler himself all alone in a dinghy."

"He didn't see me unless it was through his periscope." Amos took off his cap and put it back on again.

"He may not have seen you, but he knew you were there," said Jake. "He has a listening device that would have picked you up loud and clear. He didn't give a damn about you. He's out after big fish; you're nothing but a waste of ammo to him."

Morales made contact, and they listened, Jake with the extra headset pressed to one ear.

When he heard Morales explaining that a local fisherman had made the sighting, Amos thought that the Coast Guardsman must have made a mistake and did not realize that he was sending the message in the clear.

"He isn't using any code," he objected.

"No, hell no," said Jake.

"Then that submarine can hear exactly what he's saying. They can translate it."

"That's right."

"That's insane."

"It's not insane, it's stupid. Why don't you stay for supper, Amos? I got a nice stew and a custard pie that just now survived a surface attack in the pantry doorway." Jake put a hand on Amos's shoulder.

"No, I guess not," said the lobsterman. "I've got to get back. Why don't you come down with me and get your rum?"

When his father let him off work at five, Gus Barter sneaked a Three Musketeers from the glass case and walked over to the cove to find the *Tuna* and see how the setting out had gone. He thought that if Amos was going to set out more traps tomorrow, he could help the old man load them on the high tide later that night.

Gus looked in the window of the house, surprised not to see a light in the gathering dusk, then went down to the shore to find that Amos's boat was not in. His skiff swung on the mooring, but there was no sign of him, nor any engine sounds on the water. He never stayed out this late, thought Gus. Never. He did not like to be out in the dark. There was no sign on the wharf of his having come in and gone back out, though he must have because two tiers of traps were gone. Gus sat on the wharf with his feet resting on a ladder rung and watched it grow dark. He was cold, and he would be late for supper. He walked out on the point to look down the island toward Amos's fishing grounds, but he saw nothing. Nobody was out on the water.

Gus knew that if he hurried, he could catch his Aunt Maggie on the road. He took a deep, determined chest full of air and started out in a run over the rocks, then up the shore to the road. He was a hefty boy, at fifteen still carrying some of his baby fat. His overalls were tight on his chest; as he ran the straps flapped down off his shoulders, and he had to keep pulling them up.

He waited on a boulder by the bridge over the cove creek for Maggie to pass by on her way home from the school. By the time she came along, he had stopped breathing heavily. She saw him stand up when he spotted her, and she knew before she got to him that something was wrong with Amos.

When it comes, she had always thought, it will come like

this—as a complete surprise, in the middle of a homework lesson or dreaming up a dinner, just as the other two had. Of all
the things that could happen to Amos fishing alone, the ones
she imagined most were related to drink, as it had been with
his Uncle Walter and her grandfather: both drunk, both
drowned.

None of them could swim. She did not know one fisherman
who had ever learned. They said it was fruitless because in the
cold northern Atlantic even the best swimmer would die in minutes from hypothermia. She suspected that they never learned
out of fear, but she never said so.

"Climb in," she told Gus. "We'll drive down."

Maggie leaned across and opened the door for him. She
backed up carefully, half listening to Gus, and eased the Ford
over the lip of the paved road down onto the steep cove road,
driving in low gear all the way to the bottom and Amos's dark
house. The boy talked nervously, running through the less
frightening possibilities aloud: that Amos had run out of gas,
that he had had trouble with the driveshaft again, that his engine
had quit, forcing him to put out a sea anchor or grapple, and
wait for help.

"Maybe he's going to stay the night in Stonington," she
offered.

"If he is, it'll be the first time in his life that he's spent a night
off island."

"The second," said Maggie.

She stopped in the field and stared out at the black sea, anxious, full of regret at the idea of him out there all alone, grateful
that Gus had walked ahead of her and could not see that she
was afraid. It would not do any good to go to town for help; no
one would go out tonight in this rising wind, and Amos, she
knew, did not even have running lights—much less a radio of
any kind. Behind her, in the woods by Ava's house, hundreds of
grosbeaks chattered in the trees.

On the wharf, she sent Gus into the shack for matches and

a lantern. He was glad to have something to do—such a serious boy and so afraid to show any emotion, even to her. Maggie rolled down the sleeves of her blouse and put on the light sweater that had been tied over her shoulders. There on the cold wharf, her arms hugging herself, she had an odd impulse to tell the boy about her and Amos, but instead she moved closer to the edge and craned her neck toward the water. She said Amos's name once, softly, then hushed the boy as he clumped down the ramp with the light. She hushed him again, and he listened. To her relief, he heard it too. She stood with one hand raised toward the sound, until the *Tuna* came into view beyond the York ledges, first a ghostly shape, a black looming; then a smaller, darker form, accompanied by the increasing sound of his engine. Gus shouted and waved his lantern, though he knew Amos could not hear him.

When Amos had taken up his mooring line and shut down the engine, Maggie yelled to ask if he was all right. He answered sure, sure he was.

He knew she was angry because he had given her a scare, but he did not care—he was so glad to see her. While Amos was still tying up the skiff on the shore below, she asked him where he had been.

"I went out to the lighthouse. I saw a U-boat. And close up, I tell you. A christly submarine as big as this cove. A Standard Atlantic Boat with fourteen torpedoes." He talked standing in the mud, his arms still stretched out to the whole cove, the skiff line hanging from one, a dark idea taking shape in the increasing moonlight.

Was he drunk? She was not sure, though she normally could tell. He kept talking, describing what had happened, explaining it a little better this time having told the story twice already. He was scared, really scared; she could hear the tone of his fear even in the thin echo behind her. She had never seen him this way, not even when Walter had died, and she knew he must be telling the truth.

In his parlor, while she sat and the boy stood staring at him, Amos paced back and forth still telling snatches of it. She soon thought that it was not seeing the submarine that had him badly frightened, so she chose her questions carefully to lead him to the source of his fear. When he mentioned the second time that the sighting had been reported on the radio, in the clear, she interrupted.

"Did the man say who you were or describe your boat or say where you're from?"

"No, none of that. Not even that I'm a lobster fisherman, but just a plain fisherman. Still, now that German knows it's a local boat, and that's not far from where I fish. He didn't kill me the first time, but he sure as hell will the next time he sees me. And he's gonna know I live on this island, right here."

"Jesus!" said the boy.

Maggie gave Gus a look. Amos was avoiding her eyes.

"Don't tell anyone about this," he said.

"Good heavens. What do you mean?" He was always so secretive, she thought, at least with the living.

"If you do, people will laugh, goddamn them." He looked at Gus, who nodded his approval.

"They won't laugh, Amos; there's not a thing funny about this. Why would anyone—"

"They won't believe it," Gus said, his voice high. "They won't believe he really saw it, and they'll make jokes about it. Like the bobbing human candles."

"Maybe you're right," said Maggie. "Maybe it's better that they don't know because they might believe it. They will, even though they'll claim they don't. People out here are frightened enough as it is. If they hear that you saw a U-boat off the island, so close, they might panic. And no wonder. I'm scared too."

Neither Amos nor Gus believed her.

CHAPTER THREE

IT WAS OBVIOUS TO MAGGIE, LEAH, AND GUS THAT AMOS WAS doing anything and everything he could to avoid going out on the water on his side of the island. He rode the mail boat to Stonington twice a week, spending the whole day off island to replace a monkey wrench that had been missing for years. At Ava's, he cut spruce poles to replace the entire garden fence. He turned the garden over and started the planting. He reroofed the cabin and the hen coop. He dug a new hole for the privy and moved it. He cleaned his house from top to bottom; he cut and burned brush behind the barn and tidied up the graveyard.

The rest of the time Amos did what everyone else was doing and worked to get the rest of his lobster gear ready. Gus came over almost every evening to help him and to get his own traps ready. Neither of them mentioned that the four strings Amos had already set out had soaked by now and had probably fished. They ought to be taking the ballast stones out of them to be used in the others. Gus thought that Amos would start setting out as soon as he got over his nervousness from seeing the U-boat and when the others started setting out. This year fifty of the traps that would go in the water belonged to Gus. He would start saving money of his own—money made from lobstering, not from working in his father's store—and he would start saving toward his own boat.

They had had a hard time persuading Cecil to allow his son to go lobstering with Amos and to fish his own traps. The one-room school on Barter Island only went through the eighth grade; the few families who wanted their children to finish high school had to send them to stay with relations while they went to a school on the mainland. Gus had spent the last year with his father's sister's family in Jonesport, where he was homesick the whole time and hated the school. He thought the boys his age who were not making a living on their own, or who were clerks or laborers working for someone else and not independent fishermen, were sissies. He got Cs and was teased about his weight. After Pearl Harbor the Boyer twins, among the few students who were nice to him, announced that they were going to lie about their age and leave school to join the navy; he thought they were heroes.

Cecil did not want his son to go fishing on the *Tuna* because he thought Amos would encourage Gus to quit before he finished high school and move back to the island for good. The storekeeper wanted his son to get his diploma and stay off the island afterward in a steady paying job, as his older brother had done. Cecil had grown up on the island, and now he was stuck there; he did not want that for his boys. He knew what a mean life a lobster fisherman leads. He did not want Gus to get some dim island girl pregnant when they were both sixteen, like some people he knew, and get trapped on the island forever by her, a kid, a house, and a boat.

Amos had wanted the boy to go fishing with him, then go on his own, to keep the Coombs fishing grounds in the family, even though the name would change. He imagined Gus marrying a nice island girl and moving into the cove and raising a family, filling the place up with life again. What looked like misery in Cecil's imagination looked like the peaceable kingdom in Amos's.

Maggie had been ambivalent and so not much help to either side. She too had hoped Gus would find some work on the mainland, yet she knew that half of his father's motivation for keeping him away from fishing was Cecil's mistrust and jealousy of Amos—and something else that she did not understand. Most important, she understood that Gus had Coombs blood that drew him to the island and that there was nothing to be done about it. Like the rest of the natives, she knew it was an odd and unrealistic and backward place to live, but she would not live anywhere else, either.

Leah had reminded Cecil that he had one son already on the mainland, with a secure job in the shipyard. She did not need to remind him, but did anyway, that the price for lobsters was climbing steadily and that it would probably continue to rise. She had reminded Gus that he owed a lot to his father and that he had a duty to his family. But, afraid that he might try to enlist in the navy if she didn't, she had fixed it between them so that Gus would fish with Amos twice a week during the summer season while he finished high school, working at the store in the evenings. With a small salary from the store, and an income from fifty traps, he could start saving for his future. She put the thought of his having to go to war right out of her mind.

Leah kept things peaceful in the family by preventing Gus from going off on his rhapsodies about Amos in front of his father; it worried her that the boy praised his grandfather to hurt Cecil, or that Cecil thought as much. Amos was her father and she loved him, but she thought that Gustus was a little foolish about him. Her son would grow out of it, she told herself.

On the days when Gus was not working with him at the wharf, Amos was getting tortured by his uncles and his own mind. He did not have to go out on the water to know what was going on out there. He saw the boats passing by, and he could tell by the sound of their engines who was setting traps and where. Mornings, he stood on the wharf looking out at nothing visible on the water, with his face set and his fists clenched—like a man watching his house burn down. He could use all the excuses he wanted for the rest of the world, but it was no good: Deer Isle men were taking over his family fishing grounds, and he was not doing a goddamned thing about it. It was a betrayal of the only thing in his life that he attached any importance to. No one in the world cared where those men were fishing except the spirits in the cove, and the cove was the only place Amos could live. It was so bad it almost made him laugh, but he did not dare to because they were so disgusted with him.

The boy probably did not know that other men were setting out in Coombs waters, but he would hear soon, when they started bragging about it in Stonington and word got down to the island. Eventually, Amos knew, he would have to face Gus and explain to him why they were not going out at all. The longer he stalled, with Gus and the rest of the family knowing he was stalling, the smaller he felt.

On an evening when a long week of fog was finally blowing out to sea, taking the last of his excuses with it, Amos sat rocking on the front porch. If he did not go out and reclaim his waters, he would not get gunned down by the U-boat. Then he would surely live another twenty years, but he would live them ashamed in front of the boy and everyone else. In addition, he would spend the rest of eternity facing the family he betrayed by giving up their fishing grounds. If he did go out and got blown up, he would spend eternity with them as a hero. Well, maybe not a hero; Ava would never give him that much credit because she still blamed him for what happened to Clytie. Perhaps he wouldn't be a hero but someone who had tried, who had kept up his part of the trust. They were split, he knew, on whether he should take the boy along with him.

As for the living, he thought Maggie would be against it, but he decided to take Gus anyway, to keep his promise. He would assure her that he would stay in close to shore; in turn he would get her to promise not to tell Leah that the U-boat might know him by sight, and might be waiting to take its revenge on him— and her son along with him. Gus, he thought, might be scared too, but he was young, and he would be good for it.

Lew settled into the rocker next to him, disturbing it only slightly. He rested his cheek on his fist, his gaze toward the water.

Amos did not look at him but said, "I had a dream about you last night."

I know it.

Amos listened to Lew's breathing and waited.

You're going to tie them off. You've got no choice. So go do it for Christ's sake.

Amos waited again, then drained his cup, went down to the boat, and headed out of the cove. No one else was on the water, and it was close to the longest day of the year, so he could easily get done before dark. In the shade of the cliffs, with a watchful eye on the open sea behind him, he tied off the first string; the buoys were white with a red spindle, probably Sam Witherspoon's. He found a second and third string of ten in the Turnip Yard and tied them off too. It was a simple process and a simple statement: on each trap line he coiled ten feet of rope between the buoy and the toggle, and tied it off with the warning knot he had learned from Walter. When the intruder found the knotted coil, he knew that he had twenty-four hours to move his traps; otherwise the lines would be cut, and he'd lose everything. Amos had the old Enfield .303 to back him up if need be, but he hoped it would not come to that.

Amos and Gus started setting out their traps at the end of the week. He found that the strings he had tied off had been moved out of his waters. He had bluffed them successfully.

They set Gus's first string among the rocks beneath the cliffs.

"Didn't Sam Witherspoon have a string along here?" Gus asked.

"How'd you know that?"

"Richard Snell was talking about it in the store the other day."

"He would, that son of a bitch," said Amos, thinking that now Richard would have to eat the smirk he was wearing when he said it.

"Why'd he move? You didn't tie him off, did you?"

"Sure I did. Sure, what'd you expect? I tied off the ones in the Turnip Yard too, and I bet they're gone."

"Why didn't you tell me? Why didn't you take me with you? Some of these are my traps. Those are my colors up on the bow with yours. How am I supposed to learn how to tie somebody off?"

"I'll teach you. You're going to need to learn how to use that Enfield, too."

The Barters lived in town on the west side of the island, in one of the two yellow houses across the road from the post office and Cecil's store; theirs was the one with the fresh coat of paint and the flagpole. On the days when he and Amos went fishing, Gus got up at 4:30, an hour before his father. He ate breakfast, packed a lunch in his dinner pail, and walked over to the cove in the cool of the morning to meet Amos at the wharf at 5:30.

Since his father had started getting after him for staying up till all hours with his books, he had been reading under the blankets with a flashlight, as he had learned to do while staying with his cousins in Jonesport. There he had read all of the Leather-stocking Tales and all of the Kenneth Roberts novels about the rabble who fought the revolution. Maggie had sent him the books in Stonington, and he had brought them home with him. Now he was reading the Hornblower series. In the morning,

Gus would walk around to the east side of the island on the road, all alone, when the only sound was the deedling trill of the hermit thrush in the woods. Then, he would relive his adventures from the night before: dining with Cornwallis in his cabin, consoling Cobart for the horrible splintering of his arm, escaping in a French lobsterboat from a raid on a semaphore station. He wondered if he could ever be as hard-hearted as Hornblower, as cold and controlled.

When he got to the cove, Amos was already on the wharf fussing with a bait barrel. Gus had to squint into the peeking sun to see his figure against the horizon. Out on her mooring, the *Tuna* rolled slightly, her stern piled high with the pyramid of traps that they had loaded the night before. Twenty of them were his, stacked to go out second. When he sat down at the fish shack to pull on his high rubber boots, he had the feeling that all the dreaming that he had done about fishing as a man out of the cove was now fulfilled. In his humble cabin, Horatio Hornblower sat just that way to pull on his boots before going up on deck.

Amos had seen Gus coming, of course, because he had been watching for the boy. Still he acted surprised, and irritated.

"Well look who's here. I thought you'd given it up. I figured you were staying home with a tummyache or maybe still sleeping with your nose in a book."

"Yes, yes." Gus thumped down the wharf in his big boots. "And don't even bother with the next line; I already know it. You're going to say 'Years ago we would of been out for two hours by now and had thirty traps set. Back then we—' "

"That's right." Amos acted his part: indignant and slightly wounded. "It's true, goddamn you. Which is why I say it a lot. Years ago things were different. We were out to haul before you saw the sun. We . . ."

Gus walked by him and started down the ladder to the skiff, his dinner pail dangling from his thumb as he descended.

"Well, come on then," said the boy. "If we didn't have to

wait so long for you to get warmed up we would get out on time."

"Me? Goddamn you," said Amos, who wouldn't let on that he was pleased.

He had not felt so good in years, or at least not since the boy had gone out with him on occasion the summer before. This time it was different; it was fuller. They were going together as partners just as he and Walter had. The night before, when they were loading traps in the vague light, Amos thought for a minute that the boy was him and he was Uncle Walter. He had almost told Gus then about the feeling but decided the boy might not understand—or, worse, might not be interested.

He followed Gus down into the skiff, then had to go back up for his own dinner pail, which he had left on the wharf.

"You're getting old," Gus said from the skiff below. "You'd forget your teapot if it wasn't stuck on."

"You go straight to hell," Amos answered lovingly.

People who were fond of Gus called him "belt strong" or "big-boned"; to others he was a "hog body," or simply overweight. Nobody ever called him agile, especially on land, but aboard a boat like the *Tuna,* with little deck space to get clumsy in, he handled himself well enough. Even so, Amos liked to call him a damn farmer when he got the lines fouled or dropped the gaff overboard.

Off to the southeast, where Amos had seen the U-boat, a bank of clouds was making up, something to keep an eye on. As they passed the Seal Ledges, Amos shouted at the basking harbor seals to send them slithering into the water. He gave Gus the wheel and relieved himself over the washboard. Up in the woods on the mountainside, the maples and poplars were leafed out with the first, light blush of green.

"I hope some poor doe doesn't see that thing of yours," Gus teased. "It'll send her into heat. She'll curl her lip back and throw herself overboard trying to get to it."

Amos shook it and crouched over to tuck it back in.

"I want to set this first string here in the ledges, then we'll put yours along the Battery."

The Battery was a high ledge in deep water, one of the best places for lobsters in all of the Coombs territory—and the most dangerous to fish. Amos had not set traps along the Battery for years because it scared him to come so close to the rocks. Now, however, he would risk it again to make more money for the boy.

Traveling south and away from land, he took it slow to avoid losing the top traps on the tippy pyramid in some sudden roll. They drank tea from their thermoses in silence, watching the morning open up on the ocean around them. Occasionally a gull swept down to follow for a while, until he saw that they were not cleaning fish or emptying traps; then he'd fly off, resigned to thinner fishing elsewhere.

Gus made up for his clumsiness with strength; handling traps filled with ballast stones was nothing for him. He set each one on the washboard, baited it, and watched Amos. When Amos raised a crooked finger, Gus pushed the trap overboard and kept an eye on the line as it played out. He thought several times to watch where they set each trap, meaning to ask Amos later why he chose one spot over another. Amos knew the bottom as well as he knew his own dooryard, as well as his uncles had.

By the time they got to the Battery the wind had picked up, bringing with it a sea feeling of wet and cold from the dark bank of clouds on the horizon. It could be either fog or a line squall making up outside. It being early spring the best guess would be fog, but the wind was quite strong and the chop was picking up on the water, so they could not be sure.

Amos made one pass along the jagged wall of the Battery, riding a low swell and watching for the best spots, testing his resolve to risk the rocks to provide better fishing for Gus, who stood by his first trap on the washboard, awaiting the signal. The tide was low, adding ten fearful feet to the height of the Battery, exposing its watery skirt of rockweed and, beneath, the rocky crevices where the lobsters liked to shed.

"You ready?"

"Don't I look it?"

Amos again turned the *Tuna* in toward the rocks, knowing that closer was better. He cut her engine back, gave the signal, then as the traps struck the water, gunned the boat back out and away before the wind could draw her on and smash her to toothpicks, grinding the two of them into meatloaf.

Gus hefted two more traps into place, speared the knitted bags of rancid herring with the long needle to run the string through, and tied each trap shut, ready for the second pass.

"You ought to drizzle some of that bait oil on the trap," Amos said. "It advertises."

"Who is it that says 'Leave the boat to the captain and the gear to the sternman?' You watch out, or you're going to scrape your planking."

"Dump it."

They turned out and Gus baited two more, this time slathering both with oily gurry.

"What do the lobsters eat when they're not eating this herring?" Gus wondered out loud.

Amos looked at him, slack-jawed, his agitation overcome by utter amazement. In all his life he had never heard a more ridiculous question.

"*Something in the water*, you goddamned fool." He stared for a second, then tilted the first trap overboard himself, shaking his head sadly.

On the third pass the engine sputtered once—a little cough that weakened Amos's knees, a sound that Gus either did not hear or chose to ignore.

"I don't know," Amos said. "Maybe we better wait till this wind lets go before we set any more in here."

"We can do another," answered Gus. "We only have two more for here. You did that last run perfect."

Amos cut her around sharply to avoid coming side to the

wind, and turned back in for another run, thinking the boy was right. He was handling the boat pretty well this morning.

He took her right into the edge of the ragged wall for the next pair, and as the traps struck the water, the engine back-fired, then quit. Dead. At once the wind began to turn the *Tuna* back into the rocks.

Amos danced at the wheel. He knew exactly what it would look like: she would pound against the sharp rocks; pound, smashing barnacles; then begin to break up. They would grab for pieces of her or for the rocks themselves, and they would be smashed senseless and dragged to the bottom, bleeding and gasping for breath, beaten to a pulp and pulled under forever.

"Get the oar!" he yelled. "Get up on the bow and turn her into the wind. Oh, shit; she won't start. Oh, God; where's that grapple?"

Without a word Gus scurried onto the bow pulling the oar with him. He paddled furiously to try to turn the *Tuna* but was helpless with so much boat lying across the wind.

"Here!" Amos stretched out along the gunwale holding out the grapple hook and a coil of line. "Skulk it and throw it to windward as far as you can and pull us off when it grabs. Hurry up dammit, we're about to strike!"

Gus knelt on the bow, pinning the free end of the line, and swung the grapple over his head.

"No, you fool! Skulk it. Cleat it first."

The boy did as he was told and threw the grapple sidearm into the face of the wind. The coil failed, then snarled, and Gus started to haul it back in. Amos screamed at him to leave it alone and take up the slack.

"Did it catch?" he cried. Amos was back at the wheel turning the starter over and over, leaning out through the window, his face as red as a raspberry.

Gus hauled on the line, felt it give, then catch, then give again. Finally it held.

"It's holding!" he shouted, and scrambled back with the oar to try to push them off.

Amos ducked below with a wrench and screwdriver; as he disappeared, the hook lost its purchase, and the starboard side struck the rocks with a bang and a groan. Gus screamed that the grapple was slipping and scampered back to the bow.

Down below Amos was crouched with his tools between the engine and the hull. The *Tuna* was rolling so badly that he could not stay bent over the engine, working with both hands, but was pitched back against the hull, then thrown forward onto the engine. He tried to catch hold of the ceiling, but went flopping backward, swearing, howling in pain as his back struck the hull or he burned his hand on the manifold.

"Why's she rolling so? Aren't we into the wind?" He saw over Gus's shoulder that the wind was driving them back into the rocks.

"God!" he yelled. "We're going to strike again. I knew it wouldn't hold. Oh, damn this thing."

Gus stood staring, amazed that they were about to die, even more amazed that he thought Amos looked funny flopping back and forth down below—helpless, bent over like a question mark. Maybe this was the detachment that Hornblower felt when he was in danger.

Amos threw out a lifejacket; Gus grabbed for it, but it glanced off his arm and went overboard, splashed, and sank out of sight.

"It sank!" cried Gus. "It sank like a christly stone!"

Amos didn't answer. This time when he crossed the solenoid with the screwdriver the engine growled and turned over.

"Quick, pull out the throttle!"

The engine caught and roared, but as Amos scurried up to take the wheel, the starboard side struck the rock again, scraping horribly as they pulled away.

Neither of them spoke as he took her around in the lee of the high ledge and sat idling in the calm water, catching his breath, holding his wrist. His oilskin apron, which had softened in the heat of the engine room, lay hardening in his lap.

"I guess if that don't call for a drink, nothing does," he said.

Gus nodded. He started to shut down the engine but Amos stopped him, saying it might not start again. Somehow, Amos knew that he had seen this ahead of time—or something a lot like it. He had, in a way, but not a failed engine and not at the Battery.

Gus fetched his cup, the rum, and his thermos, too, in case he wanted to cut the Demerara with tea. He was surprised that Amos was so quiet; he expected him to be swearing and vowing never to go near the Battery again. What had just happened was exactly why he didn't fish there any more.

"How's your hand?" Gus felt that Amos had gotten burned for him.

"It's fine. Look, no blisters. Here, let's both of us have a drink if you can promise not to tell your parents, or Maggie."

Gus tried not to act too eager. He held their cups while Amos poured the dark rum and water and stirred it with the filet knife.

A one-legged gull landed on the topmost trap and watched them drink.

"I guess we shouldn't fish in so close," said Gus.

"Not until we tune this engine. We'll put your last bridle over this morning, though; tonight I'll adjust that carburetor."

"Look at that." Gus pointed out to sea. "You can see two of them at once."

Two freighters sat on the distant horizon, seemingly motionless.

"Do you suppose they'll make it across?"

"God only knows. The U-boats are out there somewhere. I can vouch for that." He shook his head sadly. "You know what we're doing, don't you? We're acting as if the worst thing that's happening anywhere is an engine going out in the rocks. We're as bad as the rest of them. German submarines are driving in and out of this bay to sink our ships, and we're acting like there's nothing going on."

"What can we do?" Gus's cheeks were plum colored; the rope burns in his palms throbbed painfully, but he would not mention them.

"They're using this bay for a safe harbor," said Amos. "They even have a working light to guide them in and out."

"As father says we just don't have the planes or ships to stop them," replied Gus. "God I wish we could do something; it feels so helpless. I wish I was eighteen."

Amos had been planning this conversation for a week, and now he had the boy where he wanted him. He had not counted on the extra edge of the burned hand, only on Gus's feeling beholden to him for risking the boat in the rocks. He was too proud to ask Maggie himself, but if Gus did, it would be all right.

"What the Coast Guard needs is people to be spotters, like the home guard in England and the guys on the west coast. They need men who can help them keep a lookout and report in; not plane spotters here, but sub spotters."

"That's what we'll do then." Gus was resolved; he stood up to show it.

Amos acted forlorn. He threw the dregs of his drink overboard. "But we can't. We can't go offshore in this boat. It's too small, too slow."

"That doesn't matter. We can handle it. We can—"

Amos shook his head. "I wasn't going to tell you this because it'll just discourage you the way it did me, but we've got to be realistic." He paused to add weight to what he was going to say.

"Jake Gardiner, who's not just a keeper but Coast Guard now, told me that if I could get a seaworthy boat, he could have a radio mounted in it, a Coast Guard radio like the one they have at the lighthouse, only smaller."

"What's discouraging about that? God, we could—"

"You didn't listen. You didn't hear me say *if* I got a seaworthy boat. Where do you suggest I get six thousand dollars— from the cookie jar?"

"Why couldn't we borrow it? Wouldn't a bank loan it to us?

They did for father. It wouldn't be that much, if you sold this one."

"I've thought of that, sure. Don't think I haven't. There's a way all right, but up to now I've been avoiding it. I can borrow against our property. But it scares me. I could have a bad season—miss some payments—then some bank would take everything."

"I get paid for working in the store. I'll help with the money from my traps, too. We can do it."

Amos paused, as if he were making up his mind just then.

"You're right. Sure we can. No, I won't take your money. Hell, if things keep going as badly as they have been, there won't be any banks to foreclose on me; some damn Hun will own the cove anyway. By Jesus, we'll do it."

"You and me," said Gus, flushed with enthusiasm. "Let's have another drink on it."

"No, let's go home. After one drink I was considering going offshore in this boat. If I have another we'll be attacking submarines. Let's see if we can't get this engine to run without it conking out again."

Amos knew Gus would tell his mother about their plan that night. And Leah would tell Maggie tomorrow when she came into the store. He guessed it would be a day, or two at the most, before Maggie stopped by on her way home and insisted that he borrow the money from her. She would not hear otherwise. He had his eye on that Nova Scotia boat in Stonington.

                              Monday evening
                              May 9, 1942

Ruth dear,
        Ernest Mattingly brought his new baseball
glove to school today, all oiled and tied snugly
with cod line wrapped around a ball nestled inside. He left it on his desk for all of us to see, in

hopes, no doubt, that someone would ask him about it. But none of the others said anything—the boys jealous or unaware, the girls indifferent. I was reminded of your Michael on my visit last spring (or was it the year before?), when he had done the same thing. How pleased and proud he was to explain to me how the leather would soften and form a permanent pocket after the ball was removed. He had read in a magazine that Phil Rizzuto did the same thing when he was a boy. So when I stopped at Ernest's desk during arithmetic and admired his glove and mentioned Phil Rizzuto for the others to hear, he turned pink with pleasure. I said a silent thank you to Michael for his lesson on your porch stoop.

The days are getting longer, and though the mud ruts in the road are firm in the morning, we haven't had a frost in weeks. The trillium are in flower, and yesterday I saw Jack in his pulpit. Soon it will be apple blossom time.

I've seen more of Amos in the last week or so than I have in a long, long time. (When I write his name, it surprises me to see it. Does it you? In script it is a shapely name.) For years I'd only seen him when he drove by the school in midmorning, going to and from the store and P.O., twice a week at most. Occasionally on his return trip we'd both look up at the same time, he with his hat pulled low and a slight smile, me in the window in mid-sentence, wanting to wave but demurring. Now I've seen him twice—no, three times—in a week, talked to him, been in his little house, stood within reach of him, close enough to see that the uncut hairs on the back of his neck are going to gray. We've changed so little, really, since we were once so close.

I made up a May basket for him (you're smiling) and planned to take it over in the dark, just as Leah and I used to after he moved out. There was a bouquet of violets blue and white, a doily painted with songbirds (not nearly so nicely done as yours), and a jar of apple butter. But I didn't deliver it. Don't ask me why.

Yes, I am still worried about poor Leah; you were nice to inquire. I wish I could report otherwise. I wish she would talk to me about it, but she is tight-lipped and avoids my eyes. When she's alone she gnaws at her fingernails and picks compulsively at the calluses on her hands. I've seen her like this before, as you know, and I hate it more each time, hate Cecil more. She's had the courage to disagree with him on something, or even (do I dare hope?) disobey him, and he is punishing her, belittling her, kicking away the frail supports of her self-worth with criticism, sarcasm, and a tone of weary disappointment in his voice. He knows that her only source of confidence comes from her efficiency as a housewife and as keeper of the store and household accounts. At supper he eats only half of what she serves him, saying that he's tired of leftovers when he knows the meal is freshly prepared. Then he criticizes her for wasting food. In the store the other day, in front of several people, he wiped the cutting board with a white towel, held it up dirty, and asked her in a voice for a forgetful child if they hadn't agreed to keep the board clean always. She answered with a submissive yes and lowered her eyes. I wanted to march around that counter, take him by his piggish earlobe, and twist until he fell to his knees and apologized to her. I wish I had.

Now I've gone on and on. But I do feel better having complained. You've always been the one I can talk to; I don't know what I'd do without your friendship.

It's growing dark, and I have a lesson to prepare and four themes to correct. I'll close now, missing you, and light the lamps. Please give my love to Adam, kiss Sarah, and muss Michael's hair for me, whether he likes it or not.

Love always,
Maggie

P.S. Mrs. Roosevelt says we'll need to be brave, and I think she is right.

CHAPTER FOUR

CECIL HAD BEEN UP SINCE FIVE, PICKING UP THE SATURDAY GROCERY shipment in Stonington with Gus, unloading it, and now—with Leah's help—storing or shelving it. His sleeves were rolled in perfect cuffs above his elbows, his tie was loosened, and his store apron was as spotless as a pillow slip.

He could see what was coming. Now that meat was to be rationed, the prices of lobster and fish were climbing faster than he had imagined it would. As the war effort increased, so would the demand for fish. Popular magazines were running long, involved recipes for housewives, explaining how to cook fish as a substitute for meat, describing all the different things that could be done with hake and cod. A *Bangor Daily News* article, which Leah had clipped and pinned to the store bulletin board, reported that it was considered patriotic to order fish and lobster in expensive restaurants in Boston and New York.

Gasoline was rationed, but not for farmers and fishermen. Ironically, Cecil's customers would finally have money to spend after so many lean years of self-rationing, but he would not have anything to sell them. He thought: The Japs bomb Pearl Harbor, the government decides to go to war against Hitler, and Cecil Barter gets cheated out of the chance to reap the rewards of long years of scraping by in the store. The government was issuing ration books, and there were already shortages of everything from sugar to linen. Cecil had heard rumors of plans to raise taxes, and there was even talk about price controls. It seemed that everything he had worked for over the past years was being yanked away from him.

But he was a Barter, and Barters knew, he liked to say, that in adversity there is opportunity, if only you are smart enough and disciplined enough to take advantage of it. Cecil had always had the discipline, in all things—hadn't he chosen a plain but competent woman to be his wife?—but until recently, when it came to him unexpectedly in a sudden brilliant realization on the town landing, his ambition had really been no more than a dream. The average citizens, even the poorer ones like the islanders, would tighten their belts for the war effort, consoled by patriotic advertising from manufacturers and by government propaganda. Their sacrifices would provide the muscle needed to strengthen American industry. The ships and tanks and planes would get built, and it would be the captains of industry who would loosen their belts. Summer people. Men like Mr. Owings, who owned a steel company and kept the big cottage on Point Lookout. Like Mr. Davidson, his summer neighbor, who had a pharmaceutical company and a sixty-foot sailboat that he brought up from Boston every Fourth of July, filled with family and friends.

There were more than a dozen such families on Point Lookout. Their wives bought incidentals at his store, but their fresh vegetables, wines, cheeses, dairy products, and almost everything else were delivered by Merrill and Hinckley in Blue Hill. Katherine Merrill, the last of either family, was retiring that summer, and would sell the store to the highest bidder in September. Cecil had three months to find a way to buy it, and he would; by Jesus, he would.

His older boy, Melvin, who was home from the shipyards for the weekend, sat chain-smoking Old Golds on an upturned milk crate by the little stove between the counter and the shelves. Unlike his parents and his brother, he could sit still while others were working around him. He had his father's long, narrow face and his mother's round, upturned nose, whose nostrils he habitually pinched as if he could narrow them to fit his face. Richard Snell had moved the only chair away from the rainy window and settled in it next to the stove. In high rubber boots and thick flannel, he sat cross-legged, facing Melvin across a basket of Bermuda onions. When Richard got too warm, as he did every few minutes, he pulled open the stained neck of his long johns to let the heat out and take an appreciative sniff. Richard's face had healed completely since Cecil saw him last. His mother, who mistrusted doctors as much as her son, had snipped the stitches with nail clippers and pulled them out. But his hand had gotten infected from the little bits of buried lobster shell, and he had been forced to go to a doctor after all to have the sores opened and sprinkled with sulfa. The hand lay curled in his lap, opening and closing slowly as he talked and scratched the little cuts.

In the center aisle, Olive Gross stood staring at the boxes of laundry soap on the top shelf, trying to remember what it was she was forgetting. Standing in profile, true to her name's shape, she filled the aisle.

When Cecil had finished unpacking the chicken and arranging it on ice under his new glass counter, he stretched, and smoothed his hair with the back of his hand. He watched Leah cutting and weighing cheese at the far end. She still kept her back to him, showing him that the argument they had had last night was not over. He had told her that she was acting like a spoiled little girl, a selfish only child, and it had hurt her into silence. That morning her hands had fumbled among the breakfast dishes as if she were still too angry to control them; now she lowered the meat cleaver onto the wheel of cheddar, placed the heel of her left palm on the end of it, and slowly cut a perfect one-pound wedge.

Gus was among the shelves by the windows, listening intently to his brother and Richard. Melvin seemed so knowledgeable about what was going on in the world. Gus thought that Richard, who never listened to anyone, respected Melvin, though he would never let on that he did.

"Gus?" It was the voice his father used to awaken him in the morning, and it sent him back to his shelving.

"I don't care how many shifts you work," Richard said. "You can't build ships as fast as they sink them. You won't out-invent them, and you won't out-produce them; they've got theirs already made, and they're using them to sink ours as soon as they come out of the harbor. No matter what you say, we're pooched unless there's a miracle."

Richard crossed his arms on his chest and leaned back to draw a Lucky Strike from the pack in his shirt pocket and tap it on his thumbnail.

"The hell we can't." Melvin moved the ashtray to the lip of the stove for both of them to use. "The unions will take over the yards completely—and the factories too, if they have to. It's the unions that will get the job done on the Fascists, not savings bond stamps. The working man will win this war, and after it's over you won't see another depression ever again."

Melvin was wearing baggy trousers and a floppy gangster hat that Gus thought was the stupidest thing he'd ever seen. Fresh from the shipyard, he sported a "Victory Union" button on which a man in overalls stood between two flags with his fist raised. This was Melvin's fourth visit home since he started working in Bath, and he was still preaching unions to the fishermen. Behind his back they called him Melvin the Red.

"The working man? For Christ's sake, what are we then?" Richard wanted to know.

"I mean organized labor, as if you didn't know. If you fishermen got organized, you'd be a hell of a lot better off, and so would the entire fishing industry."

Leah covered the wheel of cheese, took off her hair net, and shook her hair loose. Without a word, she went to the store-room to get away from the smoke, the talk, Richard's body odor, and her husband's eyes.

"You could put your lobsters in pounds and hold them off the market until the price was right. You could get your own re-frigerator trucks and sell directly to the restaurants in Boston. You could rebuild and modernize the old canning factory. You could—"

"*You* could go over to the east side and convince Amos Coombs of what you preach. The day that he comes over here to town and says: 'Hey, fellas, let's all pitch in together and mix up our lobsters and take equal shares,' that's when I'll join. When Jesus returns for his flock."

"Amos is irrelevant. He's lost in a skeleton world. He never trusted anybody he wasn't related to. Now they're gone, and he's gone with them. He says he's never heard of the labor movement and doesn't want to. He says it sounds like some-thing dirty."

Richard released a bitter laugh, and Cecil smiled. His arms filled with cans of cleanser, Gus shot his father a hurtful look and glared at the back of his brother's head. He made a noise as if to say something, but his mother called him from the store-room. Cecil watched him leave, wishing that he had not smiled.

Olive moved cautiously to the other aisle, closer to the con-versation, and locked her listless stare on the prunes and raisins.

"Now we've made him mad," said Cecil.

"I was only teasing, and he knows it," Melvin said. "He'll be okay. He takes everything grandfather says so seriously, as if he was . . . I don't know."

"Like Amos was his own father," said Richard. He lowered his eyes to the hand in his lap and picked absently at a tiny wound, as if he were sorry he had said what he had, as if he were embarrassed to have let slip what everyone else was saying.

Cecil tore a sheet of waxed paper from the roll, a slow con-trolled tear. One day soon, he thought, he would ask the boy point-blank what kind of man would walk away from his ten-year-old daughter—a girl who had just lost her mother—leaving her to be raised by someone else. He'd ask Gus why he thought Amos left Leah with Maggie in Head Harbor and moved back to the cove, and why nobody ever mentioned it.

"Trouble is," Melvin offered, "that people down here in these little towns, on these islands, don't realize how fast things are happening everywhere else. If they did, they wouldn't be so nervous."

"Oh, like what?"

"Like last month the little old Bath shipyards put two new Corvettes and three eighty-three-foot subchasers down the ways—and that with half our workforce busy on the expansion. Those ships and the ones like them that we have in the works are fitted with the new high-frequency direction finder, not to mention the new catapults for depth charges. You can't tell people things like that because they're classified; I shouldn't even be telling you."

"It's safe with us," said Richard. "But that's not what the islanders are worried about. They think the Nazis are going to come ashore here, invade them. It's comical."

Melvin, the worldlier of the two men, laughed. "Yes, I can see the headlines now." He pointed to an imaginary newspaper in the air, tracing the headline with his finger. "*Island Fortress Invaded,*" he read.

Olive thought he was pointing at the clock, which reminded her that it was getting late; she had to bake those pies so they could cool, but couldn't make the recipe without her Karo syrup.

"Karo!" she said aloud.

"*Crucial Rock Captured by German Navy; Boston Threatened,*" said Richard, laughing.

Olive had not heard enough to get the joke, but she laughed with them anyway as she approached the counter bearing her syrup.

A muffled *bang!* stopped their laughter cold. Gus stood over the box of canned peaches he had just dropped flat on the floor from waist height. He had been stewing in the storeroom about how chummy his father was with Richard Snell, whom he hated, and then had heard the mocking laughter.

"What about those four spies that came ashore on Long Island?" asked Gus. His voice was shaking. "Not spies—saboteurs. What about that kid in Machias last week? If somebody told you he saw two guys in city clothes walking up from the shore, you'd probably laugh at him. I'll bet you laugh at the people who are getting organized to patrol the shore out here. Those Germans that came ashore at Amagansett had money and detonators and timing devices and stuff like that. In crates. Enough to blow up shipyards and factories. You think that's a joke don't you?"

"I laugh at what I want to, boy," said Richard. He liked Gus all right, but he would not be talked down to. "You're right, I would laugh at someone who said the Germans would be dumb enough to put somebody ashore here on an island where they couldn't get to the mainland except on the mailboat. I haven't laughed at *that* yet, but I will, by Jesus, if I want to."

"That's enough you two," said Cecil. He slammed the register drawer shut, making Olive jump again as she opened the door.

"Gus is right," said the storekeeper. "Out here we have to do everything we can until they can build a navy to protect us. If half the rumors about the number of ships being sunk by U-boats are true, the Germans will soon cut off England's oil supply—everything—and they'll have England. Then they'll come for us."

" 'The English will fight to the last drop of American blood,' " quoted Richard. "Wasn't it you, Cecil who said that in your speech to America First? I think it was."

"That was six months ago. I wanted to stay out of the war because it was a war for Europe. But now it's for us too, and we're losing. Since we're in it, we're going to fight and win.

That's why we dissolved America First this winter—a meeting I noticed you missed."

Melvin tried to join the conversation by saying that he had not seen Amos yet on this visit.

"What's he up to these days?" he asked Gus.

"Right now?" The boy looked at his watch. "Right now he's buying Stevie Eaton's big Novi boat." There, damn them. He had said it. He had promised he would not tell anybody, but they'd find out soon enough anyway.

"What'd you say?" asked Cecil.

"You heard me." Gus pushed back a row of cans to make room for the peaches.

"Don't use that tone of voice with me, young man."

"I'm sorry," said Gus. "It's true."

"The hell you say," said Richard. "What boat? The *Quahog*? Amos bought it?"

"I only live on an island, but as far as I know the *Quahog*'s the only boat that Stevie Eaton owns." Gus took in their amazement as if it was three fingers of rum, a victory toast for Amos.

"How'd he ever manage that?" Cecil wondered.

"He sold the *Tuna* and paid the difference."

"What's Amos want with a big offshore boat like that?" Richard asked.

"He's going to go fishing."

Cecil did not believe it. "That's what he said, son, and maybe that's what he wants to believe. But Amos doesn't have the money to buy a boat like that." Cecil sounded almost frightened. "He can't be."

But he had. Amos was bringing the Novi boat around the northern end of the island in the rain at that very moment, whistling and having a little drink at the wheel. She was twice as much boat as he had ever operated—much less owned—and she handled beautifully. The rain clouds were scaling off to the

east over the darkening sea as he approached the Sheep
Ledges. There, Amos pulled the throttle back and swung her
around the first buoy in a string of blue-and-white ones. They
were the Grove boy's traps, he thought. He hooked the buoy,
then paused to take another fond look at his boat.

She was freshly painted forest green, with a white house,
white washboards, and a clean white boot stripe to show off her
lines. Though long and low aft, the sheerline rose abruptly at the
house, ending in a high bow whose straight stem was almost
plumb to the water. She would take just about any kind of heavy
sea, and she had enough deck space for three men to work with
room to spare—or for other things.

He took up each of the buoys in the string carefully, so as
not to muss the clean washboard, and tied off a coil on each before he threw it back. Maybe the Grover boy had not heard what
happened to the other Deer Isle men's gear. If he did not know
enough about where the Coombs waters were, then this was a
way to learn. Amos thought maybe he should have waited until
Gus was with him to tie these off, but there would be another
time. When he had finished the string, he took the *Quahog*
home, coming around into the cove as if he had been running
this boat all his life.

Maggie was waiting for him on the wharf, her hands deep
in the pockets of her slacks, her nose pointed to sea. As he
came into sight, she realized that she was as nervous as a young
girl, just as she had been the first time that they had embraced.
This time, though, she was not afraid. Maggie liked the looks of
the boat—this was the first time she had seen the *Quahog*—but
she knew that for Amos she would have to reserve her praise
until she had had a closer look and had taken a ride. Such a big
boat, she noticed, was made bigger by the little cove.

Maggie had known that Amos had been ashamed of himself
for being afraid to go out on the water after he had seen the submarine. She had not guessed, though she should have, how
much pressure had been put on him by the invisible ones he paid

so much attention to. Amos had told Gus that one morning he found Walter standing on the cliff in front of the cabin watching Sam Witherspoon putting his traps in Coombs waters, right where Walter had drowned. When Amos came breathless up the path, his uncle did not turn around but stood there with his hands clasped behind him, his shoulders slumped in sad defeat.

When Leah first told Maggie of Amos's plan to buy a bigger boat, she said it was for fishing offshore, but Maggie guessed the truth. She felt anxious and relieved at the same time. After thinking it through for a couple of days, she went to the cove one evening with her own plans in mind, and his replies imagined. She insisted that he let her buy into the boat; she would be half owner, and that way he would not have to borrow from anyone and would not be beholden, even to her.

He hemmed and hawed, but he did not argue. Amos wanted the option to buy her out in case anything went wrong, and Maggie agreed.

Watching him now, as he secured the new boat on the *Tuna*'s mooring, she wondered if they weren't both crazy. They probably were.

He came in to stand with her on the wharf. Maggie's bountiful chestnut hair was pinned up, covered with millions of tiny pearls of condensed fog; a damp ringlet hung over her ear. When she nodded her approval of the boat, trying—like him—not to grin too broadly, Amos put his arm around her waist.

"What do you think?" he asked.

"It's been almost twenty years since you've done that," she said quietly.

"No," he said thoughtfully. "I bought the *Tuna* in '29. What's that come to? Thirteen years."

"What?" She turned to him, her head tilted slightly.

"I haven't bought a boat in thirteen years. Remember? It was—"

"I meant since you put your arm around me," almost adding: And the first time you've ever done it without looking in every direction to make sure nobody could see.

"Oh." He blushed and let his arm drop to his side.

"I didn't mean I didn't like it," she said. His ears were deep red.

"I wasn't thinking."

"We're co-owners," she said. She would have liked to slip her arm through his but did not. "Does that make us cocaptains? No."

"It don't matter to me," he said. "Let's take her for a ride. Let's go show her to Jake, and get that radio. Wait till you see how the water curls up when her bow cuts through it."

On the way to the lighthouse, they decided to keep the name *Quahog* even though she said it had a suggestion of Massachusetts to it. He said they could call her the *Hen Clam*, as it meant almost the same thing, but she held out for *Quahog*, and Amos was glad, since he would not have to buy new brass letters for the Novi's transom.

He coaxed Maggie to take the wheel, but she said maybe later. She stood close to him under the house, their shoulders touching at times, just the two of them alone, just as she had imagined it; she shut her eyes and envisioned the huge black submarines swimming beneath them.

Harvey Gooden was looking at a Lifebuoy soap ad, examining a picture of a girl in a bathtub, when Morales came into the room to say that there was a good-looking babe coming ashore. Of course, Harvey did not believe him. How could he believe anything from a guy who called himself Mexican when he was really Portuguese? There were no Mexicans in New England and no coloreds either to speak of—only 'Gees and some Italians in the quarries. Someday he would find a way to trap Morales in his lie, calling himself part Indian, which Harvey claimed he was. He waited until Morales left before he went to the window to see for himself. There she was. He decided that she must be an island woman, but this was the first time he had ever seen one wearing slacks and displaying such a good figure.

Harvey did not recognize the boat but thought the man looked like Amos, only taller.

On the short boathouse slip, Amos watched fondly as Jake sniffed around the new boat, testing the planking with his pocketknife, revving the engine. Amos could tell that he was satisfied and nudged Maggie, who smiled in reply.

"You could mount a good-sized machine gun on her if you strengthened her planking," Jake said. "You probably have a better chance of getting one than we do. It wouldn't do much good against a U-boat, but we don't know that it's just U-boats we're looking for. Naval intelligence thinks the Germans are going to put more saboteurs and spies ashore. A fifty caliber would be just the thing. Wouldn't it be the bees knees to catch a rubber raft full of Nazis in the open with a gun like that?"

"Good God," said Maggie. "A machine gun? I thought we were hoping for a radio." She did not know Jake Gardiner very well, having only met him twice in passing; she thought he must be joking until she looked at Amos and saw that he was not.

Morales, swinging down the path in his Stetson, an osprey feather stuck in its rattlesnake band, caught Maggie's eye and gave her a wink before he got close enough to see that she could very well be in her late thirties. Her face was fair and freckled, but she was no teenager; there was a confidence there, an authority or something. He liked the way she stood posture perfect; he liked the fullness of her breasts above her folded arms, liked the way she talked to the men, looking them in the eye.

"Come aboard, Morales and take a look," said Jake. "See how the radio will go in here."

Morales introduced himself to Maggie as Seaman First Class Ernest Morales, and said she could call him Morales.

"I like your hat, Morales," she said, holding his handshake. Morales was in love with an older woman.

Jake said that he had to brief Amos and that there was paperwork to be read and signed; the lighthouse keeper invited him and Maggie to come inside for a cup of coffee. On the stony path to the house, Maggie asked Jake if she could look around while they conducted their business.

"I've wanted to come out here since I was a little girl," she said. "My father once spent two days and nights here during a terrible gale. He said that the waves broke the windows of the house, and dragged a boulder as big as a lobsterboat from one end of the rock to the other. They had to take refuge in the light-house. I suppose he was exaggerating."

"I doubt it," said Jake.

"It's so quiet now, so beautiful, everything freshly painted. You've planted pansies—I love the yellow ones—and impatiens, too; how lovely."

"Amos brought the seeds," said Jake. "And it's beautiful now because the morning fog's gone out to sea; you brought the sunshine."

Maggie laughed and Amos rolled his eyes.

"May I go up in the lighthouse?"

"Sure, I'll show you around."

"Oh no, you have business to tend to. I'd like to wander around on my own, if I may."

While Maggie explored, Morales and Harvey installed the radio. Jake and Amos hovered over a table strewn with operating manuals and stacks of government forms.

"Sign this one here," Jake said. "They're issuing eight hundred and fifty of these radios to fishermen, and it's about time. You're one of the first. It's part of a program called the Coastal Picket, to be manned by civilians and Coast Guard reservists. If you join the temporary reserves, you might get a gun to mount on her."

"How could I? I'm almost fifty years old."

"They'd take you. You know the water. You could easily pass for thirty-five—or younger if you had to. You're going to have to learn how to operate the radio anyway; Morales can teach you, or you can go to the reservist's school in Rockland for a week, get certified in navigation and gunnery, take the oath. It would make it easier to get the things you'll need."

"A week?" asked Amos. "No." Where would he sleep in Rockland? Who would watch the houses and the chickens, tend his traps? The idea of spending the night off the island made him queasy.

"Maggie's going to be doing this patrolling with me, just so you know. I can't imagine the Coast Guard liking that much," he said.

"You want to take her with you? A woman? What is it between you two anyway?"

"It isn't anything between us two," snapped Amos. "I'm taking her because she wants to go, and the boat's half hers, so she can." He surprised himself; it had only occurred to him just then that she would want to go.

"No need to get your nose out of joint," grinned Jake. "But if they find out somehow that you've got a woman aboard, I'm going to swear I didn't know anything about it. You don't want to go to the school?"

"No, no school for me."

"I don't blame you. You'll get your fuel and the radio, and we'll see about a gun. You don't have to go to the school. I, Chief Petty Officer Gardiner . . ." He puffed out his chest and hooked his thumbs in his suspenders. "Am authorized to sign you up for a stint of five months in the temporary reserves."

"Okay. How do you do that?"

"I just did it. You're official."

"Good," said Amos. He glanced at the door. "If I can't get a gun right away, how about some depth charges?"

Jake laughed. "For this boat?" The man was too timid to spend a week in Rockland but was ready to go to sea in a tub carrying depth charges to use against the Kriegsmarine.

"She could be double planked." Amos had expected him to laugh.

"You're serious. But no. They tried that last month on a sixty-foot trawler out of Boston. She was steel hulled, and the catapult still blew down through the deck."

"You could rig up a kind of runway for them and roll them off the stern," said Amos. "All they are is fifty-gallon drums with black powder in them, right? And a fuse or something?"

"Well I guess so," answered Jake. "But if you did manage to get over top of a sub and let them loose, you'd be blown to bits yourself; you couldn't get away in time."

Jake stood up when Maggie came through the door and offered her a cup of coffee. He took them into the radio room to show them the plan on the wall chart.

"The red pins are sinkings. Look at them all. The black ones are U-boat sightings," he explained.

"That one there is mine," Amos told Maggie.

"Our sonar is useless this close to shore because the water is too dense, so the U-boats can lie on the sandy bottom without a worry. It's going to take small boats like yours to spot them until we can get airplanes. The nearest air station is Salem, Massachusetts; if we can document enough activity near here, they might transfer one of their PH 2's to Owls Head near Rockland. Then we could begin to fight the Nazis. Right now all we can do is find and recover survivors.

"Our orders say that we're to use our lighthouse launch to patrol north and east of here. They want you to search to the south and west, out in the Grumpy and Gilkie fishing grounds. Another man on Vinalhaven and two more out on Matinicus have applied for radios, which they ought to get soon, but until then it's just you and us."

"Am I right to assume that the U-boats spend the daylight hours in shallow water and go out to the shipping lanes at night?" Maggie asked.

Jake nodded.

"Then we should patrol at dawn and dusk as well," she concluded.

Amos was not surprised to hear her say "we."

"You'll need to call us when you go out and maintain radio contact while you're on the water," said Jake. "And let us know when you go in. It wouldn't hurt, Amos, if you kept contact with us while you're fishing. But be careful to turn the radio off when there are other fishermen around."

Amos said he would need to practice using the thing after Morales showed him how.

"Which is exactly what he's ready to do right now." Morales stood in the doorway, hatless, brushing little curlicued wood shavings from his shirt, showing Maggie his perfect teeth.

"One more thing." Jake stopped them at the table in the front room, found a booklet entitled *The Coastal Information System*, and opened to a page with a turned-down corner. "I want you both to read this part right here."

"You do it," Amos said to Maggie.

She read it to herself first, then aloud: " 'These patrols are not intended as a military protection of our coastline, as this is the function of the army and navy. The patrols are more in the nature of lookouts, or pickets, to report activities along the coastlines, and are not to repel armed forces.' "

"You hear that, Amos?" asked Jake.

"You don't see a hearing aid, do you?"

"What about you?" Maggie asked Jake when they were outside. "Aren't you afraid they'll attack the lighthouse?"

Jake laughed bitterly. "The Germans use the light for navigation, just like our ships do. Even when our navy wises up and tells us to shut off the light and fog horn—if they ever do—the U-boats can use our radio beacon to compute their position. They need us."

"And by the looks of your pantry, you need some fresh food," Maggie said. "I hate to think of you two eating out of cans—you three, I mean."

"The tender comes back in ten days," Morales said. "Every

American serviceman between here and Europe is eating out of cans. And those poor guys in the convoys are sailing in tin cans—big, slow-moving targets just waiting to be blown up."

"We'll be back before the tender comes," said Maggie, buttoning her jacket against a freshening breeze. "Won't we Amos?"

He did not answer. His mind was on the radio, how it must look in the boat, and on what the old ones would say when he practiced on it in the cove. He was wondering what they were going to say about him and Maggie, together all of a sudden after all these years. Walter would be tickled. Ava might even soften some toward them.

CHAPTER FIVE

BASIL WALKER WAS TOO FAT TO TURN AROUND IN THE DRIVER'S SEAT to see where he was going. The mirrors on his 1932 Ford truck had long ago rusted off, as had the hinges on the door, so he had to rely on Fuddy McFarland, who had leapt down from the truck bed to guide Basil backward into the town's scrap-collection area. Iris Weed, with horn-rimmed glasses and a permanent pucker, clutched her clipboard as Basil backed toward the roped-off spot. She knew the brakes on that truck were no good, so she held her breath until Fuddy slipped a chock behind the rear wheel to hold the vehicle on the slight slope.

"Is it all iron?" she asked. She was not going to get any closer to either of the men, or their truck.

Fuddy rubbed the stubble on his chin, leaving rusty smudges like those on the crotch of his trousers.

He said it was.

"Then it goes in that pile. I'll send Betty over to write down what you've brought when it's been weighed." She pointed to the scrap-iron heap with her pencil and returned to the pile marked "Aluminum."

Basil did not want to get out of the truck because it would be too much trouble getting back in, and Fuddy was not inter-

82

ested in untangling the load of junk piece by piece. So, he tied one end of a hawser to a boulder and the other to the Model A frame at the bottom of the load and stepped aside.

"Lookit here," said Basil, pointing to the float at the end of the dock. Jake Gardiner and a miniature ensign, both in summer whites, stepped from a Coast Guard launch being secured by Morales, and walked up the dock to the scrap piles.

"I like your sign: 'Scrap the Jap.' That's clever." The little ensign, his bare forearms bright pink from the ride in the open boat, managed a deep manly voice.

Fuddy stared at them.

"We're looking for your first selectman," said Jake. "Can you tell us who he is, and where we can find him?"

"Don't know." Fuddy slapped at his pockets for his cigarettes.

"You don't know who your first selectman is? How many people live on this island?" The ensign squinted for a closer look at Fuddy.

"Don't know that either."

"I'll bet you know who the constable is," said Jake.

"Dwight Chafin," said Fuddy, glad to have an answer. "He's in the white house on the right past the alder swamp. Up the hill." He pointed toward town and the hill beyond.

"You're not going to bring that nigger ashore here, are you?" Basil motioned toward Morales with his pipe stem.

"I wasn't going to, until you said that." Jake turned, cupped his hands and yelled to Morales, waving to him to join them. "He's a Mexican-American and a Coast Guardsman, and that pistol in his holster is loaded. Why don't you wait till he gets here and call him nigger to his face?"

Basil started up his truck and ground her into first gear. The hawser strained, the boulder budged, then the hawser parted in the middle with a twang that made Fuddy jump backward and Basil curse so foully that he fogged his windshield.

When Morales joined them, Jake and the ensign introduced

themselves to Iris and asked her where they might find the first selectman. She patted her hair into place and directed them to Cecil, who she thought would be in the store. Iris offered them a ride—she loved a man in uniform, so rare on the island—but Jake said they would enjoy the walk.

Betty Chambers, in rolled-up dungarees and saddle shoes, hurried to Iris's side to meet the men in white but arrived too late. As they watched, the threesome stopped to talk to Billy Mattingly and his little brother, who were pulling a wagon load of pots and pans. Billy had a carved wooden pistol stuck in his belt, and his little brother had a wooden sword; both were wearing sailor's caps. The ensign patted Billy on the shoulder. When his superiors had turned to go, Morales stood at attention before the boys and rendered them a perfect salute. They returned it and remained at attention by their wagon until he had gone.

"Wasn't that cute?" said Iris. "That ensign is so *little,* so *young.* He still has his dimples. But that other one is some handsome," she said, referring to Jake.

"He's dreamy," said Betty, who meant Morales.

Doris Chafin was sitting in the sun on her front porch shelling peas when she looked up to see Cecil Barter and three sailors walking up her driveway. She stood up, holding the apron full of empty pods in one hand, and shouted through the screen.

"Dwight," she called. "Dwight, come out here. This minute!"

Roused from his nap, Dwight blinked in the sunlight as Cecil introduced him to the Coast Guardsmen. Doris dumped her apron over the porch railing and smoothed it out. When Cecil introduced her, the three men removed their hats. Ensign Onderdonk's hair was so blond, his body so thin, and his complexion so pale that he looked like a two year old in a sailor suit. Doris invited everyone inside, but Cecil said they would rather sit on the porch.

"I'll get another chair," said Doris. "And some refreshments."

"I'll just sit on the steps if you don't mind," said Morales. "We have a set just like them at home."

Ensign Onderdonk took a sheaf of papers from his briefcase and held it on his knees while he talked. Jake, who had already heard this spiel several times, accepted a cigarette from Dwight and leaned back in his rocker.

Cecil listened with an air of quiet authority as the ensign explained the situation and quoted the order from Coast Guard Headquarters, Naval District Seven. All districts adjacent to the coast were ordered to form a "Coastal Picket" made up of civilian volunteers. These volunteers, "hereafter Patrolmen," were to be properly armed and equipped, and fully instructed in the execution of their duties, which were to maintain a coastal or beach patrol system in all parts of their locale where terrain permitted.

Doris opened the screen door with her rear end and set a tray of coffee, chocolate cupcakes, and Pepsi on the little porch table. She excused herself to go back inside—and listen through the screen.

The ensign, who had never eaten chocolate cupcakes without a napkin, continued. He was authorized to issue a rifle; a Very pistol, which fired a flare; and other equipment to beach patrols on the islands in the Penobscot Bay region. Those without phone systems linking them to the mainland would each be issued a radio. The armed patrols were instructed to walk the beaches and shore to watch for anything suspicious and to report it immediately through proper channels.

The Mattingly boys—together with the Crowell brothers, who had joined them at the store—constituted the entire third and fifth grades of Maggie's school. They tried to hide behind the big maple in the drive, but Morales saw them and waved to them to join him on the steps. They marched up single file, Billy first. Morales put his index finger over his lips and patted the step for them to sit down.

"Can we see your gun?" Vince Crowell was the smallest and the least afraid.

"You can see it, but I can't let you hold it because it's loaded," answered Morales.

The boys nodded eagerly.

"Who's this?" Morales nodded toward Betty Chambers and another teenaged girl who were coming up the road on bicycles, standing on their pedals as they began the steep hill.

"That's Betty Chambers and Mabel Eaton," whispered Billy. "They're jerks."

"Betty has big chubbies," Vince said.

As if she had heard Vince, Betty pulled back her shoulders and stuck out her chest for a deep breath, displaying her Maidenform miracles to a gap-mouthed Morales.

"I'll say she does," he whispered reverently.

Amos patrolled every day at first—at dawn one day, in the evening the next—but he found that the first bright crack of light from the sun blinded him and made observation of anything to the east impossible. So, he settled for evening patrols, stopping at the lighthouse on his way in at dark to refuel. He had always wanted sunglasses and decided that now he would get a pair.

But Amos did not know where he was going to get the energy to do everything he had to do. Normally, lobstering from dawn to mid-afternoon and then taking care of chores in the cove for himself and the others wore him out by dark. Now he had the patrolling, as well, and he would be doing it alone until the men on Matinicus and Vinalhaven got their radios, and Maggie was done with her teaching. He read the advertisements about how to stay fit and alert for the war effort. He saw pictures of men his age or older working night shifts in airplane factories, sweating with their sleeves rolled up, looking over their heads at a picture in their minds of a young man charging through smoke and explosions on a battlefield somewhere. The advertisements listed the kinds of food an older man needs to stay fit, but he did not have most of the things they recommended, and neither did the store.

His assigned area ran from southwest to northeast, following the shoal that lay eighteen miles out. When the weather permitted, he crated his lobsters in the cove at the end of the day, cleaned the boat, and sailed back out, heading due south by west from the cove and running twenty miles to Seal Island, a bare little rock out of sight of any land. There he steered close enough to see the puffins that had gathered, then set a course of twenty-five degrees to lead him along the shoal to the lighthouse. On a good night, he was home and tied up by ten. When the sea was heavy or the wind contrary, he might not pull into the cove until midnight. On nights like those, he could only fall into bed, too tired to cook or even eat, too tired to wash up or shed his dirty clothes.

It had to be the cove that suffered, that got neglected—everything but Ava's garden, now a Victory Garden, that Maggie helped him keep. The old shed would have to wait another year for a new roof, the well cover would have to stay rotten for another season, and the field in front of Ava's house would not get scythed, which meant that the thistles would come back, bringing the bees, and choke out the hay forever. Nothing would get a fresh coat of paint. Amos knew that it galled Ava to see the place going to hell, so he avoided her. When Walter or Lew were around, he was either too busy to pay them any mind or so tired that he fell asleep in the chair next to them, which he regretted the next morning.

While school was still in session, he often came in from his patrol to find Maggie waiting for him on his wharf with a supper in a covered basket. She was always eager to hear whether he had seen anything and would ask for news of the men at the lighthouse. Maggie worried that Amos was losing weight and badgered him to get more rest. When he returned home late, he often found a lamp burning in his window, a meal warming on the stove, and a box of fresh food for the lighthouse crew on the counter. He knew what the old ones were saying about her being in his house and coming to see him so frequently, but he did not care.

June 25, 1942

Dear Ruth,

I thought of you this afternoon while I was hanging out the laundry. It was a perfect summer afternoon (as it is an evening now); the high white clouds, cobalt sky, and soft wind, made me feel an "inebriate of air." I closed my eyes and saw us, just girls, in your father's little backyard, folding all those sheets and singing that silly ditty—how did it go?

Bringing in the sheets, bringing in the sheets, Our hands smell like Clorox, bringing in the sheets.

Was that the summer that we bobbed our hair? You said I looked more like Katharine Hepburn's Jo, than any femme fatale, and I was so flattered. I miss you.

I'm afraid that I'm writing to say I can't come to visit this summer. Even out here (or especially out here) we are all astir with the war effort. I'm sure you understand. I hope you won't be disappointed, as I am. I'll miss our walks, the movies, and—most of all—you and the children, for whom photographs, though much appreciated, are poor substitutes.

You should see Gus these days; he certainly has "growed some," as Amos says. Not physically—indeed he seems to have shed some weight—but in manliness. The war has had a way of speeding everything up for all of us. Though I hate to see the boy in him diminished, watching him mature has been a treat for me and a comfort for Leah, if only she could admit it. Amos has a new boat ("a corker"!), Gus has his own traps, and together they are making good money. As always, they are making fun of one another. But I think it's Gus's new friend Morales, a Coast Guardsman at the lighthouse (a Mexican-American from Boston, of all places), who has brought him out. Morales is a captivating young man who fancies himself a rogue. Last weekend the two of them went up to Stonington for a ball game and dance at the Masonic Hall. They stayed the night with George Grindle (who *is* a rogue), and when they came back, you'd think that Gus had been in Manhattan for the weekend—or Paris or downtown Bangor.

You said it sounds as though Amos and I have "found one another" again. I try not to let myself entertain such an idea (I think it would scare him half to death), but I do admit that seeing him more often, on this business or that, has been . . . well . . . promising. And if that's not enough to tweak your curiosity and inspire you to write back, I'll add, sheepishly, that I think Amos is a tad jealous of a certain Mr. Gardiner.

I hope this finds you well, dear one. I'm off to bed, if I can stay awake long enough to get there. Kiss the little ones for me, and give my best to your dear Jack, please.

Your loving country cousin,
Maggie

The Reverend Paul Hotchkiss, the summer minister, called the schoolhouse gathering to prayer. He was a barrel-chested, sonorous man, who everyone said looked like Orson Welles. Hands clasped before him, the reverend waited for the murmuring and shuffling to cease, then addressed the Lord. He asked God to bless and watch over this group and their efforts. He informed Him, and those who might not have heard the news, that the work that this group was undertaking was made even more urgent by the fact that Herr Hitler had only the day before announced that the entire Atlantic Ocean belonged to Nazi Germany, adding that any of his enemies found on it would be destroyed.

Reverend Hotchkiss looked out one window at the bay and another to the shining sea, saying, "It is your ocean, Lord, and ours too because we are in it, out here seven miles from shore. Help us to stand tall and protect our homes and families, our country. Give us the strength to overcome fear, and help us to remember always that you are our Protector. Amen."

The minister asked Maggie, who stood by her desk at the far end of the room, to lead the group in the Pledge of Allegiance, which she did. Posted as sentinels outside the door on the porch, Morales and Gus faced the flag through the screen with their hands on their hearts.

Cecil—in a shirt and tie, and striped trousers—stood behind the table facing the rows of folded chairs, with Jake behind him and Robert Owings seated to his left. While he welcomed the group and thanked Mr. Owings, in particular, Agnes Chadwick, the wife of the governor of Connecticut, moved from her seat in the row of summer people and sat between Iris and Bernadine, as a democratic gesture.

Jake drew a large and very accurate outline of the island on the blackboard, while Cecil presented their plan for the local shore patrols.

They had split the island into four sections, bisecting it horizontally, then vertically. Each section would be the responsibility of a group with one person in charge. Cecil read from his notes: In quadrant number one, under the capable direction of Mister Owings, the group would concentrate their vigilance on the northern head, Laundry Cove, Point Lookout, the island thoroughfare, and the mountain. Group One, consisting mostly of summer people, would also be responsible for surveillance of any and all sailboats and yachts that visited the island. Jake circled an X on the map as each of the lookout points was read.

Group Two, led by Richard Snell, had the most difficult quadrant—the remote and barely accessible southwestern end of the island, with its key points at Eli Creek, Duck Harbor Mountain, and the southern cliffs from Thunder Gulch west. Group Three, with Dick Hanson as its leader, would watch at Squeaker Cove, Head Harbor, the Eastern Ear, and Boom Beach. Group Four, the smallest, would be coordinated by Amos Coombs, who was not present but had been briefed. It was responsible for the Battery, Eaton Cove, and the cliffs between Coombs and Old Coves. Chief Gardiner's lighthouse crew would assist Amos's group with the surveillance of open waters.

Jake explained that the Coast Guard would provide a radio for communication with the mainland. During patrolling hours, a watch would be mounted in the church, with all groups reporting to the radio operator. In the event of an emergency, the church bell would be rung. Jake's "very capable operator" would train an islander to use the radio.

On the porch, Gus slugged Morales in the arm, and Morales, grinning, slugged him back.

Robert Owings, dressed for action in a freshly laundered flannel shirt, rose to cover the remaining details. He said that the committee had declined the offer of weapons. They had accepted the Very pistols, binoculars, and other equipment, but to issue weapons would be a nightmare—and dangerous to boot. Those who wanted to arm themselves could do so with their own firearms—there were plenty of those on the island—or could borrow a weapon from a neighbor. Hours for the shore patrols and lookouts were to be from six to nine in the evening, at a minimum. It was acceptable, he said, for men sixteen or older to patrol alone, but women and boys under sixteen would have to be accompanied by a man, for obvious reasons.

At Maggie's shoulder a june bug the size of a small sparrow went into a dive and slammed headfirst into the window screen with all its winged might. Having struck, it fell to the ground. Within seconds the insect recovered and soared over the swings, gained air speed in a wide turn, and made another run at the screen, with the same results.

"That's it," Cecil concluded. "In a nutshell. Does anyone have any questions, or suggestions?"

Iris and Richard raised their hands. Cecil called on Iris.

"Shouldn't we teach more than one person how to use the radio? I mean . . ."

"You're right," Jake said. "That's a good point. We can teach you, too, if you want to volunteer."

"Me? Oh." Iris pressed her lips together to erase the pucker as she did in the morning mirror, and she blushed deep red.

"So what are we supposed to do if we see spies or Germans?" Richard asked.

"Report them immediately," Cecil said.

"And run away? I'm not gonna. Christ no."

"These are orders, Richard." Cecil was frosty. "We are not to engage anyone, under any circumstances. It's not your call."

"It will be if I'm alone on some cliff and I—"

Cecil said they would talk later and adjourned the meeting.

While others rose to leave or stood talking in clusters, Mrs. Chadwick read the wall chart that she had been squinting at during the meeting. It was a cursive exercise, a quote copied by a girl with a graceful hand, a blue ribbon pinned beneath.

> *The work for those who are at home seems to*
> *be obvious. First, to do our own job, whatever*
> *it is, as well as we can possibly do it. Second,*
> *to add to it everything we can do in the way*
> *of civilian defense. Now, at last, every com-*
> *munity must go to work to build up protec-*
> *tion from attack.*
> —Eleanor Roosevelt

Mrs. Chadwick, who was a Republican, nodded her approval when she was done reading. Maggie, the Democrat who had supplied the quote, saw the older woman nod and smiled to herself.

She also saw Cecil and Robert Owings in the corner by the photos of the five island school graduates who were in uniform. Mr. Owings's face was set in a false smile; he made a feint to get away, but Cecil sidestepped to block him. Mr. Owings shook his head to say no. Cecil patted his forehead with a folded handkerchief, something Maggie had never seen him do. Mr. Owings said something, then shrugged his shoulders, his palms up. Mrs. Chadwick came to his rescue. Cecil shook hands with her, then with Mr. Owings, and took his leave. He said something mean to Leah, words that made her turn away angrily. On his way out he brushed Richard aside, leaving the fisherman glaring in his wake.

She raised her hand to knock, but saw through the window that Amos was asleep and let herself in, setting on the floor a cloth-covered basket with a thermos protruding from it. Tommy Dorsey's band was swinging on the radio, and she shut it off. He must have been sleeping for a while, she thought, he hated "that boogie-woogie music."

Maggie was dressed for open water—in wool pants, rubber boots, and a tweed coat with a Very pistol riding heavily in the inside pocket. Amos's lips were parted slightly, and his face, smoothed by sleep, looked ten years younger. The poet was right, she thought: sleep is a blessed thing.

Should she wake him with a kiss, she wondered? No. It would scare and confuse him. If the soft affection they had once shared was going to be revived, it would take time. Twenty years without tenderness, and all because of unfortunate timing and a vindictive sister.

Maggie shook his shoulder gently with the hand that held her cap.

"Unh?" Amos came up from a deep sleep. "I only sat down just now."

"Yes," she said. She could tell by his eyes that he was glad to see her. "And well you should get some rest. You don't get enough."

"I'm not so old, you know."

"I didn't say that. Any man half your age would tire doing as much as you do. I'm tired too, tired of Iris Weed going on and on. I think she's found her calling in all these auxiliaries. She belongs to every one. Now she can do her talking with an audience and do it all day long. I need some air."

"Air you'll get." Amos stretched slowly and rubbed his face before he put on his glasses. "What's all this, a picnic?"

It was a gentle evening, with a warm land breeze blowing from the west. On their way past the ledges, they saw a solitary summer sailor making his way into Blue Hill Bay in a green schooner, late for cocktails in the harbor, no doubt. The captain was at the helm wearing a long-billed swordfisherman's hat; a boy in shorts waved to them from the bow chains, where he rode with his feet in the water. There were no other boats in sight. The setting sun was mottled by low, rippled clouds.

"That's a mackerel sky." He knew she knew.

"Rain tomorrow," she said. She stood on the deck behind the house, her hands deep in her coat pockets. She thought the island looked larger when seen from the east; the mountain and the spiny ridge loomed huge and dark with the sun behind them. As she watched the cove disappear and the island shrink, the sea began to swell under them, rocking the big Novi boat from side to side like a cradle.

Amos knew what she was thinking: that this was their boat, his and hers together, and would someday be Gus's. Maybe she was thinking that this is what they should have done years ago: gotten aboard his boat and sailed off to somewhere, leaving the island behind them for good. Maybe that was what they should have done.

He asked her to take the wheel for a minute while he went below. When she did, she was surprised by how hard it tugged. She hoped he was not going below for a drink. He was not, or at least he did not smell of it when he came back on deck. He took the wheel from her and reached down to open a little door in the bulkhead, releasing a rush of static that made her step back as if from a sudden swarm of flies. He put on the headset and glanced at her for approval, which he saw. Then he pushed a button on the cord and stopped the rushing noise.

"Mabel Baker One Nine this is Mabel Baker One One. Radio check."

Morales answered, loud and clear enough for her to hear his voice in Amos's earphone. "One One, this is One Nine. That's *Able*, Amos, not Mabel. Able Baker."

He turned to Maggie. "Morales has terrible radio procedure. That was a security violation saying my name, and he knows it."

"I see." She knew she had to learn to work the radio. Maggie was taking mental notes on everything. She was good with details and often thought that she would make a good police witness in a murder trial.

Amos keyed the mike again. "This is One One. Roger, radio

check. I read you loud and clear. I have negative further. Out."

He hung the headset on the bulkhead. "You get used to the static after a while," he said.

"I'll need to read the manual, I suppose, if only to learn the language," said Maggie. "You sound like Buck Rogers and what's his name."

"I didn't read the manual. Morales and Jake taught me. I can teach you. There aren't many words. I haven't learned code yet."

"Are we authorized to learn code?" she asked. "I know Morse Code, but I don't suppose . . . I have a lot to learn."

"It'll be easy for you. I've been taking a heading of a hundred and ninety-two degrees when I have the nesting island behind me like we do now. In a sea like this, with low swells and not much head wind, I try for ten knots, which will put us off Seal Island in an hour and ten minutes."

He pointed to penciled figures above the windshield. "Those are the headings: first leg, second leg, third leg, home."

"A hundred and ninety-two for the first leg," she said. "Roger."

Beyond the mouth of the bay, the swells—thick, with long but shallow trenches in between—marched evenly toward their port bow. Amos put Maggie at the wheel, and standing behind her, showed her how to ride up one side of each swell, over and down the other. She took to it easily, though the strain of the wheel was hard on her shoulders.

"The thermos is tea," she said. "Pour us a cup, would you?"

He took the wheel when Seal Island came into view, and Maggie scanned the surface with the binoculars. If a U-boat was on its way out to the shipping lanes, Amos explained, it would probably be coming from the west, to starboard. He gave the wet, desolate rock a wide berth and brought the bow around to sixty degrees in the swells.

"See? There." He pointed straight over the bow. "There, you'll see it flash again. Wait. That's the lighthouse; that's Jake. On this heading we're following the shoal up to it; the shallow water is off there, to port, about a half mile. They turn the light on at seven o'clock, and on a night like tonight you can steer for it. Only you can't count on seeing it; a thick of fog might come up at any minute, but you know that."

"Out here it seems even more ridiculous that they keep the lighthouses working," she said.

"God only knows why they don't turn them off. Jake says that the people running this war are idiots, only he used a different word."

A half hour later, with the sea down and the sun setting through a crack in the low clouds, he cut the boat's speed back to five knots, and Maggie brought out their supper. They ate in companionable silence.

She wondered how long it had been since they had been alone and as close as this, without a chance of someone surprising them. He must have had the same thought, as he looked away—suddenly awkward—fumbling with something above the wheel. Seeing his shyness opened the doors of longing and memory at once for Maggie; she felt all the old vulnerability and need. With a certain quiet joy she did not understand, she allowed herself to risk memory, wondering if Amos was doing the same thing.

It was one of the spring mornings, before the lilacs, when they were alone in her father's kitchen, eager for each other, afraid of the sound of her sister Clytie's steps on the stairs. As always, he was packing his dinner pail, and she was making breakfast while Clytie, Amos's wife, and their daughter, Leah, slept. He was as anxious as he seemed now, and Maggie as vulnerable. They did not speak then, either, but came together slowly, in warm silence. He would turn and take her face in his hands or, from his chair, take her by the waist to pull her into his lap, his hands rising timidly to her breasts, her mouth warm and wet on his.

• • •

Would he turn to her now? No, she knew he would not. The source of their guilt was dead but not gone; Clytie would always hover between them. Maggie's sister was more potent now as a spirit than she had been then as a woman, because now she could come between each of them and their memories. Their only comfort was that Clytie had not been able to come between them and their desire, then or now.

While Amos was finishing his cake, Maggie wandered aft on the deck with the binoculars around her neck. He cleaned his glasses on his shirt and watched her. He remembered another morning, in the same kitchen, when she had come to him, opening her robe, her hair and warm body smelling of flannel sheets. Now, with his glasses off, her figure back on the deck was as vague and ageless as it had been in his memory, and he wanted to touch her once more.

"Amos?"

He put his glasses on. She was facing out to sea, the binoculars in her hands, her eyes closed.

"Do you hear that?" She held her head still, her neck craned, as though listening for Clytie's feet on the stairs.

"What?" He pulled the throttle back, his hands shaking, telling himself that she did not really hear anything. He held his head out over the washboard. If there was anything, he did not hear it and shook his head at her in relief. The swells were starting to turn them.

"Shut off the engine," she said.

"I can't. We'll get turned side to."

"Amos, please, just for a second. It's a humming."

Like an electric motor, he thought. Oh, God. He shut off the engine and stared out at the empty sea, immobilized by dread. It was a humming noise, off the stern now and heading straight for them. Now running away was no longer an option; starting the engine would make too much noise.

"Out there," she said. She pointed to starboard with the binoculars. "Can you see anything? His periscope?"

They stood apart, staring, too frightened to move, as the sound grew louder and louder until it was almost directly under them. It was a huge moaning noise, all too familiar to Amos, that made the sea vibrate. He waited for the U-boat to break the surface underneath them and hurl them through the air.

"Now there's nothing," she said. "Can you still hear it? I'm not sure I do, wait, yes. Amos," she said excitedly. "Turn out that way, and let's follow it. Or I will and you get on the radio."

"Like hell. Not with you aboard."

The Quahog, dead in the water now, had swung around with her side to the swells and was rolling dangerously. The bait barrel slid across the deck and bumped against the side, a sound that would reverberate a mile through the water, like the boom of a drum. He started the engine and turned back on course, away from the humming.

"It was a submarine," she said.

"Well?"

"What else could it have been?" asked Maggie. "No creature hums like an automobile." She stood staring after it, still too excited to be afraid.

Amos was well past excited and deeply involved in afraid. He kept his eye on the lighthouse, his hands on the wheel, and the boat at a steady ten knots.

"It could have been your imagination," he said. "Our imagination."

She set her face against him. "What do you mean? Did you hear a humming noise traveling in that direction or didn't you?

"Yes I did. I thought I did." He saw Walter standing in the path by the house once in a while, too. He saw Ava in the window again just the other day. He saw bobbing human candles from thirty miles away. Sure he saw them; he thought he did.

"We did hear it. We did not imagine it, Amos." She knew

the look: his head slightly bent, his eyes averted, the posture of strict attention to the task at hand. He was getting ready to duck something, and this time he would not get away with it, she decided. The wind, a little stiffer from the west now, blew fine, cold spray in her face and this encouraged her.

"Sometimes, he said, "you see what you want to see. Sometimes what you need to see. And it's real. That noise, now that I think about it—"

"Oh no, Amos Coombs. You're afraid they'll laugh. But you can't dodge this because of what you think people will say. This is war. Remember those empty lifejackets you brought in? That's where the sub is going. To kill more of our boys. And when it's done, the Germans will enslave the rest of us."

"We'll call it a vessel heard in the distance," he said. "When we stop at the lighthouse we can explain to them what we heard. You're right. It was a U-boat."

There was no one in sight at dusk when they tied up at the slip below the boathouse, so Amos went ahead and started pumping his fuel. In a minute, the door of the keeper's house opened, and Jake and Morales came down the long wooden walk, Jake still munching a saltine. In the yellow window behind them, Harvey's face was up against the glass, wearing a foul expression of disapproval.

Pleased to see Maggie, Morales helped her up onto the landing. When Amos had his back turned, she beckoned to get Morales's attention, then opened her coat to show him the Very pistol he had given her. Morales leaned forward and whispered in her ear, then patted her shoulder. From his window, Harvey saw the woman open her coat to Morales to show him her wares, and he saw the spick's face light up when he had a look. It made him sick what this world was coming to, plain sick.

Maggie told Jake and Morales what they had heard. She described it carefully, trying not to sound like an alarmist or someone prone to wild tales. Amos nodded steadily in agreement.

"It probably was a U-boat," allowed Jake. "I'm not surprised. I'm just surprised that we haven't heard one here on the rock. I'm surprised one hasn't stopped to ask directions yet."

Maggie thought he seemed resigned to failure, defeat. She wanted to encourage him, boost his spirits. Was there another woman who might? She did not think so. Jake said he would record it as a possible sighting, and she gave Amos a look.

"A hundred ten degrees, you said?" Jake asked.

"Right out toward the shipping lanes," said Amos.

"You should have chased him, Amos." Morales said. "You could have poured a bottle of that Cemetery rum down his periscope and thrown a match behind it, though that probably wouldn't have been necessary."

"It's Demerara," Amos corrected. "Dem-Er-Rare-A."

On the way home they were quiet, thoughtful. The sun had long ago gone down over the islands and the mainland in the distance, but there was still enough light to see the gray shapes of lounging seals on the ledges they passed.

"I suppose it would be better not to say anything to anyone on the island about what we saw or heard," she said.

"God no."

"Imagine what they'll say when they hear we were out here alone. 'Wickedness' is the word Iris will use," she said.

He looked at her, half amused, half elsewhere. "After what we've been through on this island, you still care what they think? They believe what they want to believe—you know that. And when it comes to what they say to each other, it don't matter what they believe, because they say what they think others want to hear.

"And who cares? They'll never say anything to our faces; they proved that after Clytie died. It's been how many years since? And still nobody has said a word directly to either of us." He shook his head. Then he smiled, almost beamed, as if he could see the memory in the darkness.

"Remember years ago when they were whispering about Harold and Katie? They had them living in sin right away, condemned overnight: no trial, no questions, no nothing. Just wickedness. They've been talking them down for years."

She was reflective. Why was he carrying on like this? "Yes, I know. But you've picked a bad example. In this case what they believe and say are true. I know it. I saw his car parked in the road by her drive every Friday night for months. His wife was still alive, and her husband was still warm in his grave. That's fact."

"It's also fact that me and Lew and Walter put his car there. It was seven Fridays. We pushed it out of his yard as soon as he was asleep, drove it down the road to her drive, parked it, then drove it back in the wee hours, and rolled it back into place in his yard. He never realized it, and she didn't either. Everybody else on the island knew the car was there, and believed they were making thunder in her bedroom, but nobody ever said a thing to either of them."

"You didn't!"

"Didn't what?"

"You didn't really do that, did you? You're making this up to tease me."

"Sure we did," he grinned.

"I don't think that's funny! I don't think that's one darn bit funny. Look what you did to Katie's reputation—and Harold's."

"We owed him one, and it didn't hurt her any. Come on, Maggie. Everett married her anyway. If he believes that about her—and I don't know whether he does or not—he married her anyway, which means he loves her, don't you see? He does. Look at them. They've been married as happily as anybody I know, for years."

"How old were you then?" she asked. "You were almost thirty. A thirty-year-old teenager." She thought that he must not see the irony in the story; if he did, he would not take such pleasure in it.

"I don't remember. It doesn't really matter anymore."

"No," she said bitterly. "I suppose it doesn't, and that's the lamentable part."

She had to be pretty mad, he thought, to use words that he didn't understand when they were alone. To hell with her if she couldn't take a joke. Now she would be icy the rest of the night. He never should have told her.

Over tea at his house, she paced back and forth in the parlor—her coat off, sweater open, flannel cap still on—making plans out loud. Watching her, seeing again the beautiful determination in her eyes under that foolish cap, made him remember why he had loved her back then, at such risk.

"What are you smiling at?" she asked. She knew, he could tell by her face that she did. "You're not making fun of me, are you?"

"You know I'm not. Keep talking; I'm listening." He stirred his tea carefully.

"I'm more convinced now than I ever was that you should not be going out there alone. I won't let you go by yourself any more. That's out of sight of land, and the seas are heavy—they were even tonight, when you admitted it was calmer than usual. Where do those swells come from?"

"That's the sea coming in against the shoal, where the bottom comes up. You won't *let* me? Even if we were man and wife you wouldn't be talking like that."

"Oh yes I would." She was a pisser when she was being reasonable. She sat down by the cold stove.

"I'm going with you," she said. "Either Gus or I will go with you *every* night."

"I'll admit I liked having company this time, but I was more nervous than *ever* with you out there where something might happen—more than likely *will* happen from the looks of it."

"You have to take me," she said. "I'm half owner."

"I suppose I do."

"And I want you to promise me that you'll share your look-outs on the cliffs with others in your Shore Patrol group," she said.

"No, I won't do that. I don't want those people walking around up there, snooping around here in the cove—maybe in the houses—disturbing things. I'm sick of them snooping in my world. You are too. Admit it, Maggie."

She closed her eyes and nodded yes.

CHAPTER SIX

HORST WILTZIUS AND HIS SON OF THE SAME NAME LOOSENED THEIR
ties and lingered together at the long dining table on each of the
last three nights that the young Horst was at home. Frau Wiltzius, who would normally not approve, opened an extra bottle of
wine for them and left them to their tobacco. Young Horst's
older sister brought her curly headed little girl, Frankie, to say
good night to her uncle and grandfather, then she, too, left them
to their politics and naval talk. They smoked the last of the cigars that the older Horst had presented his son upon his gradua-
tion from the naval academy at Flensburg.

Unlike many fathers and sons in Germany, the Wiltzius men
agreed on most everything and loved to discuss politics and the
war. The older Horst had served in submarines in the previous
war and had known Admiral Dönitz personally, though only
briefly. He agreed with Dönitz's contention that in this new war
the chivalry of the old days was no longer practical. It was unrealistic to think that a U-boat could approach an enemy ship
with a warning, then give the crew time to escape in lifeboats
before firing torpedoes it. It was a pity, they agreed, but necessary. The older Horst approved, too, of Dönitz's insistence upon
a more democratic, less rigid relationship between the captain

and crew aboard each U-boat. How else to avoid the disastrous mutinies caused so often by tyrannical captains in the last war?

Though the Wiltzius men remained optimistic in front of the rest of the family and the workers in the vineyards, they shared a dread about the future of Germany under Adolf Hitler. But in those last nights together, they avoided talk of the Eastern Front, the excesses of the Nazi party, and the awaited arrival of Polish conscripts to help with the harvest. They talked instead of what they would do when young Horst returned from his first patrol and of the optimistic predictions for this year's wine. The older Horst could remember well the exhilarating mixture of fear and expectation that his son was feeling before his first encounter with the enemy.

In the morning, while the young man said good-bye to the rest of the family, the elder Horst waited in the automobile, for fear that he would show his emotions. They drove to the Trier station in silence and, as they had agreed the night before, said their farewells briefly at the train.

"You wear the uniform well," the older Horst said. "We are proud of you. Go with God."

The trip to Lorient, on the Brittany coast, took three days. Ensign Wiltzius's train was sidetracked more than a dozen times to make way for munitions trains and long, black lines of boxcars heading into Germany. He spent one night asleep in the corner of his third-class compartment outside Paris, another on some rural siding in western France.

His apprehension and nostalgia both disappeared when he reached Lorient and the bustling harbor where the U-boat base was being finished. He was astonished by the gigantic concrete pens being built by the Todt Corporation. If only his father could be there to see them. They had both heard rumors, but the sight of these structures was another thing altogether. The walls were twenty feet thick and built so high that the boats could be lifted out of the water below by cranes mounted in the ceilings. No bomb could penetrate them. For some reason the British had not bombed them during construction, and now it was too late to even try. How could anyone defeat a Germany that could manufacture such a miracle?

In the confusion of the harbor the young Horst felt naive and unable to hide his fear of appearing helpless. The other ensigns, no older than he, seemed so confident. They went about their business with an air of nonchalance and a knowledge of the working details of the place that made them appear to be old hands. He thought that once he was assigned to a boat, all would be well. He went to the headquarters ship on the quay and reported to Command, only to be told by a snide adjutant with an evil, hairy nose that he would have to wait three days for his boat.

Horst managed to say that he would have to make do with wine and women for a while longer, but instead of sounding jaded as he wished, he was sure that he appeared callow and that the clerk who had overheard him exchanged grins with another as he left the room.

At least the time spent waiting gave the young ensign the opportunity to learn his way around so he did not seem so clumsy and overwhelmed. He found two classmates from Flensburg at the Hotel Beausejour, and the three of them got fumbling drunk every night.

Finally, on the fourth morning, he was told to report back to Command at three in the afternoon. When he returned, still nursing a headache from the night before, he met Captain Reising, who received him warmly. He was assigned to U235, a brand new modified Type VIIC that had just arrived from her sea trials at Kiel. They would go aboard in the morning and begin their own shakedown and training of the crew. In no time, Reising said, they would be sailing into the North Atlantic to join one of the wolf packs. Horst, who would be watch and radio officer, should bring his gear aboard immediately.

Young Wiltzius was disappointed with Captain Reising at first because the man seemed so gentle, so congenial. He had hoped to serve under one of the infamous Gray Wolves, those fierce, determined U-boat heroes he had so long idolized. Reising, who looked to be in his early thirties, was a veteran of several patrols and wore the Iron Cross, but without Oak Cluster or Sword. Would he be anything like the great Gunther Prien, who had said that he got more pleasure from a good convoy exercise than he did from any furlough? Horst doubted it, but he resolved to serve his captain well and make his father proud.

They trained for two long weeks, going through every conceivable drill over and over again until the crew—only half of which had combat experience—operated as well as the precision machine they animated. On the fifteenth day the expectant men ran through yet another diving routine far out in the Bay of Biscay. The drill went as smoothly as anyone might have expected, and within minutes U235 lay on the sandy bottom, ninety meters below the choppy surface. The boat rocked gently in the current; the silence within was broken only by the soft noise of the compressors up forward.

In the control room, still wearing his red glasses at the chart table, Captain Reising turned to Horst and told him to assemble the crew in the forward torpedo room. Most of them were naked except for their black shorts and shoes, and their bodies glistened with sweat in the greenish light, as did the interior surface of the hull. Many sat on the shiny brass torpedoes, waiting wordlessly for further orders. The bunks had been folded up to make room for the crowd.

When the men were assembled, Horst went to the control room and reported to Captain Reising, who followed him back to the torpedo room, shutting the bulkhead door behind him to muffle the noise of the compressors. The wire mesh covering the bulb over his shoulder cast a spiderweb pattern of shadow on his white cap. Reising waited for a moment, looking from face to face.

"Gentlemen," he said in a low, even voice. "You have proved yourselves worthy of this boat and worthy of the sub-

marine service. I have just now received orders from Admiral,
U-boats. Tomorrow we take on food and other necessities. The
following morning we set sail for the convoy routes in the
North Atlantic."

He paused, then smiled. "Good hunting!"

When he was gone, the crew was silent until the blue-eyed
Mardsden reached across a torpedo to shake hands with the
ghastly Liebe, setting off a babble of excitement and hand-
shaking before the petty officers could disperse the men to
their stations.

All the next day, under a chilly, gray Brittany sky, U235 was
loaded with food and provisions. Below, every inch of spare
space was used to store fresh foods: sausages, hams, and
smoked bacon hung from pipes and cables everywhere. Hammocks filled with huge loaves of black bread and long French
baguettes were slung in every available space, so that the crew
had to move in a crouch. Crates of potatoes and tinned meats
were stuffed into every possible nook. Along the hull in the forward part of the galley were cases of Beck's beer ordered by
Captain Reising for special occasions. The crew was as fresh as
the food that surrounded them and eager to set out. That
evening, in his tiny bunk, Horst wrote a brief letter home, then
dreamed himself toward an anxious sleep, with images of Admiral Dönitz himself, in his long black leather coat, welcoming
them home amid the music of bands and crowds of girls with
bouquets.

At noon, U235 separated from the pier and moved slowly
out of the harbor into the open waters of the bay, where her
diesels took over. It was a dark day, threatening to storm. Horst
and several others rode with the watch on the bridge until the
increasing seas soaked them, and they went below. Even with
the weeks of training, young Wiltzius and the other new men
were still striking their shoulders on bulkhead doors and banging
their knees on exposed pipes and levers as the boat pitched and
heaved. Captain Reising kept U235 on the surface to make bet-

ter time, instead of submerging for a gentler ride. By evening, Horst was struggling with seasickness and was grateful to get out into the air when his turn for watch came, no matter how wet and cold it was.

Darkness fell early and was deepened by the thick cloud layer at the western edge of the storm. The sea was calmer, and U235 was making good speed. Wiltzius and Obersteuerman Achen were on lookout; three others were riding the perimeter of the conning tower in silence.

"Listen to that. Do you hear it?" Achen pointed skyward off the starboard bow.

Horst cupped his ears, as did the others. The heavy engines of a large aircraft reverberated in the sky. It sounded as if it was flying low and in a direction parallel to theirs.

"Captain to the bridge!" Horst shouted into the intercom.

In seconds, Captain Reising was on the bridge, straining to hear and see with the others. The noise of the aircraft changed from a deep, pounding sound to a higher-pitched roaring. They could see nothing but darkness and the gray edge of the heavy clouds.

"He can't see us any better than we can see him," Achen said.

"He's banking. He's coming around this way. What's he doing?" There was another change in the noise of the engines aloft—this time a lessening in volume but an increase in clarity.

"He's coming right at us, sir!"

As Wiltzius spoke, a giant silver beam of artificial light cut through the low clouds from the approaching aircraft, shone on the water just off their port not fifty meters away, then began to move slowly toward them.

"A porcupine!" screamed Achen.

"Alarm!"

They tumbled down through the hatch, sliding and bumping on the ladder, and striking the deck plates on the run. The noise of the alarm bell seemed to explode inside the boat. Men turned handwheels frantically, while the machinists hung their full weight on the levers to blow the air out of the ballast tanks and let the sea in.

"All hands forward to the forward torpedo room!" screamed Captain Reising. The rush of the crew through the boat swept Horst forward with it, banging him against every metal object, throwing him once to the deck plates in a full sprawl. The roar of the escaping air overwhelmed even the alarm bell until, seconds later, as young Wiltzius was recovering and following another man through the last bulkhead, a giant explosion lifted the stern of U235, shook her, and flung her off her axis. A second explosion seemed to shove the boat sideways.

"Wabos!" someone screamed. "Wabos!"

"Not depth charges," said another. "It's bombs!"

For a moment the boat was out of control, heading straight for the bottom. Men screamed at one another in the darkness, until the emergency lighting came on and the captain and steersman got the boat righted.

"Left full rudder!" Even from their position forward they could hear Captain Reising shouting orders. "Starboard motor half ahead!"

They had changed course and were righted, perhaps seventy meters down now, if Horst had guessed right. He knelt on the deck plates, holding onto a chain, looking up and listening, as were the others around him. There was only the noise of their own electric motors—nothing more. Young Wiltzius struggled to control his shaking. He thought for a moment that he would vomit but concentrated on the pain in his shoulder.

"What was it, sir?" Next to him in the feeble light, young Praeger thrust his face forward, looking for salvation. He had cut his cheek slightly; his eyes were bulging with fear. The sight of Praeger and the man's need for reassurance made Horst stand up.

"I'm sure it's all right now Praeger." He spoke aloud so that the others near him would hear. "That was a Porcupine—you know, a Sunderland flying boat. He had a light on us, but he missed us, didn't he? The incompetent boob."

Praeger and another man nearby laughed, relieved.

"He won't find us again," Horst said. "Captain Reising has already lost him, you can be sure. There, the lights are on. Back to your stations. Get this mess cleaned up."

Later, in the control room, Reising and two of his officers shared a plate of bread and jam, and talked over their tea. The boat had suffered little or no damage, unless one counted the fright to the crew. Everyone knew that the captain's quick work with the steersman had prevented them from losing the use of their hydroplanes and keeling over completely. What they did not know was how the aircraft found them in the darkness.

"It must have been coincidence," said Ensign Raeden. "What else could explain it? It must have been his luck."

"Could he have radar, sir?" asked Horst. This was on everyone's mind, though none had mentioned it until now.

"It looks that way," Reising said. "But Admiral, U-boats insists that it is impossible. I inquired in my after-action report, and the reply was unequivocal. The enemy does not have radar small enough for aircraft."

The ensigns suspected that the captain was not convinced, but would say nothing.

"Luck," repeated Reising. "His luck." Then he smiled, as if to himself. "And our luck, as well, to have had so many fresh loaves aboard." He turned the loaf of black bread around to show them the impression of a man's skull, as deep as two cupped hands.

"So many pillows and such tasty ones, too."

CHAPTER SEVEN

RICHARD SLOWED FOR A FROST HEAVE ON THE DEER ISLE ROAD, BUT it was still quite a bump, especially for his mother and Claire, who both let out a little *whoops* when they bounced on the back seat. The two widows, Lucille Snell and Claire Fickett, were cousins twice removed and neighbors who visited one another often. Lucille was wearing her new frock with the orange floral patterns; Claire compensated for the age of her own dress with her gold brooch and a new Sears and Roebuck hat adorned with a pink spray. Richard, in a fedora and Sunday suit, drove with his elbow out the window.

When Lucille had first heard that gasoline was to be rationed to three gallons a week, she despaired that they would not be able to continue their Sunday outings. Richard, however, had assured her that they would have enough gas—just leave it to him. He was telling her the truth when he added that he enjoyed their outings, too. He liked to take his '36 Desoto out on the road. The blue had faded some, but the chrome still polished bright, and there was not a spot of rust on her—unlike most of the cars in Stonington. People they passed on Sundays knew they were going to the Jed Prouty Inn, which had the nicest restaurant

113

west of Bar Harbor, and Richard knew that the women who waved envied Lucille for having such a good son.

It was the finest kind of summer day for a Sunday drive. The loosestrife was in bloom, and the purple roadside lupine, Lucille's favorite, was in full flower. On the causeway beach between Deer Isle and Little Deer Isle, Lucille saw the MacFarlands setting up for a picnic lunch and poked Richard to honk so they could wave. He did, sliding into the wide turn before the bridge over Eggemoggin Reach. Lucille had yet to ride over the span with her eyes open. Driving through the air over water was scary enough, but on a bridge that Richard said was built to sway with the wind, it was absolutely horrifying.

"With a breeze like this one—" Richard began.

"You hush!" she said, and covered her eyes with her hands as they approached the bridge.

"You should open your eyes and see all the sailboats," said Claire.

"Look at them all," Richard said. "You'd never know there was a war on."

Later, they passed a young man hitchhiking in front of the Blue Hill library. He was carrying a striped suitcase and smiled at them when they passed.

"You should've picked him up," said Claire, touched by the smile. "He might be going off to enlist. Or home to see his family. These days we have to—"

"He was a stranger," said Lucille. "We do not pick up strangers."

"He was wearing a necktie, for pity's sake. He was smiling." Claire smoothed her dress over her knees. It could be her boy Bruce, trying to get home from Maryland.

"Don't forget that it was strangers that robbed Richard and beat him up in Rockland—that nearly killed him," Lucille said. "You can't be too careful these days; it's shameful."

• • •

After dinner, they went for a walk down Bucksport's main street, Richard strolling ahead picking his teeth while the ladies looked in the shop windows. They stopped at a bench at the far end of town to rest their feet and watched a ship taking on pulp from the paper mill. A crane twice as high as a church steeple was lifting logs from railroad cars with its claws and dropping them like sticks onto a log mountain. The afternoon shift was arriving, crossing the road from the parking lot by the hundreds.

"So many people, so much going on. It makes me feel small," said Claire. "Look at how many of them are women. Everything's changing so fast."

"You should see Rockland, if you think this is something," said Richard. He folded his arms on his chest. "I'll bet the next time I go there, the harbor will be twice as big, and I won't recognize a single boat."

"Oh, but you promised," said Lucille looking over at her son and then to Claire, whose hand she took in hers. "Richard was set on going back to find those two fellows and teach them a lesson, but I made him promise he wouldn't. He's so proud."

In the quiet car on the way back to Blue Hill, Claire said that Stonington was crowded and busy enough for her. "I'll bet you miss Barter Island sometimes," she said.

"Oh, I do, a little bit," said Lucille while she watched the houses go by. "I miss some of the people and the quiet sometimes. But I don't miss cleaning summer people's houses and doing their laundry; I don't miss not having a telephone, not going to picture shows, or not taking Sunday outings."

"I doubt you miss Deacon Barter—Lord Cecil," said Richard. He mocked Cecil's somber voice: " 'Good morning. I'm Cecil Barter, and you're not. Welcome to my island.' "

"His father was a nice man," said Lucille. "He was some generous when times were bad. And Leah, poor dear, I do miss her. So unlike her mother."

"Thank God," said Richard.

• • •

At exactly three by the town hall clock, Richard dropped the ladies in front of the drugstore in Blue Hill for their ice-cream sodas. He offered to go in with them to help them get a table by the window, but Lucille said they would be fine on their own. They would look for him in an hour, as usual.

When the Desoto ground to a stop in the gravel before Carl Topp's big gray barn, Carl appeared in the side door and waved Richard inside. On Sunday afternoons, when he worked on his car, Carl dressed like an engineer: a blue-and-white striped hat and soft gloves with cuffs that stretched to his elbows. He was a spare, upright man in his early sixties, with kind eyes and an appraising, sidelong glance. He had been restoring the 1905 Buick two-cylinder touring car for eighteen years, telling Bel that all the money they put into it would be recovered ten fold when he sold it for their retirement. But now that he was nearly finished, Carl was loath to let the car go. He had promised Bel that they would ride in it in the Fourth of July parade this year with the idea of attracting an offer from one of the many summer people who liked to drive antique cars while they were rusticating in Maine.

Carl shed his gloves to pour a drink while Richard circled the bright car and peered under the open hood at the engine, his hands behind his back.

"Not a spot of dirt or grease anywhere," he said. "When Cyrus Hawkes sees this, he'll reach for his wallet. With any luck, the senator will reach for his at the same time, outbid Cyrus, and you and the missus will be off to the city in a new Cadillac."

Carl handed Richard a cup. "But her idle is still pretty ragged. That parade is slow—all that stopping and going; I'd hate to have her conk out in front of everybody. I'd hate that."

"You'd have to keep her for another year," Richard laughed. "What'd you use to make the seat leather shine so? Do you care if I sit in her?"

"Sure go ahead."

Richard climbed up onto the grand seat and held the mahogany steering wheel with both hands. He wiggled a little to settle himself in the soft leather.

"You look good up there," said Carl. "Maybe you should buy it. You could store it here."

"Sure," said Richard.

"I've got something for you, by the way. Did you bring the cigars?"

"Yes I did. And I've got something for you, too."

Lucille and Claire saw him coming from the window of the soda shop and met him at the curb. Richard held the doors for the ladies, then reached through the window into the front seat for a white box, which he set in his mother's lap.

"What's this?" she asked.

Richard got in and leaned back over the seat. "Open it," he said.

"Open it, for pity's sake," urged Claire.

Ever so carefully, Lucille opened the box to find a pair of porcelain salt and pepper shakers swaddled in tissue. The figures were meticulously painted. Salt was Jack, and pepper was Jill. Jack, dressed in blue, was seated; the salt came from his broken crown. Jill, her little red mouth open in surprise, held a bucket in each hand. It was the expensive imported set from the knickknack shop that Lucille had so long coveted as a crown for her shaker collection.

"Oh Richard," she held Jack in her palm. "I don't know what to say." Claire looked away to avoid seeing Lucille's tears. She felt like crying herself, for herself.

"No need to say anything." He started the car.

"But how could you afford them? These were . . . I'm not even going to say how much they cost."

"Lobstering's good," he said.

On the straightaway through the rocky blueberry fields,

Richard saw a car approaching fast behind him. It was a new convertible with three girls sitting up in the back, laughing in the wind, and three boys in the front. Summer people. Richard was going thirty miles an hour, which he thought fast enough for anyone, but the shouting kids in the car behind, now within twenty feet, disagreed. Lucille and Claire looked around. Two long honks from the convertible's horn turned the ladies' heads back to the front. Richard waved the car around, his right tires rumbling on the shoulder of the road as he made room.

When they sailed by laughing and waving, the nearest boy said, "Get a mule gramps!"

"Goddamn summer people," said Richard.

"These teenagers today," said Claire. "You should report them, Richard. Did you see their license number?"

Richard did not answer.

"He'll stew all the way home," Lucille whispered. "Look at her pretty little eyes; they're the same color blue as the water in her buckets. Isn't that some clever?"

Leah shook the bread out of the pan and thumped the loaf. She could hear Cecil dressing in their bedroom overhead. He had said that he was disappointed that she couldn't come to the Owings's dinner party with him, but she knew he was glad. She was on the food committee for the dance that night and had to help get things ready. It was a perfect excuse: Cecil could tell Mrs. Owings that she, Leah, was really sorry to miss the party but that civic duty called. The Owings would be impressed, Cecil would not have to be embarrassed by her shyness and nervous chewing of her nails, and she would not have to spend the afternoon listening to stuffy summer people talk about their yachts and perfect children.

Maggie and Amos were coming for supper. As Maggie had said, it would be like the Sunday afternoons in Head Harbor when Leah was a girl. Amos came for dinner then and often stayed for supper, too. After dinner he would do one of the heavy chores Maggie had saved for him—turn over the garden, shovel snow—then he'd come inside to read magazines in the parlor while Leah did her homework. The next morning, on the way to school with Maggie, Leah would feel sorry for herself that she did not have a real family all the time. She would wonder, but never ask, why Maggie and Amos never married after her mother died. When she heard Cecil come down the front steps and go out the door, she put the water on to boil and covered the bread with a dish towel.

She would not do what Cecil had asked her to do, she thought. She would not "have that talk" with her father when he came for dinner. She would not have it any time, ever, no matter what Cecil threatened or did. No matter what he called her. It was so like him not to understand them, or even try to. She shook Cecil out of her mind and began to set the table.

Maggie let herself in the back door, put a rhubarb pie on the counter, and drew four bottles of beer from a paper bag.

"What a nice table, Leah," she said, opening the icebox door.

"And who are those for?" asked Leah.

"Two for Amos." She held up a pair. "And one for each of us."

"Oh, not for me," said Leah. "Do you think he'll come? I'll bet he finds some excuse at the last minute, though he did promise."

"I'll bet he comes," Maggie said. "But I'll be surprised if he goes to the dance, too. I'll bet you a bottle of beer that he comes for supper; if he does, you'll drink one; if he doesn't, I'll drink both of them, and I'll breathe on Iris Weed at the dance."

Maggie knew that Amos had refused when Leah first invited him to supper; she also knew that Gus had told Amos that Cecil would not be there. That is what had changed his mind, not Leah's pleading or the boy's teasing. Hers was a safe bet, soon to be won.

In the garden, cutting flowers for the table, Maggie watched Amos and Gus arrive in the pickup, and Leah meet her father on the back stoop with a kiss on the cheek. She pushed him back a step to admire his new striped shirt, his best trousers and shoes. She said something that made him laugh and took him by the arm to lead him inside. Maggie thought that the weight he had lost—his trousers were gathered by his belt—made him look healthier, as did his tanned face below the white hat line. Leah, decided Maggie, looked as fresh and bright as the zinnia she bent to cut.

Amos sat in Cecil's chair, with Gus on his right, while Maggie poured three glasses of beer, and a glass of milk for the boy. She set a stack of four plates by Amos's folded hands.

"Now sit down, Maggie," said Leah. "And shut your eyes, all of you."

"What for? I don't trust you," Amos said.

"You're not getting any supper until you close your eyes," she said.

When they did, she brought a platter from the oven and set it before Amos.

"Okay, open them."

Amos looked at the platter, at Leah, then back at the platter, where six pink, uniformly shaped slabs of something lay arranged on a bed of noodles and cheese. Rectangles with rounded edges, they were sprinkled with scallions. Amos pierced the nearest slab with his fork.

"What is it?" he asked.

"Prem," she said.

"Prem," he repeated. "Laugh, damn you," he said to Gus. "I'll laugh when I watch you eat it, if that's what it's for."

"It's Swift's Premium Ham. It's been processed. It comes in a can with recipes on the back. It's new. There are other brands, all with funny names. Cecil bought a case of it from Merrill and Hinckley. Let's try it."

Amos filled and passed their plates. Maggie cut a small corner of her portion and chewed it cautiously.

"It isn't pot roast," she said wistfully. "I suppose we'll be eating processed food for a long time. We ought to be thankful for it. Mothers in Europe are feeding their children scraps from German garbage cans."

Gus, his fork poised, asked Amos if he was going to say grace.

"Maggie just did," he said, and filled his mouth. "I like this. It would make a good sandwich. You could put mustard on it."

"Let's drink a toast." Leah raised her glass of beer and winked at Maggie. "What to? To our boys. To the Fourth of July."

"To the merchantmen," Amos added.

"To Prem," said Maggie.

Amos drained his glass and filled it again.

"Dickie was in Stonington yesterday," Leah said. "He saw your boat tied up at the quarry. He wondered what you were doing over there." The women looked at Amos to show that they did too. He finished chewing and took a swallow of beer.

"I went to see Hutch, to ask him if he could turn my driveshaft on the lathe in their machine shop. Not that it's any of Dickie's damn business."

Gus smiled knowingly at Amos.

"What are you smirking about?" Leah asked him.

"Nothing!" Gus said defensively.

"Why did he give you that look, father?"

"What look?" Amos passed the bread.

Maggie washed the dishes and Gus dried, while Leah finished clearing the table and Amos finished his beer.

"I'm sorry we have to rush," Leah said. "But we have to change and go help get the food tables ready. You and Gus stay here and relax; there's another bottle of beer. I told Gus he could listen to *The Green Hornet* tonight, if you don't mind."

"I don't mind. I like that program."

"You are coming to the dance, aren't you?"

"I promised you I would, so I will, though I don't much feel like it."

He had promised Walter that he would go, too, and that he would have a little drink for him. Walter loved a good time—music, the laughter of young women, and a well-called contra dance. He had reminded Amos that Jake and Morales would be there, and Dickie too. What kind of a guy, Walter had wanted to know, would sit at home on the Fourth of July?

"Confucius say . . ." Gus mimicked the Green Hornet's Filipino valet's Asian accent. "Confucius say, 'Man who lead two lives must sleep with one eye open.' "

"Very good, Cato," said Amos.

"You *asked* him?" Rosalyn Owings stood with Agnes Chadwick on the lawn beside the town hall, watching people enter through the wide doors under a red, white, and blue banner that said "July 4. United We Stand."

"Certainly I did," Agnes said, still warm from the dinner wine. "Her name was Susan, and they were married three years. She died of fever during a nor'easter at the Boon Island lighthouse. He buried her there, and he hasn't looked at another woman since."

Rosalyn made a sorrowful noise. She could see Jake in the hall entryway, in uniform, with Morales at his side. The lighthouse keeper was shaking hands with Dwight Chafin.

"I wanted to ask him about the gold medal he wears," said Rosalyn. "But I demurred." She fanned her face with a fluttering hand.

"It's the Lifesaving Medal, given by the Lighthouse Service," Agnes said. "He says that she deserves it more than he does. A fishing boat of some kind ran aground near Boon Island in a storm. He rescued the crew—all seven of them—four in the first try, three in the second. They were frozen, two almost dead, and Susan nursed them all back to health. He wears the medal for her."

"But not a wedding band," said Rosalyn.

"No, And that won't go unnoticed tonight, will it?" Agnes nodded toward a noisy huddle of young women on the wide steps.

Inside the hall were nearly a hundred people, some sitting in folding chairs that lined the walls, most milling in chatty groups in the center of the floor and by the refreshment table under the window opposite the stage. The windows and doors of the hall were thrown open, admitting a stiff southwesterly breeze that ruffled the bunting on the walls.

Reverend Hotchkiss, visibly expanded from the generous table at the Owings' dinner party, climbed the stage, spoke to Jack Bishop at the piano and Archie on the fiddle, then called for the crowd's attention.

"We'll begin with 'The Lady of the Lake,' " he boomed. "Ladies line up on my right, please, and gentlemen on my left. Mr. and Mrs. Barter will take the lead." He bowed in the direction of Cecil and Leah, who stood in the entryway. The older couples and widows took seats along the wall; the few fishermen who had ventured inside and gathered near the door slipped out in quiet file behind Amos and Dickie Hanson.

Cecil and Leah stood ten feet apart, facing the stage in the middle of the floor. Leah smiled over her shoulder at the women who lined up behind her, most of them laughing young ones. Cecil, as straight and sharp as a pencil, kept his eyes on the reverend. Leah caught Maggie's eye and waved to her with a look that said "I'm out here; you come too." When Jake, second in line behind Cecil, noticed the exchange, and saw Maggie shake her head "No," he left his place in line and escorted her, in spite of Maggie's many whispered protests, out to stand behind Leah. Then he resumed his place behind Cecil.

Lily Scales elbowed Iris Weed, sitting in the chair next to her, and sniffed twice in the direction of Jake and Maggie.

"My, my," said Iris. "Aren't *we* the privileged one."

As they lined up, Betty Chambers counted down the line of men to Morales, and finding that she was one off, asked Mabel Eaton to trade places with her; when Mabel hesitated, Betty took her by the shoulders and moved her. The music started loud and disjointed, stopped, then started again. When the reverend called them to bow to their partners, Betty curtsied to Morales and sent him a fond smile. In return, Morales bowed to the waist—the way a matador, she thought, would bow to his senorita when offering her a red rose.

Jake bowed slightly and offered Maggie his arm for the promenade. "I was hoping you would be at the dinner party," he said.

"Was it very fancy?" she asked, eyes ahead.

"It was. And very proper. Silver spoons and crystal and violin music on the phonograph. Damn dreary," he said.

"And Morales was there too?"

He escorted her to the side, still holding her arm. "He glared at me the whole time. I got him to go by promising him you'd be there. When he saw you tonight, all dressed up, he squeezed my arm like a monkey."

"Oh, pooh," she said. "I'm much older than he is." Maggie withdrew her arm from Jake's.

"Look over your left shoulder," he said. "It seems you've got more than one admirer."

Standing on tiptoe, with their noses and fingers on the sill, were Amos and Dickie, straining to see. When she turned, Amos's face disappeared, then Dickie's after it.

"We ought to make Amos come in and dance," said Jake.

Maggie laughed. "He might join later, but he won't dance. I made him dance 'The March and Circle' with me once. He swung the wrong way and knocked Doris Chafin flat on her bottom. It didn't hurt her—she has ample padding—but everyone laughed at them. She blamed Amos, and he blamed me."

● ● ●

Jake lit a cigarette and stepped into the road, out of the realm of light from the town hall windows to let his eyes adjust to the darkness. He could make out two clusters of men among the parked cars and trucks. The farther group was loud and in motion. Lit cigarette ends sailed out of it like little distress flares. One shape pushed another backward into the alders, and several laughed while one swore loudly. Among the darker forms, he saw Morales's pale uniform. Let him get drunk, Jake thought, and laid if he's lucky; he deserves it.

He approached the nearer, quieter group. There appeared to be about six men, all but two perched on bumpers, talking and smoking toward the ground. Amos emerged from the shadows and shook Jake's hand.

"Let me get you a drink," Amos said. "It's Green River, nasty stuff, but we cut it with ginger ale. You know Dwight here, and this is Dickie Hanson; he fishes on the east side." Jake greeted the constable and shook hands with Dickie, who rose for the occasion. Amos bent over into an opened trunk to mix Jake a drink.

"I met you in Stonington last year." Dickie drew on his cigarette, illuminating his face for a second.

"You look familiar," Jake said. "Amos talks about you."

"I helped you and your ugly little mate load a couple of drums of kerosene. You cussed him the whole time," said Dickie. "He deserved it, the nasty bastard."

Jake took his drink from Amos. "That was Harvey Gooden. He isn't so bad; he's dirty himself, but he keeps everything around him clean, and I like that."

Fuddy MacFarland and Skippy Groth sat shoulder to shoulder on a bumper in the dark, their legs crossed at the thighs and again at the ankles. Each made the same adenoidal noise when Dickie introduced Jake, but neither looked up from the conversation. Cousins who shared the same father, they looked like brothers—except for Skippy's cleft palate and cruelly parted hare lip. They so clubbed his speech that only Fuddy and their parents could understand him when he ventured more than a short sentence. The two cousins were sharing a cup of rum, talking quietly; when Skippy drank, he was careful not to slurp.

"Down in Thomaston I've got relatives who are Gardiners," Dickie told Jake. "You're not from Thomaston, are you?"

"No," said Jake. "I never was. I'm from up-country originally, but I was at the Pemaquid Point lighthouse before I came here. I didn't know there were Gardiners in Thomaston."

A ratty Model A pickup truck with one headlight slowed to a crawl in the road behind them; Richard Snell was at the wheel, straining to see faces in the darkness. He parked and shined his flashlight on them as he approached.

"Jesus, Richard," said Amos shielding his eyes, "Point that damn light down."

"Sumbitch," said Fuddy.

"Nuh." Skippy hid his face behind his hand.

Amos introduced Richard to Jake; Dickie found a seat on a bumper. Someone set off a string of firecrackers in the field behind the alders, then another, and a child squealed happily.

"So who do I have to fuck to get a drink around here," asked Richard.

"You could try yourself," said Fuddy.

"I doubt he will. It's been suggested to him a million times and he's never tried it yet."

"I'd argue that he has, and he did a pretty good job of it."

Dickie laughed, waved to the trunk, and told Richard to help himself. Richard cussed them as he poured, mixed, and swallowed one cupful. Then he poured a second, saying that he was worn out from his shore patrol—unlike some others; he said he tore his pants taking a short cut through the puckerbrush at Eben's Head.

"I heard you were going to be ashore here tonight, Chief," Richard said. "I thought maybe you could help me out with something."

Jake looked at Amos, who showed nothing. "I might," said Jake.

"I want to join the temporary reserves, for the Coastal Picket, and get a radio for my boat. I don't feel like I'm doing enough just walking along the shore. The *Lucille*'s seaworthy, and I know these waters as good as anybody." Richard looked around at the others, who said nothing.

"You'll have to go to Rockland for that," said Jake, who smelled disapproval on Amos's breath. "Ask for Ensign Onderdonk. He'll give you an application, and if you qualify, the Coast Guard'll send you to their school."

"Maurice Wilkins on Vinalhaven said he got his from you," Richard said.

And Maurice told him who else had radios, Amos thought.

"Well, he did," said Jake. "But now you've got to go to Rockland."

"I guess I'll go then," Richard said. "The last time I was there dealing with the Coast Guard I . . ."

"Christ, you said you smashed one in the face with a lobster," said Fuddy.

"Chryff," said Skippy.

Skippy and Fuddy stood up.

"Got to walk the pink flamingo," Fuddy said, and launched himself toward the alders, nearly knocking Amos over. Skippy followed him, thrashing through the dark thicket, his bladder responding to Fuddy's call. Amos set his cup on the hood and withdrew into the darkness.

The musicians, refreshed by a sup on the back porch, struck up a slow waltz, and someone dimmed the lights. Amos watched the couples on the floor from the doorway, then slowly made his way through them to Maggie, who was sitting with Doris on the far side of the room. He stood before Maggie who smiled and gave him an inquisitive look.

"Hello, Doris," he said.

"Evening, Amos" said Doris. "Is Dwight still outside, or has he gone home?"

"He's listening to Richard the Lionhearted tell about his battle in Rockland. Would you like to dance, Maggie?"

She said she would love to and gave him her hand. Doris beamed as they walked away.

He held her at arm's length, leading her in a stiff box step.

"Not so far away," she said pulling him closer. "I can't follow you."

"Then I can't see my feet," he said, and laughed nervously.

Iris Weed, who had begun to wilt, sat up and unfolded in bitter blossom when she saw them together on the dance floor. Lily Scales leaned into Iris's ear. When Maggie and Amos stumbled by Iris's chair, Maggie smiled at the ladies triumphantly, causing Lily to stare in disbelief and making Iris look away.

"Can't you just hear them?" Maggie whispered.

"Yes, I can." He laughed again, softly.

She wanted to ask him to come for Sunday dinner. If he had invited her to dance, he might come to dinner, she thought. Instead she asked what he had meant at supper when he had said he had been to the quarry to get his shaft turned.

"What's wrong with the shaft? I haven't noticed anything," she said.

"It's making a funny noise, down by the stuffing box. At half throttle."

"You can't haul the boat out now; it would take a couple of days," she said.

"In the fall," he said, smiling. "I was making an appointment for the fall." He let his hand slide down her back and rest on the dimple above her buttocks.

"What are you up to, Amos?"

"Nothing," he said, and moved his hand back up to her shoulders.

She shook her head. "Will you come to dinner next Sunday," she asked.

"Yes, I'd like that. As long as it isn't Prem."

She promised that it would be something he liked.

In the dark alders at the edge of the meadow behind the church, Fuddy started to say something, but Skippy put his hand over Fuddy's mouth and held a finger to his own lips. Off to their right they could hear a boy and girl whispering excitedly, then there was a giggle and a soft moan. Skippy took Fuddy by the hand, and they crept toward the sounds. In a small clearing, lit by the thin moonlight, Morales was unbuttoning Betty Chambers's blouse with one hand and trying to tug it free from her skirt with the other. Betty stopped him, stepped back slightly and slowly removed the blouse herself, letting it fall to the ground. She kissed him and unhooked her bra, offering her firm, full breasts, their nipples straining to meet Morale's eager hands. She moaned and moved her hips eagerly as she watched him caress and squeeze her breasts, touching one nipple then the other with his tongue.

Skippy, whose mouth was wide open in wonder, felt his knees weaken; he released Fuddy's trembling hand and groped to find an alder trunk for support. Pop-eyed and breathing like a boy fogging a cold window, Fuddy held a branch aside to watch the couple sink to their knees. When Betty's fingers found Morales's belt and began to undo it, Fuddy's hand slipped inside his own trousers as if it were hers, and he held himself while Betty and the Coast Guardsman undressed each other.

She pushed Morales back slowly onto the soft grass and stroked his face softly with her swaying breasts as she mounted him. Leaning on his chest, her breasts gathered between her upper arms, she lowered herself onto him, cooing like a dove as he entered her. She rose and fell slowly at first, then with more heat as she pushed upright, her hair thrown back, her pale buttocks slapping his thighs.

"Oh," she said. "Oh, oh, yes."

Still inside her, Morales rolled her over, and she held her legs apart, hands under her knees, while he thrust into her.

"Don't stop! Don't stop!" Her voice was husky as though she could not breathe. "Keep on doing it!"

Amos was glad to find that Richard had gone when he rejoined Jake and Dickie and the others in the dark. He poured a healthy drink and sat next to Dwight, who was beyond conversation, to watch from the shadows as the older couples stood on the steps saying good night, the men pulling their wives away. The younger couples slipped past into the hall, drawn by the sound of what the musicians must have meant to be boogiewoogie. He saw Maggie and Leah come out together, Maggie's white sleeve over Leah's shoulder. They skirted the crowd and crossed in the light under the big windows on their way home. Leah's head was down, and she seemed to be shaking—maybe sobbing—as Maggie was talking to her. Amos thought to catch up with them to see what was wrong but instead accepted another drink from Dickie, who had just told the one about the fat lady picking crabs, much to Jake's delight.

When the crowd had gone and the men had finished both bottles, Jake suggested that they go inside and watch Morales dance, and see if they could guess which girl he had ended up with. Dickie went with him, and Fuddy and Skippy, who emerged from the alders making wet noises to each other, followed. Amos stood up, patted the snoring constable on the back, and started to follow. But he found he was wavering, unstable, he so walked down to Cecil's to get his truck and go home. Cecil's car was in the yard, and all the lights were on in the house; Amos climbed into the truck and drove slowly, leaning out the window to let the air revive him.

By the time he got around the island to the cove road, he felt a little better. To the south, on a sea made bright by the high summer stars, he could see Saddleback Ledge and over it, about to go down into the Atlantic, a half moon tipped like a pouring bowl.

Amos stopped at the house to get his flashlight and binoculars, then walked up the old road past the field and houses to Old Cove, which was hushed at high tide and glittering in the starlight. There he turned south along the rocky shore and went into the dark spruce woods that covered the cliffs. Still wearing his striped shirt and Sunday shoes, he walked slowly in the spruce, using his flashlight, stepping carefully over humps of glacial granite. Twice he stopped along the cliffs where the trees opened, sat on a boulder, and scanned the horizon with the binoculars. From that height, nearly one hundred feet, he could see beyond the ledges to the flat sea, where nothing showed on the surface. The only noise was the thin hissing of an occasional breeze high in the spruce, and the silence welcomed him.

As he approached the cabin, he shut off his flashlight and was careful to walk in the soft, quiet spruce needles. He thought he saw the shape of a man in the trees behind the cabin; it was too small to be Walter, so it was probably Lew. Since he felt cool—and clear now, too—Amos considered sitting on the boulder and having a sip from the bottle he kept under the cushion of moss there. But he was tired and wanted to go to bed, so he went carefully to the edge of the cliff to scan the sea once more, with one watchful eye on the cabin. He let go of the sapling he was holding onto, lifted his binoculars to his eyes, and pitched headlong onto the sharp rocks below.

PART TWO

The Coastal Picket

"If you got something outside the common run thats got to be done and cant wait, dont waste your time on the menfolks; they works on what your uncle calls the rules and the cases. Get the womens and children at it; they works on the circumstances."

—Old Ephraim,
INTRUDER IN THE DUST, William Faulkner

CHAPTER EIGHT

AFTER CHURCH, GUS WENT HOME TO CHANGE, THEN WALKED OVER TO the cove. He had fallen asleep twice in the pew. After the service his father had taken him aside and lashed into him for being a disgrace. Gus swore to himself that by God if Cecil ever tried to give him a whipping as he threatened to do, he would fight him. Gus was not a kid any more and he would not be treated like one.

Amos was not at home. He was not anywhere around the house, and the truck was parked in the yard. The cove was quiet and still in the thin fog. He went from house to house, then down to the wharf. The skiff and boat were on their moorings, and there was no sign of any activity on the wharf. A line of indifferent gulls sat on the peak of the fish shack preening and sleeping. Gus hollered into the woods beyond, rousing the gulls, and heard Amos's name echo in his own voice over the water behind him. He went back to the house to see if Amos had taken a shotgun and gone after crows. In the gun closet he found that the binoculars were missing, which made him think that Amos had headed out to patrol the shore.

There was no sign of anyone's having walked through the high, dewy grass in front of Ava's, so Gus decided that he must

135

have gone up the road, walking in the ruts to keep his feet dry. The boy hurried up the road, calling Amos's name. He went up to the old cove and came back along the cliffs through the woods. He remembered his parents whispering that morning in the kitchen about how drunk Amos had been at the dance, and Gus decided that he was in the cabin sleeping it off.

Though the fog was thick in the spruce along the cliff, the flashlight glittered at him among the brown needles where it had been dropped. Suddenly scared, he picked it up and switched it off and on. The batteries were dead. He hollered and looked around in the trees then, reluctantly, drawn by some demanding dread, he went over to the edge of the cliff and peered down into the sifting fog.

Seventy feet down, Amos's body lay on its side, the lower arm underwater, wedged in the rocks, the head rolled back, looking up. Gus shouted his name and scrambled down the incline. When he got halfway, he stopped and saw Amos's face clearly; his mouth was wide open and the eyes stared straight at him, seeing him, recognizing him, expecting him. Gus tried to go to him, but he could not. Sobbing, he climbed back up the cliff and ran home for help, carrying the flashlight to give to someone, anyone, so he would not have to hold it any longer.

Dickie Hanson, Cecil Barter, and Dwight Chafin went around to the cliffs in Dickie's boat. Maggie, Leah, and Gus went by road in Maggie's Ford, all three riding up front in terrified silence.

Leah would not look over the edge. She would not even get close to it. Maggie only glanced, to be sure that it was true, then stepped back into the spruce, where she could see the men and boats, but not Amos. She pulled Leah against her, and Leah buried her face in Maggie's shoulder. While Dickie held the boat off in deep water, Cecil and Dwight rowed ashore in a skiff, shouting at Gus to come down the cliff and help them. The boy

clambered past Amos, careful not to look at him, and waded out
to bring in the skiff. Cecil swore and sobbed once, almost chok-
ing, when he saw Amos.

Amos's skull was caved in on the left side, behind his ear. In
the salt water his blood and brains had congealed into a dark,
slippery mass that swelled out behind and over his ear. He had
died instantly, Cecil said, from the ungodly force of the fall.
Amos's forearm was broken, the grisly bone jutting out of the
ripped sleeve of his striped shirt; his left hip was torn and black
with blood that had seeped through the tattered trousers. Gus
looked once as they lifted him, then vomited into the water at
his knees. Dwight took the body out in the skiff, and he and
Dickie hauled it aboard. When Dickie went back to get Cecil, he
told Gus to come along with them, but the boy, shivering and
staring straight out to sea, said no, he would go back in the car.

"Yes," Cecil said. "You're right, son. Get the women home.
One of us will meet you there."

Late in the day, when Amos's body had been taken to the
undertaker's in Stonington, and the Barter's house had begun to
fill up with people and covered baskets of food, Maggie left and
drove home to be alone. On the way, she slowed twice to stop,
nearly blinded by her weeping, but both times she gripped the
steering wheel bitterly and drove on. Under the darkening oaks
past Boom Beach, she imagined Iris and Lily in the corner of
Leah's parlor, heard Iris say "drunk again," and saw them shake
their heads, solemn and satisfied. She had thought from the beginning that he had gone up to the cabin for a drink, but she
had not said so to anyone. Once Dwight got the coroner's report, he and God knows who else would go through the cabin
and find a bottle of booze. She turned around and went back to
the cove, dry eyed and determined that no bottle would be
found.

She parked at Ava's and went up the path to the cabin.
Halfway up, she realized that they had not found the binoculars,
either on the ground or on Amos's body. Maggie stood at the

place on the edge of the cliff where she thought he must have been standing when he slipped, where she had stood when she had seen him that morning. The tide had come in and covered the rocks where he had lain, but from no angle could she see the binoculars.

On the boulder where Gus had found the flashlight, there was a flat spot where the spruce needles had been ground to dust by someone's sitting on them—more than once. To the side of the boulder, within reach of the seat, she saw an irregular bump in a large green cushion moss. She lifted the moss to find a rum bottle and a white porcelain teacup. Maggie threw the bottle over the cliff, listened to it smash among the rocks, and put the cup in her dress pocket.

She wondered why he would sit on the boulder and not in the cabin, only a hundred feet away. He used to go inside often before he began patrolling the shore, she knew he did. He walked the cliffs in all weather, in the rain and cold, but why would he sit outdoors wet and covered with mosquitoes when he could stay dry on the porch or at the cabin window and have the same view of the sea? Perhaps he stayed outside in warm weather, inside when it was rainy.

The cabin was unlocked and unused. There were no signs of anyone's having been in it, at least not recently. In the kitchen, mice had chewed to shreds a box of baking soda and had gnawed on the bar of soap in the sink. On the bureau were scatterings of acorn shells left by the squirrels. A kerosene lamp sat on the little red table by the front window, a scallop shell full of burned kitchen matches next to it. The lamp's chimney was charred black. She trailed her finger through the thin layer of dust on the sill. From the front window she could not see the boulder seat where she had found the rum, but she could look out past the York Ledges and beyond to the far horizon. There was no rum anywhere in the cabin.

She felt herself grow warm with anger and frustration as she remembered how they had treated Walter's drowning—as sim-

ply a consequence of drink, richly deserved. The coroner had
said that the cause of death was a heart attack, but that had not
hindered them in the least. Even she had believed that he had
been drunk when he fell overboard. Now there was Amos, too.
Maggie was embarrassed for him, for Leah and Gus, and for
herself. She was angry at herself for feeling that way, angrier at
him for proving right the snide ones who had said that it had
been his imagination that had provided the sight of bobbing
human candles.

As she stepped out to shut the door behind her, she noticed
muddy prints on the floor by the sill. They were not clear footprints, and when she looked more closely she found that they
had a layer of dust over them. But some of the prints were different: they appeared to be made by a smaller shoe or boot, and
the outlines were white, spread out like a fungus and dried.
These looked like salt stains. Maggie had seen enough of them
to know, but it did not seem possible that anyone could walk all
the way up from the cove, through the grass and woods, and
still have salt on his shoes.

She shut the door and stood looking in through the window.
Now the cabin, like all the cove, would be empty for good. Now
they were all gone, the old ones erased forever by Amos's
death. Maybe it was better that he had not lingered but had left
in a hurry, unconvinced—in spite of what he said—that the old
ones would go with him, leaving only the houses themselves to
crumble or, worse, be bought by summer people. On the path
under Ava's apple trees, she surprised a feeding doe that raised
its white tail, snorted, and bounded into the woods with a fawn
following. Maggie squeezed the lifeless teacup in her pocket and
felt her heart turn as cold as clay.

They had laid Amos out in Cecil's parlor for the customary
sitting up with the open coffin the night before the burial. His
head was bound with a black cloth, his red hair oiled dark and

combed back as he never wore it. A bouquet of daisies and Indian paintbrush lay over his folded hands. Leah sat all night in her rocker by the window, receiving mumbled condolences from the mourners with a wordless nod. Dickie Hanson, the only male who stayed all night, sat by Amos's head, his legs crossed, his face locked in cold anger. The older fishermen came with their wives; those who had been Amos's friends, as well as Walter's and Lew's, lingered even after their wives left. They smoked and drank coffee, their cups and saucers balanced on their knees. In the kitchen, Maggie received the food the women brought and served those who would eat. In the hour before dawn, when the house was still and those sitting up were asleep in their chairs, she hung up her apron and tiptoed up to Gus's room. He was asleep on his back, fully dressed in his church clothes—laid out, she thought, like his grandfather. She kissed him on the forehead and spread a blanket over him.

The sun was peeking over the edge of the sea when Maggie parked next to Amos's truck in the cove. She seemed to be watching herself from a slight distance as she gathered up the skirts of her mourning dress to feed Ava's chickens. She saw herself standing in the road between the empty houses, her eyes shut, unmindful of her hair as it lifted in the morning breeze, her back warm from the first rays of sun. She thought that the woman she saw was waiting for something, though she did not know what. The sound of a boat slowing down to enter the cove turned her around. With her palm she shielded her eyes from the sun; seeing that it was the lighthouse launch, she walked down to the wharf to meet the boat.

"We only heard last night," said Jake. "I'm so sorry Maggie." Behind him, Morales—soaked to the waist with salt spray—muttered something and dropped his eyes.

"Thank you," she said. "Morales, look at you. You're drenched. You're all goosebumps. Why didn't you wear a slicker?"

"I don't know," he said, handing Jake an American flag folded in a triangle.

"For his coffin." Jake tucked in a loose fold.

"He died in the line of duty," Morales said.

"Yes, I suppose he did," she said. "Let's get you dried off."

"I don't need—"

"Come along," she said.

More than forty people came to the burial. Leah had decided against a funeral service at the church, and she was surprised by how many were there. The graveyard lay in a boggy
cleft of ground between two high smooth granite ledges, shaded
by a lonely forest of red oaks. The pallbearers carried the coffin
in from the cove road, parting the crowd and the high grass as
they approached the Reverend Hotchkiss, standing by the white
obelisk and the open grave. During the service Cecil and Gus remained by the reverend's side, both upright and dry eyed, their
hands clasped before them. Leah and Maggie stood together by
the coffin while Jake and Morales spread the flag over it. Leah
had asked the reverend to stick to the Book of Common Prayer,
to make it short, and to substitute Psalm 121 for the Sailor's
Hymn.

Afterward Jake waited for Maggie in the vague sunlight on
the road. He said he felt partly responsible for what had happened, and he hoped that she would forgive him.

"I knew how much he'd had to drink, and I should have
known he was going to head back and walk the shore," he said.
"I should have—"

"What could you have done?" she asked. "If that makes you
responsible, then we all are. You can't let yourself think like that.
You were good to come, Jake."

"If I can do anything for you," he began.

"You can." She stepped out of the road to let a car full of
mourners creep past, pulling him with her by the sleeve. "I went
up to the cliff alone yesterday afternoon. I was hoping to find
his binoculars, but instead found a cup and a bottle of rum hid-

den under a clump of moss beside a boulder he'd used for a seat. In the woods."

Jake nodded.

"Don't you see?" she asked. "He wasn't watching from the cabin. Why would he sit out in the wet and cold, a hundred feet away, when he could see just as well or better from inside? He hated to be cold.

"I looked in the cabin, which was open. Nobody's been in there for a long time—for months, by the looks of the dust. But whoever was there last, or at one time, left water stains on the floor, from wet boots or shoes. Saltwater stains. I tasted them. How could that be? The cabin is a quarter of a mile from the cove wharf, through tall grass and bay bushes that would take off salt. Those prints were left by someone who climbed the cliff to the cabin."

Jake nodded to Iris Weed and her parents as they passed. "I see what you're suggesting," he said. "But it's not likely, Maggie. Why would they risk putting people ashore here? They wouldn't land someone on this island any more than they would at the lighthouse. What could they do here? You're thinking of the saboteurs they put ashore at Machias. There they could walk to the city or take a bus. But not here, no."

"Couldn't they have landed just to snoop around? He must have seen them—or he saw the salt stains—and was waiting in the woods lest they return."

"But why?" Jake asked, then paused. "Unless they wanted to try that high ground for a radio relay of some kind."

"God."

"It's possible," he said. "I guess it is. Let me look into it. Have you told anyone else?"

"No. We feel vulnerable enough out here as it is. Here comes Leah. Will you at least report it?"

Jake said that he would, but as he watched them walk away arm in arm, led gently by islanders to Maggie's car, he knew he would not report anything. They would not give it any attention

in Rockland. They were already swamped with reported sightings of Germans ashore along the coast, and they were not
equipped to do anything about it. A salty footprint seen by a be-
reaved woman would not even get logged. She was eager to
rinse the stain of drunkenness from Amos's death, and he admired her for that, among other things.

On the way back to the car with Leah, nodding still at other
mourners, Maggie remembered something and turned to go
back to tell Jake, but Leah tugged her along. There was not a
soul on Barters Island, she thought, who did not know how to
keep a lamp wick trimmed so as not to blacken the chimney.

Early fall is the finest time of the year on the island. The
mosquitoes, summer people, and horse flies are gone. The lobsters have grown into their new shells and are plentiful. The
trees have begun to change color—the red maples on the
fringes of the spruce bogs first—and there is a smell of wood
smoke in the air, sweet-burning birch from kitchen stoves. Most
of the men go up onto the mountain to shoot a deer that they
would put in the cold cellar to cure among the growing ranks of
mason jars on the shelves. The kids are in school, and the nights
of sleep grow longer. In the old days the only thing to fear in the
fall was the hurricanes that would come up the coast and clean
out a man's traps—and perhaps his boat, too—smashing them
to bits in the rocks. That fall, the sea surrounding the island
swam with Nazi submarines, and darkening to winter, it was
more and more often discolored by ribbons of oil that spread
like bloodstains on the water.

For weeks after Amos's death, Leah kept to her house. Not
her husband, nor Maggie, nor any of her friends could get her
to go out, even to the store or post office. She stayed home
from auxiliary meetings and church functions, and failed to show
up the first time the women gathered to fold bandages, an event
she had organized herself. She cooked, kept the house, and did

some canning, but mostly she sat in the big cushioned kitchen rocker, her knitting still in her lap, staring out the window across the garden into the copse of maples. She had been too young to grieve for her mother; now with Amos gone she mourned like a girl who had just lost both her parents in one horrible, inexcusable accident.

In almost any weather, Leah could tell the conditions on the water by watching the way the wind worried the maples. When the tide was going and the wind from the southwest bent the trees toward the mountain, she knew to worry about Cecil, on his way home with freight. Other than that, she did not care.

Maggie, too, withdrew with her grief. She felt the loss of her sister anew and struggled with the anger that came from having had her hopes for a relationship with Amos rekindled, then snuffed out suddenly. She taught school and kept busy with her chores, but on weeknights and weekends she stayed by herself in her house in Head Harbor. There were two other houses in the little harbor where her grandfather had settled and three generations of Bowenses had fished. Theirs—now hers—was a high white house with a cupola, set closest to the water on the rocky western edge. In the evenings she sat in the front window, where she could look across the harbor and see the lamplights at the Sweeneys'. At seven-thirty a lamp moved up to the children's room on the dark north side, and by eight the whole house was dark except the parlor where Seth and Louise had settled and could, she knew, see her light. In a thick of fog, she was alone, the old house all her world.

Early one Sunday morning, before dawn and in just such a fog, Maggie awoke to a sound she did not understand. The wind had shifted to the southeast and came in slow and steady and soggy off the open sea. She thought the noise might be a flock of alien birds, but it was metallic, a clinking and tinkling and tonking, like the baby xylophone at school when the little ones played on it. She lay on her back under the blankets, imagining some beastly mechanical thing with treads creeping slowly out of the sea on the sandy harbor bottom, dripping black slime, heading for the road—some diabolical Nazi invention unleashed on the shore below her house.

She sat up. The sound was not in the house or on the shore out front or even, she realized suddenly, in the harbor itself. It was out along the rocks washed by the high tide.

She dressed and went out the back door cautiously, flashlight at the ready. She thought of the Eveready advertisement in *Life* magazine, where a man scared a grizzly bear out of his cabin with his light. Outside the sound was louder, distinct in the dark fog; it was a tinkling of thousands of various bells, and Maggie knew she was not dreaming. She went slowly down her father's path, feeling her way on the familiar ground. She kept the light turned off until she got down to the rocks at the water's edge, then knelt toward the noise and shined the light into the water.

They were metal canteens—thousands of them—chirping pathetically in the tide, trying to come ashore. She shined the light out into the harbor, and as far as the fog would let it, the beam showed bobbing canteens—some in clusters, others floating alone. She went back up to her father's shed, stopping once to listen long out to sea, and returned with a gaff. She used it to retrieve one of the canteens, hooking onto its cap chain. It was ice cold.

Maggie did not go to church that morning but sat with her tea in the front window, the canteen on the table beside her. After dinnertime, she drove into town to report what she had found and to visit with Leah. She asked Gus if he would go to the cove with her and help her move some lumber. On the way, he was silent and seemed anxious about something. She offered to let him drive, but he declined, choosing rather to roll the window up and down, up and down.

They had not talked since Amos's will had been read the week before. He had left the houses and property in the cove to

her, and his boat and lobster traps and gear to Gus. After the accident, the boy had turned to his father for comfort or for help
in understanding. Maggie thought that Cecil—and Melvin, who
had gone back to the shipyards—had together worked some
kind of change in Gus. It seemed as though he had softened
after the accident and as if they had remolded him in a different
form. He seemed more guarded now, defensive and cynical. He
avoided the cove, never said a word about Amos or lobster fishing, never made any reference to the hundreds of their traps the
other men had taken up and piled on the wharf. He didn't even
talk about the boat on the mooring. Today he did not look her
in the eye or ask what lumber she needed help with.

On the wharf Maggie told him that there was no lumber.
"And it just occurs to me now that you've guessed that. I want
to ask you to do something for me."

Gus was losing weight; his muscles were gaining definition.
He wore his sleeves rolled up to show his biceps like the determined farm boys in the war posters. Today he was tense and serious, arms straight down at his sides, fists balled up. Like his
father, he avoided her eyes as he talked.

"I don't know what I guessed," he said. "I wasn't sure. I
didn't think about it." He kept his back to the sea and the big
Novi boat that rocked on the mooring. "Yesterday I was going
to come down to see you, but I couldn't. I was getting ready to
visit today when you came to father's just now. I want to tell you
something. I guess this is as good a place as any. I guess this is
a good time."

She waited, watching him. She did not like the tint of piety
she saw in his demeanor. He fidgeted and gestured toward the
wharf around them.

"But first what is it you wanted help with, if it wasn't lumber?"

"No," she said. "You tell me what it is that's on your mind
first. You've been waiting longer. You look like you're about to
burst."

"No I'm not," he snapped. "What makes you say that?"

"Never mind. Nothing," Maggie said. "You tell me what you have to say, then we can get to what I need."

He drew himself up, then relaxed as he spoke, as though the last word out pulled all his anxiety with it: "I'm going to enlist."

She was not surprised. She turned to look at the *Quahog* riding on its mooring, then back at him. "You're going off to Boston or New York or someplace to lie about your age and sign up."

"First I need to change my name. That's what people do."

"God. Is that necessary?"

"I don't know for sure. I can say I lost my birth certificate. If I ever had one. I don't even know that. But they don't give you much trouble if you look old enough; they need men too bad."

Relaxed now, larger in his new role, Gus walked to an upturned trap and sat on it, as Amos used to do.

"What about your mother?"

"She won't even know I'm gone," he said. "It won't matter to her. She's lost in her grieving. It's unnatural, but there isn't anything to be done about it."

And where had he gotten the word "unnatural" Maggie wondered. Now she was mad. "That's ridiculous, and you know it. Oh, I hate to hear you talk like that. You could destroy her now, you know. Are you ready to do that? Break her heart completely to satisfy your need to get into this war and away from something you don't understand?"

"No, I'm not. *You* don't understand. I'm not going right away. I just said that about her. I'm going to wait until this winter, when she's better, when father is over this ulcer that's been making him so sick. I'll tell her I'm going to the shipyards like Melvin so she won't worry."

"Why do you tell me, and why now?" she asked. "You knew I wouldn't approve. What about this boat and the gear?"

"I'm going to sell it all."

"What? What about your future? What would Amos say?"

"What future? How can you talk about the future when

there's a war like this? You sound like my father. They're sinking ships right here in our dooryard, and you talk about the future. He talks about how good the war is for the fishing industry. Some guy said it's not a bad war if you aren't being shot at, and my father thinks that's right. Remember how he used to be against me going fishing with Amos? Now, after the will, he's all hopped up about how we can make good money fishing, with them rationing beef and the English dying for canned fish."

"It's all true, of course," she said.

"I have to go, Aunt Maggie; don't you see? I have to. If I had a family of my own or something, I might stay and go lobstering, even with Amos's gear. But I have to go. I can get in the navy or army, and get a chance to fight back at them. I'm ashamed to stay home."

Maggie stuffed her hands inside her flannel jacket and closed her eyes. She imagined him and another boy sitting alongside a dusty road, exhausted, thirsty, defeated, drinking from a canteen. Would one canteen be enough for him in the heat, she wondered? He wasn't used to hot weather.

"You can sell these traps, of course," she said finally. "I can't say anything about that. I can understand why you want to go, believe me, but I don't agree with you. You can do your part here. They also serve who only stand and wait."

Gus rolled his eyes. He hated when she quoted something. He thought it made her sound stuck up. Maggie knew and did not care; she looked at him carefully.

"But you can't sell the boat," she said. "Put that out of your mind. It's half mine, you know; it might be all mine for that matter. The boat he meant to leave to you when he made up his will was the *Tuna*, and it's gone. We bought this one since. That makes you and me co-owners—the way Amos and I were—and I won't sell. I could buy your half from you, but I haven't the money. No, don't sell the gear. Don't sell anything. You're making a mistake." She understood his need to do something but not the pride. And there was something else in his tone of voice, something unfamiliar and unfriendly lurking behind his words.

"Anyway . . . " Gus stood up, as if facing an accuser. "Anyway, I want to get out of here. I don't want to spend the rest of my life stuck on an island in the middle of nowhere, living twenty years behind the times. I want to go where I can take part, instead of listening to it on the radio, reading newspapers five days old by a kerosene lamp. Look at this gear. Here. Old, worn out rope, tarred by hand, with empty rum bottles for toggle buoys."

He stepped into a tangle of lines and buoys and cork floats and began to kick at it, again and again.

"Stop it!" she cried. "You'll cut your foot." Now she saw. "You're ashamed of him, aren't you?"

"No I'm not," he said. "I just don't want to be reminded of him. I don't know what it is that I feel except that it's bad. I don't want to live in the past like he did. I want him to leave me alone."

Maggie sat down on a trap. "Going away isn't going to do that."

"It might. If I stay here there won't be any escaping. The world's changing faster than we can tell, and the old ways don't fit in anymore. I'm almost glad for his sake that he's gone, in a way. I'm sorry, but I am."

"You're angry at him for the accident, the way he died."

"Sure," he said. "Aren't you? And I miss him. And I hate him. God, Aunt Maggie, I don't know."

"I know how you feel," she said. "It's hard for your mother and me, too, don't forget. We have the same feelings."

"But you stick by him, even now. If anybody even hints around mother that he was drunk, she acts like he's being accused of murder."

"I'm sure she does," Maggie said.

"I can talk to you about it, even though I suppose it's the worst for you, of all of us."

"No," she said quietly. "Not the worst. It's not something—"

"Melvin says Grammy Clytie committed suicide on account of you and Amos," he said. "Father didn't deny it when I asked him."

Maggie should have been surprised to hear it come out now, but she was not. "What else did Melvin say?" Her voice was low, icy. "I'm sorry you had to hear it from him first."

"It wasn't just Melvin. I've heard things before." He was defiant, justified in his right to know. "They say that you and Amos were in love—*after* him and Grammy were married. They say she wasted away, died on purpose, because you took him away from her. You moved in with them in Head Harbor when Amos was living there with her, in your grandfather's house. When mother was little."

"I'd been away at school in Bangor," she said. "I came back to help care for my father, who was dying, and I stayed in the house because there was nowhere else for me. Your grandmother was very ill, too, obese and depressed. That is when we fell in love. I resent the implication, which is idiotic and sickening, that I moved in with them to catch Amos."

Maggie explained that Amos and her sister Clytie had married young, at just seventeen; it had been a shotgun marriage and one that had quickly failed. She did not tell Gus—and never would, even lying to deny it—that Clytie had let herself go to hell after Leah was born. She had an affair with Lester Hamilton, and it was so public on the island that even she, Maggie, had heard about it while she was in school in Bangor. Clytie went to fat and ignored everything: the baby, the house, Amos, her ailing father. She was a bitter bitch by the time she was nineteen. Nothing was good enough for her. She sat at the kitchen table day and night, and gossiped with visitors or ate cookies and stirred tea and complained. To avoid squalor, Amos did the housework and changed Leah's and the old man's diapers. As a child, Leah was sickly and unruly.

"Yes, we were in love," Maggie admitted. "He said we taught each other to laugh. And I think that Clytie knew, though

I denied it then. But there's no way of knowing whether she willed herself to die, as they say. After father's funeral, she took to her bed, bloated and miserable. For months. All that laudanum. No one can claim to know whether she wanted to die, any more than they can claim to know it was drink that made Amos fall. Do you see?"

"He was drunk."

"He may have been, but—"

"Do you think Grammy wanted to die because of you and Amos? That she killed herself?" he asked.

"If she did, it was not grief at the loss of Amos as they claim," said Maggie. "She never loved him; she never even liked him. She was jealous of us, of me; she made herself sick—and maybe even die—to hurt us, make us guilty, and to make it impossible for us to ever love one another openly on this island."

"Is that what Amos thought?"

"Yes."

"So he moved back here to the cove with his family and left you and mother alone in the house when she was—how old— six or seven? Why didn't you get married and live together?" asked Gus. "You must have wanted to. Maybe not in that house—I can see that, I guess—but you could have left this damn island and taken mother with you and raised her like she was yours, which you did anyway alone."

"I don't know why we didn't leave. We were young, and we believed we were guilty. Amos could never have abandoned this place; you know that. I thought of leaving with your mother, but I couldn't. At first I cared for Leah out of duty—even guilt—but over the years I came to love her as my own daughter. Amos came to dinner on Sundays, every Sunday until your mother went off to high school; then his uncle Lew died, then Ava, then Walter, and he just, well, he just stayed with them."

Gus started to say something more, and she waited, but he only shook his head and looked out into the breeze, squinting at something unseen in the southwest.

"Now perhaps you can do me that favor I asked you to come down here for," she said.

"Okay."

"Come with me in the boat. I want to take it out for a run, for some distance," she said. "You just come along and watch me, and tell me if I do anything wrong. Can you work the radio? I'm afraid of it."

"Why do you want to do this?" he asked.

"Can't you imagine?" She untied the outhaul line and pulled the skiff in to the wharf. "I'm going to continue patrolling," she said. "He took me with him several times. I'm confident that I can handle this boat. We bought her to patrol for submarines, and patrolling she will go."

Gus went ahead of her down the ladder to take the oars, muttering his disapproval as Amos would have done, but going along anyway.

She had rehearsed this, of course. She had run through it step by step in her mind a thousand times. He was humoring her, she thought, and that was fine.

He noticed immediately upon coming aboard, as she knew he would, that she had cleaned up the boat but had left Amos's things as they had been: his slicker on the bulkhead door, his cup and new sunglasses in their places on the bulkhead, even his wool mittens, dry and folded down below.

She started the engine, revved it, then let it idle, listening. The wind was light, the tide full. She knew that the mooring chain would be heavy, but when she went forward to lift it off the bitt, she found that she had underestimated its weight and almost went overboard with it. Gus moved to help her, but she waved him away, reminding him that he had come along to watch, to see that she could do it alone. Back at the wheel, she turned the high bow slowly in the cove, and took the big Novi boat out into the York Narrows, steering with the two spokes that she had extended for better leverage.

"There are ledges over there." He pointed off the port bow.

Maggie took the *Quahog* down the east side of the island, along the lonely side toward Head Harbor, out in the cold mist. She had been this way many times—first with her father, then with Amos—so she knew when to cut back her speed when they came into heavier seas outside the ledges. She knew, too, when to swing out and around Thunder Gulch and knew to keep the Cape Ann buoy at 180 degrees. She had meant to take Gus around the southern head and into Head Harbor, but she decided that she did not need to go any farther than she had. Two hundred yards from shore, she turned into the wind and cut the engine.

Most of the flotsam near the boat was shapeless, merely broken pieces of planking, clumps of lifejacket stuffing, some garbage. But fifty feet off the stern, in a tight flock like a family of bobbing sea ducks, he saw some of the canteens and heard them clinking and tinkling against one another as they huddled together fearfully. Farther out, in a long ribbon, was another scar of debris, this one oil soaked and followed by thousands of canteens floating in dreary escort.

Off on its own, apart from the larger gathering, floated a charred life raft, and around it, victims of the same fiery end, were a gangplank, blackened raft pontoons, cans of emergency rations, and a burned lifejacket.

Gus leaned over the washboard and picked a small tin out of the water. Malted milk tablets. He threw it back in.

"What about the boys who were supposed to use those canteens?" she asked. "How will they get a drink of water? What about the men who were aboard this ship? Where are they? They're dead. Where are the men who were in that raft? They drowned, and they burned first, like human candles, just as Amos said. You don't have to go away to find the war, Gus Barter."

"God damn them," he said.

CHAPTER NINE

August 11, 1942

Dear Ruth,

Please, *please* don't feel badly for not coming to the funeral. That you might be torturing
yourself over this only makes it harder for me.
The lovely flowers you sent me and the contribution you made to the church in Amos's name
were more than enough.

As I said, and you *must* believe me, I would
have sent word to you and asked you to come
had I thought I needed you. I was too busy with
the funeral, and trying, fruitlessly, to console
poor Leah.

You're right to worry about her (though I
think she brightens just a little each day) but not
right to worry about me. I am fine. I'm as tough
(though not yet quite so wrinkly) as an old walnut.

For me the pain, as Leah said, has an "ele-
ment of blank" that I am able to ignore as long

154

as I stay busy, which we all do down here. We will not be defeated.

You asked what it's like being out at sea with the war raging on and under the water all around us. You saw the July 27th issue of *Life,* I'm sure, the one with the Atlantic Convoy on the cover. Look at the photos of the jetsam that has come ashore down south—the stove-in lifeboat, the blistered life rafts, the cargo of walnuts (for pity sake!)—and you'll have an idea of what we see here. It appalls and frightens me. It also makes me more fearful for Gus when he goes to haul each day, but ironically, it makes me less fearful and more determined when he and I go a-patrolling, or when I am walking the cliffs at night.

I don't know yet what to do about Amos's legacy to me—all that Coombs property. I felt badly for Leah when we were all surprised by the bequest, but I believe her when she insists that it's better that he gave it to me, and she believes me when I insist that it is hers for the asking.

You can imagine what Iris and the others think and say: "And just what *was* it she did to earn that inheritance, anyway?" To hell with the biddies, I say. And to hell with Cecil, too, for that matter. I relish the role of Robin Hood, protecting Leah's shire from the wicked Prince John while the rightful king is away. Though I don't watch for his return. You smile at my romantic allusion and think me a silly old girl, and you are right, as always.

I must quit. I'm glad that Jack didn't get sent to Augusta after all; I know how happy you all are in Bangor. Perhaps I'll be able to come for

a visit around Xmas time and go sledding again
on the hill behind Sherman Street. Give the kids
a hug for me, for "of such is the kingdom."
(Imagine me quoting the Book of Luke!)

Love,
Maggie

"I call this hot." Sitting on the merry-go-round in the school-
yard shade, his weight tilting the round wooden platform toward
the men on the swings, Richard rolled up the sleeves of his flannel shirt and pushed the gurried cuffs of his long johns up to his
elbows.

"It's nearly eighty by the school thermometer," said Dickie,
scouring his inky fingertips with a mixture of spit and sand, and
wiping them clean in the grass.

Fuddy, holding the chains of his favorite swing with fists at
chest level, pushed off gently with his feet, swung, and stopped
himself by dragging his contemplative soles in the furrows beneath him. Taller now and gaunt, with thriving colonies of black-
heads on either side of his nose, he did not look like the same
schoolboy who sat in that swing twenty years ago. But Fuddy
felt no different and was no more interested in the talk around
him than he had been in the fourth grade.

"You wouldn't be so hot if you weren't wearing a winter undershirt," said Dickie.

"It isn't a undershirt," said Richard. "It's long johns, and I
was damn glad to have them out on the water this morning.
What do you expect me to do, stand up here in front of half the
town and peel them off? Show my hairy bum to the summer
people and the Coast Guard?"

Dickie did not reply. He knew that Richard, who loved a
gathering of any kind, had hauled his traps early and hurried up
from his mooring to be at the schoolhouse when the registration

began at noon. He had been the first to come and would be the last to go, established on the merry-go-round to watch and listen, or—when he had an audience—to expound upon the fools who were running the war.

The Mattingly boys, armed with cap pistols and driftwood submachine guns, broke from behind the schoolhouse and ran, bent over, to take cover behind a green Pontiac. Ernest, his left arm in a sling bloodied by iodine, waited until Dwight and Doris Chafin were out of his line of fire, then opened up on the three boys holding the stone wall beyond the swings. What Ernest knew—and only Fuddy noticed—was that the Crowell brothers, led by Vince, were crawling through the bayberry and would soon flank the boys behind the wall.

Chief Petty Officer Irville Rich stepped out of the schoolhouse door, blinked in the sudden light, and sneezed. He held the screen door open for Gus, who blessed him and skipped aside as the door slammed shut. A squat, fidgety man, Chief Rich barely came up to Gus's shoulder; he wiped his brow with his handkerchief, buffed his glasses, and blew his nose. Next to Gus's T-shirt, which was bleached weekly by Leah, Chief Rich's whites looked as if they had been rinsed in old dishwater. He offered a cigarette to Gus, who declined it with a comment that made the Coast Guardsman laugh.

"Here's the man himself," Richard said to the group in the swings.

"He's not so bad that you should sniff at him," Dickie said. "He's from Jonesport."

"Which means he's related somehow to half the people on this island," said Richard.

"A third at least," Dickie said. "Perhaps even to you, Richard, but no, I guess not. I wonder if he knows anything about the *Ebb*; wasn't she out of Jonesport?"

"Why don't you ask him?"

When Chief Rich moved into the shade, Dickie stood up to shake his hand and say "Hey" to Gus. Chief Rich nodded to

Richard and Fuddy, who returned the gesture and grunted a welcome from their seats.

"I hear you're from Jonesport," Richard said. "What can
you tell us about the *Ebb*? She was out of there, wasn't she?"

"The trawler that got sunk? No. She was out of Winter Harbor, I believe. All I know is what I read in the Ellsworth paper:
that she was sunk by surface gunfire from a U-boat out past the
bay, and seventeen of the crew were lost. Out of twenty, I think.
They brought them in at Southwest Harbor, the survivors. The
Ebb was a seventy footer. They're sinking smaller and smaller
boats every day now."

"Lord, Lord," said Fuddy.

"If I knew more than what was in the papers, I couldn't tell
you anyway." Rich's belt was pulled so tight that Fuddy thought
the chief looked like a cinched marshmallow, lightly toasted the
way he liked them.

"Well, you could tell certain ones of us." Richard sat up and
adjusted his weight.

"How'd you get this ink off?" Gus asked Dickie.

"Get some of this sand here," Dickie said. "How many more
people you got to register, Chief?"

"Miss Bowen figures fourteen more of those that have any
business being on the water. We've done a hundred and seven,
including the summer people, the ones that aren't yachting. It
seems there are some people down here who weren't counted
in the last census."

"And you probably won't see those same ones coming in to
register with you today, if it's who I think it is," Richard said.
"They say the census is an attack on their freedom. Getting
fingerprinted and having to carry an identification card—they'd
probably call that slavery. The last census fellow didn't even
bother to go down into Squeaker Cove."

"Lucky he didn't," Fuddy said. He held one nostril closed
with a forefinger and cleared the other one onto the ground.

"When Satan stood up against Israel, he incited David to number the people," said Dickie.

"You sound like Cecil," Richard said.

"What makes you say that?" asked Gus.

"The Bible," Richard said. "Quoting the Bible."

"My father doesn't quote the Bible."

"No? Well he *talks* like the Bible. Don't get your hair up, Gus. I didn't mean anything insulting." Richard rubbed his chin stubble and shook his head. "If you're wondering why I haven't been in to register yet," he said to the chief. "It's because I don't have to." He watched for a reaction. Dickie rolled his eyes at Gus.

"And why is that?" the chief asked.

"Because last week I signed on with the Coastal Picket. I took the oath for the Temporary Reserves. This month I'm going to Rockland for a school and to get a radio for my boat."

Gus flinched slightly and stared at Richard for a long, surprised second before he made his face go slack again to cover his wonder. Never let a Snell see that he's surprised you.

"The Coastal Picket needs all the men down here it can get," Richard explained. "Men with seaworthy boats that is."

"Well, that's true, and that's good of you for signing up," said the chief, "but I still have to get you to register like the rest. I have my orders, and there's nothing in them about any exceptions."

"Well, I don't mind." Richard heaved himself up off the merry-go-round and hitched up his trousers.

Gus glanced at Dickie, who made a face to show that he hadn't heard anything about this. The boy watched Richard and decided that he was telling the truth. He would need to talk to Maggie—she would be surprised too—and hear what Jake had to say about it. He had been wrong—they all had—to think that Richard was only meanness and only out for himself. "Yeah," Amos would have said. "But look at him all swelled up with importance like he just won the Battle of Midway. That's Richard Snell for you."

Even so, Gus thought as he watched Richard light his cupped cigarette and the chief's, even so, it's time for us to get over our differences and work together for a greater cause. He was glad to have another Barter Island boat patrolling, even if it meant trusting the Richard Snells of the world.

Fuddy, who could hear a clam burrowing from twenty paces, looked up suddenly toward the crest of the town hill, where a truck had slowed and shifted into first gear for the descent. Dickie looked up, too, when the truck began to sputter.

"You jinxed us, Dickie," Fuddy said. "Talking about Satan and his senses. Listen. That'll be Basil."

"Coming to register?" Richard wondered.

"Coming this way at least," Dickie said. "That's the Squeaker Cove boys we were talking about, Chief, easing down the hill with nothing but a hand brake and low gear between them and glory—or them and the alder swamp. Stick around. If he's coming here, he'll use that boulder as a nudge to stop himself with. I'll bet you a soda he'll need it."

"I'll take that bet," said Richard. "You watch, Chief. Basil can stop that thing where he wants to without brakes or any boulder, and when he does there'll be a drink in it for us."

"For you, anyway." The chief flicked his cigarette into the bushes. "I got to go back in; I'm on duty."

When they heard the cough and sputter of gunfire on the hill, two of the young defenders peeked over the stone wall and ducked back down, betraying their position. Behind the green Pontiac, Ernest Mattingly seized the opportunity and led his squad in a frontal attack on the wall, screaming *Charge!* behind a hail of stone-sized grenades, waving his flankers in for the kill. Overwhelmed, pelted from two sides, the defenders beat a retreat through Miss Bitterfield's Victory garden and fell back on her garage, replenishing their ammo supply from the gravel drive as they ran.

Fuddy, their only audience, turned slowly in his swing to follow the running gunfight that swept around to his right. When
the combatants disappeared in the spruce thicket on the shoreline, Fuddy lifted his feet and swung back around to watch Basil
bring the truck in.

Basil did not need to nudge the boulder with his wooden
bumper; he did not even steer for it. He eased her over the
slight incline in the road past the school-yard drive, dropped
her into neutral, and rolled back onto the flat, grassy yard,
where he cranked back the hand brake not ten feet from the
green Pontiac.

"He ought to tie her off on that car. She might drift." Fuddy
was worried that Skippy, who was sitting with his legs dangling
off the back of the truck, might not have the sense to jump to
the side should it start to roll.

"You owe me a soda," Richard said, and ambled toward
the truck, hands in his pockets. Fuddy followed, swinging his
shoulders in the same show of indifference that he used when
another boy brought a live critter or a new knife onto the play-
ground. Skippy clambered up onto the truck bed and hefted a
five-gallon can to fill the gravity-feed gas tank that was bolted
onto a wooden scaffold behind the cab. The others gathered
around Basil in the doorless driver's seat, his bulk overflowing
the steering wheel.

"Well Jesus Christ, if it ain't Gus Barter." Basil turned his little head to look over his shoulder. "I haven't seen you since the
funeral. You quit working for your father in the store?"

"No, I work in the evenings now," Gus said, thinking, No
wonder they called him Sausage Lip. "I've been putting my
traps back out."

"Those are yours then, the red-and-white buoys down by
the Battery and in the Turnip Yard?" Basil feigned ignorance.
"Those in what was Coombs waters?"

"In what still is Coombs waters or, more rightly, Gus's waters now," Dickie said. "Amos willed him his boat and his gear,

and so rightfully he gets the Coombs fishing waters as well."

"So they're Barter waters now," Basil said. "Is that what you're telling me?"

"They're still Coombs waters, and I'm fishing them. I'm half Coombs." Gus looked at Dickie and Richard for support and saw it. "I'm painting Amos's buoys with my colors and setting them out, too. I've got three strings of his so far, and three strings of my own bridles, too. I'm in a hurry to get more out; I got three shedders today."

"They're coming all right," Dickie said. "I got a dozen today. Maybe more."

"Jesus Christ," said Basil. "Why don't you fellas step around to the other side here and open up that door." With a pretty wave to the shifting group, Rosalyn Owings climbed into the green Pontiac without assistance and drove away.

"Aaah! You got me!" The youngest defender crumpled in the puckerbrush holding his chest, and Ernest finished him with his bayonet.

"There's glasses in the glove box, Skippy. Set them on the seat to where I can reach them." Basil uncorked a bottle of Green River and sniffed it before he filled the two glasses. As Skippy reached for them, Basil lifted a heavy butt cheek with one hand and released a muffled *poot*. Skippy backed away waving a hand in front of his nose.

"Slipped out like a peeled grape," said Basil with satisfaction.

Amos had told Gus about Green River, how it burns and has an oily, kerosene kind of texture. The boy looked past Fuddy's shoulder and over the truck at the schoolhouse where Maggie might be watching out the window. He stepped behind the cab when the glass came to him, took his drink quickly, and handed it—empty—to Skippy. Compared to Amos's rum, Green River was bitter and left a foul, moldy taste in his mouth. Basil took his own share straight from the bottle and filled another glass almost to the brim.

"Watch this," said Richard. He lit a cigarette, then touched the lighted kitchen match to the glass on the seat. Fuddy and Skippy crowded into the door to watch the dancing flame.

"Blow that out! Jesus Christ." Basil waved at the flames. "That's alcohol you're burning, goddamn you."

"Oh, there's plenty in there," Richard laughed.

Fuddy reached for the glass and covered the rim with his palm to snuff the flame.

"Let's see you flatfoot it, Fuddy," Basil said. "You watch how his Adam's apple moves."

Fuddy stepped back, stood at attention, and slowly, deliberately, poured the Green River into his mouth. As he watched Fuddy's Adam's apple rise and fall and rise again, Skippy clapped his hands beneath his chin in gap-mouthed wonder.

"Noan snop! Noan snop!" He cried in a voice like Betty Chambers's. "Tsneep on nooin int!"

With a noise like an underwater explosion breaking the surface, the whisky blew out of Fuddy's mouth in a bilious brown eruption, directly into Richard's astonished face, drenching him hat to chest in regurgitated distilled corn and sputum. Fuddy bent over coughing and hacking and laughing, while Skippy danced on one foot then the other, gurgling with delight, an impressive bulge growing in the crotch of his trousers.

"Bar Har Har!" Basil slapped the dashboard as he would have slapped his knee if he could have reached it.

His eyes and mouth wide open in terrified disbelief, Richard wiped his face with the tips of his fingers, then lunged at Fuddy, lifting him by his shirt and slamming him, still laughing uncontrollably, into the side of the truck.

"Laugh, you son of a bitch!" Richard's forearms shivered with rage, as he slammed Fuddy again, striking his head this time. "I ought to break your fucking nose."

"Bar Har! Jesus Christ!" Basil shouted. "Watch you don't dent my truck. Reach me that glass, Skippy!"

Skippy dangled his fluttering hands between Richard and Fuddy as if to distract their attention, but Fuddy only laughed harder, and Richard slammed him again.

"Cut it out, Richard." As Gus took a step forward, Dickie heard the screen door slam and put out an arm to stop the boy. Maggie issued from the schoolhouse, marching toward them at a quick step, her arms straight at her sides. Gus and Dickie turned in unison and walked toward the road in a casual retreat.

"What the hell is going on here?" she asked, folding her arms across her chest. "Look at you Richard; good God, you're disgusting."

Holding a limp and quiet Fuddy with one arm, Richard mopped his face with the other. Skippy stood aside to watch Miss Bowen give her scolding, a sight that brought back a wave of fond memories.

"You're damned right it's disgusting," said Richard. "And that's why I'm about to wring his neck."

"Not here you won't." Maggie's voice was cold and condescending. "I do not abide fighting here, nor drinking either."

"Come on, Miss Bowen," Basil pleaded. "Let him wring Fuddy's neck."

"He can wring it elsewhere. Gather up your swill, and get this degraded spectacle out of my school yard. If I have to come back out here, I'll be accompanied by a Coast Guard officer, and I'll be carrying a written complaint for the constable."

Basil started the truck. Maggie did an about-face and walked slowly back to the schoolhouse. Richard, still angry and now embarrassed, too, gave Fuddy a final shove and released him to join Skippy on the back of the truck, where they giggled and whispered and slapped each other around.

"Too bad she couldn't keep somebody else we know from drinking and walking around on the cliffs in the dark a while ago," said Basil to her receding back.

"Shut up, Basil. Just shut up." Richard took off his shirt and folded the slobbered side under.

"She thinks her shit don't stink," said Basil. "How anyone could give a good goddamn for someone that thinks her shit don't stink, *I* don't know."

Maggie kept to herself that weekend. She did not feel like seeing anyone, talking to anyone, listening to anyone. On Friday the Sweeneys had gone off on the late boat to visit Louise's relatives in Deer Isle, and Maggie had Head Harbor to herself. Saturday was a fine, crisp, late summer day, with the first hint of autumn on the land breeze. She rested, puttered around the house, and thought about driving in to the post office to see if the lap table she had ordered from Sears had come. But she decided to save the gas and to save herself the noise of the women in the post office. In the afternoon she lost herself in quiet nostalgia around the house and woodshed, moving things about, blowing dust off the long-neglected tools that her father and then Amos had used. In the garden, the four fattening yellow pumpkins Maggie was growing for the school set off in her a sweet, sad longing that carried her far back, past the war and recent loss. Memory in this form, she decided, was kind, oddly satisfying, even encouraging.

But that evening, while she sipped a glass of sherry at the radio, Walter Winchell revived her thoughts of the war, and the weather report warned of gale-force winds moving up the coast. Boston was getting heavy rain, and the winds there had been clocked at seventy knots. Hull and Natick were flooded; all boats at sea were seeking safe berths up the coast. It was an early hurricane, one that should hit the Maine coast sometime Sunday evening.

Maggie loved a storm, especially the dark and wild nor'easters, though a hurricane would do. Clytie had hated them—all storms—even a glorious blizzard. She had thought her sister queer and somehow masculine for not being afraid that the house would blow down or the roads would wash out. But Maggie liked being snug in the house, with the wind howling and the sea thundering outside. Her father worried about his boat and gear, as did Amos, who had fretted even more when the *Tuna* was in Head Harbor.

She thought of the *Quahog's* mooring chain, how badly it was worn near the toggle, and shuddered to imagine what would happen if it did break loose. There would be nothing left. Perhaps Gus had riven the hawser through the chain as he had said he would. The boy might be in the cove now, she thought, having heard the gale warnings. He was alone so much these days.

She hoped that the storm was a huge one and that they would not have to go out patrolling tomorrow night, as planned. No one would. Maybe the hurricane would halt the war for a while and save some lives. The merchantmen would stay in harbor, the airplanes would get tied down, and the U-boats would settle on the bottom. The heavy seas would make it impossible for anyone to come ashore on the island. Even Clytie might have liked a storm in wartime.

The night was warm and still, but from her bedroom window Maggie could hear the sea making up outside, striking Cape Anne ledge with a distant thump. In the morning, out the kitchen window, the sky was dull with low, slow-moving clouds, and the day darkened before it began. The air grew damp and salty, making a haze on the windows and her reading glasses, which smeared when she wiped them with her hankie.

She draped a wool blanket over her head and shoulders, and gathered it around her before going out to find which of the back doors was banging in the wind and to check the others. Behind the chicken coop, the flock of crows that had been riding the wild spruce tops in the wind erupted, the birds squawking, cawing, screaming in panic as they scattered in every direction. She turned in time to see a bald eagle—an immature male— landing on the rocks uncertainly with a struggling crow in his talons. He settled, his wings flayed and spread, and with a swift strike, broke the crow's back. The other crows returned to the trees and watched him in silence, riding the wind. The eagle shivered to adjust his feathers, flapped once, and looked around at everything but the crows behind him. Maggie saw him look at her.

He turned the crow over, and with several sharp thrusts of his beak, ripped open its breast. He looked around again, then with a jab, tore off a piece of flesh and gulped it down. The first crow floated off its branch, as quiet as the approaching cloud layer, and landed ten feet from the eagle on the same rock. The raptor did not look at the crow, though he knew it was there, but continued to eat—slower now—enjoying his meal. Another crow alighted on the rock, then another, until six of them encircled the eagle to watch him eat. One walked around lifting its legs and swinging them out like Popeye the sailor, and they all croaked quietly among themselves. In a minute the crows stood still, watching the eagle enviously. One or two, their heads lowered in submission, approached the eagle, then backed away. Now he looked around himself, and in a sudden lurch that sent the crows scurrying, lifted off with his food and flew to the point of rocks across the harbor, where he could eat in peace.

Maggie thought for a moment that she had seen that very thing happen before, though she knew she had not. Who ever heard of an eagle eating a crow, especially when a nice fish would taste so much better? Her mother called a flock of crows a murder of crows.

That afternoon, as the wind picked up steadily, she filled both the wood boxes and barred the garage door. By three the rain had begun to fall in earnest, and by four night had set in. The wind moaned outside, and as Maggie sat in her chair by the front window, she listened to the rain striking the side of the house. Though she knew that there could be no one out on the water in this weather, she put up the blackout curtains. Tonight she tacked them along the sides and the bottom, too, to help keep out the wind. The leeward windows she left uncovered.

Through them she could see the vague shapes of the spruce trees trying to crouch in the wind.

Settled in her chair, she sat with a book open in her lap. The kitchen stove needed stoking, she knew, but right now, in the storm and dark, she felt a foreboding about the kitchen, one connected with Clytie sitting at the table, disheveled, staring into her cup. She closed her eyes to see herself and Amos sitting across the same table from one another during a storm, not long after she had come back from Bangor, before they had a radio. Her father was asleep under a quilt in the chair she now occupied; Clytie and Leah were upstairs. Between deep groans of gusting wind, they could hear Clytie crying quietly.

"You ought to go up to her," she told him.

"I know it," he said. "But if I do she'll only bitch and moan and blame me for something I did or didn't do. Anyway, she's not scared; she just doesn't like us sitting up together."

She covered his freckled hands with hers to still them.

"You're shaking," she said.

"Too much of that tea," he answered, pulling his hands away. He looked over his shoulder at the stairs, then out the windward kitchen window, which was plastered with wet leaves.

"Sit by the window," she said. "Finish knitting your bait bags. You can see your boat from there."

When he did, she stood up.

"Where are you going?" he asked.

"I'm going up to give her some laudanum, if she'll let me. And read to Leah or bring her down here for some hot chocolate."

Clytie did not want Amos for herself, but even more she did not want Maggie to have him—or him to have her. She wanted Maggie gone, out of the house, but the only way she could have that was to hoist her obese self out of bed and do the house-keeping, take care of her father and Leah, let Maggie go back to Bangor and finish school.

She told Maggie all she wanted in the world was to get up, throw the laudanum out the window, and look after Leah and the men, but she just couldn't. She couldn't do it. When she heard Maggie hurrying up and down the stairs, or laughing in the kitchen, Clytie hated her. It was not jealousy, as it was when they were girls, but real hatred that gnawed at her like the mouse gnawing on the laths inside the wall next to her pillow.

A gust of wind blew a scatter of hail against the house. Above Maggie, far above in the black sky, the wind kept up a steady roaring. She went into the kitchen to stoke the stove and put on some water. The news would be on in an hour. Returning to her chair, she stopped to listen. The house creaked and groaned around her; the blackout curtains on the windward side bellied out like sails. She was frozen with fear for a moment and stood stock still in the middle of the room, waiting for the whole house to blow to pieces. Perhaps this was the Big Wind itself, finally come. She gave herself a shake and went to look out behind the blackout curtain. The windows themselves, entire frames, were bellied inward by the wind. She tacked the curtain tighter against flying glass and said Amos's name plaintively. His house in the cove, deep in the cleft of ledges, under all those sturdy old oaks, was safe from the direct wind. If he were alive, she thought, he would be sitting down there safe and sound, and she found that comforting.

The new creaking was louder. It came from across the front room by her writing desk, and was steady with a thin, high-pitched screech. She knew what it was before she looked.

The old, nailed-down cellar trapdoor was moving upward slowly. It rose almost imperceptibly. Then Maggie saw the nails, shiny where they had been so long embedded in wood, stripped even cleaner now as they were pulled out slowly. She rocked purposefully and watched as the door rose. The nails came to their ends all at once, and she could see Clytie's flattened hand against the underside of the door. Then her sister's wrist, too gray and pudgy, but still unwrinkled.

Shaking, Maggie stood up and, with an eye on the trapdoor, went to the closet and took down her coat. The arm was still visible to the elbow.

"All right," she said succinctly. "If that's what you want, all right. But I'm not staying. You'll be alone. I'm not coming back."

Maggie went out through the kitchen and reached to pull the door, she caught a glimpse of the hair on the top of Clytie's head, reddish brown and thinning.

Hastily, she tamped the stove down and went out to the mudroom to put on her boots and take her slicker. Bracing herself for the wind, she turned back to the house.

"All right," she said bitterly. "The house is yours, then; this one is. But I'll have him, and to hell with you, Clytie Bowen."

CHAPTER TEN

MAGGIE HAD EXPECTED THAT THERE WOULD BE LIMBS BLOWN DOWN across the road or that there would be flooding along the low, muddy section by the old farm. But once she got inland and in the lee of the thick spruce along that part of the road, the wind was not so bad, and she could see fairly well through the clacking windshield wipers. At Amos's house, she left the car in the drive next to the front door and scurried, bent against the rain, onto the porch. Inside, with the storm shut out behind her, the house was dark and still. She let her eyes adjust to the room and listened. It did not creak and groan; there was only the sound of the wind in the oaks as though far, far away, and her own breathing. She hesitated, then began to feel her way to the stairs. In the stairwell, his oilclothes and jacket hung on hooks; she smelled him there, strong as life, as she brushed by them to climb the stairs. No need for a fire or light tonight—only his bed and the possibility of sleep.

Standing in his tiny room under the eaves, she could see the dim outline of the window and the shape of the bed, but all else was shadow. It was warm and still in the room. She shut her eyes to see him lying there, half asleep and waiting for her. This time of night his chin would be scratchy with whiskers. They

171

could sleep naked; she could surprise him by getting under the covers naked. She took off her coat and trousers and sweater. Could he see the goosebumps? She undid her hair, still wet at the edges, and shook it loose.

If Maggie had had children, her body might have been changed, but she did not think so. Her breasts were still full, her thighs and bottom still firm, her tummy almost as flat as it was when she was twenty-one. He liked it that she never got heavy like the other island women whose bums, he said, spread to the size and shape of the seats of their kitchen chairs. She turned down the covers and undressed in the dark. In the bureau drawer, she found a nightshirt, and put it on before climbing into the quiet bed.

But then she remembered those mornings in the kitchen when he had whispered, more than once, that he would love to see her, look at her. (Did he say "in all her glory"? He may have.) He told her that he would so love to lie with her in bed, all by themselves in the house, and make love slowly, peacefully, however and whenever they wanted. Now, in his room, she saw it clearly.

He would be sitting up against the headboard, the counterpane covering his pale legs and lap. He would smell of Ivory soap. At the edge of the bed, within his reach, she would spread her feet and legs apart slightly, and raise the cotton shirt slowly up over her thighs. She would look to him for reassurance and raise it farther to reveal her panties and smooth tummy. Then she would draw it slowly over her breasts, the cotton slipping soft and warm across her nipples, which would arise with her breasts as she pulled the shirt over her head and shook her hair again slightly. Turning aside in profile, she would step out of her panties, and when she bent over to retrieve them, she would feel his rough hand trace the outline of her buttocks, exploring, then settling on one, cupping it firmly, holding her, not letting go, turning her toward the bed. She would kneel beside him on the sheets, and when he stretched out, she would push back the quilt and lower herself into his arms to kiss his mouth. While he fondled her breasts, caressing with the soft back of his hand as he had done so often, she would slip a leg over his middle and feel him aroused, straining against her thigh.

Afterward she would fall asleep with her head on his chest, listening to his heart beat. She would.

Maggie awoke in the predawn dark, lying flat on her back in the undisturbed sheets. The wind had subsided, and the rain had stopped, but she was worried by an unfamiliar sound until she realized that it was the creek, swollen and indifferent, rushing by the house on its way into the cove.

Downstairs in the thin light, she got the stove going, put on some water, then tidied herself in the kitchen mirror. She wondered why she could no longer smell him, then thought that by sleeping in his bed, she had assumed his familiar odor.

In her father's kitchen, Amos had always been eager to get going in the morning, to escape the temptation of being alone with her. She was the one who was not so careful, often playing the role of the instigator. How many times since had the smell of tea reminded her of those sweet, frightening mornings. She smiled, satisfied, and lingered in the window with her hands wrapped around the warm teacup. Thank God it was Sunday, so she did not have to go to school.

There were limbs down everywhere. The ruts in the drive were flooded and overflowed into the yard, but the wind had died and the eastern sky had cleared enough to reveal the orange warmth of the sun coming up behind the clouds over the sea. She moved the car out of sight behind the ledges by the garage and walked, her shoes soaked through, down to the cove and boat. Over her shoulder, though she refused to look, he lay on his back in the graveyard, with the others.

The *Quahog* rode quietly on her mooring. From a distance, Maggie could not see any damage to the wharf or fish shacks.

The rocky edges of the cove were scoured clean of shells and sticks, but on the clam flat, above the mud under the boulders, a pile of detritus sat, soaked and bedraggled, along the high-water mark. Pieces of planking, lobster traps, ropes and buoys, oil-stained wooden crates, dismembered lifejackets—all lay tangled and forlorn in a heap. Caught alone between two boulders, almost up to the field's edge, was a bundle of brooms as big as Basil Walker, bound together for shipment to some staging area in Europe.

Aboard the boat, Maggie thought about calling the lighthouse to see how they had weathered the storm, so tiny and exposed, but she thought better of it and only turned on the radio to see that it still worked. Dropping to her knees on the bow, she found that Gus had riven the hawser through the mooring chain. When she pulled it up, she saw that he must have rowed out early the day before, at low tide when the storm was only brewing, and he had done a thorough job of it. The slow-moving tide turned the *Quahog*'s bow toward shore, so that she stood in the middle of the cove—once empty, but now inhabited again. Whether the old ones and the people in town cared or not, Maggie was there to stay. The wind, from the southwest now, was brisk and wintery cold. When she died they could drive her down to Head Harbor and bury her with her family, but until then she was here with him, with them.

Olive Gross and Doris Chafin were waiting in the post-office parlor while Miss Lizzie sorted the mail behind her door. Both women had opened their mailboxes so they could see when Miss Lizzie slipped something in from the other side. With the summer people gone, there was less mail—only one bag today. Less mail meant that Miss Lizzie would take more time to sort it, a phenomenon nobody had ever questioned. Olive had gotten up to remove a letter when Lorna Crowell, who had just come down on the mailboat from visiting her oldest daughter in

Jonesport, came in from the rain. She wore her long coat, open two extra buttons to show her new blue dress. She greeted the others cheerfully, obviously pleased to be home, and said hello to Miss Lizzie through the closed door. The postmistress replied through one of the open boxes, saying that Lorna had come home none too soon; her box was stuffed so full Lizzie couldn't get another thing in it.

"Didn't Albert come in even once to collect it?" Lorna asked. Albert was one of the most prosperous fishermen on the island; she could pose a question like that without fear of anyone thinking he was lazy. They would only assume that he was too busy making money to collect the mail. Money for new dresses, for instance.

Lorna sat down in the big chair by the stove and spread the *Ellsworth American* flat on her lap.

"I don't suppose you've heard the awful news," she said. "I mean, it hasn't been on the radio yet. It's all the talk on the mainland, though; I've never seen people so outraged."

Doris gave Olive a look. Olive was sitting in a straight-backed chair, overhanging it on both sides. She did not look up from her magazine.

"It's right here on the front page," Lorna raised her voice. "You should listen to this, Miss Lizzie."

Lizzie's voice said go ahead and read it; she couldn't help but hear.

"What is it?" Doris was impatient with Laura's little show: ruffling herself like a hen to settle in the chair, delaying the news to drag out her drama. She looked right at Lorna. Doris had bright, knowing eyes, the kind that look behind what you're saying. She gazed intently at Laura to make her nervous.

"Well, I won't read the whole thing." Laura went over the article herself, leaving her finger on a line to keep her place, then read aloud. " 'The passenger liner *Laconia*, carrying servicemen's wives and children and Italian prisoners of war was sunk off the Cape of Good Hope.' Let me see. The U-boat captain was named Hartenstein. I wonder how they know that. Anyway, the U-boat surfaced and saw all those hundreds and hundreds of helpless people in the water and just sailed away, leaving them to drown in the middle of the ocean. The only rescue ships were a day and a half away. They don't say how many died; they can't of course. They only say 'horrible losses.' There's an interview here, too, with one of the American pilots who had to fly around and around over them but couldn't go down to help. He could only watch them get fewer and fewer as they sank out of sight."

Miss Lizzie opened the top of the Dutch door and leaned her meaty forearms on the ledge. Olive, whose brother Randy was lost in the North Atlantic in March, kept her head down and held onto her magazine.

"Imagine it," said Lorna. "That German didn't make any attempt to help them. He probably laughed. Mothers with their children clinging to them, trying to stay afloat on debris. Think of the noise, the voices of those children, of those poor—"

"That's enough, Lorna. Doris got up to take a hankie to Olive, whose tears were making their way to her chin. Doris stood next to Olive and glared at Lorna until she understood.

"Oh, Olive," Lorna said. "I'm so sorry. I wasn't thinking."

Lorna started to stand up, but Olive—still face down—shook her head violently and waved the other woman away.

Lorna folded the paper. "What about the news down here? What have I been missing?"

"Well, there's Maggie," said Miss Lizzie.

"Maggie?" Lorna looked around the room at the others.

"You tell her," Miss Lizzie said to Doris. "I think I got a mouse in the closet here."

Doris shot a glance at the spot Miss Lizzie had just abandoned, then looked at Lorna. It was a rare occasion when Lorna was the last to hear island news. Doris tried not to enjoy her advantage; normally she was not one to gossip.

"The day before yesterday, she left her father's house in

Head Harbor and moved into Amos's house in the cove. Overnight, without telling a soul," Doris said.

"Well!" Lorna was delighted; her mind set sail on a sea of possibility. "Whatever for, would you imagine?"

Doris would not imagine, not with Lorna. "I don't know," she said. "I don't suppose it's any of my business; it's hers now, the house and the land. She told Leah she just decided to move there and did it. I don't know. She'll be closer to school and town."

"I wonder if that was her motive," Lorna said. "I would think—"

There was a muffled thump in the mailroom and a little scuffle before Miss Lizzie appeared in the doorway, her cheeks red with effort.

"The mouse was running on the top of the door, and I shut it on him," she said. "But it only caught his feet. He was stuck there upside down, but he got away. Didn't he squiggle though?"

Doris escaped out the front door, saying she had shopping to do.

When she was gone, Miss Lizzie told those remaining that she knew something else they didn't. When Lorna asked what that was, Miss Lizzie fussed with her hair net for a minute, then said, "Last Tuesday the Hamilton girls were walking home, and when they passed the Boutwell cottage, Susan saw a curtain move in the window—like it had been held open for someone to see out, then let closed when she looked at the house. It was dusk. There's nobody supposed to be in there.

"When they told Charles, he went over there with his gun, but he didn't find anything. It was probably their imaginations, but I tell you people are scared. I won't go out alone after dark, not me, thank you."

"I won't go walking anywhere alone any more," Olive said. "Even in daylight I'm watching to see somebody come out of the woods and jump on me."

They were silent while Olive got her mail and left. They watched her out the window as she waddled down the road toward the town landing.

"Where on earth do you suppose Maggie sleeps?" asked Lorna. "She must sleep in Amos's bed."

"I don't know," said Miss Lizzie. "Perhaps she's sleeping in one of the other ones."

"There *are* no others," said Lorna. "His is the only bed in the house."

"How do you know?"

"Oh, I was in there a few years ago, with Leah."

"Hmph," said Miss Lizzie.

Among the last of the things she brought up from her father's house were her recipe books. As she aligned them between two crocks on the kitchen counter, a clipping slipped out of one. She read it and taped it to the cabinet above the sink.

> *Thank God, few people are so poor that they do not have an inner life which feeds the true springs of thought and action. So, if I may offer a thought in consolation to others who for a time have to live in a "goldfish bowl," it is: Don't worry because people know all that you do, for the really important things about anyone are what they are and what they think and feel, and the more you live in a "goldfish bowl" the less people really know about you!*
> —E. Roosevelt

When Maggie heard the store truck come down the cove road, she thought it must be Gus, hoped that it was Leah come for a visit. But when the vehicle went by the window, she saw that it was Cecil, a cigarette stuck in his mouth, squinting in the smoke. He parked by the graveyard and walked up the drive slowly, waving at the deerfly that circled his head. Maggie had been expecting him, as he knew, but she acted surprised to see him.

Cecil looked ghostly pale—from his ulcer, she assumed. She invited him to sit, and he took the rocker, crossing his legs.

"You've lost weight," she said, standing before him. "So has Leah, for that matter; she's taking this so hard."

"I know it," he said. "I can't keep anything on my stomach, with this ulcer; that's why I've lost weight. And she just isn't eating like she used to."

"I can make you a nice cup of Postum with milk; that would agree with your stomach."

"Thank you," he said quietly.

If he had come about Gus's staying on the island to finish the lobster season, or about their patrolling, he would be gruff and acting bolder, she thought. Maggie had seen him twice in the store since the reading of Amos's will, and he had not spoken to her either time. Now he was ready, it seemed, and so was she.

"You know why I'm here?" he asked, taking the cup and saucer.

"I can guess, but I don't want to." Maggie sat in the chair opposite him, her hands in her apron. She was careful not to let herself feel sorry for him.

"I'm here about the will, the property. I'm here because she would never ask you herself," he said.

Maggie nodded, tamping down her anger, and let him go on. He lit a cigarette, using the saucer for an ashtray.

"It's just not right," he said. "That Leah, his daughter, got nothing. I'm not saying he shouldn't have given the property to you. That's not my place, and I'm grateful for Gus getting the boat and gear. But think how Leah must feel that he didn't leave her a thing."

"Go on," she said.

"You're not making this any easier. Look, before he died, Amos was thinking about deeding the other houses—Ava's and the cabin, and the land up there to her. He was—"

"Amos was thinking that?" she leaned forward. "How do you know? Did he tell you? Did Leah say he was?"

"He wanted Gus to go fishing out of this cove and to settle down here after high school. You know that," he said.

"Yes, but that's not the point is it? That's not even relevant. If Leah wanted the property for that reason, why didn't she just ask him about it? He would have given it to her, to keep it in the family; he wouldn't have blinked. Let me answer for you since you don't seem to want to talk straight yourself. She didn't ask him—even though you pestered her to tears about it—because she knew he would say yes, and she knew that you would sell the property before the ink was dry."

"Did she tell you that?" he sat up and glared at her.

"She didn't need to; I can see can't I? Katherine Merrill put her store up for sale in June. You want to sell yours and this property and buy her out. You want to move off this island to where the money is and take Leah and Gus with you. You can't stand this place. Don't butt your cigarette in that cup; I have to drink from that. Look at you, smoking one after another. This island or something about it is eating away at you, has you bent over in pain."

"My health doesn't have anything to do with this," Cecil said, his voice rising. "What I'm asking you to do is give over some of this property to Leah—or even sell it to her if you need the money, though I can't see why you would, with two houses now."

"You won't understand, will you? Or maybe you can't." Maggie closed her eyes for a moment. "Think about it. Leah didn't ask him because she wanted this cove to be his, his family's. Why hasn't she asked me to give it to her? For the same reason: It's theirs."

"No it isn't," he said. "Not any more."

"It is. It's theirs in my keeping. And that's all there is to it," she said.

"Leah's his daughter, for Christ's sake," he said bitterly. "Some of it should be hers to do what she wants with, do something for the living."

"What *she* wants?" Maggie raised her eyebrows. "If I deed a portion to her, you'll pick away at her. You'll make her so miserable that she'll give in and let you sell it. You'll belittle her until she can't stand up to you. I can't bear the way you treat her."

"That's what I thought," he said, standing. "It's not family or any of that crap. You don't want me to have that store. You want her to stay stuck on this island, slaving away. Gus too. You want them here for your own sake. You want the property for yourself, too. It's not for Amos and those spirits. You don't believe in spirits," he pointed at her. "You don't even believe in God."

Maggie stood, too, the heat rising to her cheeks.

"Don't point, Cecil," she said. "It's impolite. I think you should take your leave, so I don't have to ask you to."

She carried his cup and saucer into the kitchen, where she scrubbed them with scalding water and rinsed them with bleach. Better for Leah to slave away in a little store among her own people than to slave away in a big store among strangers.

"Hello? Excuse me. Are you open?" A thin-faced man in a flannel cap held the door ajar and peered into the store at Leah, who sat on her stool behind the counter. His voice was not timid or deferential, but habitually polite.

"Yes, of course. Come in." Leah stood up, then sat back down.

"It says you're open until six, but I didn't see any lights or activity. It's hard to guess the time in such thick fog. It's not six yet, is it?"

"No. It's just past five." Leah peeled off the thin gloves she wore to keep one hand from scratching and picking at the fingers on the other.

When he stepped inside, took off his cap, and smiled, she was surprised to see that he was so young, not much older than Gus. His polite manner made her want to straighten her hair, but instead she smiled and buried her hands in her apron.

She thought at first he had bought his overcoat two sizes too large, but when he turned aside, she thought that he must have lost weight since he bought it: the sleeve length was right, and it fit properly in the shoulders over a heavy sweater. By his speech the young man was not from Maine, and she knew no summer people who would be seen in clothes so sadly worn. His cheeks were sunken; a pale stubble showed on his chin and upper lip; his blue gray eyes were active, skittish, but unafraid. Some island family's distant relative, she guessed, though she had not heard anyone mention such.

Leah tried not to let him see that she was watching him as he went slowly down the aisle, bending to examine boxes, reading the labels on cans. Every so often he glanced at the front of the store—not at her, she saw the third time, but at the door. She thought of the Hamilton girls and the moving curtain in the Boutwell cottage and wished fervently that someone else would come in. She could hear him humming in the produce aisle.

He came to the register with his arms full and carefully, almost reverently, placed each item on the counter: an onion, three wrinkled green peppers, a cabbage, and a loaf of store bread. He was wearing street shoes—once black but now scuffed gray—and pleated trousers. His hands were not those of a working man. He glanced at the door again, smiled at her, but said nothing. She wanted to say something herself, something casual to allay her fear with conversation, but she could not.

He paid her from a leather coin purse with a snap closure and looked out the window while she bagged his groceries. Unhurried, he mumbled a thanks and started for the door, but then stopped and set the bag down on the soda cooler. Leah backed away from the register and stood as though about to open the refrigerator, watching him from the corner of her eye. He turned his back to her, took the bread from the bag, and from it drew four slices, which he set aside while he replaced the rest of the loaf. Watching out the door, up and down the road, he chewed the crust off the stack of slices, squeezed the dough into a ball with his fist, took a bite, and left.

Leah stood in the door in the lingering smell of wood smoke and watched him walk down the road nibbling, but as he disappeared in the fog she could not tell whether he was going to the town landing or had turned toward the western shore. Her first thought was to close the store and find someone to come back and sit with her in case he returned. Instead, she waited, hoping someone familiar would come along, scolding herself for being scared of a harmless boy. After a lonely hour, in which she busied herself with closing, she walked home, her eyes scanning both sides of the road. She was comforted by the light in Dickie and Edna's window, and when she got home and found Gus rooting around in the kitchen, she wondered what it was about the stranger that made her feel vaguely sad for Gus.

When Cecil opened the store just before six the next morning, he found Lorna Crowell coming up the steps. When he held the door for her, she marched by him to stand in front of the register. He thought she looked as if she hadn't slept a wink. The scarf she had thrown over her head had caught in her hair net and thrown it all askew, and she was covered with a fine, wet dew. Cecil flicked a cigarette end out the door and tamped another on his thumbnail.

"How long have you been here?" she asked. Lorna had not come to shop.

"I don't know," he said. "Maybe a half hour. Why, is something wrong?"

"I thought maybe Albert stopped to see you on his way to Dwight's."

"No. I saw him go by. He didn't come in though. What is it?" Cecil asked. His ulcer tore at him, and he blanched.

"Albert claims it's nothing, but he's just saying that so I won't worry. If he thought it wasn't anything, then he wouldn't have gone to report it to the constable, would he?" She looked at Cecil for a response and thought he grimaced.

"Last night—well, yesterday around five; it was dark enough to be night—I was watching for Albert to come home, and I saw a strange man walk past going toward town," she said. "It wasn't anybody from here. He was wearing a long, dark coat, like a detective or a gangster."

She let it sink in. Hers was the last house on the road to the uninhabited west side of the island, so where was this guy coming from, thought Cecil.

"A half hour later he came back, this time with a satchel or a suitcase, I couldn't tell, and headed down the road to nowhere. It was him all right. When Albert came home he said there weren't any but island boats moored in the thoroughfare. So he's gone to ask Dwight if anybody else has reported seeing the man, as much to check up on me as to find out for himself."

"He came in here around five," Cecil said. He slipped on his apron and tied it in front. "Leah told us about him at supper. That wasn't a suitcase you saw; that was a bag of groceries. She said that he was probably visiting somebody, that he wasn't a fisherman. According to Leah he was some polite—and young and frail looking. He was probably out for a walk."

"At dusk in a thick of fog?" Cecil could be so frustrating.

"Summer people take walks in the fog," he said.

"Oh, come on, Cecil!"

"Maybe he's a laborer hired to do some work on one of the summer cottages down in Moore's Harbor, and he's staying down there," he said. "Leah said he didn't have any accent."

"So?! If you were a spy would you go around talking like a

German? 'Ach, strudel. Guten day to you'?" Cecil, she thought, was as thick-headed as Albert.

"She did say he seemed nervous, like he was worried, kind of watchful," he allowed.

"There!" she cried. "I'm staying here until Albert comes back."

His rubber boots folded down at the knees, Richard stood on the town landing with Dwight, watching the mouth of the thoroughfare for the evening mail boat.

"We've got three hours of daylight left," said Richard. "Let's go now, at least down to Moore's Harbor."

Dwight sat on the rail at the top of the ramp puffing on his pipe, thinking that the worst part about being constable was having to actually listen to people like Richard Snell when something went wrong.

"No," he said. "No. We can't just go running around. We've got to have a meeting."

"We are having a meeting," said Richard. "There's seven men here."

Aboard Albert's boat, which was tied up next to them, Gus sat on the stern watching Albert sort lobsters while Vergil Eaton, his sternman, pumped the bilge. Behind Richard, toothless Calvin Niels, who at eighty was still known for his prodigious strength, sat on the tailgate of his truck watching his grandson Zeke, who was kneeling on a filthy canvas trying to reassemble his greasy gearbox. Calvin watched a horsefly the size of his thumb land on his forearm; he waited until it settled and felt safe enough to lift its abdomen to drive in its proboscis, then swatted it dead.

"They're not listening," said Dwight, tilting his head toward the Nielses, "And—"

"They wouldn't be listening if we were setting in rows of chairs in the town hall," Richard said.

"I've got a load of cedar shakes coming on this boat," Dwight said.

"What makes you think he's dangerous?" asked Albert as he tied shut one crate of lobsters and pushed it aside to begin filling another. When he'd had a good day fishing—as he had today—Albert tied up at the town landing to count his lobsters and enjoy the envy of those watching him.

"*I* never said he was dangerous," Dwight said. "It doesn't matter one way or the other whether he is. My wife, like several other wives I could name, isn't going to rest or let us rest until we find this guy. Your wife, Albert, is still in the store. She's been there all day; she won't go home until you come to fetch her."

"He could of gone off on the morning mail boat," said Vergil. He stopped pumping the bilge. Vergil had not gone off island to high school when he could have five years ago; he had hired on as Albert's sternman with the idea of making enough money to buy his own boat. But, living alone in the abandoned east-side schoolhouse and running around with the Squeaker Cove boys, he had squandered what Albert paid him and had yet to even buy a single string of traps for himself. Vergil was the example that Gus's parents used when the boy argued against finishing high school.

"He didn't," Gus said. "Nobody saw him this morning. He might have his own boat."

"We'd of seen it," said Richard. His wrists rested inside his suspenders, supporting his hands, which were entwined over his belly. "A dozen boats fish these shores every day, in-close all this month, too, for the shedders."

Vergil whispered under his shoulder to Gus, "And that's news?"

Gus smiled. "Maybe it's a small boat," he said. "And he has it pulled up on the shore and hidden under branches or something."

"Somebody could have put him ashore," Vergil said.

Dwight stood up and knocked out his pipe. "Here comes the mail boat. I'll ask Buster if he's seen anybody like this guy or if he's heard anything."

"How was it, Richard?" Albert assumed a fighting pose, holding a lobster in each hand. He swung the right one toward Vergil. "Like that?" he asked.

Vergil and Gus snickered; Dwight looked away.

"I was only holding one, and no it wasn't like that goddamn you," snarled Richard. "I hit him with it, hard; I didn't swing like a girl."

Buster Dodge, the gray canvas mailbag slung over his shoulder, stopped at the top of the ramp to catch his breath and rest his game leg before he began the ascent to the parking lot. Government regulations said that only he could touch the mailbag; no matter how low the tide, how heavy the bag, or how badly his leg hurt that day, it was his job to lug it up the hill and drive it to Miss Lizzie. It was a painful penance for him, every day but Sunday, and one he relished. Dwight asked him if he had seen a pale young man in an overcoat and city clothes among his passengers. Buster grunted a negative, shifted the bag to his other shoulder, and started up the wharf.

"He's his old pleasant self today, isn't he?" said Richard. "I'll give you a hand off-loading those shakes; we'll ask him again when he comes back."

Albert took his boat off to her mooring, leaving Vergil and Gus to help with Dwight's shingles.

When Buster returned, his face was full to the brim and about to overflow in laughter.

"You didn't tell me it was a German spy you were looking for," he said to Dwight.

"I didn't say it was a German spy, for Christ's sake." Dwight hated to be mocked by a Stonington man. "It's a stranger that two or three people have seen, and I want to find out who it is."

"Miss Lizzie said he's a German spy, and you're going to hunt for him, take him prisoner," Buster said.

"She's just scared like the rest of the women are," said Richard. "You say you didn't see somebody like Dwight described on the mail boat?"

"How can I be sure of that?" Buster didn't like Richard's tone, or Richard. "I've carried hundreds of people back and forth this summer. I can't tell you whether he came down here amongst all the others, but I can say I haven't had such a passenger since the summer people left. What the hell did he do wrong to have the constable after him?"

"He's trespassing, if nothing else," Dwight said. "The Hamilton girls saw somebody in the Boutwell cottage just the other day."

"The Boutwell place is on the east side. Miss Lizzie said Lorna saw him on the west side." Buster shook his head.

"That's just it," said Richard. "He's staying in one empty house until all the food is gone, then moving to another one. Skulking around, stealing and trespassing. I bet he's armed, too, an escaped convict—or worse."

Buster looked at Vergil and Gus for some sign that this was a joke but saw none.

"Don't use a monkey wrench," Calvin told Zeke. "It'll slip and skin your knuckles. Use a box end if you got one."

"Suppose he's a hunter or a camper, and he's staying in the woods," Buster said. "You got fifteen square miles of forest down here, and it belongs to Mrs. Bowditch—all of it. I doubt she'd give a rat's ass if she knew somebody was camping on her land. She lives in Boston. Maybe he's her son or nephew or something."

"Don't be foolish," said Richard.

"*Me* be foolish? You're the ones being foolish. Somebody sees someone she doesn't know, and the whole island runs for cover, forms a posse for Christ's sake. Imagine that on the mainland. Somebody comes running into a store and says 'I seen somebody I didn't know! Call out the National Guard! Deputize the menfolk! Alert the Coastal Picket!' Christ." Buster sniffed.

"Oh, I know," said Dwight. "But it could be a German. There's a war you know. A woman in Ellsworth saw two of them last month, and the police caught them."

"Well, maybe he is." Buster tucked the empty mailbag under his arm and took hold of the ramp railing. "I'll leave you fellows to take care of it, and I'll probably avoid getting shot by mistake when I do. There's a big box from Sears for Miss Bowen. Why don't you come aboard and sign for it, Gus? Maybe you can carry it over to her when you go next."

When the boy had gone aboard the mail boat, out of earshot, Vergil said, "Maybe it's one of Amos's spooks."

Dwight laughed. "Maybe it's Amos himself, taken on a ghosty form. Except I can't imagine his ghost ever leaving the cove, not while Maggie's there, at least."

"Ghosts," said Richard, still seething from Buster's attitude. "What a crock of shit."

"We'll get some men together in the morning and go looking," Dwight said.

Gus came up the ramp with a flat box and leaned it against the stack of shingles.

"What is it?" Vergil wanted to know.

"It says 'table,' " Gus said.

"Looks awful small to be a table."

"Maybe it's a small table," Calvin said.

"We can take cars down the road on both sides, checking houses. The young ones—the rugged ones—can walk down the length of the island through the woods," Richard suggested.

"In pairs," Dwight said.

"Like beaters on a tiger hunt," Gus added. "Me and Vergil will be one team."

"Well, I don't know," Vergil said.

"Sure. You don't think you and me could take care of whoever he is?" Gus wanted to know. "Hell, the two of us could—"

"This isn't a hunt," Dwight said. "We can't have people thinking that way, talking like that."

"Which is why we're waiting until the morning, until people

have calmed down." Richard pointed at Gus. "We just want to find this guy and talk to him, not gun him down."

Aboard the mail boat, Buster cast off the bow line and handed himself along toward the stern. Richard searched his pockets, muttered something that sounded like "Well hell, then," clumped in a hurry down the ramp and stepped onto the mail boat like a man who had been hurrying to catch her.

When Buster had rounded the thoroughfare buoy and turned out into the bay, he opened her up, and Richard came forward to join him at the wheel.

"That Albert Crowell thinks he's some funny," Richard said. "He pisses me off is what he does. It's high-minded sons of bitches like him I can't stand."

Buster struck a match on the thigh of his raised leg and puffed his pipe alive.

"You could use a drink," he said. "I'd offer you one if I had it, but my rum's all gone. I'm not the first person to mention that to you, am I now?"

Richard pulled down the brim of his hat to shade the setting sun. Buster pulled up his stool.

"You ought to stop in to see Lump and tell him about your stranger; ask if he knows anything about him." Buster said. "He's in his office till six."

"And get laughed at?" Richard showed his teeth. "Like hell I will."

"No need to get ugly about it."

The last of the ferryboats carrying quarrymen home was un-loading at Green Head. The Stonington fishing fleet had long since come in and been moored and washed down; the men had gone home to their tidy houses, arrayed on the ledges that rose behind the town. Parker Waite stood in his skiff, talking to Bill McDonnell on the *Nana*, but not another man was to be seen on the water. Richard looked for a light in his mother's kitchen window, but it was obscured from this angle by the roof of the Noyes house.

"I wonder if there's a movie tonight," he said.

"I think there is," Buster allowed. "It's a comedy; I don't re-member the name of it. Rose said it was good. If it made her laugh, it might cheer you up. Me, I'm going to listen to Martha Raye and Parkyakarkas."

Richard coiled the bow line on the deck. "You wouldn't want to look the other way on the matter of the fare would you? There's nobody around to know."

"No, I wouldn't." Buster waited.

Richard pulled sixteen cents from his pants pocket and looked at it in his palm.

"How about I pay you for both ways in the morning?" he asked.

"All right then," said Buster.

As he climbed the wharf ladder, Richard mumbled, "Jew," under his breath.

CHAPTER ELEVEN

SHE MUST BE BAKING A PIE, HE THOUGHT AS HE LET HIMSELF OUT of the truck and stood to stretch in the dying light. By the smell, she was burning birch in the kitchen stove, birch set aside for baking. He had parked in the tall grass beside her car and the old garage, where Amos's truck had sat undisturbed since the funeral. The sun had gone down behind the mountain, leaving the cove in a late-summer-evening shade. A cloud of little flies danced high in a late glance of sunlight. In the wide cleft between the granite ledges, under the broad canopy of oaks, the fresh mound over Amos's grave was barely visible. The pillar of smoke from the kitchen stove rose to the tops of the trees, then slipped away in the light wind. Tomorrow would be a good day on the water and a damned shame to waste. Gus slipped his knapsack onto one shoulder and balanced the flat box on his head to carry it to the house.

Maggie met him in the dooryard, smiling, her head tilted in curiosity. She had seen little of Gus since school started and they stopped patrolling every night. In the morning, she saw him on the wharf or aboard the boat as she left for class; when she returned at the end of the day he was gone, and the cove was empty. Alone in the silent evening house, she worried about his fishing so often by himself, missing nearly two months of school, and going home to a bitter father and a mother who was shrinking with grief.

"Let me guess," she said. "You knew I was baking, so you brought my lap table over thinking you'd get a dish of cobbler for your troubles."

"Is that what this is, a lap table?"

"Yes. Let me help you," she said.

"No, I got it."

She stepped ahead of him to hold the door, not saying that he hadn't come just to deliver her package, not with a knapsack on his back. The front room was warm with the smell of sweet, cooking fruit. He set the package next to the wood box and removed his cap, leaving a startled shock of red hair over his forehead. Maggie waited.

"Mother wants me to spend the night here," he said quickly. "She made me promise I would."

Maggie smiled, swept a dusting of flour from her forearm. "Why did she make you promise?"

"Because you'd be insulted that she thought you needed somebody to protect you, that she thought you might be afraid. She said you'd be angry and try to send me home." Gus smiled.

"What?" she asked.

"She pretended she was you—tucked her chin down and glared at me and talked in that frozen voice you use when you're mad. It was comical."

Maggie laughed. "Since you've already been scolded, you might as well make yourself comfortable. The truth is that I am happy to have company, yours especially." She reached to brush his hair flat, but he pulled back slightly and patted it down himself.

"Father said I should sleep in the garage, so as not to be in your way," he said.

"Don't be ridiculous. You'll sleep here."

"He said you probably don't believe there's a stranger down

here, and even if you do you're not scared of him," Gus said.

"He's right, I'm not scared—at least not any more than I normally am," she said. "How can I not believe that there's a stranger here, when your mother and perhaps others have seen him? I have *every reason* to believe it—more reason than you know—and I want him apprehended."

Gus looked quizzically at her as Amos would have.

"Caught," she said.

"I promised father that I'd look through the houses tonight, Ava's and Mineola's. The cabin, too, for any signs of him."

"That's fine. I'll go with you," she said. "But we'll want to wait fifteen minutes until the cobbler is done. We can have a late dessert when we get back."

When it was done, she set the bubbling cobbler on the shelf to cool and stood in the kitchen door rolling down her sleeves, watching him as he broke Amos's double-barreled shotgun and slipped in two shells.

"Is that necessary?" she asked. "No, don't tell me; you promised. I hope you plan to keep it broken; I'd hate to have one of my legs shot off."

"Of course I will," he said. "Don't worry. I know what I'm doing. I've been hunting plenty of times."

"Hunting for a German spy or for a ghost?" she asked.

"You don't believe in ghosts," he said. "You don't even be-lieve in God.

"No, I don't."

"Let's go." He held the screen for her.

They walked side by side in the ruts that led to the houses, following the beam of her flashlight as it danced ahead of them. The wind had backed to the south, bringing a damp chill from the open sea.

"The day before yesterday, Albert put Vergil ashore in Head Harbor so he could walk home," Gus said. "His truck's pooched again. When he was passing your house—your father's—he felt something inside it. He didn't *see* anybody; it wasn't people. He just felt something, something large and awful. He got home in record time. What do you suppose it was?"

"A bit of underdone potato," she said. She shined her beam on the houses and it blinked back from each window it passed.

"What?" he asked.

"It was his imagination," she lied. "Just as it was Amos's imagination that provided Ava and the others to keep him company here. If we run into them, we'll ignore them, won't we?"

The shed where John had once kept his little store was in near collapse; the door hung by one hinge and the wall that had held the coal bin had given way, spilling its contents onto the ground. Maggie shined her light inside as they passed and led the way around the giant forsythia. Mineola's house, the last and least sturdy of those built in the cove, was perched on a heave of granite ledge, with posts supporting its corners. In the mudroom she held the light while Gus took the key from the hook and opened the kitchen door. The floor, which had not supported human weight for seven years, sighed and buckled beneath them. A squirrel, or perhaps two of them, scampered across the floor above, fleeing to the attic.

Maggie shined her light slowly over the counters and shelves, then into the little adjoining sitting room. Gus coughed nervously.

"There's nobody here," he said. "Did you hear the squirrels?"

"Yes, but I'll look upstairs nevertheless," she said. "Such a tiny house."

Gus stood still in the damp, moldy darkness and listened to her move about on the second floor, remembering how Amos used to say what a cold house this was with no cellar, as cold as the couple that lived in it.

"No sign of anything or anybody up there," she said, coming carefully down the steep staircase.

"No, I wouldn't think so."

When they had let themselves out and found the path, Gus thought that he hadn't been afraid in Mineola's house because there was no sense or feel of anything human to it. But as they approached Ava's place, his stomach heaved up against his lungs, and his arms went weak. He stayed close behind Maggie, crowding her on the side-door stoop.

She knocked loudly three times.

"Don't do that!" he hissed. "It's not locked."

She turned the knob and pushed the door open partway, leaning ahead into the kitchen.

"Ava? Walter? Anyone home?" she called.

"Come on, cut it out," he said, and pushed her forward. There were no sounds of skittering rodents, no complaining floorboards.

Maggie took a kitchen match from the box on the wall by the stove and lit the kerosene lamp on the table. She ran her finger across the tabletop, leaving a shiny path in the dust.

"Well, Ava's not here," she said, looking at her fingertip. "She'd never allow dust to collect like that." She meant it as a joke, to encourage them both, but realized that the dust meant Amos wasn't there any longer, either.

"It's as though she just walked out," Maggie said looking around at the clean dish towels, the curled tide calendar, the icebox door held slightly open by a string. "Or gone off to the mainland for a visit." She flashed her light past the mirror on Ava's bureau, then returned it for a moment to let them see the whole room in its reflection. In the window by Ava's wicker chair, Gus saw the shivering figure of a man, caught his breath, then grinned at himself when it stepped back as he did. Maggie whacked the bed quilt with the flat of her hand to see the dust rise, then examined the closet and knelt to sweep the light under the bed.

"Mother says I used to spend whole afternoons in this parlor," said Gus, "but I don't remember them."

Maggie straightened the doily on the radio. "Don't you remember Ava's stereopticon? You loved it so."

"Yes, I guess I do," he said. "African villages. Niagara Falls. A hippopotamus."

"You called it a chowdermouse," she said. "I wonder that Amos didn't pull the hairs from her brush."

"Let's get out of here."

"I'm going to look upstairs," she said.

"Oh, all right. I'll go ahead of you. You shine the light for my feet."

The bureau and bed in Walter's little room beneath the eaves were covered with faded newspapers. The shade was drawn, its pull string secured to a nail beneath the sill.

Maggie shined the light on the bed. "What's wrong with this picture?" she asked.

"Some pages are faded and some aren't," Gus replied. "You think somebody's used his bed. It coulda been squirrels."

"A very large squirrel," she said. "One in too much of a hurry to bother to rearrange them properly."

Outside, she played the light across the meadow, then switched it off.

"There's no need to check the cabin. I was up there last night," she said. "We ought to walk the cliffs, but that cobbler is getting cold. Look how bright the first stars are."

"You check it every night?" Gus unloaded the shotgun and crooked it over his shoulder.

"Yes." She wanted to take his hand across the grassy hump between the ruts, but did not. "And, yes, your single hair is still in place, Sherlock, as if you hadn't gone to see for yourself."

"Mother's hair," he said. "I did, yesterday. I'm surprised that the paste has held so long, with the rain, or that the wind hasn't blown the screen open some and broken the hair."

"I should write a testimonial for the company, describing how its schoolroom paste has gone to war."

"It couldn't have been this guy who Amos saw, who he was watching for," said Gus. "It was too long ago. I still think it was summer people he saw or thought he saw; I think they burned the lamp chimney black."

"I know you do, and I still think you're wrong, too willing to overlook the salty footprints. Maybe it wasn't this guy, this

Goldilocks in Papa Bear's bed. I doubt it. But I won't be satisfied until I talk to him or find out otherwise."

"Mother says he's a skinny little guy, nothing rugged about him. It would take more than that to knock Amos down or throw him off of the cliff, no matter how—"

"Perhaps he's not alone, or wasn't," she said. "Perhaps he has a good reason to stay away from the cabin. Perhaps he knows we're watching it and knows damn well why."

"Or he's moved up onto the mountain with his very-low-frequency machine. Morales says it wants to be on high ground, which is why they might choose this island. And it's shelter and food that have brought him down, like the deer that show up when the summer people leave."

"I want to talk to him if they find him," she said. "Will you make sure I get a chance?"

"If I can," he said.

"Say you will. Promise it."

"I will," he said.

"Someone's here!" Lucille looked up from her knitting, her eyes round in surprise. "Who could it be?"

"A man," said Claire. "He let himself in. It must be Richard."

"On a *Thursday*?"

Richard switched on the light in the mudroom and shouted "Hello!" into the kitchen. He wiped his hat band with a gray handkerchief, mopped his brow, kicked off his heavy boots, and appeared before the ladies.

"I didn't expect you tonight, dear." Lucille set her knitting in the button box and offered her cheek for a kiss. "Have you had your supper yet? Is everything all right?"

"No I haven't eaten. I came up on the mail boat. Nothing's wrong. I just felt like visiting. Hello Claire."

"Hello, Richard. We've been all afternoon at the Nitsomsosom Club, where your mother, please, was duly elected treasurer."

Claire, president emerita, was the founder of the Nitsomsosom Club and the source of its clever name. They had begun as four, knitting socks and vests for the British Relief; now they were twenty ladies strong, sewing and knitting for the Red Cross.

Richard congratulated his mother and leaned into the icebox for a bottle of beer.

"There's a nice chowder I can heat up, and you're lucky because there's still plenty left of the bean salad I took to the meeting." Lucille stood and smoothed her dress.

"I'd like that."

"Did you see Mr. Webb's new garage?" Lucille asked. "Today was the grand opening; they unveiled the sign with the flying red horse and showed off his new pumps."

"I was just down there," Richard said.

Claire, who was known for her uncanny ability to smell drink on a man, sniffed twice audibly to say that he and Russell Webb had downed a few, hadn't they? Lucille and Richard ignored her.

"You sit down while I set you a place," Lucille said.

"It's time I went home." Claire squeezed the darning egg out of the sock into her basket and speared the ball of yarn with her needle.

"You don't have to go," Richard said. "I need to make a phone call."

"Stay and have some iced tea," said Lucille.

At the stove, stirring milk into the chowder, Lucille leaned toward the door to the front room to better hear Richard on the phone with Carl Topp in Blue Hill. He had to talk loudly because of the connection, but he was turned away from her in the far corner of the room. She heard him tell Topp that there was a commotion down on Barter Island over a stranger; when her

son asked him if he had heard anything about it, Richard
sounded relieved that he had not. There was something, too,
about a meeting, and she worried that he and Topp were still involved somehow in America First. She would get the details of
the commotion, at least, when Claire left.

While he ate his supper, blowing on each spoonful of chowder, Richard listened impassively, without reply, to the women
as they told him the paper had reported that the *Vincennes* had
been sunk and that Frances Torrey's son was unaccounted for.
They also reported that the quarry was going to close down because the Portuguese were being drafted and were disappear-
ing, no doubt to avoid the war.

Richard carried his iced tea in to the rocker by the radio,
turned it on, and settled sullenly into the chair with a cigarette.

Claire waited with the dishtowel in hand as Lucille poured
hot water over the plates in the sink.

"What's he listening to?" Claire asked.

"It sounds like the Al Jolson show—you know, with Martha
Raye and Parkyakarkas," said Lucille. "He thinks they're funny,
though I can't see why."

"What a ridiculous name," Claire said.

"I know it."

"I'm skirting it, uphill," said Vergil when he and Gus came
to the cedar bog. "I'm not going to walk around the rest of the
day soaked to the waist. Besides, he won't be hiding in a bog;
he ain't that stupid."

"Maybe he's that smart," Gus said. "Maybe he thinks that
it's the last place we'd look for a guy in street shoes and city
clothes. I'll go through it and catch up with you on the other
side. It's mostly sphagnum."

"It's deeper in the middle than you think." Vergil started
through the bay berry toward higher ground.

The soft moss held Gus's weight at first but soon gave way,

and he sank to his ankles, filling his boots with water. Up to his knees, then to his thighs in the cold, black mire, he felt his way with his feet among sunken stumps and slick bottom mud. watching all the while among the trees and tall skunk cabbage that encircled the bog. When he sank to his waist in a sudden hole, the cold shrank his privates and he gasped aloud. It was foolish to think that the man his mother saw would be hiding in a swamp, but Gus had said he'd walk a straight line and he would. He tightened his belt to hold up his now-heavy trousers and thought how Vergil would laugh when Gus emerged from the bog soaking wet.

When he reached the red maples at the far edge, their leaves bright, the first to turn, Gus scanned the spruce and boulders above him for Vergil, watching for movement, for the white bands of bedsheet that each of the searchers wore on his hat and sleeve. He waited, dripping, and thought that he must have missed his partner.

"If you get separated," Dwight had said when he dropped them off, "just keep going. On this side of the ridge, just make sure that your right foot's walking higher than your left. If that don't work and you lose your way, walk downhill to the road. But you know that already."

Riding shotgun, Dickie had lifted the forefinger on the hand he had stretched out the truck window. "Be wise as serpents, and beware of men," he had said.

"Shut up, Dickie," Dwight had responded.

Gus watched and listened for a few minutes, but the chickadees were still busy in the lower branches of the spruce where Vergil should pass. The boy decided that he had already gone on, and started out himself, picking his way among the boulders and bushes. Gus would not yell for Vergil; it would warn the stranger and might alarm the others farther up the mountain. He carried his shotgun cradled at the ready across his chest and felt very much alone in the thickening forest.

• • •

Dwight turned down the road to Squeaker Cove, where the two old Walker houses and a dozen outbuildings—some collapsed, some leaning toward the same—hunched near the shore and wharf. Basil's broad-beamed boat, *Eliza B.*, rode on her mooring.

"I thought he'd be out to haul today," said Dickie.

"Not with Fuddy and Skippy, his sternmen, walking the ridge," Dwight said. "He wouldn't go alone. He doesn't have a pot hauler. If he did the work those two guys do hauling and baiting his traps, he'd fill his boots with sweat in an hour. He runs short of breath when he walks to the outhouse. I wonder where he is."

They parked at the near house, and as they got out of the truck, Basil hove into view from the garden with an armful of green tomatoes. The slobber-stained bib of his overalls lay limp on his great gut.

"Let me guess," said Basil, pointing at Dwight's pistol belt. "It's Halloween, and you're going as Hopalong Cassidy."

"You haven't seen a stranger down around here, have you Basil?" Dickie asked. "We're looking for a guy—"

"I know what you're doing. How could I not know, for Christ's sake?" He set the large tomatoes out on a sawhorse in the sun. "You've got both my sternmen walking around on the mountain when they could be out to haul with me, making some money. They're so excited, Skippy was up all night preparing for battle."

"You'll make up your day fishing," Dwight said. He had no use for Basil Walker, and Basil knew it. "All we're asking is that you keep an eye out for this guy and if he comes down around here—"

"If he sees that thing, he'll scamper off so fast I won't see him." Basil's wet mouth formed a smile as he pointed to the wide door of an old garage.

A man-sized figure—one arm raised, legs wide apart—was outlined in black on the paintless door, its chest and head blasted to splinters by double-ought buckshot and any number of small-arms rounds.

"He had a Hitler mustache, but it got blowed away," Basil explained.

"Target practice?" Dwight asked.

"More like a warning; lookit here." Basil caressed the edges of the torn chest cavity with his stubby fingers. "it's my contribution to the war effort. There's two dollars' worth of lead in this."

"And another two dollars' worth of lead in whatever you had stored in the garage," Dickie said. "I hope you remembered to take the car out."

"These here," Basil pointed to two holes that had missed the figure by inches, "Are Fuddy from the porch rocker with the navy Colt, only two misses out of six in rapid fire—some impressive."

"I'm surprised you got Skippy to hold still long enough to paint around him like that," said Dickie.

"We didn't," Basil said seriously. "We tried to. That's Fuddy. Longer arms."

Dwight smiled and shook his head. "I guess if the stranger comes around here I won't have to worry about taking a statement or any of the other pain-in-the-ass details of my office, like arrest papers or—"

Basil threw back his shoulders to increase his girth. "All you'll need is a big old canvas bag," he said proudly.

Gus tried to keep to the low shoulder of the ridge, where the boulders were huge and worn smooth, and there were fewer spruces. But growing among the boulders were vast, waist-high thickets of puckerbrush and juniper. Fighting through the cover, trying to keep a footing on the boulders underneath, he could not look around as he moved, and he did not dare cock the hammers on the gun, lest he slip. He took off his flannel jacket and tied it around his waist, but still he sweated through his shirt. He stopped and waited, stopped and waited, breathing through his open mouth to hear better, listening for Vergil—or anyone else.

After Gus crossed the trickle that would widen into Bridge Creek, he found himself in an unfamiliar, dense thicket of young spruce trees, their lower limbs dead and entangled. The only way through the vicious branches was to go crabwise, leading with a shoulder, squinting his eyes nearly shut to avoid getting them poked out. He had to go the last few yards on his hands and knees, finally emerging in a stand of scrub oaks. He sat on a boulder, brushing himself off, catching his breath, thinking that if he came to another such stand, he would skirt it. To hell with the straight line.

He either felt or heard the figure moving in the densest part of the thicket, just below him. It was man-sized and dark, and it moved a few steps, then stopped, then moved again, unhampered by the dense brake of limbs. It hitched when it moved, sniffed when it stopped; it was coming straight for him. Gus could not look straight at it, did not dare to, but he knew it was not wearing white bands. When it moved again, his bladder emptied into his trousers, hot and sudden, and he lowered himself into the brush beneath the boulder face down, his cheek pressed into the sharp juniper, the woody little trunks of bay bush digging into this ribs. Drenched in fear, mouth agape like a dead fish, he listened to the wispy footsteps as they came near, stopped abreast of him, then continued in the spruce, receding like a soft sigh.

After what may have been a half hour, he raised himself onto shaky elbows, his cheek afire from the prickly juniper, thinking that he should shout to warn Vergil, but knowing he would not. He stank of urine and the rich reek of the squashed and warmed salami sandwich in his breast pocket. His hands shook, and his face was wet with sweat and tears. He ran. He scrambled downhill through the brush, bent over as though under fire, oblivious of the granite edges that cut his shins and knees, determined to reach the road before the shape saw him and turned back. Just north of the Needle's Eye, where the road was washboarded, he emerged in the sunlit stretch and walked ten yards in the road. Then he crawled into the ferns to hide himself, sitting cross-legged in the dark, his head in his hands, catching his sobbing breath.

Three miles and a mountain away, Richard guided his truck over the gravel and bumps and ruts of the road on the west side of the island. Even in first gear, at less than five miles an hour, he scraped bottom on exposed knobs of granite ledge where the road was only fill. Cecil smoked in the passenger seat, staring down through the woods on the water side of the road. The piece of plank that Richard had fixed over the hole in the cab floor had worked loose, and dust rose between Cecil's knees. It and his cigarette smoke helped cover Richard's ripe, protein stench.

"This is stupid, and you know it," Richard said as he tried to scan each clump of trees, every jagged cleft of the mountainside as they passed. He steered with is right hand, his shotgun leaning out the window on his left forearm, where it could be seen.

"For somebody that thinks it's stupid, you're taking it pretty seriously," Cecil said.

"Well, we might run into him, but it will only be if he wants to be found," said Richard. "Look at those woods, those crannies; anybody could hide out in twenty square miles of that. It would take teams of bloodhounds, like they hunt niggers down South, to run somebody to ground on this island."

"We should have brought more people to ride in back and watch; this is the direction he was going when Lorna saw him coming back from the store," Cecil said a second time.

"What difference would it make?" Richard asked. "He isn't in Moore's Harbor; we can swear to that. Now it's only Eli's cabin and the Hamilton sheds in Duck Harbor; we'll have to set all afternoon at the Bowens place waiting for the guys to come off the mountain."

"Maybe he has a tent, or he built a lean-to." Cecil handed Richard a lit cigarette to increase the smoke in the cab. "Leah said he smelled like a campfire."

"She said he was clean shaven, too."

Richard stopped over a mossy creek that ran under the road and got out with a teacup for a drink. Cecil peed in the road, then climbed down to the creek to kneel and drink from his hand. The truck sputtered on idle, and Richard sprang into the seat to rev her up and clear her throat. Cecil stretched his legs and took his time getting back in, pulling the door shut as Richard began to roll.

His double barrels arranged in the window again, Richard looked at Cecil from the corner of his eye. He said he had been to visit his mother last night, and she had asked after Leah.

"Mother thinks her grief for Amos was made worse by the way he treated her in his will; but I told her no, she's not that kind of woman."

"And what kind of woman would that be?" Cecil acted offended to show that he had taken the bait, a little tug on Richard's line.

"Not the kind of woman to care more about inheritance than her father's death, that's all; not the kind to take being left out of his will the wrong way." Richard tugged back and thought he set the hook.

"Leah wouldn't want anyone to know, but your mother is right, at least about her being hurt—deeply hurt—to be left out like that."

Cecil confessed in a meek, crestfallen tone to let Richard think that he had been landed. He had traded places in the trucks with Dickie that morning in order to be alone with Richard, knowing full well that the lobster fisherman would bring up the subject of the will at some time just for the pleasure of feeding his rage. Cecil hadn't thought it would come this easily. What better way to play on Maggie's conscience than to have her hear that even the women in Stonington believed Leah was wasting away not only from the loss of Amos, but also because of Maggie's greed? What better way to retaliate to Richard's meanness than to use it to get that store in Blue Hill? Cecil was nothing if not practical. He lit a cigarette.

"Mother asked because she cares about Leah," Richard said. "She always has. Lots of people do. You hate to see someone like her, not a nasty bone in her body, brought so low."

"She'll be all right," Cecil confided. "She's eating regular again. She worries about Gus fishing alone; she's afraid that he won't finish school."

"You ought to get her off this island—move off, all three of you," Richard said sympathetically. "She could put her sorrow behind her and put that boy in school before he knocks up some dimwitted island girl and gets trapped down here."

"You're preaching to the choir," Cecil said, satisfied. "Here's the path to Eli Creek. Pull over there."

Richard followed Cecil down the windy path to the cabin, his shotgun loaded and riding in the crook of his arm. He wondered out loud to Cecil's stiff, unresponsive shoulders, how old Eli's cabin must be. He guessed fifty years. Richard said the last time he had been down here, an easy ten years ago, the place was leaking, and the chinking was dried and falling out. "Who the hell was Eli anyway," he asked, not expecting a reply and not getting one.

The path came out behind the cabin, which faced down the ledge toward the mouth of the creek and tide. Before he reached the little window, Cecil stopped suddenly, one hand up to signal a halt, and drew his revolver from his belt. Richard smelled the smoke, too, and stepped backward, surprised and nearly unmanned by fright. He took a deep breath, raised his shotgun to the level of Cecil's back, and followed slowly.

The door was propped wide open by a smooth brown

stone. Without a blink, Cecil stepped inside and whispered "Nobody here," before Richard had joined him.

The dark little room had been dusted and swept; the ashes in the fireplace were still too hot to touch. Richard watched, amazed, as Cecil climbed the ladder to the loft and peered over, exposing his helpless head to who knows what.

"Not here now," Cecil whispered.

"Christ God!" Richard said. "Look Cecil, a half a cabbage and store bread. It's him."

"He must have heard the truck," Cecil whispered. "He can't be far, but look—there's no gear, no clothes around. We should go get some help."

"No," said Richard abruptly. "No. Let's look around. Let's go down to the shore; he might have a boat."

At the edge of the creek, Cecil stopped to look upstream, then down toward the stony shore. The water, icy and clear and shallow, flowed from a dark pool in rivulets over a wide swath of granite onto the beach. On the far side, not twenty feet away, a man stood up suddenly from the brush, his arms limp at his sides.

"You're looking for me," he said, with a tone of finality.

Cecil raised a shaking pistol and pointed it at the man; Richard hopped away, leveled his shotgun at Cecil's back, and cocked both hammers.

"Put your hands up," Cecil said.

"I'm not armed." Pale and thin and clearly harmless, the man—or boy—hunched his delicate shoulders. "I won't give you any trouble. I'm ready to turn myself in. I have a suitcase."

"Leave it there and come out in the open, on the creek ledge," Cecil said, still covering the stranger, unaware that the muzzles of Richard's twelve-gauge was aimed at the small of his back.

The man slipped on the moss but gained his balance and stood in two inches of water in the middle of the ledge.

"Who are you and what the hell are you doing here?" asked Cecil.

"I'm Henry Fairlee," he said. "I'm AWOL from my unit—the First Division. I came here to hide. I've been here nearly a month, and now I want to give up. I have to face it."

Cecil lowered his pistol, and behind him, Richard released his breath and lowered his gun, easing the hammers into place.

"The First Division's shipped overseas," Richard said. "You're a deserter, a goddamned coward."

"Yes," said Henry Fairlee.

"You'll have to face a court martial," said Cecil.

"Or worse," said Richard with some satisfaction.

"Yes, worse," Henry Fairlee said. "I'll have to face my father."

"Get your suitcase," Cecil said. "We'll take you to the constable and he'll take you to wherever it is you're supposed to go."

Richard stepped forward to stand with Cecil; he lifted his shotgun. "Hold open that coat and turn around so we can see you aren't armed," he said.

"All right, let's go then."

Friday,
September 9, 1942

Dear Ruth,

    I should be out patrolling tonight, but it's been such an odd and busy day that Gus and I decided to take a night off, to leave the cold waters for the Vinalhaven and Swan's Island patrol boats. It's nice to be home, or I should say nice to be here in this house and feel that it's home, even though I am here alone, and not with him, as I allowed myself to dream. In daylight I wrestle with my anger and try to keep it at bay; in twilight I abide with grief.

Did I tell you that I moved his kitchen table to the western window in the parlor and that I write to you on it in the late afternoon light? I do. I am now, and it is a consolation for me.

Yes, of course my precipitous move stirred up the biddies. (No, I can't explain why I did it; it just happened.) They were already clucking about his leaving it to me; when I moved in, they reacted with a frenzy of indignation. Gus keeps me informed. No one says anything to me, of course, nor I to them. I will not give them the satisfaction of allowing their disapproval to embitter me. Their other target is Betty Chambers, who had the gall to dance cheek to cheek with Morales at the Labor Day Social and is reputed to have been seen smooching with him afterward. They consider Morales nothing better than a Negro, and the words "wicked" and "strumpet" have been used for her. Gus is outraged for Morales's sake and almost got into a fight with Fuddy because of a smarmy comment. He can't understand how they can behave so, and I am at a loss to explain.

At least Gus and I can talk. I think he's being teased about Mabel Eaton, whom he swears (falsely) he is not sweet on. I wish I had gone to the social and seen him dancing "close" with her. I would have attended if I had thought that Mr. Gardinier was going to be there. I would like to have seen him and thank him personally for the kind notes he's sent since the funeral. (No, I am *not* sweet on him.)

I realized this afternoon how successfully I have been deluding myself about Amos's fall these past weeks. I had myself convinced (it's so easy to do when we need to) that someone or something, other than that damned rum was responsible for the accident. I even reported my suspicions to the Coast Guard. There was a rumor of a stranger hiding out on the island, and I thought that would somehow prove me right. But our men found the poor fellow today, and after I quizzed him (privately in the cab of Richard's truck), I came away believing that he was not on the island that night, nor had he seen anyone suspicious in his weeks of hiding out. He was as forlorn and frightened a young man as I have ever seen (AWOL from his unit and his fellow man). His plight made me angry and ashamed of myself and deeply saddened for all of us.

But I'll ignore my shame, as I try to ignore my grief, and direct my anger at the Hun, as we all must. Damn him, as Gus is wont to say. And damn the ones who are more interested in vilifying their neighbors than they are in the war and what lurks in the water all around us.

Now I've gone on and on, and ended on a sour note. I'll not start another page but send you my love briefly here in the margin. Thank you, as always, for listening.

Love,
Maggie

CHAPTER TWELVE

AFTER LUNCH, HARVEY GOODS CLIMBED THE CIRCLING IRON STAIRS of the cold stone tower toward the light. At the halfway window, he stopped, belched tunafish, remembered his mother (who had warned him that it made him "repeat"), and idly watched two dory-looking boats drifting, together, about a half-mile east. He thought they must be handlining for haddock beyond the shoal, but saw that they were awfully far from shore without a mother boat. At the door to the light, he tied on the linen apron he wore to protect the lens and brasswork from his soiled clothes, slapped the dust from his pant legs, and let himself in.

They said that the worst thing about being a lighthouse keeper was that you had too much time to think, but for Harvey the worst thing was Morales: his whorehouse-sweet hair oil, his wiggling ass, his fucking cowboy hat, his ease with codes and signal equipment and electrical gadgets, his Hawaiian shirts. Harvey didn't believe him for a minute when he hinted that he was ding-ing Betty Chambers, but it galled him unmercifully to think of Morales rubbing up against her, maybe even seeing and feeling her white titties. He wished Chief Gardiner would tell Morales to shut up once in a while, but the chief let him rattle on in his fake Boston accent and even seemed to like him sometimes.

Other than the little bedroom, which was nothing more than a place to sleep or lie awake dreaming of home, the light was Harvey's domain, and keeping it and the lens working and clean was his specialty; this job was, as he said in a letter home, where he shined. The light was also where he could be alone for a few hours every afternoon, away from Morales's preening and the chief's instruction manual, away from all of their annoying little habits. Inside the lens, where the world outside was refracted in a hundred bright angles, where the lonely rock and sea around was broken into hundreds of harmless little postcard images that all changed in unison as he moved, he polished the brasswork and oiled the fittings with sleepy, habitual care. Standing on a footstool, Harvey polished the outside of the lens with soft diapers, wiping each of the angled refractors with a smooth sweep. If the government did order the lighthouses to go dark, as the chief kept predicting, the Germans wouldn't have any more use for them and would probably use them for target practice. If they went dark, Morales would probably stay to keep up the weather reports and for communications; they'd let Harvey—the light man—go, and he'd be drafted sure as shit. He wouldn't miss the rock or them or this godforsaken Maine coast, but he would miss his light and lens. He hated the thought that someone else might be hired to care for it when they turned it back on.

Outside, on the gallery, he walked around into the lee, lit a cigarette, and leaned on the railing. Below, the chief was on his knees, weeding the edge of the bed of marigolds by the boat slip. The sea was nearly flat calm; if Harvey spat there wouldn't be breeze enough to carry the saliva beyond the broad base of the tower. The two boats he had seen earlier had moved in some, and he could tell that they were dories after all. They drifted close together, coming in on the tide, and in the closer one there was a little figure making some kind of motion. Through the binoculars he could just make out a man waving something back and forth over his head—back and forth, in a slow arc.

Through cupped hands, his burning cigarette between the fingers of one, he shouted to the chief, sending half the basking harbor seal colony sliding into the water. Jake stood and brushed his knees, looking up, trowel in hand, the crows' feet gathered in the corners of his eyes.

"There's somebody in trouble out there, to the east'ard," Harvey shouted. "He's waving something. Two dories."

"You sure it's not lifeboats?" Jake's voice sent the rest of the seals into the sea. "It could be survivors from the Norwegian freighter."

"It's dories," Harvey shouted. "Come see."

"You come down here, PDQ," Jake yelled. "Collect the blankets, and bring them down to the slip. Morales!" he turned to the house. "Get your ass in gear; we're going to launch her."

When Giuseppe Clarrutaro saw the gray launch making its way toward them, rising and sinking on the low swells beyond the shoals, he slumped to the dory seat and wept like a child into his wrinkled hands.

"What is it, cappie?" Akers nudged Clarrutaro's knee with the bailing scoop but got no response. He steadied himself on the gunwale and rose on aching legs to squint toward the distant lighthouse, barely visible against the dark shoreline.

"Jesus! Oh, Jesus!" he cried, waving the scoop. "Ship your oars. Look there, a cutter; no, a launch. Johnson, Buchard!" he shouted to the other dory, "Look to port. A boat. We're saved!"

At once, the oarsmen in both dories rose, shouting, poking at the heavens with their oars, then in pairs and in threes, the rest of the eighteen were on their uncertain feet, screaming like gulls, hugging one another, waving, weeping. A leaping pair in Johnson's boat fell onto the gunwale, and the dory shipped a foot of water before their mates pulled them in. Clarrutaro, his crucifix between his pressed palms, sank to his knees in the bilge and with the believing half of his crew, offered a prayer of thanksgiving.

"They're fishermen all right," Morales said. "But how can there be so many? What kind of fishing boat has a crew that size?" He stood ready with the gaff on the starboard side of the launch while Jake brought the boat around on a swell.

"What happened?" Jake asked the dory they gaffed. "Who are you?"

"You're the most beautiful men I've ever seen, both of you," said an oarsman.

"You're captains," said another. "Admirals."

"Angels," rasped a man whose hands were wrapped in strips of undershirt. "Fucking saints."

"Hard down on that, Wakefield; shut your foul mouth." Clarrutaro reached across the gunwales to take Morales's hand. "We're trawlermen," he said. "I'm Giuseppe Clarrutaro, skipper of the *Ben and Josephine*; this is my crew here. That's Oscar Johnson, captain of the *Aeolus*, and his crew. U-boats sank both of us yesterday at dawn with their deck guns."

"Did you lose anybody?"

"Grindle and Pisano got burned. Oscar lost his dog, Spook; the rest of us are okay, thanks to God."

"A U-boat?" Morales was incredulous. "I never heard of a U-boat attacking a fisherman."

"Not a U-boat, son," Clarrutaro said. "Two of them. They sent both our boats to the bottom, and we never did a damn thing to deserve it."

"We can take a few of you aboard here, but we'll have to tow the rest of you," Jake said. "Let's get going before the wind picks up. If you'd had a breeze, you never would've gotten in this close."

"If we'd had any weather at all," said the oarsman, "We would all have been drowned. Look what we got for freeboard— no more than two hands of it; we'd of swamped, sure."

Praise God," Clarrutaro said.

Jake nosed the bow of the launch into the cradle, and Morales threw the bow line to Harvey, who secured it to the winch.

"Get these fellows up to the house where they can lie down, and pour some coffee into them," Jake said. "We'll pull the dories ashore."

Harvey waded in to help the three boys and older man—one at a time—off the launch and up through the slippery rock-weed to dry ground. Unlike the others, who were shouting and laughing and kissing the ground as they tried to drag the dories ashore, these four were wrapped in blankets as they shivered silently; the limpest of them, a man about Harvey's age, got Morales's blanket with the bucking broncos on it. When Harvey led him—almost carried him—to dry land, he started crying. Harvey didn't know what to say as he sat him down, so he simply told the man that he would be right back with the last guy and would take them all inside.

He offered them bunks, but they smiled, shook their heads, and sank into the chairs in the front room; outside, someone let out a war whoop, and another answered him. Harvey left the four with a pack of Luckies and went to fetch them coffee. When he came back, the weepy one was asleep, his chin on his chest. They carried him into Morales's bunk, where the old man pulled off his shoes and socks and tucked him in, smoothing his salty hair.

Outside there were men everywhere, some sitting on the stoop smoking, others washing each other down with buckets of fresh water. Three, with raised V signs, were posing for Morales's camera at the base of the lighthouse. Harvey found Jake talking to a dark-skinned man, whom he introduced as Captain something. They were talking quietly and watching a man in skivvies as he wrung out his shirt and called for another bucket over his head.

"The Coast Guard's sending out a cutter first thing in the morning," Harvey interrupted. "I told them we could get them to the mainland with the help of fishermen from the mainland, but they want them to wait here. I guess they don't want anybody talking until after the ensign debriefs them. I opened up all the beans, and they're cooking now. I'm going to get a stew going here right away."

"That's okay for tonight," Jake said. "But what about to-morrow? They won't get here until late in the day, if they get here tomorrow at all. Our pantry's nearly empty," he told Clar-rutaro. "It's the end of the month, and the tender doesn't come for another four days."

"We'll be all right, Chief." Clarrutaro put his hand on Jake's shoulder.

"Hold that pose, Captain," said Morales looking down into his Brownie. Harvey's mossy smile faded when he saw Morales move the camera to exclude him from the picture.

"The food problem's been taken care of," Harvey said. "I called Barter Island's Coastal Picket station at the church. I talked to a Miss Chambers (he gave Morales a look) and told her we had survivors ashore and they were hungry. I didn't say a num-ber in the clear, just a lot of them. She said they'd be here at first light with food, and I bet they will."

"If you have flour," Clarrutaro said, "I've got a man, Dias, who makes the best biscuits in New England."

"Dias?" Harvey said.

"You go make that stew," said Jake.

"He used his deck gun?" Jake continued, when Harvey and Morales had left. "At what distance?"

"He took our bow clean off with the second shot. When we got everybody overboard, he moved in and blew her to bits with the 88 and the machine guns. Then he just steamed off. In a minute we heard the other one open up on the *Aeolus* the same way, and we could see her go down. Oscar got his men into the boat, but he went back aboard to find his dog. It's a little Spitz. Spook must have been hiding from the noise; he couldn't find him. When Oscar finally jumped for it, they hit his fuel tank; that's how Pisano and Grindle got burned—the dory was so close to the explosion."

"Two of them," said Jake. "The Coast Guard's going to have a hard time believing that."

Clarrutaro shrugged his shoulders. "We've seen them in pairs before. Everybody who fishes off the Grand Banks has

seen U-boats. We didn't bother them by reporting their posi-
tions and they didn't bother us. At least, not until now."

Jake looked at Oscar Johnson, who sat leaning against the
boathouse, smoking in the shade near a man sleeping face
down on his forearm. The lighthouse keeper said Johnson
looked like a man who had just lost his best friend.

"He has," said Clarrutaro. "And his boat, too, the poor
bastard."

"But he saved his crew—you both did, for Christ's sake. I
think we ought to have a drink on that, don't you?" Jake asked.

"I thought you'd never ask."

Betty Chambers set one of her market baskets on the stoop
and pushed open the north door to the keeper's house to meet
a moist, malodorous cloud of body odor, salt, and other fester-
ing things. She stepped back and wiped her nose on her sleeve.
When she stood inside among the sprawl of sleeping figures,
she thought that there was something sweet beneath the stink—
the smell of her brother's little bedroom in the morning, of the
stuff the sandman left in the corners of his eyes. Some of the
survivors were covered with coats on the couch and in chairs,
but most were wrapped in blankets on the floor. The three in the
center of the room slept curled up together like spoons for the
warmth.

Harvey sat up on the couch, full of wonder. He blinked and
squished his lips with his fingers.

"You must be Betty Chambers," he said.

"Yes, I am." Her light brown hair was parted in the middle and
rested like soft wings over her ears. Her knee-length skirt showed
legs the likes of which Harvey had seen only in magazines.

"Jeekers," he said.

Betty looked over her shoulder for Maggie, who was coming up the path with a covered laundry basket.

"I'm Harvey Goods," Harvey combed his hair with his hand. "I talked to you on the radio yesterday."

"I'm pleased to meet you, Harvey," she said. "Where's the kitchen?" She scanned the sleeping faces for a dark one and was surprised to see several—none of them Morales. Harvey pointed to the kitchen and hurried to relieve Maggie of the heavy basket; she thanked him and went down the dark hallway to rouse Jake. Maggie stepped over sleeping forms, some of which were beginning to stir, and began to open the windows. In the east, the very tip of the sun, pumpkin colored, showed itself on the watery horizon. For the first time, she was surprised, and a little afraid, to be on so small a rock in the middle of the ocean. Once in Jake's room, she smelled his soap and hair oil, and turned to greet him, her hand extended.

"Good morning, Maggie," Jake said, shaking her hand. "You were very good to come, thank you. Was it cold on the water?"

Gus passed, leaning backward with a heavy box that he rode on his belt.

"No, just dark," she said. "Were there any lost? Are any of them hurt?"

"Nobody was killed," he answered. "U-boats with deck guns and machine guns blew their boats to bits; it's a miracle they're all alive. Two have burns. Let me get these guys up and give you a hand; one of them's a damn good cook."

"No, don't wake them up." said Maggie. "This is our department. You can help carrying in the rest of it and clearing these tables. Leave the kitchen to us, just keep people out while we're cooking."

"There's more? asked Jake. "Christ almighty." He waved to a man who sat up in the middle of the floor rubbing his eyes. "Come give us a hand Akers," he said. "Where did it all come from?"

Gus and Betty stood in the kitchen entrance listening wide-eyed to Morales's solemn account of the rescue.

"Look at them," Maggie said, "They are rapt withal."

"What?"

"Nothing," said Maggie. "The casseroles and baked goods are from the island ladies, as fresh as can be, some still warm. The store goods—the coffee, sugar, milk, bacon, butter, cigarettes—are from Gus's father Cecil, a contribution, made, I might say, quite sincerely."

"Coffee and cigarettes, too?" he asked. "I thought you said Cecil was—"

She shot him a look and nodded toward Gus.

"Ah," he said. "Well, he's damn generous. At least you can let me take your coat."

"Thank you." She pulled her scarf free. "But first take this." From the Very gun holster inside her coat, Maggie brought forth a bottle in a paper bag. Jake grinned.

"All ours got drunk up last night," he said.

"We thought so," she said.

"Is this from Cecil too," he asked.

"No, it's from Amos. Where are those boys with the burns?"

The patter of shoes, the smell of food, and the sound of women's voices soon had the crewmen rising from their ghostly sleep on the floor. Guiseppe Clarrutaro's announcement that the kitchen was off limits while the ladies were cooking only created a logjam of shoulders in the doorway, so he and Jake herded the crewmen outside to wait until they were called. Only Caetano and Akers, in charge of clearing and setting the table—and Dias the biscuit man—were allowed to stay inside. When the men were invited back in, one at a time, to take a plate of bacon and eggs and biscuits and pancakes passed from the women to Dias in the doorway, the house no longer smelled of sweat and cigarettes and fear, but of coffee and bacon and longing.

While Gus and Morales washed the returning plates, Maggie and Betty served coffee and muffins and dishes of pie to the quiet ones who languished in the front room and to the noisier smokers on the stoop, who begged Betty to sit with them. A skinny man with blue eyes and a salt-starched shirt knelt on one knee clutching a bouquet of uprooted marigolds and asked her to marry him; she turned him down, saying that she was too young.

George Grindle, whose scalded cheek and hands were freshly wrapped in bandages white as snow, followed Maggie outside and invited her and Harvey to come see the dories; two other crewmen saw Jake headed toward them and fell in behind him. The tide was full; disturbed by an increasing westerly breeze, it lapped and splashed at the dory rudders at the water's edge.

Maggie leaned over the gunwale of the dory Grindle said was his. The half-foot of water in the boat's bottom had ripened in the sun and smelled vaguely of dead sea things and vomit. Jake stood behind her, his feet awash.

"So much for Richard Snell and those like him who swear that U-boats won't go after fishermen," he said.

"Yes," she agreed. "And when they find out that it was U-boats—two of them, and innocent fishermen—Gus's parents aren't going to let him fish offshore or go patrolling any more."

"How could they keep him from it?"

"Why, they'd make him promise," she said, a little surprised. "What could he possibly say to dissuade them?"

"I guess he could say there's a war on," suggested Jake. "What about you? Isn't that what you'd say if I asked you to quit?"

Maggie pursed her lips and turned her head, smiling to herself. She had thought while they were feeding the men that she would invite Jake to dinner but realized that she couldn't entertain him in Amos's house. She just couldn't, however nonsensical the reason.

Harvey and Akers tacked a faded flag onto the blade of one of the twelve-foot oars and raised it above the dories. While Harvey held it in place, other crewmen brought rocks to shore it up.

"Where'd Miss Betty go?" asked the blue-eyed suitor as he set down two skull-shaped stones.

Harvey looked around for brown faces within earshot.

"Don't ask," he said. "You don't want to know; it'd turn your stomach. You'd upchuck your blueberry pancakes."

"Don't tell me," said the suitor. "She's gone off with the guy in the Stetson."

"The spick in the Stetson, you mean." Harvey shook his head sadly and stood back to admire the flag that flapped and rippled in the breeze.

Jake rolled the paper bag down the neck of the bottle, uncorked it, and held it poised over Giuseppe Clarrutaro's coffee cup.

"Hair of the dog?" he asked.

"I don't mind if I do."

Jake poured slowly, reverently.

"That's good," said the captain.

Jake kept pouring. "It is, isn't it?"

The trawlerman said whoa and held up his hand when his cup was half full. Jake sat down at the table, pushed a brimming ashtray aside, and poured two fingers for himself.

"She doesn't look like any schoolteacher I've ever seen," said Clarrutaro. "Schoolteachers are fat and ugly or mean and twisted. If I was in her school, I'd misbehave so she'd keep me after." The skipper took a sip and flapped his eyelids in appreciation.

"She's a fucking saint." Wakefield stood at the table with an empty cup.

"You know I hate that," the captain said. "And I hate a moocher."

Jake poured Wakefield a cup and waved him away.

"She likes you some," said the trawlerman. "I can tell by the way she looks at you and stands up close when she's talking to you, brushes against you. I won't mention how you look at her."

"She's just friendly, and sort of neighborly and polite," Jake stared into his cup. "She does that with Morales too. She's too much a lady for a guy like me. More important, she lost the only man she cared about this summer and she hasn't gotten over him."

"She will."

"I don't believe it," said Jake.

A lone gull, on his own evening patrol, scaled along the cliffs eighty feet above the water; it passed Maggie and Gus at shoulder height, flapped once, and turned out to the darkening sea. Maggie stopped in a clearing where only a few dead and blasted spruce were left among the boulders. She knew without looking down—something she hadn't done since he fell—that the tide was high by the sound of the water on the rocks. She and Gus had come to walk the cliff patrol together tonight to see if what they heard was true. They watched seaward and waited, counting the eighteen seconds to themselves.

"It's true," Gus said. "The light's out."

"Yes it is," she said quietly. "Like the lights of Europe."

"It's creepy. I wonder what will happen to those guys."

"I don't know. Harvey was worried that having lost the lighthouse for navigation, the U-boats wouldn't have any use for it and would blow it up because of the radio."

"Now they have good reason to put up blackout curtains," said Gus.

"Look how bright the moon is on the water," she said. "I'm tired tonight; I wish I'd brought a thermos."

They followed Amos's path, widened by their own use; it favored the stands of birch and maple over the impenetrable spruce, and avoided the more dangerous granite upheavals.

"She made me promise again this morning, as if I didn't already," said Gus. "I got mad."

"I'm not surprised," she said. "That she asked you again, I mean. Try to understand her. You'll be leaving for Jonesport in less than a month anyway."

"She's treating me like a kid," he said.

Maggie laughed. "It's Fuddy, and the others, isn't it? You're worried that they'll call you a mama's boy. If Fuddy does, knock him overboard, and when he comes to the surface ask him how many nights *he's* spent out on the cold water this year. You're not a mama's boy, and you know it."

"Who will you take with you?" he asked.

"I want to ask Betty Chambers—she's not afraid to get things done—but I know they wouldn't permit it, two women. I don't know yet."

"You won't go alone."

"I promise I won't," she said.

Maggie sat on the boulder on the cushion moss while Gus went ahead with the light to check the cabin. When he returned in the gathering dark, he sat next to her, reclining on his elbows on the moss.

Maggie wondered if the changes wrought in Gus by the events of the summer would make his last year of high school an easier one.

"Do you think he's here?" Gus asked.

"Only in memory."

Gus lay silent for a long minute. "It wasn't memory that made me see the figure of a man up on the mountain," he said.

"You didn't tell me about that."

"He didn't make any noise in the spruce branches when he pushed through them. He didn't stumble on the rocks. I was so scared I hid on the ground when he walked by," he said. "I peed my pants."

"It was fear that created that shape," she said. "Though perhaps memory, too, and regret."

"What memory? Of Amos's spirits, of him? It was more than memory," Gus said. "Besides, you don't believe in anything after life; you called ghosts 'hundred-ton potatoes,' whatever that means."

She smiled. Was he teasing her for always quoting things, or did he really hear 'a hundred ton'?

"Underdone," she articulated. "A fragment of underdone potato. Don't you remember Scrooge and Marley?"

"Sort of." He did now. "But not the potato."

"He meant that the ghost only existed because of indigestion," she said. "A dangerous thing to say to a shade, he soon learned."

Gus's eyelids grew as heavy as they did at his school desk. "Uh-huh," he said. His eyes closed, he slipped his mooring, went adrift, then to sleep.

She poked him awake with the binoculars and said, "Look at this," pointing to their left, north of the Sheep Ledges.

He took the binoculars and focused on the black silhouette of a large lobsterboat making its slow way seaward in the moonlight.

"It's not memory?" he asked innocently. "Or fear?"

"No, smart aleck, it's a boat," she said. "Perhaps he's going to the lighthouse."

"If he is, he's steering too far north. It's not an island boat; none of the ones down here have that much house on them. Coming from the northwest, he could be from anywhere—Stonington, Castine, any of the Deer Isle harbors. He's too small to be going fishing—offshore, look how he pitches already—and there's no shoals where he's headed, not to fish."

"He could be going to Bar Harbor," she said. "Or somewhere else along the coast. It couldn't be the Swan's Island patrol boat; he's too far south."

"Or he could be a new patroller we don't know about." Gus put the binoculars in her lap. "I'm going down to the boat and try to raise him on the radio, or call Morales if that doesn't work. Morales would know; it's probably nothing, but it won't hurt to check. You wait here."

He was gone for what seemed a long hour. When he returned, he said he had lost the path in the dark, not wanting to show a light. He couldn't raise the boat on the radio, and Jake knew nothing about a new patrol boat, or any boat for that matter. He certainly wasn't expecting company.

"No," Maggie said. "He didn't go toward the lighthouse. I lost sight of him ten minutes ago, but he was holding a steady course, a little south of east—ninety-five degrees I'd guess." She pointed.

"He could have gone anywhere. Jake says not to worry about it."

"Nevertheless, I'm going to stay here to see if he comes back," Maggie said. "You ought to go home and get some sleep."

"I'm not going," he said. "I want to see for myself. We can take watches."

"I'll go to the house and get some tea and some warm clothes; no need to hide a light now, I guess."

When the boat returned in the hour before the false dawn, Maggie used the binoculars to follow him, barely visible in the last of the moonlight. He was on the same heading and would pass just north of the island.

"Damn it," she said.

"What is it?" Gus sat up. "Him? Why are you cussing?"

"Yes, the same boat." She passed him the binoculars. "Because if we'd had our wits about us, we would have moved to the northern head and seen him better when he passed by."

Perhaps he's a smuggler of some kind, though I can't imagine what he'd be smuggling. He can't have gone to the border and back in six hours; I doubt he even went as far as Bar Harbor."

"Or he went to see his girl and traveled by water so no one would stop him for using gas illegally," he said. "I just thought of that."

"How romantic," she said. "A nocturnal tryst."

"A what?"

His dinner pail dangling from the handlebars, Gus dragged his feet in the gravelly road to slow his descent into the cove. He had come an hour early this morning to catch her before she left for school at six. He'd gone to bed early, tired from their watch the night before, but had awakened at three and had lain on his back chasing stray thoughts until he rose to wash at five. As he passed his parents' room, his father's grinding snore—he felt, or rather knew for certain—that Maggie had not slept either and that she knew he'd show up early, before first light.

He knocked and let himself in to find her at her writing table, marking someone's homework with a red pencil. When she rose to greet him, he saw that her eyes were as red as the bright spot on her lips where she'd wetted the pencil.

"Did you see him again?" he asked.

"Yes, I did." She pushed the pencil into her gathered hair. "He went out at the same time, on the same heading. Sit down and I'll get us some tea; mine's gone cold." She gestured at the rocker, but he followed her into the kitchen.

"And came back?" he asked.

She lifted the cozy from the teapot and poured two strong cups. "Around midnight it grew hazy and hid the moon, so I went up to the head in hopes that I could hear him returning, even if I couldn't see him. And I did—hear him, I mean. He woke me up, I must confess. He went around the head, through the Burnt Island Thorofare, and up into the bay. I couldn't see him; he must have been hugging the far shore, though he sounded so close."

"There," he said. "Damn it. I knew it. I should have gone with you."

"What good would that have done? Well, perhaps two witnesses rather than. . . . What are you so jittery about? For heaven's sake, take your tea and sit down. You haven't slept either, have you?"

"Jesus Christ don't you see what damn fools we've been? No, I didn't either until last night."

"Stop swearing and explain, please."

He drew a folded chart from inside his shirt, and made room for it on the kitchen table, weighting the folds with two lamps.

"I'm sorry, but look." His index finger started at the northern tip of Barter Island and moved slowly seaward. "You go ten miles on a heading of ninety-five degrees, and you either turn north toward Bar Harbor or . . ." He tapped the chart. "Or you go five more miles on the same heading, and you end up here."

He looked at Maggie for some sign of understanding, but she only nodded, waiting.

"This is the end of the shoal, and this," he drew an oblong circle, "is the flat, sandy bottom. Remember?"

"Where Amos saw the U-boat," she whispered.

"Yes," he lied. "And it may be where he saw this same lobsterboat going out and coming back in."

"May be?" she asked. "You're only inferring that, guessing. He didn't tell you? Why didn't he?"

"No, and he didn't tell me that he was watching the cabin from a distance, either. Maybe he was tired of not being believed and wanted to be sure."

Gus watched her as she pumped a rush of fresh water into the kettle and set it back on the stove. In the shaving mirror she saw the red smear on her lip and wiped it away with a washcloth.

"So, you think," she said, "that the submarine Amos saw, or another, is using the same hiding place, the sandy bottom, and that this boat is meeting him there as he departs for his nightly hunt in the Halifax lane."

"I think he's taking the Germans supplies—food, water, fuel, I don't know what—and maybe information about ship movements," Gus said slowly. "I think there's a good chance they'll meet up again tonight."

"A spy," she said. "A traitor. We'll call Mr. Gardiner and tell him we've seen the boat again, going to the same place. He'll report it to Rockland this time, I'm sure."

"I'm not." Gus folded the chart and turned the lamp down, then cupped his hand over the chimney to blow it out and let the vague morning light increase in the kitchen. "Even if he does call it in, it won't amount to anything; with the thousand other sightings they can't do anything about, it won't even get marked on some coastal chart."

"Perhaps we can do something," she said, "But what?" She closed her eyes, and when she did, Gus smiled, knowing that once he had gotten her this far, she would not turn back.

"We—the Quahog, and the lighthouse launch—could lie in wait for this fellow and intercept him," she said, opening her eyes anew. "But no, you promised your mother."

"Come with me," he said.

"Where to?" She glanced at her watch.

"To the shore. It won't take but a few minutes; you won't be late for school."

"Can't you just tell me what it is?"

"No," he said. "You have to see it."

The fog bank that had hidden the moon in the night had retreated to the open sea, where it hid the sun but not the light that spread over it toward the land. Maggie followed him down the dewy path, past the pile of rotting lobster traps and broken barrels behind the fish shacks.

"Gus, I haven't even packed my lunch yet; I still have six more tests to grade."

"Please," he said. He offered her his hand and led her across a plank behind Amos's shack, over tar-covered boulders to a small path that led uphill into the spruces.

"You have to duck to get through here." He released her hand and disappeared into a tunnel of limbs. She hesitated, folded her arms across her chest, then shook her head and followed—like Alice, she thought, following the white rabbit.

When she emerged from the scratchy tunnel, she found Gus standing in a small clearing next to a huge pile of dead brush, his hands behind his back like an impresario waiting for his audience to settle. She looked at her watch to get the show going, then stood impatiently while he removed the cover of fading branches from the mound to slowly reveal a tarred and tattered canvas. Beyond the trees behind her, the sound of a lobsterboat on its way south to the Turnip Yard reverberated in the cove.

"What is it?" she demanded. She imagined a large machine—a boiler of some kind—with odd curves and awkward angles.

"Help me with this tarp; it's Christly heavy." Gus wiped his face on his sleeve.

On a rough base made of heavy, hewn spruce and piling spikes, two blue, fifty-five-gallon fuel drums rested on a slanted structure, one drum above the other, angled upward, each held in place on the runners by knee chocks and a wide plank. On top of the drums, tied in place with cod line, were coils of black cord painted with evenly spaced red stripes. Gus stood with his hands in his armpits while she walked the length, then the width, in a close inspection. It was Amos's work, not Gus's, she saw.

"What's in them?" she finally asked.

"Black powder packed around a stick of dynamite. The fuses are waterproof; each of the marks is for ten fathoms. We worked out the timing with other drums filled with sand and gravel that we rolled overboard with measuring lines on them."

"Do you intend to use this on the *Quahog*?" She was surprised by the thought.

"Why do you think he wanted a bigger boat?" he asked. "We measured a hundred times if we measured once to make sure it's built to fit just right, and it is. See those holes in the runners? We'll cut a path through the trees, then put a block and tackle on the launcher up here and a winch down below; at high tide, we'll ease it down on log rollers, winch it aboard, and clench it down with lag bolts. Just like that."

"Just like that," Maggie said. "And then set sail to do battle with a U-boat."

Gus nodded. "We'll need luck to get over him and even more to hit him, but we've got the speed and—"

"Exactly who is this *we*?" She knew too well.

"You know," he said.

Maggie laughed. "Oh no," she said, raising her palm to halt his talk. "We're under orders to observe, to report—not to engage. You promised your mother. This would be ridiculous; it would be suicide; I won't have any part of it."

Gus had prepared for her arguments, but was angry nevertheless. "It isn't patrolling, and it's not the *Quahog* anymore," he said. "When Jake sees this and how well it's rigged, he'll go along with it."

Maggie didn't understand what he meant about the name, but she knew where Jake would stand. "No he won't. Nor will I. It's out of the question."

"I'll get Vergil to go with me," he said. "I'll go it alone if I have to, goddammit."

They locked eyes, and neither blinked.

"I forbid it," she said evenly. "The *Quahog* is my boat. The half share he left you was in the *Tuna*, before we bought this one. Do you dare dispute that?"

"No," he said, his face set against her. "The *Quahog*'s yours. And you're going to be late to school."

She thought to respond in kind to the snide tone in his voice but would not. She turned her back on him and made her way down to the shore. As she passed between the shacks at the foot of the wharf, she noticed that the *Quahog*'s transom had been freshly painted; the brass letters had been removed and replaced with the name *Amos Coombs*.

PART THREE

The Battle of the Atlantic

"But remember this. You'll find it hard to perform your duty unless you risk your ship. There's folly and there's foolhardiness on one side, and there's daring and calculation on the other. Make the right choice."

—Admiral Cornwallis to
Commander Hornblower,
HORNBLOWER AND THE HOTSPUR, C. S. Forester

CHAPTER THIRTEEN

U235 WAS OPERATING ON THE CONVOY ROUTE BETWEEN HALIFAX and St. John's, patrolling slowly, running on one diesel engine at a time to conserve fuel. So far this had been Captain Reising's most disappointing patrol. The radio reports he had monitored from other U-boat captains boasted of the greatest successes anyone had yet heard of, but after four weeks out, U235 had fired only four of her torpedoes and sunk only three freighters for a total of 15,100 tons. Six months ago, three sinkings would have been remarkable, but now it was commonplace. Though he was determined to continue patrolling while he still had a little fuel left, Reising was worried about his crew: a fight had broken out in the torpedo room, half of them were wrenched with diarrhea, and even the old timers were surly and grumbling. He hoped for one sighting, one radio report from another U-boat of a convoy, one stroke of good luck to send him back to Lorient with respectable tonnage. He would never match Prien and Kretchmer at this pace; he would never even make 100,000 tons.

His officers collected every ounce of data and argued over their conclusions twice before they agreed that the boat could stay on patrol until 0700 hours the next day. At that time, all things taken into account, they would have to begin the return trip across the Atlantic. With the fuel they had left, they could travel on the surface with both diesels and make a relatively quick crossing. Even Obersteuerman Achen, who lived for the hunt, had turned his fierce eyes homeward. For two weeks, what food they had left had been running out, one commodity at a time; the loaves of black bread still strung in hammocks had turned so hoary with mold that the crew called them white rabbits. The men were lucky to have a thin soup that tasted of diesel fuel; they had long ago eaten the last of the canned meat. They smothered everything they ate with strawberry preserves, trying to kill the taste of diesel and decay.

When word got around among the crew that they would be sailing home in the morning, the men began to smile for the first time in a week. Praeger resurrected his accordion. In the crew's quarters, blond, wavy-haired Mardsden, who still had not managed to grow a beard, began cutting white pennants from his bedding. Kung and Siegemann, both naked but for a pair of shorts and both covered with grease like painted Indians, rigged a table on top of the two forward torpedoes. They painted the tonnage of each of their three kills on the pennants: 7,000; 4,000; and 4,100. When they came into Lorient, they would be proud to fly the pennants from the conning-tower cable. It might not be a record, or win the Knight's Cross for the captain, but it was a successful patrol, and they had contributed that many more tons to the Third Reich's goal of wringing England's neck.

That night, when things had settled back into routine, Liebe, the radioman, found Captain Reising asleep in the control room. He shook his superior's shoulder gently and handed him the message he had just decoded. U235 was to break off its patrol immediately and proceed to grid square BC43, ninety-five miles east of the Newfoundland coast, there to rendezvous with U413, a milch cow, for refueling and further orders. Captain Reising rubbed his face, adjusted his white cap, and told the radioman to send his watch officers to him straightaway.

Huddled over the chart table in the control room, he and his officers plotted their course in silence, each shutting down any hopes he may have had for going home.

"Now we'll have another chance," Reising said. "And we'll make the best of it. Our orders say only fuel; they don't mention food or fresh water, so we must warn the men not to get their hopes up in that regard. Be firm with those who were most eager to return, especially the enlisted men. Tell them we'll have more pennants to fly before we're done."

In the designated grid square, where the cold Labrador current met the warmer Gulf Stream, the sea was riled but the air was warm for the North Atlantic. Banks of fog slid across the horizon. On the pitching bridge, Reising, Wiltzius, and two warrant officers scanned the sea for sight of the milch cow. Reising directed the steersman below him, visible through the hatch at his feet, maintaining a zigzagging search pattern, waiting impatiently for the supply boat to make radio contact or show himself.

Wiltzius sighted the milch cow as she surfaced less than a mile away, her bridge outlined against a distant, white bank of fog.

"There, captain," he said. "There at twenty degrees. It's one of ours, clearly a Type IX; he must be our man." Wiltzius had grown a thin red beard on the voyage.

Though she measured over two hundred feet long and displaced almost eight hundred tons, U235 seemed diminished as she moved parallel to the milch cow, like one of the canoe boats they had seen in the Kiel harbor. The two submarines came together in a splashing dance, bowing and curtseying to one another as the captains and officers exchanged shouted greetings from the conning towers, twenty yards apart. The crews, awash on the narrow decks, struggled to secure the refueling lines and crossing cables, while the watchmen scanned the sky and horizon.

The crew on the bridge of U235 nudged one another as the

captain of the milch cow descended the ladder from his bridge and—with the help of two crewmen on lifelines—buckled himself into the bosun's chair and gave the signal to be hauled across. When the first wave broke over him, he brayed like a steer and clamped his hat down. Reising called below for dry towels and reached out to hand the captain up onto his bridge. When he'd dried himself above the shoulders and replaced his cap, the round-faced commander of the milch cow shook himself, laughed, and did a little marching dance in his full boots. His roseate nose was of the variety that Wiltzius's father called the Grog Blossom. He shook hands with Reising and his officers, introducing himself as Captain Kung. Wiltzius had met the man in a club in Lorient one drunken night—how could he forget that chafing laugh?—but he didn't remember the circumstances and thought it clear that the captain didn't remember meeting him.

"God, what a stench!" Captain Kung laughed nervously, waving an arm back and forth over the open hatch. "How long have you been out, captain?"

"Not long enough, thank you," said Reising. "And you, sir, smell of tobacco; I believe I smelled it even as you were bathing just now. I think I smelled sausage, too, and fresh bread."

Captain Kung laughed again. He drew a waterproof envelope from inside his soggy coat and from it offered a pack of cigarettes. Reising thanked him and took one.

"No," Kung said. "Keep them. I can send a few extra over with your package. I wish I could do more. My orders are to refuel you and make the delivery—expeditiously. No mention was made of food. Are your supplies very low?"

"Quite low," Reising said.

Captain Kung laughed. "You're not a man to beg. Nor am I one to be stingy." He cupped his hands and leaned toward his own boat. "Mierke!" he shouted. "Mierke! See to it that these men get all the food we can spare—and fresh water. There are hungry, filthy sailors over here; do what you can."

"Thank you," said Reising.

"Thank you, sir," Wiltzius said.

"But what is this delivery, this package, if not orders?" Reising asked. "I assumed you came across to deliver orders."

"Your package is a man, I'm afraid, and he's carrying your orders," said Kung.

"I don't have room for another man. Who the hell is he?"

"He's a pain in the neck, and I'm glad to be rid of him," Kung said, laughing. "He's a Nazi, a spy or saboteur is our guess, so you probably won't have him long. For your sake I hope you get rid of him soon. He takes notes. He sniffs around looking for mistakes or incompetence, and makes notes in a little book. He tries to be chums with the enlisted men and feeds their discontent. I recommend that you keep him in your cabin, if he'll agree."

"Agree?" Reising was wide-eyed. "Who the hell does he think he is?"

"If you're not a Nazi, be careful what you said around him. I'm afraid he heard me say things that could hurt me, and he wrote them down before I realized what he was doing, what he is." Kung laughed again. "But we've decided that he'll be caught and shot wherever it is he's going. Merten thinks he will salute a nun or a firefighter; he's not too subtle."

"I'll be careful," said Reising.

"Here comes a load that looks to be food," Kung said. "I'll go back on this pass and send him over on the next. We're sitting ducks out here. I'm off to the south, and I wish you good hunting."

He shook their hands, Wiltzius's last. "And luck to you, too, Ensign Wiltzius. Perhaps we'll meet again over a drink in Lorient. This time it will be my turn to buy."

That evening they ate boiled meat and potatoes, with fresh turnips. Some of the crew had as many as three helpings of buttered beans. Within an hour there was a scuffle between two torpedomen waiting to get into the head.

"I'll shit myself if I don't go in next. I will!"

"Good, then shit yourself. You couldn't stink any worse than you do now."

The cook served Captain Reising, Wiltzius, and the new man in the captain's cabin. Wiltzius was careful to eat slowly, relishing the taste of the meat, the firm texture of the sharp turnips. He held his face low over his plate, as low as politely possible, to smell only the food and nothing else. He tried to imagine his mother's kitchen but could not. The new man declined food with a rude noise and waved the cook away as he would a fly, saying he wasn't hungry. Wiltzius suspected that the stench of the boat had taken away his appetite, and the thought gave him some pleasure. The man's German was perfect; he was a native speaker, probably from Berlin. Wiltzius wondered if his English could be as good.

"Wilhelm Shaeffer," Captain Reising chewed appreciatively while he read from the papers before him. The saboteur rose and closed the cabin curtain. Reising read to himself: he would not be joining a Wolf Pack, would not even go hunting. Instead he was to taxi an American Nazi to some rendezvous on the coast between two islands, and these orders were subject to revision at any time.

"Gridsquare BA 95," he read aloud. Wiltzius pointed to the sector on the chart with his fork, and Reising leaned over to see in the dull light. Then he continued reading. "There to meet with a vessel whose identity is to be verified by the bearer of these orders. What the hell?" Reising lifted his plate to rotate the chart on the table. "Do we have a class C chart of this area?"

"I don't think so," Wiltzius said. "If we do it is—"

"I have the chart," said Shaeffer, unfolding it. "Tomorrow night we're to meet with my contact here," he pointed. "He will signal us with a light—on for four seconds, off for four seconds, three repetitions."

"What kind of vessel? Are we to transfer you? We can't stay long so close to shore, to this lighthouse."

"I'm sorry," Shaeffer said, easing back his little shoulders. He looked at Reising and Wiltzius, superior to both of them in his access to information, his devotion to his Fuerher, his indifference to fear. "I am not authorized to provide any more details until we reach our destination. Where will you have me sleep, Captain?"

"Here," said Reising. "My cabin is yours. We'll be busy in the control room."

"I can't take your cabin."

"Please," said Reising, collecting his chart and plate as Wiltzius ducked through the curtain. "I would be honored."

• • •

September 22, 1942

Dear Ruth,

    If I wax incoherent here, it's not because I've been imbibing (I'm at my school desk listening to the children beating erasers). It's because of two nearly sleepless nights and a rush of events that makes everything seem sped up, as in an old cinematograph. As a matter of fact, the Keystone Kops is an apt allusion for describing our bustling island these days. I hate noise and confusion, as you know, and especially wasted effort. If this island were my schoolroom (and it is, in a way, as I've taught half the inhabitants) I'd have everyone sitting quietly at his desk minding his own business. The knuckles I would rap!

    No, I don't see Leah much, now that school has started. But I can tell you that she's much improved. I think Cecil has stopped hectoring her, at least for the time being. She'll be relieved—as will I—when Gus goes to school in

Jonesport, where he won't be out on the water.

Did the Bangor paper mention the two trawlers that were sunk by U-boats and whose survivors came ashore here? Probably not, as it was only a tiny incident in this huge war and meant little or nothing to those ashore. But to our fishermen and their wives—indeed, to all of us out here, surrounded by the sea—it was as momentous an event as a bombing raid or amphibious invasion. They are after *us*. We feel so helpless, so vulnerable. We are tempted to hide, to pretend that nothing is happening, to pray for salvation. But I fear we must fight back, however futilely.

Do I tell you often enough how much I love your letters? I take them home to read, so that I can have you all to myself. I loved your description of you and Jack at Michael's school play—the awful music, and the tear of pride on Jack's cheek.

Yes, Gus is fine. He's been getting a pound a trap this last month and feels quite flush, all boyish bluster. I like to mention Mabel Eaton's name and watch him blush. Right now he's mad at me for something else, and I am on my way to the cove to make amends.

So I close quickly, dear Ruth, and bustle off to the P.O. on my way home. Please give all my love to all of yours—to Jack, especially.

Love,
Maggie

She found a place among the rocks, on the rise behind the fish shacks, where she could watch him without being seen.

He'd been at it all day, she thought; he couldn't have gone to haul and gotten so much done. He had cut a wide, defiant pathway through the spruces, and it must have taken him most of the day—sawing each tree at ground level and dragging it away, clearing the deadwood and stones, filling holes and fissures with gravel. The uphill end of the apparatus that crouched under the tarp, was secured to two block and tackles attached to sturdy trunks. The hawser on the lower end, taut and shivering with the strain, ran to a winch on the wharf, where Gus stood wiping his face in his undershirt. Leaning backward, he pulled with all his weight on the crank handle; it clicked ahead one notch, then would move no more. The runner nearer Maggie had slipped off the log roller and lodged behind a boulder. She stepped out into the open as he came up the pathway; when he saw her, he didn't seem at all surprised. He looked at her as though she were tardy, a look she thought she deserved.

"You can't do it alone," she said. She was holding a pair of work gloves, which he pretended not to notice.

"I've done this much alone; I can finish it alone," he said.

"Let me turn the winch while you use your lever to ease it over these boulders," she said.

"Why? You told me—"

"I was wrong," she said pulling on her gloves. "Or, if not wrong, then wrong-headed. If you don't blow yourself up dragging this ungodly thing down to the boat, you'll get blown up trying to use it alone. I'm going with you. There's no time to discuss my motives—or to argue."

She gripped the running hawser and tried to budge it but could not. "You pry that runner up, and I'll work the log back under it. Then go work the winch."

He smiled and nodded, as Amos would have done, then fetched the long spruce pole he'd been using as a lever and waited while she slipped on her gloves.

Perhaps he did believe that they could do some damage to a U-boat with this contraption, she thought. Perhaps Amos had told Gus something to make him believe, as Amos must have believed, that they could somehow get over a submerged U-boat and drop these charges. But if there was a meeting of some kind with the lobsterboat, the German would be on the surface, wouldn't he? And he would stay on the surface to go out to the convoy lanes, as Amos had seen him do. Catching the sub underwater might be possible, but she thought it was far more likely that Amos hadn't thought the whole thing through. This, suspected Maggie, was a brave gesture, little more, and she was resolved to keep it that way. She would go with Gus just this time, and they would watch for the lobsterboat on the water, see who he was and what he was doing. They would enlist the help of Mr. Gardiner, who she hoped would either go with them or send out his launch. That way, if there was a confrontation, the Coast Guard could take charge as it was meant to. And if Maggie was true to Leah, she would find a way to convince Gus to dump the terrible machine overboard tonight.

He used a wood block as a fulcrum, and though the spruce pole bent some, he lifted the platform enough for her to reposition the log roller beneath it, freeing the runner.

"Let's uncover it," she said. "I'm afraid one of those drums will break loose and blow us to kingdom come."

"It takes a fuse to make it blow," he said scornfully. Was it real disdain she heard in his voice, or was it the playful, contemptuous tone that he and Amos used for one another? She decided that it was the latter.

"That may be, Mister Weapons Expert," she replied. "But I'd still like to see. Here, put that pole down and give me a hand with this damned tarp."

He looked at her, surprised now, and laughed.

"You," was all he said.

Once they had inched the apparatus over the slight rise in the ledge—twice having to double up on the winch handle—the heavy cradle began its slow descent. Maggie worked the block and tackle, giving Gus a foot or two of slack at a time, while he moved the log rolls into its path and guided it with the spruce pole. As she watched him work, so tired that he moved like a man waist deep in water, she thought that this was more to Gus than a fulfillment of his and Amos's plan: It was a way to ease the guilt he felt for having cursed Amos after he died and a way to prove to himself that though he ran away from whatever he saw on the mountain, he was not a coward. If this dark little part of Amos's legacy to them went wrong, it would undo everything else he left behind, and Cecil would have his store in Blue Hill.

Then again, the plan just might work.

William "Lump" Muggins thought that if he had to sit across the table from Ethel and listen to her gums slurp and slap at gobs of rice pudding one more night, he would commit suicide. Harry Carry.

Chin in his palm, he watched her clear the table and waddle away with the armload of dishes that she would leave in the sink. With two hooked fingers, she scooped a dollop of pudding and sodden raisins from the bowl and rolled it around in her mouth before she swallowed it and burped like an old seal. This being Sunday, he didn't need to ask her what she was going to listen to: the All Girl Orchestra and the program about the crossroads of a million private lives, the one he pretended to hate. Nor did he need to remind her that he would want to listen to Walter Winchell at nine-thirty. She didn't care that U.S. forces had taken Guadalcanal and were holding it; she asked how she could care about a place she couldn't even pronounce. Years ago, when she was the pretty girl in the wedding picture, with him in his uniform, she could pronounce Belleau Wood and Meuse-Argonne well enough. She could chew her food, too.

After a little nap in the kitchen rocker, Lump built himself to his feet, found his white Civil Defense helmet and flashlight, and went out the side door with a wave to her and Jack Benny in the parlor. Neither of them noticed. He lit a cigarette and surveyed the town and harbor below him. In the first light of the moon he could see the sleepy fishing boats of the Stonington fleet, their bows pointing into a westerly wind that seemed to be freshening. The sweet scent of burning leaves still lingered in the air on High Street, where he passed three then four houses whose owners hadn't put up their blackout curtains. The harbor and Main Street were dark, as was the opera house, but on the hillside above, half the homes were lit up like Christmas trees. It was no use knocking on doors to tell people to put their curtains up, not any more. As Lump often said, if they could see the picture he had in his mind of Thurlow Green lying wide-eyed in the frozen mud with a German bullet hole through his forehead, they wouldn't be so Quakerish. Low Green wasn't any more to them than a name on a monument—if that—and the hundred or more ships sunk off their coast in the last month might as well have gone down off Hawaii. It griped him so.

At Russell's garage, he shined his light on the flying red horse and into the windows, then walked down Main Street trying doors and peering into the windows of dark shops on his way to the town landing. Bruce Carr's Dodge, its headlights lidded, stuttered homeward up the hill past the rooming house. There, two old Portuguese stonecutters sat smoking on the porch, where there had been twenty men the week before. They waved, and he drew an arc over his head with his light in reply.

Once in his skiff, Lump shut off the lantern and let his eyes adjust to the moonlight. There was no sight or sound of anyone on the wharves or among the moored boats. He drew a bottle of Demerara from beneath the seat and held it up to the moon, only to find not even two fingers' worth in the bottom. He shrugged, flatfooted it, and shivered as the rum went down. With a sad sigh, he tossed the bottle overboard and took up his oars.

Richard saw the white helmet as Lump rowed past the stern of the *Nana* and cursed under his breath. He quietly stowed the section of cedar sheathing he'd been about to attach and thought to hide below. But he realized that Lump would see his skiff, so he hailed him.

"Christ, Richard," Lump said. "You scared the living shit out of me."

He shipped his starboard oar and bumped alongside the *Lucille* to catch hold of the washboard and ask Richard whether he was coming or going. Richard said he was going out for a night patrol; it took little effort for him to sound tired and resigned to his fatigue.

"Christ, I got to hand it to you," Lump said. "You know you're about the only other one around here that's doing anything. You were out last night, too. You must be some tired."

"I was down on the island last night, so I could haul today," Richard said. He made busy with his stern line to show that he didn't intend to linger.

"The night before that, too," said Lump, bailing the skiff with his free hand.

"That's right," Richard said. "That was patrolling. Tuesday. I'd go out every night if I could. It's good to know somebody here in Stonington has got his eyes open. Funny that us older guys who wore the uniform in the last war are the only ones paying attention."

"It's not funny, it's disgusting." The white helmet shook sadly. "Where is it you go, anyway? The night before last I thought you were headed out north of Barter Island."

Richard laughed. "That's what I want you to think—or somebody else who might be watching. Once I get out of sight, I cut through Merchant's Row and patrol south of the island out by the Gilkie," he lied.

Lump nodded wisely. "Three on a match," he said. He remembered a night in a communications trench in France. He had struck a match that Richard covered with cupped hands while he lit his cigarette; then Richard did the same for Lump as he lit his. When a third man butted in for a light, Richard had pinched the flame with muddy fingers, saying two on a match was dangerous enough with snipers just yonder. Three, he said, was curtains. It actually hadn't been Richard in the trench—he had served in the navy—but Lump believed it had been, having told the story so many times with Richard in it—twice to Richard himself. Richard corrected Lump the first time but let it stand when he heard it told again.

"Three on a match," Richard said. He sat on the washboard and offered Lump a cigarette. Lump cupped the match, and they smoked in a knowledgeable silence, two old comrades-in-arms enjoying a quiet smoke, afloat on the same memories.

"The truth is," Richard said. "I can tell you. The truth is that it's not so much patrolling I'm doing tonight as picking something up. If you watch, you'll see me go out past Green Head toward Mark Island and the bay."

"As far east as Rockland?" asked Lump.

Richard said nothing.

"And would that something you're picking up be aboard the smack *Kingfisher*, Mister Prentiss Phinney, master?" asked Lump. He pronounced the names slowly, reverently, smacking his lips.

"I don't say yes, and I don't say no." Richard smiled.

Lump heard his lieutenant's shrill whistle signaling the attack. "Christ," he said and stood in the skiff. "Christ I'd like to go with you. Like old times."

Richard stroked his chin as though considering the possibility.

"No, I guess I'd better go alone."

"Suppose you run into that son of a bitch you treated to a lobster facial last spring—him and his friends? You won't—"

"I won't see him. Or I ought to say he won't see me." Richard scratched the scars in his palm, refreshing his anger. "If there's a god, that guy is blind as a bat, both his eyeballs popped and poked out by sharp climbing claws, shriveled up like prunes in their sockets."

Lump thought of the boiled raisins headed for Ethel's

mouth, then of what she'd do if he took off for Rockland in the middle of the night with Richard Snell. He sat back down on the skiff seat.

"I'd like to go," he said wistfully. "I'd like to see old Prentiss Phinney again."

"I might be staying there for a while. I need to get that radio they've been promising me," Richard said. "It was supposed to be there two weeks ago; maybe tomorrow I can get it."

"Could you save out a couple of bottles for me?" Lump asked. "I don't know how long it's been, early summer, since I had a taste of that Demerara."

"I can do you one better than that," allowed Richard. "I've got one bottle left that I saved from the last run. You take it tonight and just pay me when I bring the other two. That's if you want it."

Lump did. He stretched his neck to watch Richard go below with a flashlight; but Richard kept his back turned, so Lump did not see that he removed a bottle from a full case.

"I'm much obliged, Captain." Lump tucked the bottle under his stern seat.

"It'd be best if you didn't say anything about this," said Richard. "I told Russell Webb and Buster and a half-dozen others that I was dry. Better not mention seeing me tonight, either."

"Not a word." Lump crossed his heart with a finger. "Hope to die," he said.

CHAPTER FOURTEEN

JAKE GARDINER HELD ASIDE THE BLANKET THAT SERVED AS A black-out curtain in the parlor of the keeper's house. He had heard and then seen the Novi boat approaching, her outline sharp on the moonlit water. Jake thought that she was riding low in the water, her bulk increased somehow. With the binoculars he saw what looked like bales of hay on a scaffold rising from her deck. When she veered off to come around into the slip, he saw more clearly.

"I'm looking at the curled up knees of Jesus," he said. "I swear I am."

On his way to the door, he called to Morales to bring a light and meet him at the slip. Harvey lit a storm lantern and followed them.

On the landing, Jake stood with his hands in his pockets and followed the yellow circle of Morales's light as it moved slowly over the framework on the stern, lingering on the chocks, the runners, and the sledgehammer with its handle tied to a brace with a slip knot. Maggie stood on the deck, hands in her own pockets, and watched Jake hopefully.

"Come aboard," Gus said to Morales.

"I'm afraid I'll sink her if I do." Morales shined the light on the stern, where the hull rode so low that the sea lapped at the scupper drains.

"Suit yourself," said Gus. "Take these then." He handed Morales a packet of letters which the Coast Guardsman sniffed fondly as he slipped them inside his shirt. Gus gave him a shoe box, too, tied with the same yellow ribbon. "If those are Betty's gingersnaps, you'll find they make wicked good clay pigeons."

Morales thanked him for the advice and with the light leaned ahead to better see how the fuses were attached and marked. Gus drew a fat cigar from his shirt pocket and puffed on it as he would when it came time to light them. Morales grinned.

"This could work," he said over his shoulder to Jake.

"It does work," Gus said. "We tried it twice, me and Amos. Oh, it works all right."

"How much does the rig weigh? It must be a ton. If you ran into a rough sea you'd sink like a goddamned stone," said Morales.

"If it had been rough tonight, we wouldn't have come out," Maggie said.

"I don't believe this. I cannot believe this." The hard anger in Jake's voice startled them all. "Not of you, Maggie Bowen. I thought you were a sensible woman. I'd laugh if I could; I swear I would. Just what in the hell do you think you're doing?"

"You know . . ."

"No, I want to hear it from you," he said. "I want you to tell me. Give me that light, Morales."

She was taken aback, affronted. On the way out she had insisted, over Gus's protests, that they stop at the lighthouse to inform the crew of what they were doing and perhaps enlist their help, hoping secretly that Jake would dissuade Gus with a voice of reason. Now she saw that his reaction would not be reason, but abuse, and she would not brook that.

"We did not come here, Mister Gardiner, to be insulted. We came as a courtesy, and in hopes that we might coordinate our efforts to—"

"Well, in this case your good manners saved your life," he said. "Because I'm going to impound this boat and take it off-shore myself and dump that lunatic contraption overboard. I'll put you under arrest if I need to."

"Let's go," Gus said.

Maggie's hands curled into fists, then relaxed. "You'll do nothing of the kind," she said.

"I won't let you leave here with that thing aboard," he said. "Don't you understand how dangerous it is, how one of those drums could come loose, how one swell could capsize you? Don't you see that it's you—your safety—I care about?"

"I'm flattered," she said cynically. "I truly am."

"You believe that this fishing boat you saw, or think you saw, is going out night after night to some place at sea and meeting a U-boat," he said scornfully. "And you're going to surprise them or attack them or somehow get the U-boat to submerge so you can get over top him and drop a half-ton of home-made bombs on him. What makes you think there's a U-boat out there anyway? No, don't tell me," he laughed cruelly. "It's Amos's U-boat you're after, the one he claimed he saw ten miles from here, the one you thought you heard way the hell south of here. You don't—"

"I don't have to listen to you any longer," she said. "Cast off that line, Gus. Go to hell, Mister Gardiner."

"I'll see you there, Miss Bowen."

As they pulled away, Morales held the light on the blue barrels and shouted to Gus to keep in radio contact. Cigar jammed in his mouth, Gus flashed a V for victory.

"Look at the transom," Morales said. "It's not the *Quahog* any more."

"God damn her," Jake said. "Let me have that lantern, Goods."

"What are you going to do?"

"I'm going to put the launch in the water," said Jake. "Morales is going to get our gear, and you're going to hustle

your sorry ass up into the light to see what heading they're taking. What the hell did you think?"

He'd been lucky with the tide, Richard thought. If it had
been low when he was going and coming through the maze of
island channels, he would have had to use a light. Not that there
were any houses near his water route to see it, but there was the
possibility of coastal pickets wandering around on the populated
islands, and using a light would have added to his jitters. Coming around the northern head of Barter Island, he took a bearing on the white splashing of the surf on the rocks, and pointed
his bow out into the wide darkness of the open sea beyond. He
pushed the throttle to twelve knots, turned slightly south to
ninety-eight degrees, and in the soft quicksilver light on the
open deck, set his stopwatch.

With a grim smile, he remembered the cold sweat and sudden weakness he'd suffered that first night when he'd come
around the head to find that the Mt. Desert Light was out. He'd
been sure that it had been darkened because of him, that they
knew about the meeting and had laid a trap. Even so, he had
kept on his azimuth, cussing the moonlight, and had waited
four hours at the rendezvous point, signaling at precisely timed
intervals. All the while he was expecting the hum of a Civil Air
Patrol plane or the approach of a cutter that could outrun and
outgun him. Twice—fooled by the moonlight flashing on a
swell—he had thought he'd seen the blink of a return signal
from the east. All that night, idling alone on the gentle swells,
he'd sweated in doubt and fear: Maybe he'd waited in the
wrong place. Maybe he'd been seen in the harbor adding extra
cedar sheathing to disguise his boat's house. Maybe he'd got
the message wrong, or the message itself was part of an elab-
orate trap. He hadn't known then—and still didn't on this, the
last of the "three consecutive nights"—where the return signal
would be coming from. He assumed it would be from the con-

ning tower of a U-boat, and the image still made him shiver in apprehension.

Richard was calmer tonight than he had been on the first two runs, maybe because he was bone tired but more likely because this was the last run, no matter what happened. If there was no meeting tonight, no "transfer of package," it would not be his fault. He had checked his calculations a dozen times and was sure of them; he hadn't been seen by anyone—unless you counted Lump, which he didn't. He had waited out there, alone with only his iron will for company, as faithfully as any man could. Richard would have done his duty, risked his life to make his contribution to victory. He almost allowed himself to wish that they wouldn't show up tonight, that there would be no "further orders for phase two," but he brought that hope to heel. Instead, he reminded himself of the godlike efficiency of the German war machine and imagined himself exchanging salutes with a white-capped captain on the bridge, responding to the officer's apologies for being late with a gift of rum and a show of quiet, selfless courage.

Since there couldn't be a full case, he thought there might just as well be two bottles missing and brought one up to stiffen his tea. Maybe they'd invite him aboard for a little drink. How they'd laugh when he described the coastal defenses: fuzzy old men in rowboats who could be bought off with a quart; drunken ghost chasers tumbling off cliffs; women and children; Mexicans, for Christ's sake, with binoculars. No, he'd say, *aber nicht*, he wanted no reward or recognition for his service, only the Right to Prevail. When England was starved and subdued, and America was isolated and brought to terms, then he and the others who now worked in secret would be appreciated. The proud ones, the ones that sneered, might not like him then any more than they ever did, but they would have to admit respect for his courage and persistence. It wouldn't be Low Green with a bullet through his head that they'd talk about, but poor Homer Topp, stripped and blindfolded, facing a firing squad of his fellow Americans. Then they would see; even she would. Richard couldn't remember the German word for prevail just then, but he knew it would come to him when he needed it.

Wiltzius's sister Romi, in a shimmering black skirt and high heels, stood in the pantry with her back to him. She was talking to her husband in what sounded like French, almost as though she was softly singing to him. Though Wiltzius couldn't see it, he knew she was patting him on the chest with her palm, tapping out a slow, repetitive message that they both understood. In the doorway, facing Wiltzius, little Frankie—all in white wool—opened and closed her hand to him in a wave, while taking plums from the basket on the shelf and dropping them to the floor one at a time. Behind her, in a ghastly gray window gallery, two skull-like Slavic faces with brittle noses watched the scene within—Hansel and Gretel peeking into the witch's house.

As Frankie dropped the plums, they rolled, one following the other on the same winding route around his table, through the pantry, and across the kitchen tiles to an intake pipe in the wall beneath the calendar. There they were sucked in, *foop*, one at a time.

Mardsden, a dribble of dried oatmeal in his beard, tapped Wiltzius's sternum to awaken him.

"All right, all right," the ensign responded groggily.

"The captain wants you on the bridge," Mardsden said. He was the oldest man on the boat, and his breath smelled like embalming fluid. "He has something he wants you to see. Very good."

Climbing the ladder, Wiltzius met the odor of pine and damp earth even before he passed through the hatch and felt suddenly, deeply sad. He stood next to Reising, who clapped him on the shoulder and presented, with a flourish of his hand, the high, dark outline of the North American coast.

"Not like home, eh, Wiltzius?" Reising asked. "No gentle

vineyards and wide river valleys; it's all rocks and evergreens, but—ah, the smell!"

One of the forward watchmen said that it looked like the Norway coast.

"The mountain to starboard is actually two, called Cadillac and Sargent, and they're on an island." Reising was delighted. "How like the Americans to name mountains after their cars."

An occasional tiny twinkle on a hillside off the port bow was the only light visible on the dark horizon. U235 was making six knots on one diesel on a bearing that pointed the sub straight toward a smaller island's mountainous spine, a giant hunchback floating face down in the sparkling sea.

In a black leather jacket and dark watch cap—his hands and cheeks covered with dark face paint, and his eyes sunk in binoculars—Herr Shaeffer, Das Packet, was almost invisible, as silent as the horizon he scanned. Wiltzius thought that he must be afraid to be going ashore, unarmed and burdened with two bulky cases. But, when Shaeffer lowered the binoculars and nodded to Wiltzius, the man seemed unmoved, his eyes even a little merry. He is a bastard, Wiltzius thought, a self-important fool, but he is unafraid.

"You air-watch men keep a strain on your eyeballs," said Reising. "We've had reports of small civilian aircraft patrolling the coast; twice in the last week they've bombed our boats, though farther south. I want to be steaming out of here as soon as possible. Wiltzius, call up the gun crews, both of them; we'll take no chances. We can be out of here in an hour, eh, Herr Shaeffer?"

"In less than that, if my man is on time and in the right place," Shaeffer said beneath his binoculars. "Don't worry, captain. We'll need a strong light up here as well."

"I'm not worried," Reising said curtly. He'd be happy to see the black backside of this son of a bitch. The man was eating up his fuel and soiling his sheets, and he looked and acted as if he'd just jumped off the devil's shovel.

"According to the chart, we have a lighthouse ten kilometers to port," Wiltzius said. "It must be true that they've finally turned them off. I'm going to write a letter to Roosevelt and complain about—"

"There!" said Shaeffer. "There he is. Dead ahead. Four shorts, two longs, repeated." He turned to the man behind him, who was on his knees, hauling the barrel of the Breda machine gun through the hatch. "Get me a light up here," he said. The seaman looked at his captain, who nodded, then called below for the signal light to be passed up.

Jake raised the collar of his pea coat, turned his back to the wet spray coming over the port side, and strained to see beyond the rising and falling bow of the launch. Morales kept his eyes on the boat and compass, but his mind was on Betty's soft mounds of joy, whose familiar scent rose from his shirt. He held a course of 350 degrees.

"There they are!" Jake said, pointing. "Off the starboard bow. Cut her back to half throttle, and let's keep them in sight."

"Half throttle?" Morales asked. "Don't we want to catch up to them and make them dump those damn barrels? Call them on the radio, and tell them to heave to."

"No," Jake said evenly. "She won't listen—not now, not to me. If I had seen Amos's name on the transom sooner or realized that it must have been him who made those depth charges, I wouldn't have lost my temper like that, I would have understood . . ."

"You ought to call her right now and apologize and ask her to wait for us to catch up," Morales said. "She would, then." He tucked his chin for a whiff of essence of Betty. "Tell her again it's her safety you care about, and maybe even admit that it was jealousy that made you lose your temper, then she'd—"

"Half throttle," Jake said. "We'll watch from a distance, see what they see—if anything. And if there is another boat, we'll get involved; to hell with her pride."

"Gus said that boat was on a heading of ninety-five degrees

both times they saw it; that ought to put it about a mile from here. If he's armed and we're still this far back when they run into him, the only involved we'll be is as witnesses to one ungodly explosion. Then you *will* go to hell, like she suggested."

"Two-thirds throttle," said Jake. He wiped the lenses of his binoculars. "She knows something she hasn't told us, and now maybe never will. Something to do with what Amos was watching for at the cabin when he fell. She told me then she thought people were coming ashore to use the cabin, and I never even reported it."

"No, but I did," said Morales. "I can see them now. Jesus, she's low in the water. So now maybe you all of a sudden believe them and don't think it's all a fragment of their imagination like you said?"

"I don't know what I believe any more," Jake replied.

"How about the flashing light three points off the port bow," Morales pointed. "You believe that?"

Jake swung his binoculars toward land. "Sweet mother of God," he said.

He shouldered Morales aside to take the wheel and push the throttle to full. Morales ducked below and came back up with the Springfield rifle and a handful of clips.

"There's his answer," Jake handed Morales the binoculars. "Four shorts, two longs from both of them."

"That's a conning tower," Morales said. "I can see his periscope. Maggie and Gus have seen him too, and they're headed straight for him."

"Run up that flag, Mister Morales," Jake said. "Then get on the horn, and call Goods. Have him report a U-boat in the open at these coordinates."

When Richard drew close enough to U235 to see that her deck guns were leveled at him, he stepped out from behind the wheelhouse and waved his arms up and down, up and down.

Captain Reising handed the bullhorn to Shaeffer. "Tell him to stop doing that and to bring his boat around to run on our starboard side. I'm going to start a turn here."

"He looks as if he's trying to fly," Wiltzius said. "Strachmeyer, stand by to take his line."

When the *Lucille* was broadside to U235's deck, not thirty feet away, Shaeffer called to Richard through the bullhorn: "Trenton New Jersey" he boomed. Reising and Wiltzius exchanged a curious glance.

Richard leaned back from the wheel with one hand cupped to his mouth: "Christmas Eve," he said.

"We are turning to port," Shaeffer told him. "Swing around and come alongside." He drew a circle in the air for Richard, who saluted in reply and turned hard over to dance in his own wake.

On the first throw, Richard's line fell on the deck but washed overboard before Strachmeyer could reach it.

"Clumsy ass," said one of the gunners.

Strachmeyer unhooked his lifeline from the jumping wire to reach Richard's second toss; he stepped on the snaking line and tied it to the railing.

"*Danke schön,*" said Richard in his grandmother's German.

Strachmeyer didn't reply, but reattached himself to the jumping wire and said something to the gunners, words that Richard did not understand. He held the *Lucille* off the sub's steep, slippery hull with his gaff and dropped his fenders into place. When he leaned back to look up at the men in the tower, he saw no white cap but saluted the bridge nevertheless. Only Wiltzius, who felt sorry for the man though he couldn't think why, returned the salute. Reising looked at Richard for a second, then told Shaeffer to make haste.

"One minute," Shaeffer shouted to Richard. He gave Wiltzius his binoculars and asked the ensign to have his boxes sent up right away. He saluted Wiltzius formally, shook his hand, and did the same with Reising, who nodded and wished him good luck.

Shaeffer descended the stern ladder to the deck and—helped along by the gun crew—made his way gingerly toward Richard's proffered gaff. Reaching down for the pole, he crouched as if preparing to jump onto the *Lucille*'s deck, but instead he sat down in the wash and slid clumsily into Richard's arms.

As Wiltzius and Praeger attached a line to the handle of the first of Shaeffer's heavy black boxes, a cry came from below.

"Two vessels approaching south by east," said a man in the control room. "One kilometer out; estimated speed ten knots."

"God damn it," spat Reising. The two boats, whoever they were, had to have radios; they would have seen the signal lights and alerted the air patrols. Reising's decision was a simple one.

"Gun crews below!" he shouted. "Get that box out of the way. Prepare to dive."

The alarm sounded, and the surface crew scrambled to secure their guns and clear the deck. Wiltzius and Praeger balanced the box on the railing to make way for the running men, then lowered it onto the deck.

"Captain, what are you doing?" Shaeffer shouted from the *Lucille*.

"We have two vessels approaching and probable enemy aircraft, Herr Packet," Reising said. "You are compromised. I advise you and your friend to get out of here as fast as you can."

"My boxes!" Shaeffer cried. As U235's speed increased, the *Lucille* stretched her bow line and slammed against the huge hull. For three seconds that seemed a half-hour, Richard and his camouflaged companion stood astonished on the deck, then Richard jumped forward to push up his throttle and shouted at Shaeffer to cast off the line when it slackened.

The last man on the bridge, Wiltzius watched in horror as Shaeffer, standing on the *Lucille*'s washboard, uncleated the line and clung to it, desperately pulling himself hand over hand up the side of the U-boat, thrashed by the sea as the vessel's bow began to submerge, his legs flailing for a foothold.

"Sir, for Christ's sake!" Praeger yelled from the hatchway.

Wiltzius vaulted over the railing and slid down the line that was still attached to the box. Immediately after he reached the deck, a wave knocked him off his feet, but he held onto the line and managed to scramble crab-wise toward Shaeffer and with his right hand catch the collar of the man's jacket. Wiltzius hauled him onto the deck like a great fish, then ran him up the ladder, his shoulder pushing Schaeffer's buttocks, and feeding him, head first, into the hatch. Wiltzius then fell through himself in a cascade of sea water, turning quickly to secure the hatch cover as U235 dove and disappeared.

"Baker One One, this is Baker Six. Do you read me Baker One One? Over." Maggie stepped back from the little door in the bulkhead, startled by the volume and clarity of Jake's voice.

"He sounds like he's next door," said Gus, as surprised as she was.

"Baker Six this is Baker One One," Maggie answered. "Where are you, Six?"

Gus told her to say "over," but she ignored him.

"We're off your port side; I'm not sure how far. I'm going to show you a light."

"The hell," said Gus.

"Baker Six this is One One," Maggie said. "What are you doing out here? Yes, I see your light. You're passing us. What are you doing? Did you see what we saw? Over."

"Yes we did, One One, and we are in pursuit of the fishing boat. He's dead ahead of us, on a course for shore. We'll need your help. Over."

"Do you want us to follow you, Baker Six? I don't think we could keep up with you. Over."

Maggie held the handset against her chest and looked at Gus. "I know what's coming next," she said. Gus smiled.

"Then you've got to launch your extra weight, One One.

Push it overboard now, and you can catch up with me and we can overtake him no problem—"

"We—"

"You have to wait til he says 'Over,' " Gus said.

"One One, are you there? This is Six."

"Yes, we're here. Over."

"Please comply, One One," Jake said. "Promise me you will comply. Please. Over."

"Say 'Willco,' " Gus advised.

"Baker Six, this is Baker One One," Maggie replied. "Willco. Over."

"What now?" Gus asked.

"We'll do what we were about to do, and we will comply as well," she said. "Full speed for five minutes at forty-five degrees, and if he keeps his course and the gods are smiling, we'll cross right over him. You'll want to light that cigar."

"You take the wheel," he said. "I'll cut the fuses first."

Gus ducked under the scaffold, untied the striped coils, and with tin snips poised, hesitated.

"One at twenty, the other at twenty-five?" he asked her.

"You're the expert," she said. "I have no idea."

Maggie pushed the throttle ahead two notches, but Gus cried from the stern that she should cut it back; they were taking on water.

"Willco," she said. With one eye on *Amos Coombs's* plunging bow and the other on Gus, crouched behind the bulkhead, puffing his cigar alive, she thought she must certainly be mad and wondered if Ruth would ever believe her—if she lived to tell about it. She looked at Gus's boyish face, eyes closed in the smoke and cheeks lighted by the glowing cigar, and she prayed that she would be forgiven.

"You said Amos could hear it—and feel it—when he passed over that one in the spring." Gus held onto the house and leaned over the dark water. "He has sixty fathoms in here," he said. "I don't hear anything, do you?"

"No I don't." She was too afraid to let go of the wheel. "Sixty seconds," she said.

Gus stood behind the barrels, cigar in mouth, sledgehammer at the ready. "You got to hang onto her when these go over," he said, fairly shouting. "The bow's going to rise then come crashing down. Run her up to full speed as soon as they're overboard, and hold on.

"There he is. Look!" Gus cried. "See how his bulk heaves the surface and how his periscope leaves that thin bubble wake, like Amos said? We're going to cross right over him all right!"

"Ten seconds," she said.

He held the cigar to the first fuse and jumped away as it spat and sparkled, leaning over to light the second. He spit on each of the barrels for luck, shouted, and knocked away the chocks with two quick blows of the sledgehammer. Red-and-white fire sprayed from the whirling fuses as the barrels rolled off the stern and dropped, one on top of the other, into the darkness below. The bow came down so quickly that it cut through a swell that broke over the windshield and house. Her legs apart and weight forward, Maggie opened the throttle and held the wheel, waiting for the explosions. The first one, a gigantic, sudden thunder below, heaved the boat up beneath them, then ruptured the surface behind them in a huge, round cloud with two wide wings of spray, the concussion knocking Gus to the deck and throwing Maggie against the wheel and bulkhead. We are going to die, she thought. Then the second drum erupted in the same way, striking them like a giant fist. She turned in time to see the final white ball of water break the surface as Gus pulled himself to his feet.

She closed her eyes, then covered her mouth with her hand in horror. "Oh, dear God," she said into her hand. "Oh my God, what have we done?"

"We're all right!" Gus shouted. He held his mouth wide open and pummeled his temples as he did at the pond when he had water in his ears. "Goddamn, are you okay? I can't hear a damn thing. We did it, by Jesus, Maggie, we did it!"

He scrambled over the washboard and onto the house where he could see two huge, overlapping circles of flattened sea, one of them a bright metallic sheen in the moonlight.

"Oil, Maggie!" he shouted as he swung down onto the deck beside her.

"Give me the wheel!" he yelled. "Go up and take a look. It's an oil slick. We hit him!"

"Don't shout so." She did not let go of the wheel or even turn aside.

"Those poor boys," she said.

CHAPTER FIFTEEN

WHEN THE DOUBLE PUNCH OF THE DEPTH CHARGES STRUCK THE launch, Jake spun around as if to see, and Morales—his hands spread wide at his sides—brayed like a mule.

"Ha Ha!" he cried. "V for victory! V for revenge!" He slapped Jake on the back, nearly upending him.

"Baker One One this is Baker Six," Jake shouted into the handset. "Are you there One One? Good God what have you done? Answer me! Over."

"Baker Six this is One One," replied Gus even louder. "We're fine. The boat's okay. How about that, hey Morales?"

Morales reached for the handset, but Jake held on to it, in no mood for a war dance. He thought Maggie must be smirking, but then realized that she wouldn't be. "This is Six," he said, calmer now. "We're still in pursuit of the boat; we're closing on him; it looks like he's headed for Swan's Island, around there. You're too far back to catch us, so why don't you take it on in. Over."

"We're going to try to catch up to you, Six, like you said," Gus answered. "Since we complied, we're a lot lighter. Over."

"Roger that," Jake conceded. "Do what you want, but keep in radio contact. Over."

"Hello, Six," said Maggie. "This is One One. Do you have the boat in sight? Over."

"Hello One One. Affirmative. At least we saw him a minute ago. We'll keep you posted," Jake said. "Negative further. Out."

"He's pissed," laughed Gus.

"He'll get over it," Maggie said. "Do you really think we can catch up to him?"

"Look back there, Maggie," he said. As if smoothed by the swipe of a hand, the swath of sea where the charges had erupted lay flat on the choppy surface, reflecting the moon like burnished pewter as it diminished. "Goddamn, but that was terrific," he said reverently.

Maggie thought of the terror in terrific and nodded in agreement. Let Jake be angry, she thought; she was too relieved to care. Her part was done, and it was all in his hands now; she need only follow along. No longer top heavy, the *Amos Coombs* rode effortlessly at full throttle; her high, sharp bow cut through the chop and occasional swell like a knife through frosting. This is why Amos wanted the Novi boat, she thought. The *Tuna* would be pitching and rolling, barely making way. How he had hated it when Cecil and Richard had made jokes in the store about the *Tuna*'s name: *The Chicken of the Sea,* they called it. If he was here now, she'd see that thin, satisfied smile he wore for quiet victories.

"She's not doing what she could," Gus said, leaning over to watch the boat's bow wake. "She's still too heavy. I'm going to cut that thing loose. I'll make another one, a better one this time, so the weight is farther forward, so as not to bring the stern down."

"Very well," she said. She would be glad to see it go.

When he had removed the lag screws that held the scaffold in place, she cut back on the throttle; Gus braced himself to push, shouted "Go!" and she gunned the engine. The structure groaned, and tried to hold on, but Gus forced it overboard. It sank momentarily, then rose to the surface to bob and dip in a sad, awkward dance before it turned over and floated face down.

Richard understood "zwei Boote" and "raus" and "schnell" when the captain shouted down at them, and in the man's voice he heard what he would call fear if he wasn't a U-boat captain. So, when the little bastard—the spy or whatever he was—made a jump for it, Richard turned his back on the whole deal and steamed for shore. He didn't wait around to see if the guy made it into the U-boat; he hoped he did, or if he didn't, he hoped he and his goddamned box got dragged down with it and he was drowned on the bottom where nobody would find him. Richard's undershirt was drenched with sweat; he held it open at the collar to cool himself down.

If the approaching boats were Coast Guard cutters they would overtake him in open water, sure as hell. He ran the broom handle through his wheel to hold the *Lucille* on a heading for the nearest land and dismantled the walls and roof of the fake wheelhouse, throwing the pieces overboard. He tore off the canvas that had hidden the *Lucille's* name and numbers, and jettisoned every bit of ballast and weight he could find. All but the case of rum, which would be his alibi if he could get far enough away—among the islands and on a different course—before they caught him.

When he heard the explosions, he thought of the big, dark mouth of the barrel of the sub's deck gun and what it would do to a little cutter or launch. Only two shots, one for each of them. The U-boat wasn't running from them, of course he wasn't; he submerged to get around them for better shooting. If one of those boats was from the lighthouse, he was sorry about that, but they got what they deserved. He struck a match on the bulkhead and cupped it to light a cigarette.

He didn't actually see the boat following him; he felt it, as he used to feel his father standing next to his bed while he slept. All he could tell through the binoculars was that it wasn't a fisherman and that it was gaining on him slowly but surely. The U-boat missed one of them, Richard thought, or there had been a third. He would have to lose his pursuer among the familiar islands and ledges between Marshall and Swan's if he could get there first, get into the shadows first. If not, he'd give the son of a bitch a fight.

Running against the tide, which grew stronger as he approached the larger islands, he kept the flashing ripple caused by the Sally Prude Ledges off his starboard side and headed into Toothacher Bay to make it look as if he was going to put in at Swan's Island. When he saw flashes of rifle fire on the boat behind, he swung hard to port between Little Heron Island and the Brimstone Ledge. Now Richard headed southwest at full speed on a course that a daredevil wouldn't take in daylight at half throttle. He stood on tiptoe to watch for signs of ledges ahead in the tidal rip; looking over his shoulder, he saw that he had lost his pursuer, so he was smiling when the *Lucille* slammed into Job's Ledge, cracking Richard's shoulder against the wheel with a sound like a dog crunching a chicken bone. The *Lucille* ground her stem and skeg on the barnacles, then heeled sharply and spilled Richard's limp and senseless skeleton under her washboard.

Guided by Maggie, who read the chart with a flashlight, and by Morales's voice on the radio, Gus brought the *Amos Coombs* around the dark shoulder of Heron Island to find the launch riding at anchor among the ledges in the shadow of the forested end of Marshall Island. Maggie blinked her light at the boat, whose red-and-green running lights were a welcome sight. But the return signal came from a spot fifty feet to the right. As Gus and Maggie approached, Jake played his light over the scene around him so they could see. He and Morales appeared to be standing on the water next to a fishing boat that lay careened on its side. Maggie wondered what she would see next.

"They're on a ledge; it's just underwater," said Gus as they drew nearer. "He sure struck it hard; he's run right up onto it. Good God, Maggie, it's the *Lucille*."

"It is not," she murmured, then shined her light on the name.

"Is it Richard?" she asked. "Where is he?" Jake stretched his arm up over the slanted deck next to him and pointed down under the washboard.

"He's all stove up," Jake said. "We're going to need your help getting him aboard the launch. I'm glad you came."

"Is he alive?" she asked. Gus tried to nose his bow in closer between the launch and the wreck for a better look.

"Yes, but he's got a broken shoulder and maybe a busted collarbone, too. If you could make up a litter with oars and a piece of canvas, the four of us could get him aboard."

"And the quicker the better," said Morales. "I'm freezing my ass off here." He wore the Springfield rifle over his shoulder, the sling crossing his chest, which Gus thought looked just right. "You should've seen him when we found him: he looked like the guy in the cartoon with the birds circling his head and his eyes xed out."

"We couldn't even touch him before," Jake said. "Christ, how he howled when Morales shook him, didn't you Richard?"

An angry moan came from beneath the washboard when Jake pounded on it.

He waded cautiously down the ledge toward the *Amos Coombs* until he was dark to the waist. "Why don't you hand me those oars, Gus, and come ashore here with us. Maggie, if you can keep her in close here without too much pounding, we should be able to lift him aboard. Morales stuck him with morphine, so there won't be so much howling."

"What was he doing?" Maggie asked. Gus lowered himself

over the side, let go, and sank to his neck before he found footing. Gasping, he took Jake's hand.

"You'll have to ask him," said Jake. "He won't tell us a
damn thing."

"The asshole says he's a prisoner of war." Morales had
climbed aboard the *Lucille* and stood on the deck above
Richard like a man on a steep roof. "He's wedged in under here,
aren't you Herr Snell?" Morales looked down at him. "If you
wasn't so fat, we wouldn't have to put a line on you, like a pig
in a tub."

"Fuck you, spick," said Richard.

Morales stomped on Richard's crumbled shoulder twice,
hard, as if he was trying to start a motorcycle or kill a snake. A
sharp cry cut Richard's tongue before he passed out.

"Morales, please," Maggie shouted. "Please don't."

"Sorry, I slipped."

They did have to pull him out from beneath the washboard
with a line. They laid him perpendicular on the deck, his insen-
sate legs barely supporting his bulk on the slant, and lashed him
to the canvas and oars. They lifted and shouldered him across
Maggie's deck and into the launch, where he came to with
Morales standing over him. Richard moaned and cursed in his
teeth. Maggie pushed Morales gently aside and folded a shirt to
put under Richard's head, then covered him with a blanket. She
said his name, but he didn't reply.

"The Coast Guard wants us all to go into Stonington and
meet them there," said Jake. "They want all three boats, but
they're going to have to settle for two."

"We could haul it off and tow it," Gus said.

"To hell with that; she's sprung her garboards and probably
worse," said Jake. "All the rum is smashed, splattered all over
his deck."

"I'll ride with you, Mr. Gardiner, if you don't mind," said
Maggie. "I'm afraid he's going into shock. Morales can go with
Gus."

"I don't mind one bit," Jake said. "I'd like that."

"Hot damn!" Morales scampered across to the *Amos Coombs*; Gus ran the throttle up, and they pranced out toward open water.

"Don't give him any of my ginger snaps," said Morales.

"You stay with us," Jake yelled.

"I'm going to warm a blanket down below," Maggie said. "Will you watch him?"

"He doesn't deserve it," Jake said. "You should have heard him. He cried like a baby. He cried for his mother, I swear to God he did. He says that he was just picking up some rum, that he only tried to run from us because we fired a couple of rounds over his bow. Right, Richard?"

Richard didn't reply.

With the *Amos Coombs* following in the last of the moonlight, Jake set his course for Merchant's Row. When Maggie came up from the engine compartment hugging a warmed blanket to her chest, Jake said he was sorry.

"I was obnoxious back there, about the depth charges," he said.

"You were." She looked at him. She could hurt him now by saying she'd been disappointed, but she wouldn't. "Thank you for saying something. But never mind. We're all touchy, and you were provoked. I'm just glad that it's over, and I hope it turned out no worse than just this. How happy I will be to get off the water and away from the smell of rum."

She knelt to tuck the blanket around Richard, taking care not to touch his shoulder, and she wiped his cold, wet brow with her kerchief. While Jake talked on the radio in Coast Guard jargon, she sat next to Richard, her knees tucked up under her chin.

"I know you're conscious, Richard," she said. "Are you warm enough. You're shivering."

"I'm all right," he said. He didn't look at her but spoke to the dark sky. "Thank you."

"What were you doing?" she asked.

"I already told them," he said. The defiance was leaking out of him.

"We saw you, Richard. Gus recognized the *Lucille* by her silhouette, even with the false house you built on her." She was the tired teacher behind her desk after school, and he the truant boy; she lied for his sake.

"We saw you meet a submarine. I'm not going to ask you what your business was with him; I'm not sure I want to find out. But I want to know who came ashore last spring, who it was that Amos was watching for; tell me that at least. Were you involved?"

"I don't know anything about that, nothing at all," he said. "When we get to wherever it is they're taking me, will you call my mother?"

"I will if you will swear to God—no, swear on Lucille's eternal soul—that you don't know anything about people coming ashore at the cabin in the spring."

"I swear it."

"I believe you," she said. "What should I tell her?"

"Tell her the truth. Tell her I've been hurt in an accident, my boat's stove up, and I'm going to the hospital."

"Nothing more?"

Richard didn't answer. She wanted to get up and stand with Jake in the warmth of the exhaust pipe, but she couldn't summon the strength; instead she rested her forehead on her knees.

"What were those explosions," Richard asked. "Morales said they were thunder, but that's crap."

"Gus and I were dropping depth charges on your friend," she said. "We hit him, too." She closed her eyes.

The Stonington fishermen who had set out between false dawn and first light had disturbed the smoky haze on the water in the harbor, but a cold whisp—a ghostly mare's tail—hung over the town wharf as they loaded Richard into an ambulance. A half-dozen men, all of whom knew Richard, watched in silence. They had been told by the two Coast Guardsmen who'd arrived in a government car, that there had been an accident and that nothing more was going to be said about it until after an investigation. Maggie sat by herself on a lobster crate, a blanket over her shoulders and her hands wrapped around a hot cup of coffee. Her jaw was clamped to keep her from shivering as she watched Jake, who stood smoking and nodding in agreement as he listened to one of the men in uniform at the car door. The county sheriff, his headlights dimmed by the emerging sun, drove onto the wharf and joined the solemn conference. While they talked, they looked over at Maggie and at Gus and Morales aboard the boat. She wondered why she was so cold—deep-down cold—while the others, who had been soaked to the skin, were not.

"I can't go to Rockland," she told Jake and the young man with the pistol belt. "It's Wednesday. I have school."

"We have to go," Jake said. The armed Coast Guardsman clasped his hands behind his back. "I've been ordered to, and these guys were sent to get us. We have to give them a statement is all. They want us there yesterday."

"Can't that be done here in Stonington?" She knew by their faces that it could not be, and she imagined the warm back seat of the sedan. "Then I have to make a phone call and get a message down to the island. You can wait fifteen minutes, can't you?"

"Well, Ma'am—"

"Thank you," she said, and rose to fold her blanket.

Rockland was on its lunch break when Maggie awoke in the back seat of the sedan and looked out at Main Street. At the Korner Kafé more than a dozen people, most of them young, waited in line on the sidewalk for a space at the counter. Three girls in saddle shoes and wide skirts came out, and while two of them stopped to chat with some uniformed women in the line, the third stood at the curb and redid her lipstick in her compact mirror while a little fat man watched her over his newspaper. At the stoplight, a pimply delivery boy on a bicycle adorned with flags steered between the sedan and the ambulance ahead. While he waited for a truck to pass, he gawked at the unlikely passengers who were riding in such style. Gus rolled down his window to let in the noise and exhaust fumes.

"Hell of a lot of people," he said, as the light changed. "There's the Harbor Inn. I wonder if Richard knows he's passing it."

"You should see it on Saturday night," the driver said into the rearview mirror, "I don't know where they all come from. Sorry to wake you up, ma'am, but we're almost there anyway." He put on his hat and straightened his shirt front as they turned right and headed downhill to the Coast Guard station.

At the gate, two armed guards stepped onto the running boards of the ambulance, then it turned on to a gravel drive that ran between rows of Quonset huts. The guard saluted the sedan and told the driver to go directly to headquarters, waving the sheriff's car to follow.

"I look a fright," Maggie said to Gus. "And so do you. Especially your eyes; you look as if you've been up all night drinking."

"You look just fine," he said.

At headquarters—a low, drab cinder-block building—Maggie's door was opened by a short woman who couldn't have been more than twenty. She wore a blue overcoat and cap with a shiny brass crest. "I'm Evelyn Pullin," she said. "I'm a SPAR. I'm to see that you have a chance to powder your nose and get something to eat. Your meeting is at 1300 hours, which gives us some time."

A little dazed, Maggie introduced herself and thanked Evelyn. Nearby, two men in dungarees were brushing white paint onto the row of rocks that marked the border of the headquarters yard. Maggie thought that she had tumbled into another world, then felt sure of it when she saw the lascivious look that Evelyn Pullin gave Morales as she caught his eye.

"What about my nephew?" Maggie asked uncertainly. Gus stood with Morales on the other side of the sedan.

"Oh, he'll go with the men," said Evelyn. "You'll take care of him, seaman, won't you?" She smiled gaily at Morales and patted her blonde curls to accentuate her sunny disposition. Morales offered his perfect white teeth in reply. Gus groaned.

When the sheriff's car pulled away, she saw Jake talking to a man in khakis. He waved to her, pointed to his watch, and held up one finger. Evelyn offered Maggie her arm, which she declined.

"Thirteen hundred must be one in the afternoon," Maggie said as they walked toward the row of Quonset huts. "But I'm embarrassed to admit that I don't know what a SPAR is."

"Oh don't be," Evelyn chirped. "It's ever so new—the name, the whole thing. SPAR is the Coast Guard ladies' auxiliary. It's short for *Semper Paratus,* always prepared, which is our motto. We're new here, five of us. It's all so exciting, isn't it? I mean look at me—in charge of base affairs. Ha, ha, just a girl from Kittery with a year of college."

They passed a Quonset hut from which came the sound of rhumba music and someone beating time on a metal surface.

"That's the canteen," Evelyn said. "Don't you just love Cugat?"

"Oh, brave new world," Maggie said.

Evelyn cocked her head like a curious bird.

"Stick of gum?" she asked.

In addition to his duties as deputy base commander at Rockland, Lieutenant Oscar (Oz) Grover was the Coast Guard intelligence officer for Naval Region Seven. He hated both jobs: the first because it was all details and no command, the second because, though it promised to be more interesting and of some importance, it had so far been nothing more than reporting the alleged sightings of U-boats and saboteurs—and in one case a German destroyer—by zealous Coastal Pickets and inarticulate fishermen. But today the alleged sighting was by Chief Gardiner, whom he knew to be trustworthy, and there was a prisoner involved, which meant that he would soon get to test the interrogation methods he had learned at the intelligence school in New London. With his elbows on the desk, and his chin resting on a steeple of fingers, he listened as dreary little Ensign Onderdonk explained the process of giving and taking statements.

While Onderdonk delighted himself with military and legal terminology, Gus sat upright, rubbing his palms between his thighs, glancing from the clerk who sat prepared at a little side table to the imposing lieutenant behind the flag-framed desk. Maggie listened with some interest, thinking that poor Onderdonk could never make a good teacher and wondering if she would tell the whole story to this lieutenant, who appeared to be an intelligent young man. Jake, in a set of fresh, borrowed khakis, struggled to keep his eyes open; Morales, in similar uniform, requested permission to stand, which he was granted.

"Very good, ensign," the lieutenant said, sitting back. "I haven't met your—our—detainee, only seen him in the infirmary, so before I question him, it's paramount that I get every detail from you." He looked at the papers before him. "Richard Snell, if that's his real name."

"It is," said Jake.

'Paramount,' thought Maggie; he must be a college boy.

The lieutenant looked at Jake, then at Maggie, whose smile sent his hand up to straighten his hair. He asked Jake to begin and told the others to feel free to comment, then nodded to the clerk.

With his hands spread over his knees, Jake told the lieutenant and pale Onderdonk, who loitered behind him, about Amos's sighting of a U-boat in the spring, and his own conse-

quent confirmation (and reporting) of it after the lobster fisherman had identified the outline as a Type VIIC. Amos Coombs,
he added, had since died.

"Did this Mister Coombs, or anyone else, report other sightings afterward?" the lieutenant asked.

"Captain Coombs, sir," said Gus.

Jake looked at Maggie, who nodded.

"Not sightings per se, lieutenant," she said, holding his eyes
with hers. "But evidence—and, it must be said, suspicion—of
something of this nature."

The lieutenant leaned forward to appear interested; Onderdonk, the arm behind his back clasping the far elbow, turned to
gaze out the window. Maggie explained, slowly and with care
for the clerk's sake, how she and Gus had assumed Amos's patrolling responsibilities after his death, both on the water and
along the shoreline. She told the lieutenant about discovering
that Amos had been watching not only the water from the cliffs
at night, but also the cabin itself. While she described what she
had found inside—the salty footprints, the blackened lamp
chimney—Jake noticed the light chestnut curl that had fallen
over her ear and imagined her unpinning her hair in the lamplight to let it fall on her bare shoulders.

Then they saw the strange boat, she continued, on both
nights, going out at the same time on the same azimuth, and returning the same way.

"So you decided to go out and have a look, the two of you,
and maybe intercept this boat," the lieutenant said. "What made
you think he'd make the same run a third time?"

"Intuition," she said, and smiled. "But it wasn't just the two
of us, not at first. We went to the lighthouse to tell them what
we were doing, and . . ." She looked at Jake. "To enlist their
help."

"And what was it, Chief," the lieutenant asked Jake, "that
made you go along with them? Intuition?"

A wet, supercilious smile spread across Onderdonk's face, a

look that Morales would have blotted out if he hadn't distracted himself by trying to reach his own elbow behind his back, which he couldn't do.

"We had two depth charges aboard, sir." Gus folded his arms on his chest. "It's not for the chief to say. He was afraid we'd—"

"I'm sorry?" The lieutenant looked as if he had suddenly smelled something burning. Onderdonk puffed out his soft chest.

"Not depth charges, not military issue," said Maggie apologetically. "They were fifty-gallon drums packed with black powder and detonated by a stick of dynamite on a fuse. Mounted on a ramp sort of contraption." She held her forearm at a slant. "We had tested it; we knew it could work. Mister Gardiner tried his best to dissuade us; he ordered us to push the whole thing overboard; he even threatened to arrest us if we didn't. So we did, of course. Eventually. We complied."

"Detonated?" The lieutenant was on his feet. "Are you writing this down?" he asked the clerk. "Yes, I guess you should, so we can see it in black and white and then maybe . . . this isn't some kind of goddamned joke is it, Chief?"

"No, sir," Jake said placidly. "Let us explain what happened."

He described the signals they'd seen, the silhouettes of the lobsterboat and U-boat, his radioed orders to Maggie and Gus, his request for an aircraft on station.

"The U-boat crew must have picked up our radio signals and seen us approaching on their sonar screen," he said. "And they must have decided to *macht shnell* out of there; the sub dove and took off in what looked like an easterly direction. We went after the lobsterboat."

"And you, Miss Bowen?" The lieutenant came around the desk and sat on its edge in front of Maggie, his shoulders slightly hunched. Jake thought about moving closer to her but saw that he didn't need to.

"We took a heading that we hoped would intercept him," she said. "And when we saw his periscope wake, we dropped the charges. The explosions were quite remarkable."

Lieutenant Grover stared, then shook his head. "No, a four-hundred-pound charge would blow a fishing boat clear out of the water. I don't believe this."

"It nearly did," Maggie said. And she wondered how many times in the last few days she had heard someone say he didn't believe what had happened, how many times she had said it to herself, how many times she would hear it again.

She watched Onderdonk pacing a private circle in the corner while Jake described his chase, the boat's desperate mistake among the ledges, and their taking Richard into custody.

"He denied it was him that met the U-boat," Jake said. "He says he's innocent; he was on a rum run, is all. It's going to be up to you to find out what he was doing; and we'd sure as hell like to know."

"Depth charges," repeated the lieutenant. He looked at Gus, then at Maggie, who smiled and nodded at him in return; Gus's smile was thin and satisfied.

"Depth charges," he said again, still wagging his head. Then he laughed. "Damn, I wish I could have seen it. Where the hell did you get black powder and dynamite and fuses?"

"Amos got them from a friend who worked at the Stonington quarry when it was still going," Gus said. "He didn't have to pay because his friend pilfered it. Amos loaned him money once years ago, when he couldn't afford to."

"Did you get everything, Hawkes?" the lieutenant asked the clerk, who replied that he had. "Then how about some coffee for us?"

Morales took the clerk's seat to use his ashtray.

"They're going to love this at Regional Headquarters," the lieutenant said. He walked around his desk. "But can you swear in court that it was this Snell you saw meeting the German sub? You said his boat was disguised."

"It was him we followed out of there and had in sight the whole way," said Jake. "Christ, I'll swear to that."

"On the way into Stonington, I told Richard that Gus and I had recognized the *Lucille* with the U-boat, and he didn't deny it—not then," Maggie added.

"Did you recognize him?" the lieutenant asked.

"No, that was a lie," she said. "Told to find the truth."

Maggie took a breath, crossed her legs, and let her hands rest in her lap, palms up. "There's one more thing, lieutenant," she said.

"Good," he said. "Every bit helps. We should wait until Hawkes gets back so he can get it down."

"I don't think so." She was careful not to look at the others. "I'm going to risk censure, and even ridicule, but I've decided to tell you nevertheless. I only ask that you listen."

"Of course." He sat down and rebuilt his steeple.

"When I heard the first explosion, I shut my eyes, and on the second one I saw them—the men in the U-boat—saw and heard what was happening, as clear as can be." She held up her hand. "I heard the explosion and felt it—from inside the submarine, from beneath. I saw a lightbulb explode. I saw fire squirt from a wall covered with dials. A boy with a red beard was clinging to an overhead lamp, another to a pole striped like a barber's. They were screaming; the one with the greasy black hair and quivering lip was shouting, 'Wabos! Wabos!' or something similar. One man stood in gushing water striking something with a hammer. There was smoke, and creaking noises, red and yellow wheels or valves. And . . ." She spread out her hands. "And three wrinkled, wet fingers pressed against a gray metal strut."

She waited. The lieutenant said nothing, only stared. Morales looked at Gus for an explanation; Gus shrugged his shoulders.

"What did you say he was shouting?" the lieutenant finally asked.

"I thought it sounded like 'Wabos Wabos.' I don't know German; I'm not even sure that's what it was," she conceded.

"Wabos is the German submariners' slang for *Wasser-bomben,* depth charges," he said incredulously. "How the hell did you know that? Did you know that, chief?"

Jake shook his head.

"I *didn't* know." Maggie regretted that she'd ever spoken.

"They're going to have a hard enough time believing that you attacked a U-boat. But that's possible. This is not. This is impossible." The lieutenant sounded tired.

"No it's not," said Maggie. "It happened. Just because we can't explain it doesn't mean that it didn't. This whole adventure has made that quite obvious, hasn't it Gus?"

Gus looked at her as though for the first time and agreed.

While Betty and Mabel held the checkered tablecloths in place, Iris Weed folded and fixed the corners with clothespins to hold them down in the breeze. On the grassy half-acre peninsula between the store and the town landing, Iris's church social committee had covered four eating tables and was busy arranging the pies, cakes, and casseroles on the long serving table under Leah's supervision. Though the clambake wasn't supposed to begin until three, some thirty people were already busy around the flagpole on the point, and more were arriving by car and foot, the young men carrying hods filled with clams, others toting crates of skittering lobsters. In the rocks below the tide line, Dwight and Reverend Hotchkiss stirred the big fire with poles, while the Mattingly boys brought driftwood and tossed it in to raise a shower of sparks. Seated in a semicircle on the rocks with their mother, all four Crowell children were busy sorting corn; Vince flicked a handful of silk into the wind so it would blow into his sister's hair, earning him a whack on the head with a roasting ear. The osprey from the nest on the spindle beyond the parsonage soared in a wide circle overhead, chirping loudly. When Iris shielded her eyes to see the bird, she said a little thank-you for such fine clambake weather so late in the season. She waved to the McDonnell and Waite families, who were arriving aboard the *Nana* from Stonington. The committee would not only meet its goal of fifty dollars for War Bonds, Iris thought, but the event would also be a dandy send-off for Vergil, who was joining the Marines in the morning, and for Gus, who was going back to school.

In her bright new canary yellow sweater, Betty was setting places with Mabel when Ernest Mattingly tugged on her skirt and pointed to the road. With a fistful of spoons and Mabel following, Betty hurried through the crowd and cars, and stood at the roadside by an overturned dory. She handed Mabel the spoons and adjusted her hair under her bandanna. On the road from the landing, beneath a canopy of red maples and golden birch, she saw Jake, in khakis and an overseas cap. A step behind him, walking with his knees, was Harvey Goods, his red flannel shirt buttoned to the throat and his hair so well oiled that it glistened in the shade.

"He's not with them," said Mabel. "Perhaps he's tying up the launch. But, no, they had to leave somebody at the lighthouse. Oh, Betty."

Betty took back the spoons and clenched them to keep from shaking. She clasped Jake's hand, managing a smile, and introduced him and Harvey to Mabel.

"Isn't Ernesto coming?" she asked afraid to hear. "He said he would. He said—"

"He tried to," Jake said. "But it was Harvey here's turn to get off the rock. Morales offered him twenty bucks, but Harvey wasn't hearing of it."

Betty stretched her neck toward Harvey, her blue eyes wide with fury. Harvey smiled weakly and tried to touch his ears with his shoulders.

"He wanted to say good-bye to Gus," she hissed. "We were . . ."

Harvey shrugged again, and she felt the tears coming.

"Oh," she croaked in utter disgust. She stamped her foot in Harvey's direction, did an about-face, and disappeared among the cars, with Mabel following.

"When she hears that Morales and I put in for sea duty, your ass is grass," said Jake.

Harvey sniffed.

Dwight and the Reverend Hotchkiss, both peeled down to shirts and suspenders, stirred the big fire, spreading the larger pieces of driftwood over the bed of coals. Cecil and Gus, wearing Leah's knit sweater vests, sat on lobster crates with Albert, waiting for the fire to burn down. The Mattingly boys struggled over the rocks with a drift log, Ernest walking backward with his end.

"We won't need that one," Cecil told them. "It'll take too long to burn. Why don't you start bringing up some rockweed?"

Approaching the bank of seaweed exposed by the tide, the boys surprised a swimming ribbon of black ducks riding the current in the lee of the shore. The Mattinglys released a salvo of rocks that scattered the swimmers in furious paddle and sent a dozen up into flight.

"Here, cut that out, damn you," Dwight shouted.

Albert said he wished he had his shotgun.

"We'll get some next week," said Dwight.

With long-handled spades, Dwight and the reverend shoveled a pile of coals onto the sand by the pit and began to smooth over the layer left beneath. Cecil and Gus went down to the tide line with bushel baskets to join the boys in collecting rockweed.

Dwight leaned on his shovel, his chin on his hands. "What I want to know is why nobody's heard from Richard—not even Lucille. They won't even tell her what hospital he's in."

"I talked to Mark Cassady, her pastor, in Stonington yesterday," said the reverend. "When I went to get the corn. He called Rockland Coast Guard for Lucille, and they said they couldn't tell him anything; they acted like they didn't know, but when he pressed the subject they said it was classified. I saw Richard's boat at Caldwell's pier; it's half under water."

"Bill McDonnell said Friday that federal marshals came and arrested Carl Topp in Blue Hill," reported Albert. "Wouldn't tell his wife a thing; just left her standing in the dooryard. Phew, that's hot!" He fanned his face with his hat.

"You could move to windward," said Dwight.

"I heard the same thing." The reverend looked over his shoulder at Cecil and Gus and the boys. "Just who is Carl Topp, anyway? I heard that he and Richard were in America First." He glanced again toward Cecil. "And it's rumored that they were mixed up in the German-American Bund."

"They were," said Albert with authority. "But they quit it, and they quit America First too, like everyone else did in '41." He nodded in Cecil's direction. "Richard and Carl, they used to talk about Carl's brother Homer, who got executed by an American firing squad in France. Bitter talk when they were drinking."

"A spy, eh?" asked Dwight.

"No," Albert said. "And that's a lot of the problem. To hear them tell it, he was shell-shocked and couldn't bear the thought of going back to the lines. He was guarding German prisoners, and he changed uniforms with one to get sent to the rear. They caught him and shot him. Christly thing—his own army."

Gus and Ernest Mattingly shook a heaping basket of rock-weed onto the bed of coals, which steamed and popped and sizzled as the reverend spread it out with a garden rake. "I love that smell," he said.

"I'll like it better when everything's in there cooking," Gus said.

Cecil and Vince Mattingly dumped another basket onto the fire, to be spread this time by Dwight, who declared the pit ready for the lobsters. Albert and Gus dragged the crates to the edge of the coals and began dropping lobsters, two by two, onto the smoky seaweed, where they flopped and thrashed in the fearful heat.

"That's a generous lot of lobbies," said Dwight wiping his brow. "How many you got, fifty?"

"Half of them is Gus's," said Albert.

"It's very generous of both of you," said the reverend.

Gus shook the last two lobsters and several shot claws out of his crate, then he, Cecil, and the boys went back with baskets for the next layer.

"Gus knows something we don't know," said Albert when they had gone. "And Maggie too, even though they say they don't."

"You ought to just forget about it," Dwight said.

On the next layer of seaweed they spread the clams, eight hods full. Iris brought tall glasses of iced lemonade for Dwight and the reverend.

"It's fresh squeezed," she said. "And the mint is from Leah's garden. Come join us when you've got it covered; I hope you're hungry. Miss Lizzie made her butter biscuits just for you, reverend. There must be sixty people here by now."

With the last baskets of rockweed standing by, they scattered the ears of corn. Dickie Hanson, a mug of coffee in one hand and a cruller in the other, came to watch.

"What I want to know, Gus," said Dwight. "Is why they took you and Maggie to Rockland with Richard, when it was for bootlegging that he got arrested."

"To testify, like I said. And that's what we did." Gus spoke evenly. "We told them what we saw—his boat run up on a ledge and him stove up, his deck awash in rum."

"Why'd they arrest Carl Topp?" Albert asked.

"I have no idea; I swear to God I don't," said Gus.

"There," said Cecil standing back from the heat and brushing his hands. "We're ready for the other coals to go on."

As they shoveled the last of the covering layer, Fuddy and Skippy, each carrying a hod full of clams and dressed for a backwoods funeral, appeared behind Dickie and Cecil. Basil Walker's starving dog, Bender, collapsed in the sand, his tongue muddy with dust.

"You *would* wait until we got the whole thing covered with this tarp, wouldn't you?" Dwight said.

Skippy ducked and hid his mouth with his hand. Fuddy took his partner's clam hod and set it on the ground next to his. "The truck wouldn't go," he said. "Sentiment bulb's clogged, and we wore the battery down, so we walked it. Basil couldn't, but he sent his money, and we're going to take him a supper."

"Suppah," said Skippy.

"You'll want a wheelbarrow to take *his* supper back," Dwight said.

"We got one; it's parked in the school yard."

"One other thing I don't understand, Gus," said Albert. "We heard—"

Cecil, who had started toward the tables, spun around into Albert's face. "Let it be, Albert," he snapped. "Gus told you what he knows, and he told you it's the truth. What the hell are you suggesting anyway?"

"Whatever happened, I say Richard Snell got what he deserved, and my money says that was his last damn rum run." Dwight drove his spade into the sand and rolled down his sleeves.

"The wages of sin is death, eh reverend?" Dickie slurped his coffee.

"Well, yes . . ."

"Rum ain't sin," Dwight said. "The wages of rum is only more trouble."

The head table, which had a splendid spray of New England asters as a centerpiece, was set a little apart on the lawn, between the flagpole and the serving line. The guests of honor—Vergil and Gus, and their parents—were first through the line.

They carried their plates to the table and sat, with Vergil at one
end facing the other tables, his parents on either side of him,
and Gus at the other, with Cecil and Leah. Two seats were left
empty in the center, one for the reverend. They waited in awkward silence until the other tables began to fill, then started eating. The younger families settled in little clusters on the grass to
eat picnic style. Dwight and Doris sat apart in the same spot and
on the same quilt they had used when they were courting twenty
years before.

Ladling iced tea into glasses at the serving table, Iris told Maggie, who was pouring coffee, that Leah looked better—healthier
and happier—than she had in months. She was laughing!

Maggie filled Dickie's cup. "She's so relieved that Gus is
going to school and won't be on the water, in any way, for another year. I'm relieved, too, though my cheeks aren't quite as
rosy as hers."

Harvey, who had just been called an "S.O.B." and had been
abandoned when he tried to join the girls on the stone wall, took
a seat at a table with Albert and Lorna. He parked his gum on
his plate, tucked a napkin into his collar, and began to tear apart
his lobster.

Albert told Harvey that they hadn't seen him in ages and
wondered why he didn't get ashore more often. Harvey squinted
when he bit down on the war claw. Lorna said it must get terri-
bly lonely out on that little rock, especially now that the light was
out, and she wondered where Chief Gardiner was. Harvey
pointed to the serving table, where Jake stood talking to Maggie and Iris.

"They've become quite friendly, haven't they? Maggie and
the chief I mean," Lorna spooned jam onto a piece of muffin.

"I guess so," Harvey allowed. "They seem to get along just
fine most of the time."

"Most of the time?" she asked.

"The other night when they chased Richard, were you on
the radio with them?" asked Albert.

Harvey didn't look up from his plate. "Sure I was. I was base and relay both, at the same time," he said cautiously.

"Funny that we didn't pick up anything, any transmissions, on the church radio—the Coastal Picket. Iris didn't hear a thing, and she's particular," said Albert.

"We was on a different frequency." Harvey cracked the carapace and looked down at the green tomalley that had splattered onto his shirt.

Iris joined them. She complimented Lorna on the little gourd centerpieces, declaring them "some cunnin'." She looked at the wad of gum on Harvey's plate, then at him, and tried not to pucker her lips but must have.

"It's my last piece," Harvey told her.

"Even funnier is that Maggie and Gus said they didn't hear the explosions," said Albert. "Christ, they woke up half the town, here on the far side of the mountain. *Ba-boom.* And you didn't hear anything?"

Elbows on either side of his plate, roasting ear held aloft, Harvey ate down a double row of kernels, slid the furrow across his front teeth, and nibbled down a second row.

"Didn't hear a damned thing," he said, and winked so only Albert could see.

When Jake brought his empty dessert plate to the serving line, Maggie suggested that he try a slice of Leah's lemon meringue. Jake said he couldn't take another bite; he hadn't eaten so well in months. "I'm going to need to walk it off." He patted his belt line. "Or else lie down on the ground and sleep it off like those boys are doing."

"You ought to see our Columbus Day mural at the school," she said. "I'll come with you."

By the old blacksmith shop, where the road rose toward the town hall and school, Jake offered her his arm, which she took.

Barbara Brown waved from the doorway of her tidy cottage, and Maggie waved back.

"You hear that?" he asked.

"The rivers of wind in the trees, you mean?"

"No. The nudging and winking and whispering going on behind us," he said.

She laughed. "It's just the wind," she said. "See how it bends the tall grass and goldenrod."

"Makes me sneeze," he said.

"How long do you think it will be before you get your orders? Weeks?" she asked. "You'll both be missed."

He looked away, then at her. "Months maybe," he said. "Would you ever think of living any place but out here?"

"I thought about it every morning, like a man giving up smoking, for years until about ten years ago," she said. "Now I think of it, though not nearly so often."

"Why not so much any more?"

"I once believed that when Leah married, I would move off to Bangor to finish college, perhaps to live. I have several good friends there; one is especially dear. I missed the culture, movie theaters, music, telephones, the train to Boston." She shut her eyes and smiled. "But I stayed. This is home. I'm tied here, moored."

"To Amos or to the island?"

"To both, to one as much as the other."

Skippy was sitting on his swing, eating what looked to be a brick from a plate in his lap, shoveling with a spoon held knuckles up. Maggie recognized Doris's carrot cake and guessed that he had half of it. Fuddy sat against the base of the big maple, his legs splayed. In the wheelbarrow were two clam hods, one filled with ears of corn, the other with packages wrapped in waxed paper. Next to it Bender lay on his side, his pink belly so swollen with scraps and gurry that he couldn't lie flat.

She held the school door for Jake and showed him in. The

late afternoon light shone on the far wall, illuminating the Nina and Pinta and Santa Maria as they rode on cut out waves of ocean blue. Beneath the water, in letters cut in various colors, were the words "God Bless the Coast Guard."

"It's very nice," he said.

"I should thank you for not asking why a woman like me never married—someone who is so devoted to children and hasn't any of her own."

"I've wondered for that reason and others."

"And you," she asked. "Did you ever marry? I've heard that you are a widower and heard the story that goes with it, but it sounds like something concocted to make summer ladies' eyes rheumy and make you . . ."

He laughed. "Romantic?"

"Yes, and inaccessible in a very attractive way."

"Like you?" he asked.

She smiled and walked to the window. Fuddy and Skippy were making their way up the town hill, headed home. Fuddy carried a clam hod in each hand; behind him Skippy pushed Bender in the wheelbarrow.

"Poor Skippy," she said.

CHAPTER SIXTEEN

BEFORE THEY COULD HAVE ANY WORK DONE ON THE REST OF THE house, the Harpers had to have the sills replaced. The building had to be jacked up, and the old timbers, which had rotted because of the detritus that had settled around the foundation, had to be dug out and replaced atop the block granite walls of the cellar. When they bought the house, the Harpers joined the Point Lookout Association; this allowed them to hire the summer colony's maintenance crew, which was skilled at remodeling old homes.

On the north side of the house, they added a wing with an extra bedroom and a paneled den with a deep stone fireplace, bookshelves, and a leather couch. They bulldozed the decrepit out-buildings, built an insulated generator shed, and wired the house for electricity. The old icebox and kerosene range were replaced with propane appliances. On the south side, which faced the cove, they built a brick patio with kitchen access and formidable granite stairs leading down to the dooryard and meadow beyond. They added storm windows and had the house scraped and painted. They took up the carpeting and had the exposed pine planks sanded and finished. They kept the beds, bureaus, and tables, and they replaced the weaker furniture—all but Ava's wicker chair, which they left in state by the parlor window.

July 14, 1957

Dear Ruth,

Cecil has died. You were right when you said that he couldn't last much longer. Even the morphine failed to ease his pain in the last few days, so it was a blessing when he finally succumbed yesterday at noon. Through it all Leah was a model of courage (or should I say composure? Is there a difference?). Though she could not ease his pain, she eased his fear and anger with loving care. I am so proud of her and have told her so. The funeral and service are scheduled for Tuesday. Melvin is with Leah now, and Gus, we are told, is on his way. I doubt he will bring Susan and the children, as she is due to deliver their third any day now. I'd love to see them (it's been almost a year) but will be happy to see Gus, even in these circumstances.

Yes, it is odd to have strangers in the cove, especially in Ava's house, though it's hardly recognizable as hers any longer. The peaceful solitude that I have come to cherish (and that worries you so much) is still mine in the winter months, but in summer I'll have to get used to sharing the cove. And so I shall—I think with some unexpected pleasure, despite their two boys, both "juvenile delinquents" in coonskin caps. As I told you, Marion Harper and I have had tea together several times, both here and in their kitchen, and I enjoy her company. She has a sharp mind (they are both members of Mensa) and pursues the history of the cove and island with an insatiable interest that I find endearing. I know you can imagine me spinning tales of the old days, creating (by omitting so much) an image of a happier, simpler time, a Currier and Ives history of the cove. ("Over the river and through the woods, to grandmother's house we go." Never mind that the hag has no teeth, aches with rheumatism, and dreads our arrival.) Marion is making a scrapbook of cove history and is working on a Coombs family tree.

Professor Harper (Ed) is writing a book in defense of Dewey's theory of pragmatic education. Last Sunday, over a glass of sherry on their patio (imagine me taking spirits not ten feet from Ava's glaring window—how brazen!), he explained that children do not learn by rote but by experience. I wanted to ask how one experiences one's sums, but demurred. Though he wears silk bow ties and can be a tad condescending, Ed is a personable and articulate man, and conversation with him is good exercise for my flabby intellect. We exchange magazines, my *Scottish Fields* for his *New Yorker,* and he recently loaned me Senator Kennedy's very fine *Profiles in Courage,* fresh off the press. He's made Walter's cabin his studio and goes there every morning to work.

How impressive that Michael has been made a partner in Armistead and McClaw! I sent him a note. When I saw the clipping, I didn't recognize him at first (he looked so severe!), and I imagined a little tear of pride on Jack's cheek as I read the text. And Sarah a senior at Cornell!

You mustn't scold me for sending her little gifts; they are indeed small, barely enough for a dinner or two in town—pathetic recompense for all the meals I took with your family while I was in school. I can't wait to see the campus she describes so beautifully and to see her graduate. That will be a day to "lift one's hat to."

Did I tell you that I often see Marion on her patio with binoculars? She is an avid bird watcher and keeps one eye on her boys, who run wild in the cove (I forbid them to play on the cliff in front of my house, and they think me a perfect witch for it). On several occasions, however, it's been quite obvious that it's me Marion's watching, as I take out the compost, empty the honey buckets, collect twigs, putter in the garden. It's an odd and disconcerting feeling; it unsettles me because I feel my privacy violated, and for others reasons that I don't yet understand.

I'm sorry you've been having tummy troubles. Dry toast, tea, and Pepto Bismol have always worked for me, but then I eat like a wren, and you are so hardy. You are also my dearest friend, and one I miss very much.

Love,
Maggie

P.S. We are told President Eisenhower has decreed that "one nation under God" be added to our Pledge of Allegiance. Don't you find that curious? I mean, if it *is* under God, why mention it and be told to pledge it? I'll ask the professor.

• • •

With care, Ed Harper set a tray on the patio table and poured four Manhattans into glasses that sat on paper napkins decorated with blueberries and red lobsters. Fashionably late and dying of thirst from an afternoon of tennis, Robert and Rosalyn Owings settled with their drinks in deck chairs and surveyed the meadow and cove beyond, where the Harper's little sailboat *Rosinante* sat on her quiet mooring. The patio table, which Rosalyn admired, was made of two upturned and weathered lobster traps topped with heavy glass; the runners of the traps were branded with the initials A.C. Marion, in a white turtleneck, flannel shirt, and khakis, emerged from the new kitchen entrance with a plate of hors d'oevres in each hand—crabmeat and crackers, and pigs-in-a-blanket straight from the oven.

"Nothing fancy," she said. "Not here on the island."

"No," said Rosalyn piling a Ritz cracker high with tender lumps of crab. "But simple and wholesome, like everything else down here."

"Why we love it so," said Robert. "No jangling phones, no traffic, no blaring TV, and best of all, no pretense."

"No teenagers with record players," said his wife. "No Elvis Presley, thank God."

"Just listen," Marion said, and they sipped in appreciative silence, listening to the distant wash of waves on the ledges and the titter of the swallows that rose and dove and skimmed across the meadow.

"You know, Ed, I think you got the nicest piece of property on the island." Robert popped a maraschino cherry into his mouth and flicked the stem into the grass. "Far from town, far from the road, a view of the open sea, a safe mooring."

"And there's so much history here; it's so genuine. I love your name for it." Rosalyn nodded to the rustic signpost by the forsythia. " 'Sealedge.' Is it Sea Ledge or Seal Edge? Oh, I see, it's both; how clever."

"I tried to buy this property once, you know, years ago during the war," Robert said. "Chad Barrett and I thought we would build a hotel on the cliffs like the one just south of here that burned down in the teens. Cecil Barter told me, God rest his soul, that he had or would soon have the deed, and his asking price was deliciously low." Robert sighed.

"Then old Amos died—you know that story, I'm sure—and to everyone's surprise, especially Cecil's, Amos left the land and houses, all of it, to Maggie. Cecil tried to get her to sell, but she wouldn't budge. We never knew why. We didn't pursue it."

"Speak of the devil," Ed pointed.

Carrying a galvanized bucket, Maggie walked through the hay-scented fern at the edge of her lawn and into the rutted road that passed her house on its way to Ava's, not a hundred yards from the patio. Unaware of those watching her, she plucked a lacy fern and sniffed it.

She walked one way on the road for fifty feet, then in the other rut, back toward her house; she seemed to be looking for something she'd dropped, even scraping spots with the side of her shoe. In a sunken place in the turn, she stopped and sprinkled mussel shells over it, then went to the creek to rinse the bucket.

"She's made a chowder," said Marion. She passed the plate to Robert. "Better eat up these little piggies before they get cold," she said.

"They do that to keep the road free of mud," Rosalyn said, not to be outdone in island lore by a newcomer.

"But there is no mud," said Marion. "Not in this road."

"Because it runs by a house," said Robert. "A hundred and fifty years of chowders and shells, you know."

Ed refilled the glasses all around. "I guess we just got lucky," he said. "When we heard that her house in Head Harbor was for sale, we made her an offer for this place, and she accepted. Didn't blink an eye."

"For Gus," said Marion. She looked at her watch. "Remind me to check the soufflé. If the G.I. Bill hadn't paid for his college, she would have sold them in '45. Later, when he had a chance to buy a marine-supplies business in Portland, she did sell the houses and bought the company with him. She calls it a partnership.

"The other day, when it was so foggy, I had been out for a walk when she invited me in for tea," Marion said. "We talked for a long time at her kitchen table; I think we can get to be friends. I hope so. While she was telling about the year she had to leave college to come home to care for her father in Head Harbor, she was toying with a little beetle of some kind that had wandered onto the tablecloth. I would have died if it had been my table. Not toying with him, really, but herding him, corralling him with her finger, ever so gently, like this."

She brushed the glass table top slowly with her fingers.

"Then suddenly, for no apparent reason, she crushed it."

Marion pressed her thumb on the table and twisted it.

"She's an interesting woman; she always has been," Rosalyn Owings said knowledgeably. "So businesslike, so strict, but ever so polite and friendly, and very much at ease with herself."

Ed wondered why she never married. "She must have been a knockout in her time," he said to Robert.

"Not a knockout, you know," Robert said. "But she was a damn handsome woman. She still is."

"It's a pity," Rosalyn said.

"Oh, I don't know about that," said Marion. "She seems quite content to me. I love it when she shuts her eyes while she's talking."

Gus was still in dark suit and tie when he knocked on Maggie's screen door. She had changed when she got home but wore a black band of mourning on her sleeve. His red hair had faded to ginger and was showing a little gray over the ears. They embraced without a word.

"Let's sit on the porch, shall we? Take off your coat; it's warm. I'll get us something," she said.

"No, thanks," he said and took her hand. "Let's just sit. The wind will pick up soon with the coming tide. I've missed these old oak trees."

"You've put on weight since I saw you last," she said. "When was it, Thanksgiving? But it becomes you. You look robust . . . successful."

He laughed. "You look the same as ever."

"You should never say that to someone over fifty," she said. "Tell me what you thought of Paul Hotchkiss's sermon for your father."

Gus rocked and loosened his tie, saying that he thought it was very nice and that Leah liked it even more.

"I met your new neighbors. They were outside church afterward," he said. "They invited me to come visit and see what they've done with Ava's house, but I said I couldn't this time. I don't want to."

"You should," she said. "You'd like them—and the way they've fixed up the house."

"I wish you hadn't sold it. I mean I wish you hadn't thought you had to." He waved his hand as if to erase what he'd said. "I mean I wish the cove was still the way it always was."

"It's still the same. New faces and such changes don't matter to me," she lied. "It's your legacy, the way we'd hoped it would be, all of us. Now show me the photos of Susan and the little ones; you did bring them didn't you?"

"Yes," he said and reached behind to his coat pocket. "And something else as well."

He handed her a packet of photos and laid an envelope face down on the arm of his rocker. When she'd seen the snapshots and predicted that the next child would be a girl, he handed her the envelope. It was addressed to her, in pencil, in Cecil's uncertain hand.

"Mother asked me to bring it over; it was among his papers."

She put on her glasses and read it slowly, a single page,

then closed her eyes and handed it to Gus. It was dated the month before. Gus read, then read again.

Dear Maggie

You never liked me and never respected me. You thought I was cruel to Leah, and it's true. I was. I can only say that I believe I have made it up to her since, and I think if you ask her she will say the same thing. She has forgiven me, God bless her.

But not Leah, or any other mortal, can forgive me for the reason I am writing this letter. That night after the dance I followed Amos home. I wanted to beg him to deed the cove property to Leah. My reasons were selfish. I wanted to buy the Merrill and Hinckley store in Blue Hill, but it wasn't just for me. It was for Leah and Gus, too, a chance for a better life off this island. I hope you believe that.

Amos wasn't home when I got to the cove. God, how I wish I had turned back then. Up at Ava's I saw a light in the trees near the cabin. I thought he saw me coming, I swear he looked at me. I thought that when he turned away he was giving me the cold shoulder. He must not have heard me when I walked up to him. I said his name—that's all, just his name—and he started and lost his footing and fell. I can still see his arms waving, trying to get his balance.

How could I tell anyone—Leah, Gus, or you? The shame was too great. I thought the guilt would kill me; maybe it did. The longer I kept silent, the more impossible it was to tell anyone, and the more I hated myself. Please show this to Gus and Leah. I know that God will forgive me, and I hope that they, and you, will too.

That's all.

Cecil Barter

Gus squeezed the bridge of his nose and said he would like something to drink after all if she didn't mind.

"I can give you a glass of sherry," she said as he folded the letter and returned it to the envelope.

Gus didn't respond. He stood up, leaned on the porch railing for a second, then walked across the dooryard to disappear among the out buildings behind the high ledge. He returned carrying a bottle of Demerara rum by the neck.

"It's aged," he said, tilting it in the light.

"Wherever did you find it?"

"Under the floorboards in the toolshed," he said. "I only now remembered. His woodpile reserve, he called it. Let's have a toddy, for both of them."

"And for Morales and the other poor lost souls on the *Indianapolis*," she said. "Jake Gardiner, too, wherever he may be."

At dusk, Marion Harper tapped rapidly on Ava's window and waved to Ed to come outside. She walked him to the far edge of the patio, handed him the binoculars, and pointed down toward Maggie's front yard. He saw her dim figure standing by the well, shaded from the last rays of skipping sunlight above by the shifting canopy of oaks.

"What's she doing," Marion asked.

"She's pouring something into her well," he said, disappointed. "From a bottle."

"What could that be?" Marion wondered. "Why would she do that? What is she putting in her drinking water?"

"How would I know?" he asked, and handed her the binoculars.

Maggie walked up the slope of the lawn and onto the smooth granite outcropping that rose between the house and the cove. She stood for a minute on the highest point over the water, then with a powerful underhand, she sent the empty bottle aloft, timed to the second to catch the blink of the lighthouse before it fell.